MARCH OF THE MYSTICS

DAVID SCHWEITZER

authorHOUSE

AuthorHouse™
1663 Liberty Drive
Bloomington, IN 47403
www.authorhouse.com
Phone: 833-262-8899

© 2024 David Schweitzer. All rights reserved.

No part of this book may be reproduced, stored in a retrieval system, or transmitted by any means without the written permission of the author.

This is a work of fiction. All of the characters, names, incidents, organizations, and dialogue in this novel are either the products of the author's imagination or are used fictitiously.

Published by AuthorHouse 06/17/2024

ISBN: 979-8-8230-2712-0 (sc)
ISBN: 979-8-8230-2713-7 (hc)
ISBN: 979-8-8230-2714-4 (e)

Library of Congress Control Number: 2024910570

Print information available on the last page.

Any people depicted in stock imagery provided by Getty Images are models, and such images are being used for illustrative purposes only.
Certain stock imagery © Getty Images.

Map Artist: Rena Violet
Colorist: Angel R.D
Cover Artist: Renan Shody

This book is printed on acid-free paper.

Because of the dynamic nature of the Internet, any web addresses or links contained in this book may have changed since publication and may no longer be valid. The views expressed in this work are solely those of the author and do not necessarily reflect the views of the publisher, and the publisher hereby disclaims any responsibility for them.

Before the story, I want to take a moment to show appreciation to a few people.

Mom and Dad, you have always been supportive and loving, and I truly feel grateful to be your child.

Mama Jo and Meg Larkin, Liam tells me you've both helped write with me from the beyond, and I'd like to believe that. Thank you for helping.

Renan, Angel, and Rena, thank you for creating the art that has brought this world to life. I couldn't have dreamed everything would look this good, and I can't express show incredible you are.

Tara and India, thank you for your notes and encouragement.

Finally, thank *you* for reading.

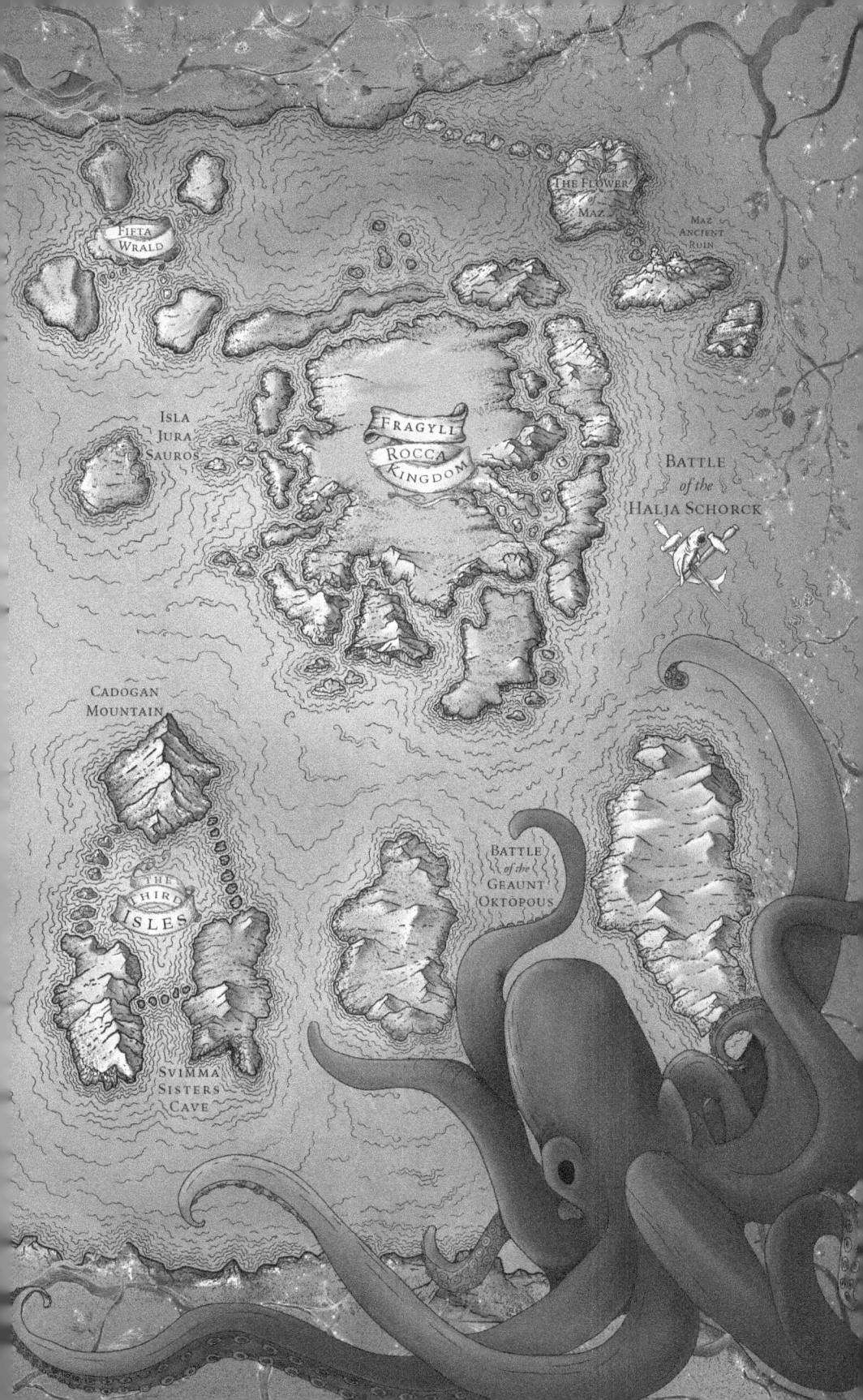

1
RAMPAGE OF THE SAUROS

CHAPTER 1

CIVIS: THE HAPPY HOOLIGAN TAVERN
DAY
••

"**TECHNICALLY, I WAS** surrounded but I could still see my exit." Gala Goda grabbed his cocktail and took a swig. For hours, he regaled the other patrons with stories of his heroics to satiate his ego. "Y'all know how expensive the Jade Flower of Maz[1] is, right? I just want to make sure I'm making it very clear—this was a big get. It's probably the most valuable treasure I've ever held. I mean, there's a whole group of us who were after it, so it's not like most of the rubbish relics I usually stumble across. This is a legendary artifact from the start of time! Well, anyway, they went to tackle me and I booked it!"

"You have to use that there revolver?" Lheni asked, pointing at the pistol on his hip. She was an elderly wrinkle of a woman, the type who spent their life at bars.

"This thing?" Gala showed off the pistol. "Nah, it's junk. Never shoots where I want it to." He stashed it back into the holster. His father gave him the gun when he was ten, and it was junk back then too. The chamber housed eight bullets, but the trigger often malfunctioned. "Thankfully, as I left, the cavalry arrived. They fought 'em off while I made my daring escape. It couldn't have worked out better … for me."

The Happy Hooligan Tavern dilapidated over the years, yet it was still one of Gala's favorite spots. It was a fun but dangerous atmosphere that smelled of sawdust. The massive, tree-stump bar was nicer than expected

---

[1] See Section V: Myths for more information.

and sat dozens. The whole place was covered in wood and could be lit ablaze with the faintest spark.

Gala was in his forties but claimed he looked younger. He had a great, full head of shaggy hair, which he was very proud of. His white skin was often covered in dirt and his face hid behind a five o'clock shadow. Small scars covered his person, the most noticeable being on his chin. He wouldn't admit it, but his body usually ached from taking too many tumbles and spending too many nights at the bar.

He typically wore an old, broken-in, yellow leather jacket. White outlined the straps and pockets. Underneath was a dirty safari shirt with the top few buttons undone exposing a small cluster of chest hair. On the left side of his belt hung a whip, while his pistol was holstered to his right. His jeans were a darker blue with few rips around the ankles. His red shoes were a hybrid sneaker and hiking boot. They were flexible, yet sturdy, and were currently his favorite possession.

The bartender, Link, walked over with more drinks. "He tell you about how he survived the Battle of the Omega Soldiers[2]?" She gave a mischievous smile as she dispersed their next round.

One of the bar's other patrons, Khurl, perked up when he heard mention of the battle. "He wasn't there," Khurl snarled.

"Yes, I kinda was," Gala told him as he took the first sip of his new drink.

"You run when the going got tough?"

"Hey, I wasn't there for that fight, man. I was there collecting the Runes of McGrath. A war happened to break out around me! Those omega soldiers were something else, I tell ya. If I hadn't found a gassed-up motorbike, I would have never made it."

"You didn't even try to help them!" Khurl screamed in Gala's face.

"Do you really think if I had chipped in that the outcome would have been any different? It was a slaughter! There was nothing I could do. All I could do was survive and get out … and bring along the super valuable artifact I went there for. Sold it for quite a bit, by the way." Gala raised his glass in honor of the sale.

"That's not what a real man would have done."

"Don't have to call me a real man, but you can call me alive." Gala toasted a second time.

---

[2] See Section V: Myths for more information.

"What brings you to Civis today?" Link asked.

Gala had spent the better part of a year traveling out to this metropolis known as Civis. Before arriving, he gathered maps and codes from his various contacts. It was not an easy feat; the codes in particular set him back weeks. In an ideal world, he would have arrived months ago, but now, with just a few days to spare, he had everything he needed. "Ever hear of the Diamond of Farrokh[3]?" Gala asked Link.

"Not familiar with it. Where you gotta go for that?"

"The Pimar Temple out in Streawberige Field."

Link's face dropped as her eyes went wide. "You know a Sauros haunts there, right?"

"That's just a myth." Gala dismissed her with a bat of his hand, even though others had warned him of the same.

"My cousin was killed by what lurks in those shadows," Lheni said. "We were kids playing there, not knowing any better. Had to have been eighteen feet tall back then. Probably twenty-five feet now. Only a fool would go there willingly."

"Hey, if I survived the Battle of the Omega Soldiers, then I think I can survive one Sauros," the fool replied.

"This diamond must be pretty expensive," Link said.

"Eh, it's not worth that much."

"Oh no," she bemoaned. "You're getting this thing to impress a woman, ain't ya?"

"Oh, Link …" Gala shook his head with a smirk. "Everything I do is to impress a woman." He reached into his pocket and pulled out some gold coins. "What's my tab?"

"It's on the house … seeing as you're about to die."

"I'm not going to die!" He gulped down the remainder of his drink. "But I will accept your generous gratuity." He turned and went for the door.

"You were a good customer," Link hollered after him. "We're gonna miss you comin' 'round these parts!"

"I'm not gonna die!" This wasn't the first time Gala yelled that while leaving a room. As far as he could tell, this was just another day in the life, but unbeknownst to him, today would be the start of something new.

---

[3] See Section V: Myths for more information.

CHAPTER 2

**STREAWBERIGE FIELD: NEAR PIMAR TEMPLE
DAY**

"**AH, *NERTZ*, LOOKS** like rain," Gala cussed to himself as he left the tavern.

Dark, ominous clouds plastered the sky as if the heavens were about to drown the world. Wind whistled and pushed every which way. If he weren't in such a hurry, Gala would have stopped to find shelter.

You're in the orange borough; the temple can't be that far a walk, he thought as he set off.

Civis was a circular city divided into seven boroughs. Each was color coded with corresponding architecture and culture. Red was dead center. This area was populated with skyscrapers, including the Five Towers of Prospect. Red was an area for the rich to live and look down on everyone. The blue borough was the next ring in the city. With this layer, they stopped building the towers so tall. Next came the green borough; that's when they stopped using sturdy material. Each layer was shoddier but larger than the last. The purple borough was the final one that had any wonder to it. Brown, yellow, and orange all looked the same, minus their coloring. They were occupied by homes that were poorly built and in need of reconstruction. Expenses no one could afford multiplied in every direction. There were no skyscrapers, but that did not mean people weren't living on top of each other.

Sitting between the cities southern border and the temple was Streawberige Field. A once lush land was now disturbed by divots and craters. Many wars had been fought there. Most of this was from the

Flaumer Titanikos attack. That behemoth had caused so much damage, it was as if the soil gave up, too scarred to ever flourish again. Gala walked through the battlefield, amazed at how grand the destruction was.

The Pimar Temple was a three-sided pyramid, stretching five hundred feet into the sky. The very tip was made of glass, but the rest was brick. The structure was chipped with scratches so massive they were even visible from a distance.

At the base stood wide doors that would allow an army to pass through. Soldiers would march out and see Civis as one last reminder of what they were fighting for. To the side of those doors was a flight of stairs that led to a platform with a smaller entrance for individuals.

As Gala approached the temple, he realized the atmosphere had changed. Bellowing thunder clacked overhead. Violent flashes of multicolored lightning exploded all around. This storm felt as if it was not from this world but from the cosmos itself.

Scarlet, emerald, and violet streaked across this grandiose, intergalactic gathering in the sky. Gala watched in amazement as three swirling clouds began to form around the temple. The sky felt a hundred miles away. His surroundings seemed small and insignificant.

A flash to Gala's left grabbed his attention. A violet cloud opened in the center and light gleamed forth. A woman appeared in that light, and the world went silent for a second before she dropped. She wore a lavender cloak, which made things a bungled mess. Her curly black hair was the only indication which way she was pointing. She was heading toward the temple and would make impact in seconds.

Gala gasped and ran toward her.

Her foot was the first thing to make contact with the pyramid. Without losing a beat, she began sliding down it. She weaved back and forth, narrowly avoiding the balconies and dents. Smoke billowed behind her feet as she gained speed. Her face showed no fear, just exhilaration. When she reached the base, her momentum pushed her across the field. She landed feet from a bewildered Gala.

"Buenos días, señor. Que tal?" The woman spoke with a smile on her face.

"Are you okay?" Gala stammered. He walked around her, looking for a trail of blood. "Do you speak what I'm speaking? I'm sorry, I'm terrible with languages."

"Yes, I can speak your language. I can speak almost anything if I set my mind to it. And I'm fine; thank you for asking." She took a few steps to stretch her legs.

"So … what just happened? It's not every day someone falls out of a cloud like that."

"To be honest, I can't really remember much. Suddenly … I was here. If I think really hard, I kind of remember being on a boat. Something in the sea." She turned back to face the clouds. "I do know that I am from somewhere … beyond."

That last statement gave Gala pause. "Do you at least remember your name?"

She thought for a second. "Dagnarone." She beamed after saying it.

"Nice to meet ya, Dag. I'm Gala Goda." He smiled and shook her hand. He had an outlandish theory, and there was no point in beating around the bush. "So, uh … are you one of those ancient Mystic warriors?"

Mystics were a part of legend. Gala didn't know of any in the modern world. They were cosmic beings who could wield the energy of the universe. Lands, objects, and people were cursed and cured because of them. They explored the planet, making it a magical place. Some Mystics played major roles on the old-world political stage, while others became exemplary warriors. Regardless of what path they went down, they all strove for the preservation of peace.

"First off, do I look ancient to you?" She raised her voice in a playful manner.

"Absolutely not! If anything, we look around the same age."

"Mmm … you look a little older." Gala's smile waned. "And no, I am no warrior. Not anymore. I cannot let fighting be my life again." Dagnarone's face became sullen as she searched her thoughts. "My soul is engrained with my past life's trauma. I've seen volcanoes erupt and icebergs melt, more bodies dismembered than whole, and young sacrificing themselves for some foolish ideals that will never materialize. I've seen more innocents become victims because of leaders' actions." She shook her head. "I will not put myself through it again."

"Good for you for taking charge of your own life like that. Not enough people do." Gala began concocting an idea on how she could help him.

She turned toward Streawberige Field and pointed at it. "What happened there?"

"Oh, a Titanikos tore it up during a war and no one ever bothered to fix it."

She leaned down and scooped up some dirt. "Hmm … it would take too long to fix now." She stood back up and faced Gala. "I could really go for some coffee. You don't happen to know where we can get some, do you?"

"Uh …" Gala looked around, hinting that they were in the middle of nowhere. "I don't see a place right now, but if you'll hear me out … I think I can get you some."

Once again, the world around them went quiet.

Instinctively, Gala and Dagnarone looked to the cloud hovering on the south side of the temple.

Scarlet light poured out as another figure began her descent.

Unlike Dagnarone, this woman had control and fell gingerly. Her body was upright and rigid. Gently closed eyes accompanied a peaceful face. Her skin was light brown and her long hair black. Her robes were crimson and gracefully swayed in the breeze. She was the definition of ethereal.

Powerful thunder snapped and vicious lightning cracked.

When her feet touched the ground, she curled to sit cross-legged. Her back stayed straight, and she began to meditate.

She opened her eyes to see Gala and Dagnarone running toward her. A smile spread across her face as she stood. "Namaste," she greeted. A second later, her eyes went wide in disbelief. "Dagnarone!" She ran over to her friend.

"Sephra?" Dagnarone replied, as if questioning whether she got the name right.

The two embraced with warm smiles across their faces.

"So, you two … know each other?" Gala asked.

"Yes." Dagnarone's eyes searched Sephra's face, as if struggling to grasp memories too far out of reach.

"It's like seeing someone you know, but you can't recall how you met," Sephra added.

"I remember something about us on vacation. We were at some lagoon and … well … I don't remember any other details, but I feel it was stressful."

"Oh, that's not good. Any idea why it felt that way?" Sephra replied.

"I think we got into an argument."

"Well, I'm sure it got resolved." Sephra changed the subject. "I have this memory of us fighting some beast atop a mountain. We worked really well as a team that day."

"Oh … you remember us literally fighting something?"

"Fighting and killing," Sephra boasted.

"And killing … great," Dagnarone mumbled.

Sephra took a few steps and looked around. "Have you noticed everything here feels … familiar?"

"It's been like a constant sense of déjà vu."

Sephra looked up at the sky. "Dropping down really is a refreshing feeling." She turned back to her companions, "So, have you figured out what the mission is yet?"

"The mission?" Dagnarone sounded concerned.

"I assume we were sent here to save the world. Have you any clue how to do that yet?"

"Whoa, whoa, whoa," Gala interjected. "Save the world? What does it need saving from?"

"All worlds need saving," Sephra's smile was replaced with a look of determination. "I don't know what dangers lurk here, but I know we can do something to help. In my moment of meditation, I saw past lives wherein I led armies—tens of thousands at my command, riding horses, dragons, and other beasts. I saw the hundreds of wars I've ever been a part of. This fight is in my soul, as I feel pain etched into my pores. The only thing drowning it out is my sense of righteousness. If I was sent here, then I was sent here to save this world."

"Okay … you got all that from the fifteen seconds you were sitting on the ground? Admittedly, you made your point, but listen, before you go off and save the world, you'll need to gain some experience, right? 'Cause I think I've got the perfect little challenge you both can help me with."

Sephra did not reply to Gala. She turned her head and looked up at another swirling cloud.

The emerald vortex released a third person. This man dropped straight down and slammed into the ground. A poof of smoke rose upon impact. He was in no pain, just a daze.

For a moment, he saw the last seconds of his previous life. He was at war, fighting a loved one. He didn't know who she was or what she meant to him. Still, that pain and failure traveled with him to this life.

He was a black man with neatly trimmed hair and beard. His robes were forest green with a golden trim. Other than the color, the robes looked identical to the two women beside him.

Everything seemed familiar as he looked around. There were little variations, but it felt like he had been there before.

He wanted to know more. There was a lot for him to be curious about.

The man stood and saw people approach him. He didn't know why, but he was excited to see them.

"Are you able to remember anything?" The woman in red asked. "Do you know your name?"

Like the women, he only had vague memories of what came before. He suspected it was a life lived in longing. For a moment he stood silent, pondering his own existence. "I am Jerlone," he told them, his name being the only thing he knew about himself with certainty.

"That sounds familiar," Dagnarone confirmed.

They each shared their names with him. It was a lot for Jerlone to take in. He paced as he considered what to say. A part of him needed to mourn right then, but he knew it wasn't the time or place. Instead, he tried to focus on the positive. "I can feel this world has a certain energy and I want to learn more about it." He gazed at the temple and the cosmic storm brewing behind it. "Such wonderment. So many possibilities." He looked at Sephra. "You just dropped too?"

"Dagnarone and I did minutes ago," Sephra replied.

"Do you remember where we came from?"

"Somewhere greater than the sky. We are from the cosmos themselves."

Jerlone knew this to be true. "I saw my life for a second. It was right there, then … gone. A whole lifetime of lessons learned from my mistakes wasted. I never got to wrap up my loose ends. I want to reach out to those I left behind and apologize. I wouldn't know the words, but … I'd find something to say. Expressing myself wasn't my modus operandi, and I regret that now."

"You mustn't focus on that," Sephra put her hand on his shoulder and looked him in the eyes. "We all leave behind unsaid sentiments. During your time together you could say a million things, but when the time is over, you'll think of a million other things you wish to say. It's impossible for that feeling to go away. Right now, you've started a new journey. Focus on the here and now and manifest a future you want."

"You can let go of your past that easy? Did those you left behind mean so little to you?" His voice raised as the weight of the emotion overcame him.

Sephra took a moment to respond. It appeared as if she were suppressing a whimper. "They mean more to me than I would care to admit."

Jerlone realized her hard exterior was a front. While he was still struggling to grasp the situation, she had already found a way to cope. He hoped it meant he would also come to terms with the situation soon enough.

"Do you like coffee?" Dagnarone asked him. "Cause this guy said he'd help us find some." She pointed to Gala.

CHAPTER 3

PIMAR TEMPLE: ENTRANCE
EVENING
. . . .

GALA WAS TOO busy scheming to hear the promise of coffee thrust upon another.

More thunder and lightning danced in the sky while rain began to drizzle.

"Alright, everyone," Gala began, grabbing the group's attention. "I know there's been a great promise of coffee, but that's going to have to go on the back burner. It should be pretty obvious that a hard rain's gonna fall any second now. Once it starts pouring, lightning is gonna strike, creating a dangerous situation. It would take us too long to reach Civis, and then we'd have to find shelter. By then we'd be soaked … and maybe even struck by lightning. So, hear me out, if you will, and answer me this: how would you like to achieve financial independence?"

The three Mystics stared at him blankly.

"Why would we need financial independence?" Sephra asked. "We didn't come to this world to soak in riches."

"Speak for yourself," Dagnarone clarified.

"Hey, if you want to achieve anything in this world then you've gotta have cash flow." Gala pointed to the temple behind them. "You see this? It's an ancient ruin, and ruins are filled with treasures! I've spent my life raiding places like this and—"

"So, you're rich?" Dagnarone interrupted.

"Well, uh … I mean … who's to say what rich is? I don't go hungry."

"Then you're poor?"

"No, I'm somewhere in between … but closer to the poor side than the rich side."

"Then why should we trust you?" Jerlone questioned.

"Because, regardless of my financial … savvy … I know something's value and where to sell it. I was on my way here to find a diamond. If you were to help me, I can get you started on a path of financial security." Gala expected their faces to light up, but they did not. "So, what do you say? You're either in or out … right now."

"If there are treasures inside, then why hasn't someone else plundered them yet?"

"Because … because …" Gala searched for an excuse. "Because you can't just walk on in! You've got to have codes and maps, which I happen to have. With the four of us working together, we can score some serious booty! Trust me, you don't want to miss out on this opportunity of a lifetime."

"I don't know," Sephra cautioned. "I feel like there's danger afoot. My intuition is advising me against going in there."

"I feel the same," Jerlone concurred.

"Come on." Gala gestured with his hands, as he often did. "Of course, it's safe! Well, okay, it's not entirely safe. It is an ancient ruin after all, but I mean, the three of you dropped out of the sky and don't have a scratch on you! Do you really think there's something in there to worry about? And even if we did run into something problematic, I think with the four of us working in tandem we could handle it. You may not realize it, but you are powerful beings."

"No, we realize it," Sephra corrected him.

"Oh … okay, good. It's important to believe in yourself … but also to have modesty." An ironic statement coming from Gala.

"I don't know what you two are talking about." Dagnarone walked toward the temple. "I don't sense anything. Besides, Gala wouldn't willingly put us in danger." She looked to him for confirmation.

He stared at her and blinked a few times before answering. "Exactly … I would never do that."

"Dag, if you're interested in some coffee, you could join me," Sephra enticed. "We can head into the city. I can't imagine it will be that hard to find."

"Keep in mind," Gala interrupted, "you have no money to pay for it. You don't really know where you are or what your plan is. But, like I said, I can get you all set up. We can get everything you need inside. Then, tomorrow, we start you fresh."

"I have this feeling we're supposed to go in there," Dagnarone proclaimed. The rain started to pick up.

"I hate to concede," Jerlone shook his head, "but he might be on to something. If we can get ourselves set up, it may be worth the risk."

"And what about the danger we both sense?" Sephra challenged.

He nodded and smiled at the question. "I think we both know this would not be the first time we've had to face a danger that was dwelling in the dark."

"Very well," Sephra paused. "Let us take shelter from the storm."

• • • •

Sephra led the group up the stairs to the entrance. As the rain picked up, it made for a slippery ascent. The higher they climbed, the harder the wind shoved.

Sephra sensed Dagnarone was about to slip. She turned and grabbed the other woman's arm just in time. No one was going to fall under her watch.

After an arduous climb, they reached the entrance platform. There was a door with a keypad, covered by an awning. The four huddled underneath.

Gala pulled out some paper from his pockets and looked for the right one. He found it, mumbled something to himself, and then entered a code into the keypad. The door slid open five inches and stopped. "Aww, come on," he groaned. He entered the code again, but the door did not budge. "Stupid, lousy code," he grumbled.

"Do you need help?" Sephra moved toward him. "Perhaps we can finish pulling the door open." She didn't know why he seemed so frustrated at such a simple task.

Gala gave it a little tug. "I'm not sure we'll be strong enough."

"I think we will." Sephra turned to Dagnarone and Jerlone. "Alright, let's get to it."

They walked over, and Sephra arranged them. Gala and Dagnarone would pull while Sephra and Jerlone pushed. Everyone was at a slightly different angle, but they were all able to squeeze in and grab a chunk of door.

"On three!" Sephra barked. "One … two … *three!*"

At first, the door did not budge, but they fought on. The three Mystics closed their eyes and focused their energy. A faint, golden glow covered their hands, and the door began to slide. Soon, there was enough of an opening to squeeze through.

Even though he played a minimal part overall, Gala seemed exhausted. He dropped to the ground and gasped for air. "Alright … good job team. Let's just catch our breath here." He looked up at the others. "Or … okay … we all look around the same age, but I guess it's only me that feels it, huh?"

"You gonna make it?" Jerlone feigned concern.

"Yeah, let's go," Gala attempted to get up but fell down. "I mean, just gimme another second." He continued panting.

CHAPTER 4

PIMAR TEMPLE: HALLWAY
EVENING

D**AGNARONE WAS THE** last to squeeze through the door and enter the long hallway.

At the end of this half-mile corridor was another door. Torches lined the walls and ignited one after another. The light was dim but showed them the way.

As she walked the halls, Dagnarone had vague memories of something awful occurring there. Someone died. She didn't know who, but still, she felt it. Her knees buckled and she was on the ground. The anxiety of being there made it hard to breathe. She had no idea why she felt this way; her memories of the event were too hazy. Nothing was clear, but the emotions were gripping.

"Dag?" Sephra turned her head toward her companion, and then she ran to where Dagnarone rested on the ground. "Are you okay?" Sephra knelt beside her.

"Yes," Dagnarone answered through deep breaths. "I just have a memory from this hall—losing someone who meant the world to me. I have this sense that I never really recovered from it." She was caught off guard feeling this way. "If it's haunting me in this life, I wonder if I will ever get over it."

"I'm sorry. I think I also lost someone important here once."

"Do you know who?" Dagnarone asked.

"No, but I think they were someone I could be cozy with." Sephra paused. "Do you know who you lost?"

"I think they were my student, but also … more than that. Almost someone I could call family."

"I'm so sorry." Sephra replied empathetically.

Dagnarone sat there for another second thinking about it. "I don't want to keep living in this moment." She stood and began walking.

Sephra followed her. "You know, I was thinking, and I owe you an apology."

"For what?"

"The lagoon. I'm sorry for making it a stressful trip."

"Oh …" Dagnarone was caught off guard once more. "Do you know why it was stressful? I don't really remember the details. I just remember the emotion."

"I'm not at my best when I'm sitting around. Vacations aren't my strong suit. I found an … excursion … for us to attend. You weren't happy I dragged you into it."

"Oh, it's coming back to me. We ended up captives of pirates?"

"I recall us overpowering them with ease," Sephra said with levity. "We were never captured, just inconvenienced."

"Can I be honest with you about something?" Dagnarone scratched the back of her head. She was nervous about broaching the subject but knew she had to. "I'm not thrilled to hear we fought and killed a beast."

"It was trying to eat us."

"Well, uh, perhaps there was an alternative. Could we have fed it something else?"

"Feed it something else? Your suggestion is to take the monster out to dinner?" Sephra condescendingly chuckled.

"Not to a restaurant, but maybe we could have helped it gather food?"

"Do you remember what this beast looked like? This was not something that dealt in reason. It was reacting on pure, terrified instinct." Sephra was starting to sound frustrated. "Why does it matter, anyway? We did this in a past life."

"Because that's not the type of life I want to live again. All my lives I've had to fight. I don't want to go on some mission to save the world. I want to plant trees and clean oceans. Swashbuckling and violence are not for me."

Sephra shook her head. "There's so much we can do to change the world and you want to plant flowers?"

"First off, I said trees, but now that you say it, yes flowers too. Second, what's wrong with that? You don't think the world needs nature tended too?"

"Of course, it does, but not from cosmic beings!"

"Well, have you ever considered there's more than one way to save the world? Violence isn't the only way to make things better. In fact, I would say it often has the opposite effect! Also, who's to say this world needs saving from cosmic beings? Maybe these people are supposed to save themselves!"

"It would be irresponsible to stand by and not take action," Sephra replied dismissively.

"That's great for you, but it doesn't change my stance. I don't want to live a life of violence."

"And what if the world needs you?"

"World won't need me. World's got you."

The two stopped walking and looked at each other. Dagnarone wasn't surprised Sephra was causing her to feel flustered. The glare in her eyes said a lot.

"I misspoke," Sephra apologized. "I understand your intentions." She reached out a hand in forgiveness.

Dagnarone wasn't sure how sincere the apology was. The right words were said, but she couldn't tell if she meant it. Regardless, she did not want to create conflict. "Thank you." Dagnarone smiled and shook her friend's hand.

They began walking again, this time in silence.

• • • •

"You really shouldn't worry about the skeletons," Gala advised Jerlone as they walked past a few gnarled remains. "These things have probably been here hundreds or thousands of years. Remember: just because you see a skeleton, it doesn't mean you're in trouble—it means they were in trouble a long time ago."

"Just because you don't see the danger doesn't mean it's not there." Jerlone stopped and looked at some of the nearby bones. "We're all skeletons in trouble, one way or the other."

"Well, that's a bit of a grim way to look at things."

"Grim but honest." Jerlone walked away from him.

"So, tell me, Jerlone, what do you remember about your life?" Gala hustled over to him, hoping to win him over. "You into anything exciting?"

"Books. I like to learn."

"Can't say I'm much of a reader."

"Didn't think you were."

"I mean, I see the appeal." Gala tried to course correct. "I'm just so busy out on the road. Having experiences and … living it to the max." The lingering silence that followed indicated to Gala his attempt at bragging failed.

"I've always felt there's so much we don't know about the world around us and so few willing to learn. I see something and I want to know how it works. I want to hear people's theories about how our dimension differs from others. Finding those answers is the way I 'live life to the max.' The rewards are few and far—but worth it."

"We're not too dissimilar. We're both trying to find something. You're just looking for ideas, and I'm looking for golden objects." Gala started to feel a kinship. "What are you searching for in this life?"

"Where we came from. What is our great purpose? I want to know why beings of great power fall from the sky."

"I'm sure you can find lots of resources—and books—on that. It's a pretty well researched subject with scholars. Yes, a couple of quacks have written their thoughts, too, but I think you're smart enough to sniff those out."

"Kind words, thanks," Jerlone said with a hint of sarcasm. "So, how long you been in this line of work?"

"Whole life," Gala answered. "Parents were adventurers too. Taught me everything I know. They were good, but not as good as me." His demeanor started cocky but became somber the more he spoke. "We had some fun times. They were kind people. They, uh, they really loved me. Sometimes I was just too stupid to realize how much." Gala could not make eye contact with Jerlone. It was not easy for him to open up about. He took out a flask from his breast pocket. Alcohol always helped him handle the pain a little better. "But that's what happens in this line of work. People die. People die, and then … we realize what we had." He took a swig and offered it to Jerlone.

Jerlone's shoulders slouched forward. "No one ever realizes what they have until it's gone." He declined the flask. "I don't have parents. I've lived thousands of lives, and all of them have been the same. I'm always born as this solitary individual who has to figure it out for himself. I've found my kinships; some were so strong that people have felt like siblings, but still, never a parent. I've never known what it's like to have someone love and care for you unconditionally, to be there in all those ways … no one else could. I've lived over and over never having that. Do you know what that does to a soul? It's tantamount to torture." Jerlone paused, and Gala suspected he was lost in thought for a moment. Then, Jerlone said, "You're a lucky man to have had them. Truly, I am sorry for your loss."

Gala looked him in the eye and smiled. "Thank you."

"How old were you when they passed?"

"About thirteen." Gala took another swig of his flask and put it away. "We were in a cave trying to retrieve the Chest of King Khirby[4]. When we grabbed it, the place started crumbling around us. Ground opened up and we got separated. Lucky for me, I got to the exit … but they couldn't. Rocks were falling everywhere, and … they told me to go and save myself, and … I got a lot of guilt about that."

"You shouldn't. They wanted you to get out; they didn't care if they died. They're in the afterlife right now, happy to be there." Jerlone said.

Gala looked at Jerlone, as though the Mystic were a vessel for his parents. "I know … but it's still how I feel." The pain Gala felt over their absence grew.

"Well, if it's any consolation, you look back at your time with them fondly. To me, that's a sign things were good. You have to live with grief, but you also had love and kindness in your life. Besides, now they are spirit, and they are always with you."

"Yeah, yeah, yeah, I get it. I pray at the peace pagoda, I know all that." Gala waved his hands dismissively. He was feeling overwhelmed and didn't want anyone to see him in that state. He walked away from Jerlone and ran his hand through his hair. After a sip from his flask, he walked back over. "And who's to say I want them with me all the time?" He sounded angry to overcompensate for being emotional.

"Worried you've made decisions they would judge you for?"

---

[4] See Section V: Myths for more information.

"Ain't we all worried 'bout just that?" Gala stopped walking. It had been a while since he was this reflective. "You know, my parents taught me to help others …" His voice drifted. "After they passed, that's exactly what I did. Went out there and looked for people in need. Helped 'em out, even if it was in a small way. I guess eventually the pressures of adulthood overpowered that. I needed to make money and survive. Took on some treasure hunting jobs that weren't exactly for the betterment of society. Had to make a few bad calls. People got hurt. There were times I could have helped someone and chose not to. I figured it would have put me in harm's way. Worse, sometimes I just couldn't be bothered to stop. I think back to those decisions and am glad my parents aren't around to lecture me about it."

"Ever consider a new line of work?"

"And live the quiet life somewhere?" Gala hesitated. "I don't know. Maybe. But it'd be hard to step away from the adventure. It's a thrill unlike anything else, and I don't know if I'd survive without it. There's something about it that keeps my blood circulating. I need that for my life to feel like it has any meaning."

At that moment, the group was two thirds of the way down the hall. The monotonous bricks were beyond repetitive at this point. It was as if they were walking past the same spot over and over and over.

No longer paying attention to his surroundings, Gala stepped on a red tile. His foot sank two inches into the ground, and he froze. He knew that had to have set off a trap, but he was unsure from where. A quick gust of air flit past him, enveloping him in a musky smell of death. As he looked up, he saw a spear hurtling down the hallway toward him.

CHAPTER 5

PIMAR TEMPLE: WAR ROOM
EVENING

S**EPHRA JUMPED IN** front of the group and moved her arm in a crescent motion. A blue energy followed her hand and created a shield. The projectile smashed into the wall of light and shattered. The shield dissipated seconds after.

The three Mystics glared at Gala.

"So." Gala regained his composure. "Remember how I said these places can be a little dangerous? It's things like that you've gotta watch out for. The red tiles are the ones we wanna avoid." He looked around to realize there were no other red tiles in the room. When he looked back to his partners, he saw frustrated and judgmental faces. "I did say I'm used to working alone."

"I'm just really surprised you haven't gotten yourself killed yet," Sephra lectured.

"You're not the first person to say that to me."

• • • •

"Dios Mío!" Dagnarone exclaimed as she walked into the war room. Her eyes marveled as she swirled around, taking it all in.

In bygone eras, the war room would have been reserved for generals and royalty to strategize in. It had thrones, round tables, battle maps, paintings of the four great queens, and chests with the finest weapons the world had ever seen.

Candelabras burst on, illuminating everything with a golden effect.

The war room overlooked the ground floor. There, soldiers would assemble before marching to war. It was a bare space besides the columns that held up the structure. The light did not illuminate that area well, but they could still see the dirt. The center of the ground was glass and allowed them to see the levels below.

Right then, they could not see anything down there except a terrifying darkness.

Above them, the pyramid stretched to its glass tip. On a clear day, the sun would illuminate the whole facility, but that was not today.

Along the slanted walls were the upper levels. Stairways and walkways could be seen with some larger landings, allowing more space. Doors leading to various rooms were scattered all the way up.

"Alrighty then." Gala put his hands on his hips as he looked around. "This is a good spot to get yourself something to attack and defend with. Take a bit of time to look around and find something real sharp."

Sephra and Jerlone walked away to begin their search.

"You're not wearing armor, so why do we need it?" Dagnarone asked as she walked toward Gala.

"Well, I care more about my style than my safety." He gave himself a once over, making sure everything still looked good.

"If I need to protect myself, I can do it without a weapon. I am a force of nature. A weapon is nothing but an instrument to channel our magic. I do not need such a steroid. Besides, once you pick it up, you're doomed to use it."

"Force of nature huh?" Gala rolled his eyes. "And yet, some say I'm egotistic."

"We attract like-minded people into our orbit." Dagnarone smiled as she walked away from Gala.

"At least get yourself some armor!" Gala hollered after her.

Dagnarone didn't care about finding weapons or armor; she just wanted to explore and see what else she could find.

There were four round tables—one before each throne. They were covered with maps and other official documents. Upon seeing the drab and dour paperwork, Dagnarone made a dismissive noise and walked away. She couldn't be bothered with such nonsense.

To the side of the thrones were treasure chests. Dagnarone approached the nearest one and opened it. There were rings, earrings, and necklaces filling it to the very top. She dug through, finding an assortment of jewelry she liked. A pair of teal and gold gauntlets were the first to catch her eye. Soon, a crystal necklace hung around her neck, adding layers to her elegance. She felt a stronger connection to nearby energy after putting it on.

When she twirled her hands in the air, it felt like swirling them through a sea of magic. The world became clearer. She truly felt like a force of nature.

After closing the chest and standing, she tripped over her cloak. She wanted to make alterations to the stuffy thing, already knowing what she would change. Of all the things she saw before her, she didn't see anything that would help her make those modifications. Until later, she would have to deal with its inconveniences.

Jerlone sat on a throne, reading from a leather-bound journal.

"What're you reading?" Dagnarone approached him.

"It's from one of the great queens," Jerlone answered. He shut the book and looked at her. "She talks of magical people who fell from the sky. Mystics. Do you have any idea just how powerful they were? Some of the stories I'm reading …" Jerlone shook his head in disbelief. "We are not humans; we are forces of nature."

"Could you do me a favor? Can you please use that exact phrasing to Gala? He laughed when I called us that."

"I need to find others who've fallen from the sky. They could have answers about where we come from."

"Why is it so important for you to know where we come from?" Her face scrunched up, not seeing his point of view. "Yes, we were from somewhere, but now we are here. We can't go back; we've been reborn. It's time for our souls to start anew. Whether we like it or not, we have to live in this moment. It's the only way to make things better."

Jerlone leaned forward, his face dead serious. "I understand we've been reborn. Still. I want to know what lies beyond. I need to believe in something. I can't describe it, but this … this means something to me."

Dagnarone walked up to the throne and put her hand on the armrest. Jerlone was not looking at her, but she didn't need him to. "I know you feel alone, but remember: we fell with you. I don't know if you'd agree, but you and Sephra are like my siblings." She would be embarrassed if neither shared the sentiment. "I know you're searching for others to figure out what our place is in the cosmos. I just don't want you to forget we're here too. We can figure this out together."

He hesitated before replying. "Yes, but I fear we all have different agendas."

• • • •

Sephra couldn't take her eyes off the art.

The walls were covered with paintings of the four great queens. Their greatest battles were depicted with the most vivid colors. Before them were monsters of unimaginable heights. Weapons glowed with a magical energy, while they stood statuesque. Thousands of troops rallied at their command. When looking at this art, dark skies felt conquerable.

Sephra daydreamed about the events being depicted. She could see these grand wars unfold before her eyes. This was her moment of inspiration. This showed that a person could become something larger than just themselves. People could work together to save the world, and it would be beautiful.

Sephra turned around, wanting to share this moment with someone. Gala was sitting nearby at one of the round tables, looking over his notes. She walked over and took a seat across from him. "Isn't this art stunning?"

Gala looked up and took a quick glance around the room. He nodded his head. "Yeah, if we could get it off the wall, it would fetch a real pretty penny."

"I can't get over how larger-than-life they feel." Her voice was still lost in a world of imagination.

"Do you have a favorite?"

"Yes." She smiled wide and stood up. "Come, let me show you."

Sephra was halfway to the painting before Gala could stand. She was captivated as soon as she turned her attention toward it. When she got there, she stopped and stared. Gala stood behind her and gave it the once-over.

The painting showed a great queen with her bow drawn, ready for battle, the weapon encompassed by a blue energy. She wore a red cape and a golden tiara. There was a very subtle smirk on her face, showing her confidence and sense of adventure.

"Do you know who she is?" Sephra tilted her head.

"Queen Swifan of Wundrian." Gala scratched his chin. "She was one of the four great queens of this temple. They went down fighting for their people. It's said they saved the world by doing so."

Sephra stepped toward Gala with a smile. "That's who I want to be."

"Little early for you to be talkin' about dying, ain't it?"

"It won't happen anytime soon, but it will one day." She turned and faced him. "Did you not know that?"

Gala chuckled. "I think I got something of an idea." He looked around at the other art. "So, you want to die for your people, eh? You even know who your people are yet?"

"No, but once I find them, I will die for them."

Sephra looked over to the nearest throne. By its side was a small rack of bows. She went to it and looked them over. All were smooth and finely crafted. Intricate designs and details were etched all over. She weighed them in her hands and toyed around with each one until she came to a decision.

The bow was a light blue. Glowing white lights were encrusted above and below the handle. A few scattered jewels decorated the rest. It was elegant, yet dangerous.

She smiled, knowing she now carried a weapon of Queen Swifan.

● ● ● ●

Gala felt enough time had passed and they needed to get moving.

"Alright, everyone, gather 'round," he shouted to his companions. He held tight to one piece of paper. It had the access codes for the doors leading to the lower levels. If he lost it, then he wouldn't know what to do.

Gala saw Sephra's weapon and was curious what Jerlone would scrounge up. He doubted Dagnarone would take his advice. If he was lucky, she would at least be wearing some armor.

Jerlone and Dagnarone both walked over without any weapons in hand.

"What the hell?" Gala groaned. "Neither of you grabbed anything?"

"Nothing really called out to me." Jerlone shrugged.

"Called out to you? Who cares if it calls out to you! Not every weapon has to have some meaning of great significance!"

"Speaking of weapons of great significance," Sephra chimed in, "look at my bow. It's from Queen Swifan of Wundrian. She's my new role model."

Gala rolled his eyes and glared at Sephra. "You're not helping right now!" He went back to addressing the group. "Regardless, let's go over the plan again. We need to go down two levels. We've got a staircase here that should lead us down, nice and easy. When we reach Lower Level 2, I need everyone to be on the lookout for a green diamond. My understanding is it's sitting atop a spiral staircase made of rock. Biggest thing I'll need from y'all is to have my back. Place like this could have some kinda rodent, reptile, or ghost that could get in our way."

"Ghost?" Dagnarone raised an eyebrow.

"Yeah, but it's not likely. Seen a couple in my time. Always a pain to deal with. Sometimes they wanna fight you, and other times they want you to solve riddles or some other nonsense. Not sure which is more infuriating." Gala broke eye contact with the group. "Anyway, my sources didn't say anything about ghosts."

The room rumbled, throwing everyone off balance. No one fell over, but there was an undeniable impact. This was not from the storm outside; there was something inside the temple.

The three Mystics looked to Gala, all showing various levels of concern.

"It's fine!" Gala lied. "It's just the foundation. These ancient ruins lose their … foundation and … they get … the shakes." He paused, hoping his excuse was believable. Then, for good measure, he added, "It's really nothing to worry about."

"No," Jerlone cautioned. "Something feels wrong. If we venture further down, we will encounter trouble. We're safe here and should stay."

"Come on, I do this all the time, and it's a perfectly normal sound and rumble. These places aren't always safe, but it'll be safe enough! Remember: all of you fell from the sky today and landed without any injuries."

"There were psychological injuries."

"Okay, well, I meant physical injuries. Obviously. I don't think going down there is going to give you too many emotional injuries." Gala walked over to the stairwell. It was at the edge of the platform. A wide spiral led down to the lower levels. "Listen, I wouldn't intentionally lead you into danger. These places sound a lot more dangerous than they are." He shook his head a little. "But, also, be prepared in case something does happen, 'cause really, anything can happen." He pointed at them, hoping to emphasize his final remark.

There were three consecutive slams down below.

Everyone still looked at Gala with caution.

Gala took his first steps down the stairs. "Once again, I really don't think we have anything to worry about. I'm pretty sure it's just the foundation."

CHAPTER 6

PIMAR TEMPLE: STAIRWELL
EVENING

"**HACHI MACHI!**" **GALA** exclaimed as the stairwell door opened.

A massive, circular staircase stretched from the war room down to Lower Level 3. It was wide enough to fit fifteen people side by side.

The Mystics peered through the door and saw only darkness. There were no magic torches to light their way. It was unlikely their eyes could even adjust to that type of abyss.

Sephra raised her hand, palm facing up. A faint light formed, no larger than a speck of dust. When she rotated her wrist, it grew. Like a magnet, little strands of white energy zipped over to it. When she stopped swirling her hand, the globe of light was the size of her fist. It floated up and settled a foot above her head. There was enough illumination for their immediate vicinity.

Gala had seen his share of small magic spells over the years, but he had never seen someone conjure light. As glad as he was for the visibility, this was the first time he'd felt nervous around the Mystics. It was a subtle reminder that they had the power to obliterate him if they so pleased.

As they passed through the door, the atmosphere changed. They walked into a room that felt infinite and cold. It was an enclosed space that somehow had a breeze. The ground was too far below for them to see, but then again, there was really nothing for them to see. Blackness dominated outside their little bubble of light.

"We just gotta take it nice and easy," Gala advised. "My sources tell me we're a couple stories up, so it'll take a bit to get down. I'd avoid tripping, 'cause that will be a whole ordeal."

Their descent was slow. Stairs felt unstable, and at times, the whole room experienced minor tremors.

Soon, they could see the ground. Jewels and bones covered a dusty, golden concrete.

Dagnarone sniffed the air. "What's that smell?"

"These dungeons get a musk," Gala lied.

"That's no musk." Jerlone inhaled loudly. "That— that's the smell of death."

Gala bat a hand toward Jerlone. *How would he even know what death smells like?* He asked himself.

The stairwell wound into the ground. Engrained seven feet down was the door to Lower Level 2.

Gala walked to the keypad with his notes in hand. "The diamond should be one more level down. We're probably going to have to spend some time looking for it. Once we have it, we can call it a day. Maybe we'll find some of that coffee Dag's been craving. Always fun to treat yourself with something nice after one of these ordeals." He smiled, excited at the thought of the reward.

There was a loud stomp, and the ground shook.

The group looked to each other, their panicked silence almost palpable.

Every second, a low, breathy growl grew louder. The energy surrounding them shifted to make room for a monstrous threat.

Gala had to get the door open. He looked at his notes and saw the first two numbers of the access code. He entered them and looked back at the paper.

From above, a powerful blast of wind came crashing down. Gala lost his grip on the notes and watched as they floated up into the never-ending gloom.

"Oh, no, no, no, no, no," Gala yammered while jumping after them.

He couldn't see it, but he could sense there was something above them. It had to be the Sauros. They were known to be great runners who did not have to rely on their vision to be effective hunters.

For a brief second, Gala considered telling the others the truth, but fearing it would affect the mission, he reneged the decision.

"Please, tell me we aren't stuck here without that paper." Sephra sounded more annoyed than concerned.

"Well," Gala started, "I wouldn't say we're stuck, but we do need to find it to continue on."

"Continue on?" Jerlone scoffed. "There's something down here! We need to evacuate!"

"First off, let's not shout." Gala looked up and around, trying to get an idea if the Sauros was still stalking them. "Sephra, do you think you can split this light of ours into four pieces? We can cover more ground that way."

"I don't think it's wise to split up," Sephra suggested. "Jerlone is right; there's something down here. Danger is imminent."

"I will admit, it seems as if there's—something—with us. That's why I think we need to split up. If we stick together, then it may just look at us as one big threat. If we break apart, it may just see us as four smaller … inconveniences?" Gala wasn't sure if this logic would work on them. He knew they were wise enough to see through him.

"We need to be ready to face this challenge together." Sephra countered.

"Okay, I get what you're saying, but if we are together, it will take us four times longer to find what I need. Honestly, it's best if we split up so we cover more ground. That gets us out faster, which is the safest thing we could do."

Sephra glared at Gala. He could tell she did not want to venture further. Yet, as far as he was concerned, there was no other option. If they'd made it this far, they had to go all the way. As a last resort, he gave her his best smile.

Sephra sighed and waved her hand. The globe of light split into four pieces and floated over to each of the adventurers.

"We shouldn't be here." Jerlone crossed his arms. "It's too dangerous, and we all know it."

"You're overreacting," Dagnarone chimed in. "Yes, there is something down here, but I'm not sensing a threat."

Jerlone's face was incredulous. "Are you daft? You really don't feel the evil among us?"

A harrowing roar echoed throughout the chamber.

Jerlone and Sephra glared at Gala.

"What?" Gala asked. "You're worried about that? That could have been anything. Probably just the foundation again."

"It sounded dangerous," Jerlone emphasized.

"It didn't sound dangerous; it sounded scared," Dagnarone retorted.

"Things are at their most dangerous when they're scared."

"I don't know how you could have interpreted what you heard as anything other than a gentle soul crying out."

"Are you insane?" Jerlone nervously laughed while shaking his head. "We shouldn't be here!"

"We've just got to see what it wants in a nonthreatening way." Dagnarone spoke with conviction.

Gala couldn't wait for their debate to end. Every second, the paper blew further away. This wasn't the first time he'd abandoned a group, and it probably wouldn't be the last. As the argument raged on, he quietly snuck out.

CHAPTER 7

**PIMAR TEMPLE: LOWER LEVEL 1
EVENING**
. . . .

JERLONE CONTINUED TO bicker with Dagnarone for several minutes. He was genuinely baffled by her stance that nothing was wrong. The more they talked, the more frustrated he became. At one point, he debated walking back up the stairs and abandoning them.

"You need to learn to communicate," Dagnarone lectured. "Things can be hard and scary in life, but you can't just try to kill those problems!"

Jerlone rolled his eyes. "This is nonsense," he told her. "Gala, we need to—" He turned to find the sly adventurer gone. He sighed and shook his head. "Great, now he's left us. Can't say I'm surprised." He looked over to Sephra. "What do you think? Do we chase after him or get out and save our hides?"

Sephra paused to consider their options. "Leaving Gala is enticing," she opined, "but also wrong. Besides, Dag, you said you don't sense a threat down here, right?"

"With all my heart and soul, I don't believe we are in danger." Dagnarone nodded.

Sephra looked back to Jerlone, her face bleeding compassion. "We said we would help. If we can't be true to our word, then what good are we?"

"You've gotta be kidding me!" Jerlone snorted.

"I understand it's foolish, but this also seems really important to Gala. Besides, you said this probably isn't the first danger we've faced in the dark. Whatever challenges are thrown at us, I think we can handle them."

Jerlone was speechless. To him, it made no sense to stick their necks out for Gala. "This has to be the worst decision you've ever made."

"It's one of the only decisions I've ever made."

"Then, I guess you're not off to a good start." Jerlone shrugged. He knew it would be a waste of time to try to continue the debate. He walked away to begin searching for the parchment.

Jerlone was annoyed enough to forget about the lurking danger. He grumbled to himself as he dragged his feet about. His shoulders slouched and his head pointed down.

His glimmering globe only provided a three-foot radius of light. Otherwise, the room was an abyss. If he focused his eyes, he could see other little dots of light in the distance. It was a relief to be able to get some idea of where his companions stood. This area was so unfamiliar and substantial, it would be easy to get lost.

There were a lot of bones on the ground. Some were human-shaped and human-sized, while others were quite different. Skulls five feet tall were ripped apart. Ribcages ten feet wide leaned against giant columns. The more he saw, the more the place felt like a massive graveyard.

A familiar rush of wind passed over Jerlone.

He froze.

Something growled on his left.

Lightning and thunder erupted with three strikes. The room lit up, thanks to the skylights. With each flash of light, he could see the mighty Sauros. The reptilian monster stood twenty-five feet tall when on its hind legs. In those moments, its long, gangly arms dangled before it. Each appendage had three fingers or toes, all accompanied by razor sharp claws. The beast's snout was large and allowed for too many teeth, which pointed every which way with no uniformity. Steam poured from the nostrils, while a faint, orange glow simmered within.

The Sauros roared and slammed its arms and feet against the ground.

The lightning stopped and the room went pitch black.

Jerlone knew there was no chance of fighting it off. He turned and ran with no clear destination or plan.

He turned his head, hoping to see it. There was only darkness. With a flash of lightning, the monster was revealed, only feet away and closing in.

Jerlone picked up the pace as he noticed a light approaching.

The beast lurched its jaws forward.

At that moment, the other light collided into Jerlone, missing the teeth by inches. He and the other adventurer hurtled off to the side.

Lightning flashed as the Sauros ran past them. It was going too fast to stop and follow them.

Jerlone saw it was Gala who saved him. His eyes went wide, and his face scrunched up.

"Phew, that was a close one." Gala said, in a clear attempt to break the tension. "You, uh, didn't happen to find that paper, did you?"

"You knew this damn thing was down here the whole time!" Jerlone exploded.

"Whoa, whoa, whoa. I didn't *know* nothing! Sure, I had heard the myth but, you know, I assumed it was a myth!"

Rage boiled inside Jerlone. He was incensed at Gala for lying to them. He pointed at Gala, channeling all his frustration into the action. "If anyone gets hurt, you'll have to deal with me."

• • • •

Dagnarone heard the commotion in the distance but paid no attention to it. Bloodcurdling roars meant nothing to her, as she wasn't one to judge a situation by a horrible sound. She kept her nose down and continued looking for Gala's note.

When the ground shook, she knew the creature approached. Even with all the terror and chaos it caused, she was not worried.

Still hidden in the darkness, the Sauros came to a stop.

She could hear and feel it breathing. The orange glow within its nostrils was eye level. The creature was at rest, almost lying on its stomach.

Dagnarone twirled her left hand, and the light increased. The Sauros's head was right next to her, but it showed no signs of aggression. She patted its scaly hide and smiled.

"What's wrong?" Dagnarone soothed the Sauros. "Are you the one causing all this noise?" It whimpered as she pet it. "You're lonely," she empathized. "It's not your intention to harm anyone. You just don't know better. Been hurt too many times, haven't ya?" The two basked in a moment of silence. "I won't let them bother you. It's okay, you can be yourself."

• • • •

Sephra knew it was a bad idea to split up. It was likely to cost someone their life. Next time, she would have to be more commanding.

When the lightning flashed, she saw the monster they were dealing with. Victory didn't seem possible; they needed to evacuate.

She ran over to the two lights and was relieved to find Gala and Jerlone unharmed. There was something off about them though; tensions felt high. "Has anyone seen Dagnarone?" Sephra asked.

"I think she's over there," Jerlone pointed.

In the middle of the darkness was one little light. It expanded and brightened, revealing Dagnarone with the Sauros lying next to her. While the beast seemed docile, it was hard to tell if it actually was. Logic indicated it should still be on the hunt. They were too far away to get a good read.

Sephra grabbed her bow and nocked an arrow. She aimed high, so it would close the distance. After a few adjustments, she became steady as a rock. A small, red energy formed in her hands and slid off onto her weapon. It spread to the tip of the arrow, ready to enhance the strike.

"You sure you should attack it?" Gala questioned.

"Can't risk it hurting Dagnarone." Sephra released the arrow.

A small, red trail of energy followed the arrow through the darkness. It struck the Sauros ribcage, a particularly sensitive area.

The beast roared and attempted to stand. Flames shot from its nose. It shifted its focus to where the attack came from and readied itself for the next strike.

Sephra saw Dagnarone running around the beast and waving her arms but did not know what she was trying to convey. Surprisingly, the Sauros seemed to be avoiding her during its dance of destruction.

Sephra shot another arrow, but the monster snatched it out of the air. She fired a few consecutively and some pierced it while others were bat aside.

Jerlone put his hands toward the enemy and charged them up. Red globes of energy shot forth, burning through the monster's scales.

The Sauros was fed up. It spit fire in between its dominant roars. Drool splashed out its mouth. Feet stomped in place as it hyped itself up. It charged and disappeared into the dark.

With a flutter of lightning, they saw the monster airborne. No one expected an attack from above. It would crash down on them in seconds.

"Move!" Sephra shouted.

As the three adventurers tried to escape, they slipped. The ground didn't feel like concrete. There was something cool pressing against their skin.

With another flash of lightning, Sephra saw they were on a glass floor. Below them was Lower Level 2, a significant drop from this height.

When the Sauros slammed into the glass, cracks formed and spread to the edges. With this weight, it would not hold long.

The glass continued to vibrate for half a minute, while everyone struggled to get up.

Sephra was the first on her feet. She could see the glass cracking below her and knew there was no time to help anyone else. She pushed off and didn't stop til she made solid ground. There, she saw a bewildered Dagnarone.

"What are you idiots doing?" Dagnarone scolded.

"Trying to save your life!" Sephra snapped back.

"How? By getting us killed?"

"Hey, that thing was ready to eat you!"

Dagnarone scrunched her face. "What are you talking about? It doesn't want to eat us! We taste terrible! It's just scared and trying to defend itself! I was almost done explaining our situation until you morons had to ruin it!"

Sephra paused. "You almost convinced it to stop?"

"*Yes!*"

Sephra went silent. "Uh … sorry about that."

Dagnarone shook her head. "I would have expected something like this from Gala, but you?"

Without hesitating, Dagnarone walked onto the glass and headed for the Sauros.

"Dag!" Sephra shouted after her. "It's not safe! We need to go!"

"Don't worry," Dagnarone hollered back. "I'm going to get it to stop!"

Sephra did not like how this was going. She looked for the guys and saw a disheartening sight. Jerlone was still out in the middle of the glass. He was walking incredibly slowly; a look of terror covered his face. Gala was closer, but the cracks were getting worse with each step he took.

The Sauros thrashed about. Flames shot from its mouth and nose, making the room feel like Hell.

The glass was at a breaking point. One wrong move and it would all come crashing down.

Sephra watched as Dagnarone stood feet from the beast, trying to grab its attention. "You have to stop," Dagnarone begged. "The more you struggle the greater the danger you create. We aren't here for you; we just need to find something and we'll leave." The desperation in her voice increased with each word. "Please! Just calm down for one moment! We need to show them that this can be resolved without violence!"

That's when the glass shattered, sending the Sauros, Dagnarone and Jerlone down to Lower Level 2.

CHAPTER 8

PIMAR TEMPLE: LOWER-LEVEL DOOR
EVENING
· ·

GALA JUMPED TOWARD the concrete as the glass fell out from under him. He landed with his torso clinging to the edge, his feet dangling down.

Below him was Lower Level 2. Torches sufficiently lit the space. He could see the Sauros was breathing but immobile. Dagnarone and Jerlone were not moving either.

Then, Gala saw what he came there for. Sitting atop a rocky pedestal was the Diamond of Farrokh. The green crystal was unmistakable. Seeing it made his heart flutter and injected a new sense of stupid courage into him. If he was ready to retreat before, then he was ready to charge forward now.

Sephra raced over to Gala and hoisted him up. "Are they okay?" she asked, her words more urgent than ever.

"Hard to say from this height," Gala informed her. "Regardless, we've gotta get down there. You didn't happen to find my note with the passcode, did you?"

"Of course not!"

"Damn." Gala looked over the edge to assess the height. The drop was too great. "Alright, maybe you can pry the door open with your powers."

"What? How would I even do that?" Sephra grimaced like that was the worst idea she'd ever heard.

"You just kinda, I don't know, dig your magic into it? There's gotta be something in your bag of tricks you can use. Dagnarone said y'all are forces of nature. If that's the case, it should be real easy to rip a door open."

She rolled her eyes. "This doesn't sound like the most well thought out plan."

"They never do when you're in a jam like this." Gala smirked.

• • • •

Sephra stood ten feet from the stairwell door, looking for a weakness or opening. It was only a little larger than an average door but was made of fine metals. Otherwise, it wasn't anything special.

"What's the hold up?" Gala pressed. "Just dig your astral nails in and pull or something. I don't know. You're the Mystic, so you would probably have a better idea than me."

"It would be best if you stayed quiet and let me handle it." Sephra did not look at him.

"Got it. You're totally right. People are always telling me they can't concentrate when I'm yapping my flap." She shot him a glare, hoping it would silence him. "Sorry."

Sephra raised her arms and began conjuring a spell. Dots of magic floated through the air and seeped into the doors. She moved her hands and arms about as though it were a dance.

The doors shifted and budged but not much else.

Sephra needed to give her arms a rest. She put in enough effort to exhaust herself.

"So, you think you're getting the hang of it?" Gala asked with little confidence.

Sephra was competitive, and his comment set her off. She would show him. Without saying anything, she stood and took a few steps forward. With her eyes closed, she conducted the spell again.

It seemed easier to manipulate the doors that time. They jostled around ferociously with each wave of her arms.

She got dizzy and slumped down to breathe. Victory was close, and she could feel it. She was exhausted but not defeated. Her siblings needed her, and that gave her the strength to stand.

She took another few steps toward the door. She summoned her magic and pushed harder than before. Needing just a little more, she stepped forward. When her magic increased, it shot one of the doors down the stairwell.

Sephra had to take a moment to rest or else she would be no good to anyone. She collapsed onto the stairs.

"That was amazing!" Gala complimented her. "I knew you could do it. Now, listen, when we get down there, you get the others to safety, okay? I'll take care of everything else."

She thought his phrasing odd, then it hit her. "You're going for the crystal, aren't you!"

"You know it," he told her with a wink. He reached for his pistol and began loading it.

"It's not worth it!"

"Don't worry, darling, I ain't defenseless." He smirked. "I got ol' faithful here." Gala spun the pistol chamber and took off down the stairs.

CHAPTER 9

PIMAR TEMPLE: LOWER LEVEL 2
EVENING

"How did that drop hurt more than the other?" Jerlone groaned.

Shards of glass surrounded him, and one cut his side. Placing his hand on the wound, his palm glowed gold. He winced as the wound sealed itself back up. After the spell faded, he looked at his hand, which was now covered in blood. It was worth it, for the bleeding stopped. There was still pain, but at least it was beginning to subside.

There wasn't much light, but Jerlone could make out the details around him. Treasure and diamonds littered the floor. Everything in this room seemed majestic. The plundering would be plentiful, but they still had to get out.

Thankfully, the Sauros was still incapacitated, but it was unlikely to stay that way for long. Dagnarone was passed out beside its stomach.

Jerlone knew it would be inappropriate to save his neck and not help her. Carefully, he pulled himself up. The first few steps were with a slight limp, until he could straighten himself out. Pain coursed through his body, but he pushed through.

The Sauros's breathing picked up. A weak growl formed in its throat as it attempted to roar.

When Jerlone reached Dagnarone, he nudged her with his foot. She attempted to bat it away, and he continued prodding her.

"Dag, get up," Jerlone pleaded.

"Wha … ?" a disoriented Dagnarone mumbled. "Wha's … going on?"

The Sauros twisted its head to look at them. Every second, it gained more energy.

"This thing will be up any minute, and we need to be out before that happens." Jerlone told her.

She looked around, her eyes half-open. She did not seem cognizant enough to realize the severity of the situation.

"Dag, we've gotta move!" He reached down to give her a hand.

Like he'd flipped a switch, she became self-aware. With a jolt, she sprang up. "Get yourself to the stairs," she commanded. "It should be somewhat safe there."

Jerlone studied her face, trying to figure out her plan. "And what exactly are you going to do?"

"Try to reason with it."

He rolled his eyes and threw his arms in the air. "No, you aren't! There is no reasoning with this monster!"

The Sauros wagged its tail, which came dangerously close to smashing the two Mystics.

Jerlone grabbed her hand. "Please, I know you want to try to help it, but that's not going to work. We need to get out." Dagnarone looked at Jerlone's hand and then to the Sauros. It seemed as though tears were forming in her eyes, though her face looked as indecisive as possible. "Dag, please." Jerlone knew this wasn't easy for her.

She conceded and stepped away.

The Sauros began to rally. It lumbered onto its hind legs and screeched a deafening roar. Flames once again shot from its nostrils.

The two Mystics quickly, but cautiously, maneuvered through the field of glass barefoot, each step a little faster than the last. Once they cleared that area, it would be a straight shot to the stairs.

The beast crouched onto all fours. It kicked back its hind legs then leapt forward.

Dagnarone turned her head and saw it approaching. She fell a few steps behind.

"Faster, faster!" Jerlone yelled at her. "Must go faster!"

Lightning flashed, enhancing the terror of the situation.

They were closing in on the stairs as fast as the Sauros was closing in on them.

Gala Goda stood atop the stairwell and cracked his whip. The snap was loud as thunder.

The Sauros froze.

In Gala's other hand was his pistol. He aimed it at the Sauros and fired. The bullet cut way to the left, missing his target entirely. "Damn," he grumbled. Keeping his eyes on the Sauros, he cracked his whip again and walked down the steps.

Jerlone and Dagnarone climbed the stairs, now a safe distance from their stalker. They reached Gala and stopped to reconvene.

"Everyone alright?" Gala asked.

"Mostly." Jerlone checked his side, the blood already slowing down.

"Good. Sephra is up by the door. Go to her and get yourselves to safety."

"You say that like you're not coming with us."

"Well, I see what I'm looking for. No point going through all this to go home empty handed."

"Gala!" Jerlone yelled at him. "It is not worth it!"

"Maybe for you it ain't, which is why I'm doing this by myself!" Gala smiled and jumped off the side of the stairwell.

Hiding behind a column, he waited for the Sauros to meander over. If he could distract the beast there, he could then run to the diamond. Once he started running, he would need to keep the pace. These days, that was a task easier said than done.

Peering around the column, he saw the Sauros nearing in on him. It was slow and moved strategically. Keeping its nose down, it sniffed to find the right spot, inching closer and closer.

It was time for Gala to make his mad dash. With the monster's head directly to his right, he turned to his left and booked it.

Upon realizing the deception, the Sauros snapped back to an upright position and roared.

Gala only had a head start for a few seconds. When he looked back, he saw the Sauros closing in on him. A helpful jolt of scared energy propelled him forward. He regretted not stretching prior, because his legs were burning.

The Diamond of Farrokh sat atop a rocky pillar. Stairs etched into the stone ascended in a counterclockwise direction. Some steps had crumbled over the years, making it a difficult trek. Gala wasn't sure how that would go, but he intended to find out.

Upon reaching the pillar, he stopped and cracked his whip. The Sauros froze. The two combatants locked eyes as Gala backed up the first step. After making it up a few more, the Sauros leaned in and snapped its jaws. Gala whipped its snout and it retreated.

The beast circled the pillar in a clockwise direction. It would swipe and bite at Gala as it passed him. Each time, the whip deterred a successful strike.

As Gala approached the top, he slipped. Hanging onto the side, he saw the Sauros round the pillar and scrambled to regain his footing.

Jaws snapped inches from Gala's body. He cracked his whip and struck the beast's eye. As the monster reeled in pain, Gala raced to the top.

The diamond sat in the middle of a small landing. It only took Gala a few steps to reach it. Grabbing it, he realized it was heavier than expected. Diamond in one hand and whip in the other, he raced for the edge.

Gala jumped off the pillar and cracked his whip. It wrapped around a nearby flagpole, allowing him to swing toward the stairs. When he hit the ground, he rolled and sprang right back to his feet.

The Sauros saw this act of bravado and, without wasting a second, went for him.

Gala never ran faster in his life. He turned his head and saw the monster approach. Looking ahead, he saw the stairs in the distance.

● ○ ◦ ●

Jerlone and Dagnarone did not get to safety. They watched the events unfold and agreed it did not look promising.

Jerlone knew Gala would only survive if he stepped in to help. He also knew Dagnarone would not approve his method either. Without saying a word or looking at her, he walked down the stairs.

"Where are you going?" Dagnarone chased after him.

He wasn't ignoring her to be rude; he was summoning a spell that used his surroundings to assist. The magic required all his concentration.

The thunder and lightning increased while the air became humid.

Jerlone took a breath and shot his arm up into the air. It lingered there for a second before he snapped it down. A second later, lighting pierced through the temple walls and struck the Sauros.

A final, harrowing screech left the beast's body as it fell to the ground.

"No!" Dagnarone screamed as she took off for the creature.

It was too late by the time she reached it. The Sauros had passed and was at peace.

CHAPTER 10

PIMAR TEMPLE: QUEEN SWIFAN'S CHAMBERS
NIGHT
. . . .

"YOU DIDN'T HAVE to kill it!" Dagnarone screamed at Jerlone from the royal bed. With an ancient pair of straighteners and a touch of magic, she focused on her hair. Her natural curls were soon looking smooth and stylized.

"There was no other choice!" Jerlone objected. "I'm mad at Gala, but I don't think it warrants us watching him die!" Their conversation became so intense he had to pace around the room to try to calm down.

The three Mystics were in Queen Swifan's room, located in the upper levels. It was beautifully garnished with burgundy velvet and lavish wooden furniture. Diamond chandeliers cast a hypnotic multicolored atmosphere. A grand balcony faced Civis. The city was exquisitely lit and seemed so peaceful in the distance.

They wore bathrobes while they made alterations to their cloaks. Fabrics, belts, jackets, and even hats cluttered the floor. It took hours for them to find this assortment of materials.

"I was this close—*this close*—to talking it down!" Dagnarone gestured a minuscule distance with her fingers.

"No, you weren't!" Jerlone shot back. "It was on a bloody rampage!"

"I could have calmed it down if *someone* hadn't dragged me away!"

"Dragged you? I did no such thing!" He stomped his foot one step forward.

"Do we need to be this heated?" Sephra questioned her companions. She was sitting at a table, working on a red cape. Of the three, she was the furthest ahead and most organized. "I think we all need to take a moment and calm down. Obviously, there was a lot going on. We can all agree mistakes were made."

"I didn't make any mistakes," Jerlone corrected her.

"That's not helping." Sephra pointed at him.

"We shouldn't go around killing animals that are scared by our actions." A red energy swirled around Dagnarone's straighteners. Steam billowed from her hair, making her seem all the angrier. "They might not be human, but murder is still murder."

"Did you not see all the bones lying around?" Jerlone asked her. "You think that thing was innocent? Let me tell you something: it killed. It may not have wanted to, but it did it to survive. That's all we did. We killed something to survive."

"We didn't kill it; you did."

"Then your conscience should be clear." Jerlone glared at her.

Dagnarone looked down and went back to altering her robes. She hated herself for not being able to save the Sauros. This life was supposed to be a nonviolent one, yet here she was already mourning.

She felt like a failure.

• • • •

An hour later, their outfits were still far from done. It was a quiet hour, as everyone reflected on the fight preceding it.

Sephra found the silence deafening and decided it could no longer continue. "Anyone given thought to what they want to do with their lives?"

"Haven't really had the chance yet," Jerlone eventually grumbled. He sat in a chair, sewing buttons to his cloak.

"Same," Dagnarone mumbled, not bothering to look up.

"Well, if you're willing to hear me out, I have a suggestion," Sephra said.

Jerlone shook his head. "I may not know what I want to do, but I do know one thing: I don't want to do what you want to do."

"Oh, really, and what is it I want to do?"

"I don't know your exact plan, but you're gonna get into some trouble.

You're going to get in over your head for some idealized reality that doesn't exist, and I don't want any part of it."

Sephra did not know what to say. "You don't know that I'll get in over my head," she replied defensively.

"Everyone gets in over their head."

Sephra grimaced.

"Fine." Jerlone rolled his eyes. "Why don't you tell us your idea."

"Thank you." Sephra smiled and stood to address her colleagues. "As you know, we have a power, and I think our purpose is to help people with it. I know what you're going to say. We don't have to use our magic for violence. We can help the world in other ways. If we work together, we can make things better for these people."

"Interesting," Dagnarone spoke up. "We said we didn't want to lead violent lives, so you thought of some other way to use us."

"Come on," Sephra shot back. "It's not like that! What's wrong with wanting to spend time with you? I see your potential, and I think if we work together, we can do great things! I don't want you to do something you're uncomfortable with, but is it so wrong to want to continue our relationship?"

Dagnarone did not reply.

"Do you have anything specific in mind?" Jerlone asked.

"I don't know." Sephra grimaced. "Something simple. We are not corrupt like politicians, nor ruined by the spoils of money. We can really start a revolution for the people!"

Jerlone laughed. "Start a revolution for the people? How is that something simple? Besides, you don't even know what troubles plague them! Who are you looking to start a war with?"

"Just because I don't know them right now, doesn't mean there aren't evils that need vanquishing!" She motioned to the three of them. "Together, we could change the power balance and make the world a better place!"

Gala walked in, adorned in a fluffy, pink bathrobe. He was drying his wet mop of hair with a towel. "Can't believe they still had hot, running water here. It must be one good heater they got in the place. Wouldn't build 'em like that today, I tell ya."

"Gala, I've a question for you." Sephra turned to him. "If I wanted to save this world, who would I need to … fight?"

"Having asked for my qualified, albeit biased, opinion, I would say

Fascio is the biggest threat. His family has always given the world something to fear."

"What are his crimes?"

"He's the king of a damned land. His family has ruled there since the end of the Early Wars, and every one of them has been a brutal dictator. The land there is very rocky, and because of it, they don't have many natural resources. They've found the best way to get what they want is invasion. They pillage and slaughter, then move on. Most of the wars throughout recorded history have been because of them. I mean, don't get me wrong, there's always other wars that don't involve them, but those tend to die down after a while. All in all, he's got every deplorable quality a leader can have. If he were gone, everyone would prosper."

"Or would an even worse enemy take his place?" Jerlone questioned.

"Can't imagine anyone worse than him." Gala shrugged.

"Why has no one put an end to their reign?" Sephra stepped onto the balcony and looked up to the sky. The storm had passed and the night stars were visible. Spots of the sky glistened with interstellar bodies of cosmic light. The universal roof felt infinite and inspiring.

"World politics are complicated. There were some good reasons for their inaction. At one point, Fascio had the Crown of Karbank. That would have been a mess. If they'd used that … game over. Another time, the Fascios had a few Mystics on their side. They cursed crops and dried rivers. Some scary stuff. It took a while for other Mystics to unite and fight."

Sephra turned to Dagnarone and Jerlone. "Sounds like this world needs Mystics to step up and save the day here and there." They rolled their eyes in response. Sephra turned back to Gala. "What's the current excuse for not dealing with this vermin?"

"King Coart is a lazy slob who has no interest in solving a problem like Fascio." Gala sighed. "As long as he's not attacked, he doesn't care."

"Then he shouldn't be leading you."

"Eh, he's barely leading us." Gala ran his hand through his hair. "The title of king is more a ceremonial title than anything. It's really the senators and congress running the show."

"Then, why aren't they doing anything?"

"'Cause, they're the same as him. I wouldn't expect them to lift a finger. You know, if Coart took a little interest and tried to persuade them, it would probably get done. The only other way they would do something is if they could profit off it, and there's a lot of profit with wars—until you end them. So, if they were to remove him from power, the war money stops, and then they can't afford their extravagant treasures."

"Perhaps I can persuade this king to change his mind. Where can I find him?" Sephra walked back inside.

"You think you'll get him to change his mind?" Gala chuckled.

"Yes," she said without hesitation.

Gala nodded respectfully. "The Hidden Castle in the Forest of Light."

"Is it easy to find?"

"It has the word 'hidden' in the name, so … no."

"Oh," she fell back down into her chair. She was not expecting it to be so hard to speak to a king.

Gala looked at Jerlone and Dagnarone. "You know, you two could benefit from going there. A lot of Mystics have visited the kingdom, probably a lot you can learn about, and Dag, you would love walking through the Forest of Light. The closer you get to the castle, the brighter the trees buzz."

"What makes them do that?" Dagnarone ripped the sleeves off her cloak.

"Ancient Mystics' spells," Gala answered. "Same reason it's 'hidden.' The forest moves around and rearranges itself. The light is a guide to help you know you're going the right way. I went there once as a kid, and it was really a sight to see, like walking through the stars."

"That does sound exciting," Dagnarone conceded.

"Look," Sephra addressed her fellow Mystics, "I understand you don't want to fight, but what if you accompanied me to the castle? I think we're meant to be together, and what if this journey gives us a little more time to discover our purpose as a team?" Her heart pounded. She was terrified they would abandon her. As strong as she was, she wasn't strong enough to be alone.

Jerlone and Dagnarone looked at one another.

"I don't think we will get what we want out of this," Jerlone told Dagnarone.

"I think you're right," Dagnarone conceded.

"But … you feel it, don't you?"

"Like we have to go with her?"

"Yes."

Dagnarone paused. "I hate to say it, but a part of me is looking forward to it."

"I don't know why that is."

"Nostalgia I guess." She shrugged.

"Does that mean you'll join me?" Sephra asked. A smile slowly crept across her face.

"As long as you don't expect me to fight for you," Dagnarone answered.

"There's still a lot we can learn together." Jerlone rubbed his chin. "Don't plan to use me for your own means, but yes, I will join."

Sephra smiled and turned to Gala. "Would you be able to guide us to the castle?"

Gala sighed. "Under other circumstances, I would love to, but I got places to be." He walked out to the balcony and looked around. "Well, maybe I can get you to the forest. It's a little bit out of my way—but I'll do it for you."

"Are you sure?" Sephra's eyes lit up.

"You really helped me out getting the diamond. I owe you that much. How about this: tomorrow, we go into Civis and I get you set up with a few things, we catch a train, and you should be sleeping on dirt forty-eight hours from now."

CHAPTER 11

ONE WEEK PRIOR
THE THRONE ROOM OF LORD FASCIO
NIGHT
....

"**YOU BECKONED, MY** lord?" Constable Zawkins bowed toward the throne. His stomach churned, as it always did before his King.

The room was dark and dank. Sharp, rusted metals cluttered together, decorating the space. Broken picture frames and discarded food trashed the ground. The carpet and wallpaper were torn to shreds. There was nothing royal about this place.

"*Yes*, my dear," Lord Fascio squealed. "Yes, indeed. It would seem I have had one of my moments of ... inspiration."

The throne was made of a Sauros skull. The mouth was agape and a chair sat within in lieu of a tongue. Jagged teeth surrounded Fascio as he lounged. He was dressed in a black-and-orange royal garb that was in tatters.

Lord Fascio was known as Mountain Folk. Slender features defined them, though they stood nine feet tall. Hairless, their skin was a sickly shade of white. Pointed, mangled teeth were normal and desired. The eyes were two black holes, presenting no emotion, just despair.

"Wonderful. We love your vision." Zawkins mustered enough enthusiasm to sound convincing. He stood and began pacing. "How can I make your dreams come to fruition?" He withdrew a notepad and pen.

"That's a good boy." Fascio grinned like the devil. "Now, listen close.

First, we're going to attack the province of Larkin. You're familiar with that dreadful land?"

"Yes, your excellency. The beach town where King Coart vacations. It's not a strategic location, if I may say." Zawkins made sure to choose his words carefully. "No crops, nor an industrious city. Their population is not fit for hard labor. Of all the places I would recommend attacking, it would be far from the top."

"I know, which is why we will send a teensy army." Fascio pinched his gangly fingers together; the nails were cracked and brown. "Next, our mole will inform Coart of the impending attack. He'll respond the same way I would—with ego. His property will need protecting, and they'll deploy troops. I'm banking on him being the whelp I know him to be and send too many. Then, our second, larger army attacks the Hidden Castle. The reserves protecting it should be easily overpowered. We lay claim to the castle and put Coart's head on a pike."

Zawkins tapped his chin with an index finger while contemplating things. He believed in Fascio but was not sold on this plan. It seemed simplistic. "There are four matters I would like to address," he finally said. "The first is the most obvious to me: the Forest of Light. We know how the landscape changes. You really think it possible to lead an army through there?"

"Yes, I do." Fascio stood. He lifted his arms and grabbed hold of the skull. Hoisting himself up, he began crawling over it. Mountain Folk were natural climbers, and this often helped them think. "I take it you're familiar with General Trekken? Twenty years ago, he navigated our people through the Valley of Despisen. That has become one of our proudest victories. Recently, he's been scouting the forest, learning its ways. He has assured me, through penalty of death, that he can lead our troops through that wooden labyrinth. He has been studying the notes of General Piety and learning from Piety's journey forty years ago. As I told him, we've done it once and we will do it again."

"I see. Very good." Zawkins nodded, factoring that information into his analysis. "Now, once we've taken the castle … then what? Outside of the significance of the occupation, I don't see much opportunity coming from it."

"The castle isn't important; killing Coart is. As long as we accomplish that, our mission will be a success. If we're able to take out any of their other politicians, then that's just icing on the delicious cake."

"Got it. Makes perfect sense." Zawkins stopped pacing. He made eye contact with Fascio. "What about retaliation, my liege? I find it very unlikely Wundrian will sit around after their closest ally is assassinated."

"Who are they to threaten me?" Fascio laughed. "Mervelliere is the strongest country, and they will be in disarray. Other kingdoms may be allies, but only to a point. Do you think Wundrian will sacrifice their people to avenge another leader? I find it unlikely. Should they retaliate, it would be with a smaller force. I know these people. They are weak cowards. We have nothing to worry about."

"Of course, sir. They will be no problem for us." Zawkins resumed pacing. "I believe the only other matter for me to discuss is how many troops you want deployed."

"Ten thousand are to be sent to the Hidden Castle." Fascio crawled to the front of the skull. "Two thousand will be sent to the province of Larkin."

Zawkins paused and contemplated. With trepidation, he spoke. "That's a lot of troops to lose at the province."

"There's plenty to spare. Our people are loyal. They will understand the sacrifice I'm asking of them."

"Just please keep in mind, they are not an unlimited resource."

Fascio raised his voice. "You think I don't know that?"

"I think you don't care to acknowledge that fact." It took all his courage to say so, but it was for the good of the people. Zawkins had to convince his king to make the best decision, even if it put himself at risk. "You're a brilliant mind, yet you sometimes get lost in the forest for all the trees."

Fascio flashed a crooked grin. "That's true, I do have that tendency. One of my … *charms*."

"And a lovely charm it is. We wouldn't want you any other way." Zawkins forced a smile. He looked down at his notepad, once again going through everything they discussed. "Before I depart, do you have any final requests?"

"Send the filthy humans for this. Mountain Folk and Mossitaurs are too valuable."

"Excellent point, much more expendable." Zawkins was human and these comments did bother him, but he was used to it by now. He wouldn't have reached this rank if he wasn't the utmost professional.

"I've already informed Emissary Mortar to contact our mole and inform her the wheels are in motion."

Zawkins nodded and turned for the door. There were still concerns on his mind, but he did not know how to express them. Before exiting, he stopped and turned to his ruler. "If I may give you an alternative point of view," Zawkins backtracked and walked toward the throne. "You're relying on your enemy responding the way you hope he will, which from my experience, is rarely ever the case. If everything goes according to plan, it will be a beautiful victory. But please remember: you've put me in this position to question you and make sure all possibilities have been discussed. I will always follow you to the very end. The very darkest of ends if I must. But I have to know … is this attack truly worth the risk?"

Fascio dismounted the skull. He marched toward Zawkins with an imposing step. "My family's dynasty has outlasted any other by thousands of years. Yet, for some reason, we are looked at as weak. Some misguided child, lashing out when we don't get our way. And why is that? We've managed to endure! Is it jealousy? Do they refuse to acknowledge our success because they know they can never attain it themselves? They have to accuse us of cheating and stealing and being in the wrong, even though they do the same things! My family has defined this world's history, yet they talk of us as if we're simply spit in a trashcan! I cannot tolerate such disrespect anymore! They mock us!" Saliva flew from his mouth, landing on his subordinate. "Their laughing and sneering, it haunts my days and my dreams! It will not go on any longer! When they say our name, they should feel a pit in their stomach so strong they would rather die than face us!" Fascio regained his composure. "And that is what I plan to achieve. I will take out the world's most protected leader and show them that no one is beyond my reach. Fascios are not the outcasts … we are the rulers." He let that statement linger. "So, yes, they are all worth sacrificing if it shows my enemy that I am not to be trifled with."

Zawkins took a moment to let that sink in before responding. "Completely understood, sir. I will begin our preparations. I look forward to our inevitable victory."

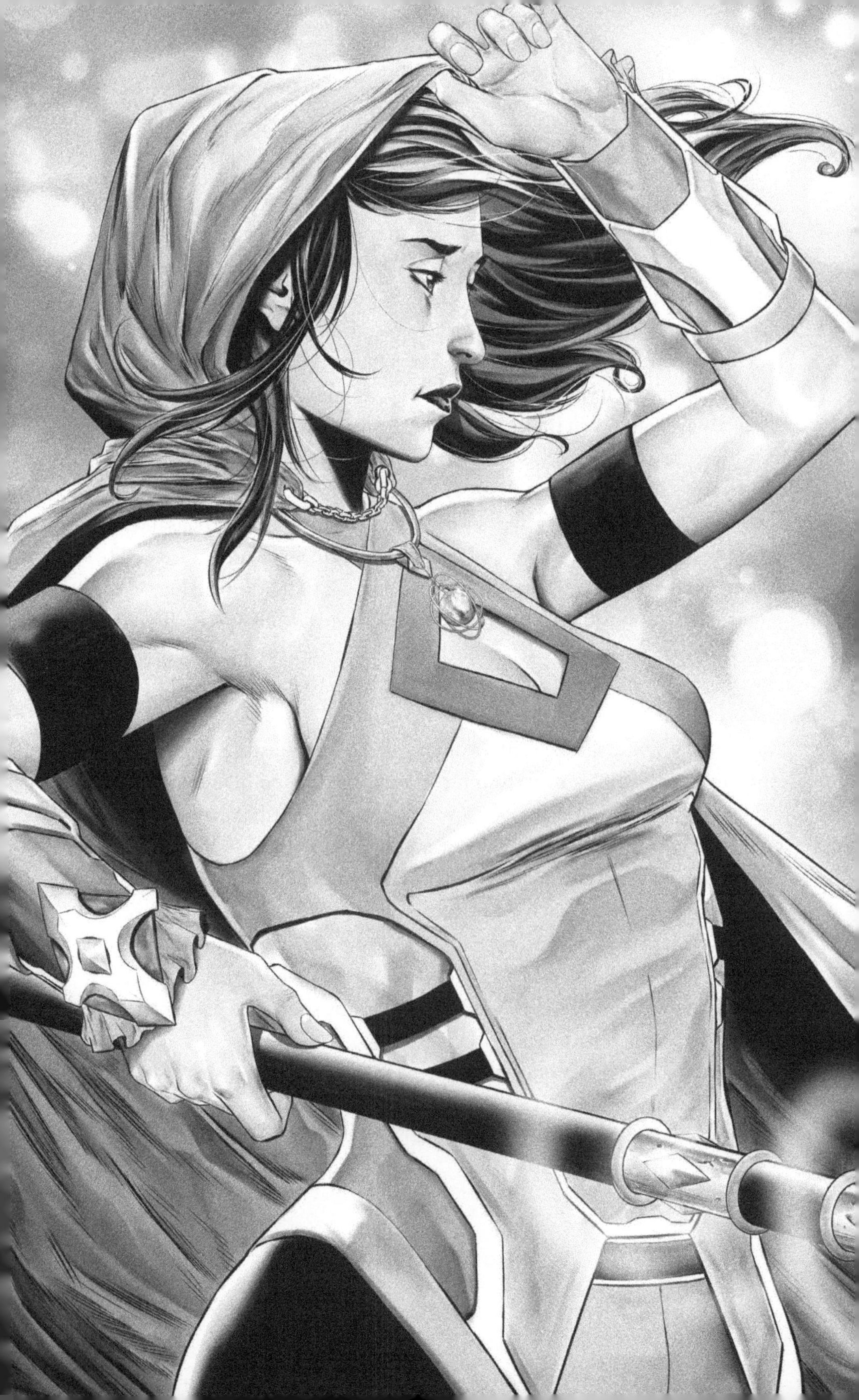

2
JOURNEY TO THE FOREST OF LIGHT

CHAPTER 12

STREAWBERIGE FIELD
DAWN

THE FIELD WAS a muddy mess. The storm did a number that would take days to dry out.

The morning itself was beautiful. Few clouds lingered from the storm as the sun rose. The temperature was comfortable and the wind nonexistent.

Dagnarone and Gala walked ahead of the other two.

Even though Dagnarone's boot occasionally got stuck in the mud, she didn't mind. Unlike Gala, she didn't care if her footwear got a little dirty. She found it childish that Gala gave his own so much attention. It was especially silly since, as far as she could tell, his shoes were nothing special. If anything, she thought the mud plastering the red added some character.

Dagnarone looked like a brand-new person. Her magenta robes had been transformed into a cloak. She wore the hood up, unlike before. Underneath was a matching sleeveless tunic. A purple armband wrapped around her bicep. Her pants and boots continued the purple look. She was comfortable and happy.

"Then, about two years after they died, I joined a fishing crew," Gala droned on. "The ship was called *The Belafont*, and we were … really not that well put together."

Luckily for Gala, Dagnarone cared about his story. She enjoyed his company and wanted to get to know him better. She felt bad she didn't have much to share with him. "Big boat?" Dagnarone asked.

"Nah, needed a bigger one, but you take what ya can sometimes. I did that from fifteen to nineteen. Everyone called me 'the intern.' I hated it. Even when I saved their hides, they'd still call me that. So, one day when we made port, I left and never turned back."

"It's surprising you were a fisherman and not a pirate."

"Is that supposed to be an insult?" Gala cocked his head.

"A little bit, yes."

"Well, you'll be happy to know that—hmm, wait—I guess we did steal from some other boats. Does that count as pirating?"

"I'm assuming there was a good excuse?"

Gala took a second to answer. "Does petty revenge count?"

"Did you kill the innocent?"

"Hey, I'm not like that!" Gala pointed at her. "I only kill someone if I know they're tryin' to kill me!"

"I would say you dabbled in piracy then." She smiled.

"Just to be clear, we did a lot of fishing too."

"And which did you enjoy more?"

"I think you know that answer." Gala smirked. "You said you used to sail around on a boat?"

She looked at him with a raised eyebrow. "Yeah, in another life. If you haven't seen me do it in the last fifteen hours, you can assume I have no real memories of it."

"Come on, you know what I mean. You people remember things. Maybe not the clearest, but if you think about things, you get glimpses."

Dagnarone thought about the sea and a feeling flooded her. It was like her soul was riding the ocean waves. Thinking of it made her long to be back out there. "I can remember a few details, but they're hazy."

"Fishing? You look like a fisher."

"No, I was a protector of the ocean. We saved aquatic life and cleaned spills. It was an adventure fighting the elements. I met the great love of my life doing that." She stopped and looked to the horizon. Her eyes longed for another. "I miss her terribly."

Gala patted her back. "I'm sorry."

"Thank you." She wiped a tear from her cheek, hoping Gala didn't see. "It's odd. I can't recall her name or see her face, but I just know I have this love in my soul for her."

"They say love travels with us from one life to the next."

"I believe it."

They began walking.

"So, you want us to try to get you on a boat? See if lightning strikes twice?" Gala chuckled.

"It's not like I fell for her because she worked on a boat." Dagnarone rolled her eyes. "I would have fallen for her anywhere. Besides, I need to figure out my own life first. That would be a terrible first date. She asks what I want to do with myself and I'm clueless. Real desirable."

Gala laughed. "You think people ever know what they want? You'd sit down on that date and bond over both of you having no clue. No one's got any idea about what will make them happy." He shook his head. "You not having a clear path … that's nothing special. You're unique in many ways, but not there."

"You seem like you know what you want."

Gala shrugged. "I wouldn't be too sure about that. Could be time for a change." He sighed. "Who's to say I don't go around wanting … something else." He looked off toward the rising sun.

• • • •

Sephra and Jerlone were still a few steps behind. They needed a reprieve from hearing Gala talk about his glory days.

Sephra's robes were now a cape. The vivid red drew the eye. A black shirt peeked out from underneath her golden armor. A skirt flowed down to her knees, while sturdy boots kept her feet dry. She had her blue bow and a brown quiver of arrows strapped to her back. Two *sai* hung from her belt. Thick bracelets hugged her wrists. Her hair was pulled into a braided ponytail. All in all, she looked majestic.

Jerlone had turned his emerald cloak into a trench coat with golden trim. Beneath was a light-purple shirt with a red collar and a dark pair of pants. No weapons or armor adorned him. He looked handsome and inconspicuous.

In general, the two did not spend a lot of their time talking.

After a period of silence, Sephra realized it was best to try to form some sense of comradery. The problem was she had nothing to talk about. "Dagnarone still mad at you?" she eventually asked.

"Would seem it," Jerlone answered.

She got the sense he didn't want to talk about it. Thinking of how his frustrations toward Dagnarone could sour the group, Sephra found it best to try to defend her. "She's just really passionate."

"Too passionate."

"I was very impressed when you killed the Sauros. I wouldn't have thought to use the elements like that."

"Not sure where I got the idea. I guess I consider it divine inspiration at this point, but it sure wasn't easy."

"It's difficult to conjure a spell for the first time. But when you cast it a second time, it's easier. A third attempt is even easier, and so on. It's hard to break through that barrier, but once you do, it begins to flow."

"I have noticed that," Jerlone agreed. "We need to build up our endurance. The wave of exhaustion that hits after summoning is crippling. Even with it getting easier, I still need a minute to catch my breath."

"It'll make us stronger in the end." A smile spread across her face. She was starting to feel something between them. It was obvious it would still take a while to get him to open up all the way, but she felt she was on the right path.

Jerlone nodded. "Mmm."

They went back to walking in silence for a time.

Jerlone broke the stillness. "Where do you think we come from?"

Sephra froze, worried how her response would come across. "I think … you're not going to like my answer," she said.

"And why's that?"

"Because I don't think it matters where we come from. I know that issue is important to you, but it's not to me. I assume we came from the ether of the universe. For me, it's not about where we've been but the journey we are on. It's best to look ahead and strive for tomorrow rather than relive yesterday."

"Dagnarone said the same thing." He scoffed.

"Then, maybe we know what we're talking about," Sephra articulated with a level of authority.

"You can't strive for a better tomorrow if you forget your past. We've lived … who knows how many lives. Do you realize how many mistakes we've made? How many lessons we could have learned from all of them? But, no, we have none of that knowledge. There was potentially so much art we experienced, and we can't appreciate any of it now." He went silent for a moment. "I have to ask, if that's happened before … what's to stop it from happening again? Don't you worry that this life will be a forgotten waste sooner or later?"

Sephra shook her head. "Life is only a waste if we squander our time. If I spend it helping others, then it will be a worthy life. I don't care if I remember it three thousand years from now or not."

"Fine. Regardless of my personal desire to remember my life, aren't you curious about what lies past the great beyond? The inner workings of our universe don't interest you? We come from someplace … exquisite. A place of meaning. I want to understand that better. I want to know where *all* of this comes from." His hands motioned to everything around them.

"But why do you need to know that?"

"For knowledge! Humanity evolves the more they know. I want to help people understand the spectacle that surrounds them."

Sephra saw his sincerity. This conversation showed her how he wanted to learn about this world just as much as she wanted to protect it. She realized she had almost immediately asked him for help in her quest, yet offered nothing to him in return. Guilt coursed through her. "Is there something I can do to help you?"

"What?" He looked at her with his head tilted.

"When we get to the Hidden Castle, maybe I can help you do some research. Gala said they have an extensive library. I'm not sure what I would be looking for, but if I can help you, I'd like to."

"Why would you want to help?"

"I know you and Dagnarone don't want to follow me into battle. When you agreed to accompany me to the castle, I was relieved. I'm not ready to part from the two of you. Call me silly or sentimental, but you're my family. You're helping me, and I want to repay the favor. So, I don't know how you can best put me to use, but I'm here for you. And thank you for being here for me."

Jerlone looked her over, still not sure what to think. "You're not getting on my good side just to take advantage of me, are you?"

"I would never do that. I'm not Gala!"

They laughed.

Sephra put her hand on his shoulder. "All of us are trying to find ourselves," she said. "I, personally, think we have a better shot if we do that together."

Jerlone looked her in the eye. "Thank you for your offer. Once we get to the castle, we'll figure something out."

Sephra stuck her hand out and Jerlone shook it. For the first time, she got a true taste of leadership.

CHAPTER 13

CIVIS: BLEAKER STREET
MORNING

"**HERE'S THE PLAN,**" Gala sauntered before everyone. "Dagnarone and I are going to go off and get bank accounts set up for y'all. Then, we're going to grab supplies and meet with some of my fellow contemporaries. Sephra and Jerlone, I need you two asking people for directions to the Hidden Castle."

"I thought you were bringing us there?" Jerlone questioned him.

"I'm only getting you to the forest. I got places to be and can't go all the way. Besides … I don't know how to get to the castle. Last time I went, I was a kid. Forest has changed and moved about since then."

Bleaker Street was in the brown borough of Civis. Huts and cozy houses lined the streets. Brick apartment complexes were scattered throughout as well. There were spots of grass and trees, but it was mostly homes crammed together. A few beat-up cars drove by. The streets were not paved; they were made of dirt, which caused a lot of dust to kick into the air.

"You want us to just ask strangers for directions?" Sephra's face radiated concern.

"Yeah, why not? I do it all the time." Gala assured her. "It's always worked out for me. Eventually. A couple misdirects along the way, but I figured it out—more or less."

"Gala, why am I going with you?" Dagnarone queried.

"Because, I need to bring a witness." She was the most important part of his plan, as far as he was concerned. The jerks at Happy Hooligan never believed his outlandish stories. Surviving a Sauros would definitely garner some skepticism. He hoped a witness would help build credibility.

"A witness? For what?"

"Don't worry, it'll be fun."

"Fun like stealing the diamond?" Her words were coated in sarcasm.

"Surviving death is always fun in retrospect. A little scary in the moment, but afterward you look back fondly." Gala smirked, thinking of other times he almost died, some as recent as the prior week.

Sephra took charge of the conversation. "We need a time and place to reconvene. Gala, you mentioned taking a train to our next destination. I suggest we get there by dusk at the latest."

"The Emit train station is in the western outskirts. Sun sets at five, so I'd recommend we get there around four." He thought about it. "Y'all do know how to tell time, right? I know you can do a lot of amazing things, but … not sure if that's a concept you grasp or not."

"Yes, we can tell time," an unamused Sephra answered.

"Analog and digital?" Gala asked. She responded with a cold glare. "You'll figure it out."

They reached an intersection and stopped walking.

"This is where we part ways," Gala announced. He pointed down one of the streets. "Sephra and Jerlone, follow this road and it will eventually lead to the blue and red boroughs. That population will probably provide better directions. People from out here tend to stay out here. Also, they can't afford to travel." He muttered that last part to himself. "Anyway, don't get nervous approaching strangers. City folk are very … welcoming."

CHAPTER 14

CIVIS: ART DISTRICT
LATE MORNING

"**I DON'T THINK CURSING** is needed," Sephra lectured a woman. They had only been talking for a minute, but the stranger was irate.

"Everyone thinks I just got all the time in the world, don't they?" The woman spat toward Sephra. "Surely, there's nowhere I could be in a rush to get to! I don't have anything going on, do I? Everyone acts like I got time to draw them a diagram!" The woman was causing a bit of a scene. "We're not all here for you, sweetie!" She pushed past Sephra and walked down the sidewalk.

Sephra grimaced. Gala had implied this would be easier. She spent her whole morning and most of the afternoon talking to people, all of whom were rude. In total, she had accumulated around three notes, none of which even seemed helpful.

The art district was part of the blue borough. Everything on display was some shade of the color. Buildings, chairs, trees, outfits, and anything in between all conformed to the look.

Skyscrapers leaned and swayed with strong gusts of wind. Past them, they could see taller, sturdier red skyscrapers in the next borough.

Painted art the size of billboards hung from the sides of buildings. Some pieces were abstract; others depicted the land or historical figures. A variety of sculptures lined the sidewalks. Everywhere they looked there was art, even in small, unseen spots. Any open space warranted creativity.

This was a crowded part of the city. Lot of people had to cross through to get to their jobs. Horses pulled carriages through the streets while small, clanky cars rattled past them. The sidewalks bustled with nonstop activity day and night. It never slowed down around there.

Sephra was discouraged but refused to let that stop her. She searched for someone else.

Walking through the crowd was a tall man with a bushy beard—brown with a couple of grays scattered throughout. Even through all that, they could see him smiling.

"Excuse me, sir." Sephra walked alongside him. "I need a little help, and I was wondering if you would be able to spare a moment?"

"I'll see what I can do," the man replied. His clothes looked like he was ready for a hike. They were brown and white, instead of the blue that surrounded them in that borough.

"Thank you. Honestly, not many people are willing to even hear me out."

"Oh, yeah, people are jerks."

"Yeah, I'm a little surprised, but anyway, first off, I'm Sephra." She put her hand out and they shook.

"I'm Babineau. It's nice to meet you."

"Nice to meet you too." Sephra readied her pen and notepad. "I understand this is a shot in the dark, but I need to get to the Hidden Castle and I don't know how to get there. Is that something you would have any idea how to do?"

"You asked the right person. The wife and I just got back from there. Forest shouldn't have changed much since then."

"It's so frustrating how it moves around."

"Yeah, absolutely. They say it's to protect the castle, but it's been invaded before."

"Oh, really?"

"Not often, but it's happened."

"Interesting." Sephra would have thought that, with the forest trails moving about, it would be near impossible for an army to invade. Her understanding was that it was the whole point of the forest moving.

"Anyway, first thing you want to do is enter from the Hill Valley of Ignatuski. It will seem a little out of the way, but it can save you a lot of time. There's a trail you can take. Follow the river, don't cross the bridge. There's a blue barn, and it should be a good stopping point. It's at a fork in the road, and I can't exactly remember which way to go there. There was a kind of … aroma … that drew us in the right direction. It was really faint, though. We picked incorrectly at first and had to backtrack. If you go the wrong way, you're going to eventually end up at a dilapidated bridge. No way you can cross it with the shape it's in. If you make that mistake, it can take a few days to backtrack and get on course, so be careful. There is a bridge you can cross with ease. It's over the chasm, but it's nice and sturdy. Once you cross it, you should find Letta Trail and be on your merry way. Would have taken us three days if we did everything right."

Sephra finished taking notes. "Thank you. This is a tremendous help." She put her pen away. "Three days to get there? How were the camping conditions?"

"I thought they were fine. This time of year starts getting cool but not too cold. Wife wasn't a big fan of it."

"Kind of dreading it myself."

"You'll be fine. I think you're capable of handling any critters that crawl your way." He gave her a once-over. No one around them was decked out in armor or carrying weapons like Sephra. "Why are you heading out there?"

"I have a proposal for the king."

"A proposal?"

"Yes." She beamed. "I want to help him save the world from Fascio."

"Oh, wow. Well, I wish you luck. You didn't hear it from me, but Coart's kind of a bad guy to deal with. He's not one to take other people's ideas, typically, but … maybe he'll listen to you. Who knows."

"Huh. And why is he like that?" She cocked her head.

"Because of his ego. He wants to say he was the person who solved the problem."

"Then, he should just steal the idea and claim it as his own."

"I'm sure he has."

Sephra thought of how to handle it. "When I present my idea, I will just have to make it seem like it was his idea. I can try to lead him on so he acts like the person who came up with everything. What do I care? I don't need the credit."

"Mighty noble of you, offering to save the world anonymously. Now, correct me if I'm wrong, but you said you'd accomplish that by getting rid of Fascio?"

"Yes."

"I'm no fan of his by any means, but how do you know someone worse wouldn't replace him?"

"We shouldn't keep a monster in power out of fear that someone worse will replace them."

"Ideally, yes, but even without that evil, the world would still need saving. There would still be the poverty and corruption that tears our citizens apart. The world is filled with pollutants that rot away our natural resources. Swords can't fix those problems. How do you stop poisonous ideologies from spreading? You wanna save the world? It's gotta be on a much larger scale."

Sephra put a hand to her chin, considering his words. "I see what you mean. The fall of one kingdom can't undo all the pain and misery that's tied to the world."

"If you really wanted to right all wrongs, you'd have to challenge your own people at one point, and when do you cross that line? When do you become so blind to your objective that you forget to be objective?"

They walked in silence.

"You've given me a lot to consider," Sephra gently said. There was a lot bouncing around in her head. She rubbed her hands together as she thought everything through.

"Don't be discouraged." Babineau stopped walking, and she followed suit. "I wasn't trying to dissuade you from forging ahead. I just wanted to give you some other things to think about—the things that get overshadowed by war."

"You've been a huge help. I didn't realize how much was on my plate."

"Good." He stared at her. "I don't know what your plan is, and I don't want to know, but if you're fighting for a better tomorrow, then I wish you luck. We could use a few like you going out and saving the world for us. I won't complain about that."

CHAPTER 15

CIVIS: THE HAPPY HOOLIGAN TAVERN
AFTERNOON

"**I TOLD YOU SO!**" Gala exclaimed as he pushed open the saloon door. "Two of your finest wines, Link."

Once again, the bar was only occupied by Link, Lheni, and Khurl. Dagnarone shuffled in behind Gala.

"I take it you didn't make it to the temple?" Link said from behind the bar.

"Of course, I did! You really think I'd coward out?"

Link looked at Lheni and Khurl. "Yes," they answered in unison.

"Well, I'll have you know that …" Gala searched through his satchel, unable to find what he was looking for. "Y'all refused to believe in me, but—where the hell did I put it?" He mumbled and grumbled as he dug deeper. "For someone who played out this moment in his head a hundred times, you sure didn't get the timing right—oh! Here it is!" Gala pulled out the Diamond of Farrokh. His audience looked bored and unimpressed.

Khurl broke the silence. "Probably a fake."

"It's not fake!" Gala retorted. "Ask my friend, Dag. She'll tell ya what happened."

They turned to Dagnarone.

"It's real, and he almost died a few times," she told them. "If my friends and I weren't there to save him, he wouldn't have made it."

"Alright, I think that's enough." An embarrassed Gala silenced her.

They walked to the bar and sat down.

Link brought their drinks. "Since you survived, you owe me for that last drink."

"What?" Gala cried, incredulous. "You said it was on the house!"

"Yeah, because I thought you were gonna die! It was a death drink, but seeing as you're alive, you owe me for it!"

"You know, this is exactly why I don't spend the holidays here!" Gala waved her off.

"Eh, what do you know?" Link cursed and walked away.

Gala shook his head. Then, like the flip of a switch, his energy changed. He smiled, turned to Dagnarone, and lifted his glass to toast. "Anyway, here's to our bright future!"

They clinked drinks.

Gala wafted his wine, taking in the aroma. With a small sip, he swished it around and enjoyed all the flavor. For a dinky place, they had a perfect blend.

He looked to Dagnarone as she downed her glass in one shot. His face dropped.

"That was delicious." She motioned to Link. "Another, please!"

"Yeah, just … put it on my tab," a disgruntled Gala uttered. "You're supposed to savor it, just so you know."

Link walked over with the drink. "So, you like the diamond, sweetheart?"

"It's not for her," Gala interjected. "We just met, and she happened to help out."

Link rolled her eyes, sighed, and walked away.

"Wait, wait, wait." Dagnarone's eyes went wide, and a toothy smile appeared. "You got this diamond for a woman? What's her name? How do you know her? What's her career? How do you see the relationship progressing over the next five to ten years?"

"Okay, slow down, and please be cool," Gala pleaded.

"I'm sorry," she replied. "Sorry, sorry, sorry. I just got really excited. I had no idea! Well, I had some idea. I figured you had to be stealing it for something good. Oh my god. Did she make you steal that diamond? Is she a delinquent like you?"

"Hey, I ain't a delinquent and neither is she." He took a sip of his drink. "Her name's Isra. I met her five years ago at the Third Island Festival. You should go sometime and see all the food and music they got going on there.

Place is damn near perfect. Anyway, she was performing at this bar, and we got to talking. Spent the whole night walking around and sitting on the beach. Can't even remember what the conversations were, but ... they just felt good. For the first time in a while, it was just nice to connect with someone like that."

"I'm surprised you're the kind of guy mentioning a connection and not a physical trait."

Gala pointed at her. "I'm a gentleman through and through!" He put his hand down. "And like I said, she was different. We actually had something to connect on. The next year, I saw her again. Another great couple of nights spent adventuring and getting to know each other. We were able to share our childhood trauma with one another." He looked away from Dagnarone. Isra was the only person he could really look in the eye to reveal his vulnerabilities. "As terrible as those feelings were, we could relate because of it."

"You kiss?"

Gala hesitated to answer. "No. There've been moments, but they slipped away." He stared off, haunted by his inaction.

"If it's any consolation, it's always easy to look back and criticize yourself, but for all you know, kissing her that night wouldn't have gone your way. Maybe it would have ruined everything."

Gala raised an eyebrow. "Is that supposed to be encouraging?"

"It isn't? I'm just saying, everything happens at a time for a reason. Maybe it just wasn't your time yet."

"Huh ... maybe." Gala took a sip of his drink. "Anyway, this has been going on a while. Every year, I'd get there early and stay late in hopes of spending a little more time with her. Last year, we took a canoe through the water caves to steal the Treasure of the Svimma Sisters[5]. It was amazing. There was a shorthand, and we just understood each other. She brought a set of skills that I could never have. We had to solve a puzzle, and it only took her seconds to figure it out—got it right first try. I'm terrible at puzzles, but she's great. I tell ya, that day ... I wished that could have been the rest of my life. I've never felt such excitement."

"You did say earlier that you were looking for 'something else' in life. I would say it's her."

---

[5] See Section V: Myths for more information.

"Maybe." Gala shrugged.

"Maybe? What do you mean, 'maybe'?" Dagnarone threw her hands about. "You just raved about her!"

"Yes, but … you know how relationships go. Any of these feelings for her would be part of a honeymoon stage. People grow out of that, and it doesn't always work." He drank.

"Oh, I get it." Dagnarone smirked. "You had a prior relationship that ended messy, and now you assume they all will."

"I never said that."

"Heavily implied by context clues."

Gala thought about it. "Alright, you want to hear about it don't you?"

"The one who screwed you up? Yes! I live for this type of drama. Give me *all* the dirt."

Gala kicked back his drink and waved for another. "I'm twenty-five and in a weird spot. Adventuring wasn't doing it for me anymore. I was making money, but it wasn't fulfilling. Then I met Núba Nomme, and she changed my life. We had a frenetic energy. Obviously, we started off strong. She was a museum curator and knew I needed a job. There was an opening in her department, and I interviewed. It wasn't for me. Something about it felt off. All these years later I can't remember the details, but it was a job behind a desk. Maybe I'd walk through a few halls of a museum to get to my office, but nothing to truly appreciate this art, ya know? So, I didn't take the job, and that caused some issues. She couldn't understand that I wanted something else. I think she took it as me demeaning her work. As if I was saying it wasn't worthy of me or some nonsense. I was just saying it wasn't for *me*, but I respected the hell out of anyone doing the job. That was the first big fight, and that was about half a year into the relationship."

Link brought over another round to Gala and Dagnarone.

"First fight always feels like the worst one," Dagnarone assured him.

"Wish I could agree, but that was just the start. Our energy shifted, and every fight was worse than the last. We'd stay up all night arguing. Neither of us liked how the other communicated—and don't get me wrong, I was aware of my own faults. She set me off, and I was stubborn about things. Maybe even low-key vindictive at times, I don't know. There were things she hoped I would change, and I didn't. She wanted me to drink less, but I wouldn't even entertain the thought. Realizing this, I didn't like who I was becoming." Gala went quiet for a moment. "The good moments were great, but those bad moments were crushing and common. Don't get me wrong, she was not a bad person. She did nothing wrong; she deserves all the happiness in the world. We just didn't work." He looked around. "I began to yearn for the adventure again. Coordinating your life with someone is difficult. Takes a lot of work. I wanted to venture out and be my own person. I missed myself."

"Relationships fizzle. Not all of them are supposed to last. Some are only meant for a short period. Sometimes we just need to learn about ourselves through their failures. That way when the next one comes along, we can try to do better."

Gala nodded. "Saying goodbye was just so hard. Like I said, she wasn't a bad person. I still loved her, but we knew it wasn't best to continue. I walked out, and I felt great, but then I felt terrible for feeling that way. I was excited to be completely me again, but I know it's not healthy to feel that way. I shouldn't want to be alone in life."

Dagnarone shook her head. "That's a normal reaction after a breakup. You need time to yourself, and there's nothing wrong with that."

"It wasn't that. It was this feeling of independence and … isolation. It's like I thrived on it. I went back out into the world to raid temples on endless crusades. If I got too lonely, I found someone to be less lonely with—just enough dopamine to keep me happy. I would say it's truly living in the moment, but a wiser person disagreed."

"I think it's living in the moment but at the expense of your future."

"I know." Gala took a sip of his drink. "So, I guess what I'm saying is, because of Núba, I'm afraid to tell Isra how I feel. Right now, she's this perfect escape from reality. Even if it's just for one long weekend a year, why ruin that? Eventually, there will be resentment or jealousy or some other emotion you should be ashamed to feel."

They were silent for a moment.

"I think your previous relationship is influencing you too much," Dagnarone said. "Whatever issues there were, that was between you and her."

"Yes, but what I'm saying is there would be new, different issues with Isra," Gala countered. "Everyone has issues. We all have drama and junk we bring to the table. It's frustrating, because they start with so much potential and end in such … hurt."

"Love is complicated. It's not just joy. It's accepting pain and helping sadness. It isn't always beautiful; it's only that way in our imaginations. When you go through it, you understand why they say love is hell."

"See, solitude isn't hell." Gala pointed at her. "It's why I've yearned for it."

"So, what good is stealing this diamond? If you're this worried about being vulnerable with her and committing, why do this?"

"Hey, I never said I felt one way entirely. Part of me wants to be with her, but I'm also scared about what that really entails. I'm just here expressing my concerns." Gala paused. "And yes, I stole the diamond to impress her. I just wanna show her how great I can be."

"You just can't help it, can you?" Dagnarone chuckled.

"I can't."

"You're getting older. Don't waste your chances."

"Yeah, yeah, yeah." Gala drank. "The Third Island Festival is this weekend. That's why I can't go all the way to the Hidden Castle with you."

"You really cut the timing close on that, huh?"

"I had to track down information first. Those codes took months to get, and they really sidetracked me."

"Yeah, they were really helpful," she said bluntly.

"They helped a little! Besides that, it was a busy year too. There were a lot of time-sensitive treasures to hunt. Some planets had to align for spells to be broken. That type of stuff got in my way."

"I guess if you showed up earlier, you would have been killed by the Sauros anyway. Without us, you couldn't have done it. Are you going to mention to her how close you came to dying?"

"Oh, absolutely. The best stories always involve someone dying or coming close."

"You're a natural showman." Dagnarone rolled her eyes.

"Alright, it's your turn."

"My turn for what?"

"I told you my biggest heartbreak; now you tell me about yours." He slapped her on the shoulder as a sign of comradery.

Dagnarone sat quietly, clearly thinking. "Okay, I remember someone not liking my powers. She didn't feel like we were equals because of it. It's not like I can turn them off and on, per se, nor did I choose to have them in this life. She didn't feel like we were equals. I never saw her as lesser, but she saw herself that way. I offered to teach her how to conjure magic, just to see if that would help."

Gala was intrigued. "You can teach someone how to do that?"

"Yeah, but it only works if the person believes in themself. She didn't. That really made things worse. She felt inadequate. I assured her that wasn't the case, but you know how we get in our heads. It's difficult feeling you're not living up to your partner's standard. Her feelings of inadequacy corrupted more of the relationship. She formed trust issues. Games were played." Dagnarone got quiet. "Yeah, it wasn't good."

"So, where does the heartbreak come in? You remember the bad times, but how'd she mess you up?"

Dagnarone was silent for a moment. "I couldn't let her go. Right now, I can't remember her name or face, but … I still feel a part of me missing. I didn't want to say bye, and that's what kept me around. I knew things weren't at their best, but I didn't want to lose another part of my life that I once cherished. It's hard to make these connections, and I'm not one to walk with ease. A few times, we broke up but always ended back in each other's arms."

"That's how it always goes."

"It's silly. We should be better than that."

"Yup," Gala concurred, "but we'll be falling for that trap till the end of time."

"When all was said and done, yeah, I was worried about getting hurt again. And, by the way, I'm sure I could have been better in the relationship, but I get focused on something and put others to the side. A couple times, I probably bought into the power trip and felt like the superior one. I'm not above those childish emotions. If I could remember more about myself, I'm sure I'd have more traits to add to that list."

"There's nothing like the highs and lows of love."

"Agreed, but as much hassle as they can be, they are worth it. Life needs that companionship, even if you have moments when you want to be alone."

"You're right." Gala thought about things. "And I'm sorry for your misfortunes."

"It's fine. New life, new me, ya know?"

They clinked their glasses and continued to drink.

CHAPTER 16

CIVIS: THE CHURCH OF THE WAND
AFTERNOON
••

E**VEN THOUGH GALA** recommended the blue and red boroughs, something led Jerlone to the orange borough instead. For hours, he walked the streets, taking in the shabby houses and dirt roads.

He spent time talking to the locals, but no one had any idea how to get to the Hidden Castle. This lack of progress did not bother him. At the end of the day, he didn't really care if he got there. In fact, he felt a little anxious when thinking about arriving.

An exquisite, albeit run down, church sat in the distance. To the left and right of the entrance were two towering, green domes. They needed painting, as the color faded over the years. Regardless of its age, the church was an impressive building that was much larger than anything else in that borough.

Jerlone reached the church, staring at it with the wonderment of a child. It was a powerful image; something about this place felt special.

A woman dressed in black cleric robes sat on a bench outside the main entrance. Curly, red hair masked her pale face, yet some wrinkles poked through. Even though she looked disheveled, she emanated a calming presence. "You look lost," she said.

Jerlone stopped gazing at the church towers and brought his attention down to her. "Not lost, just trying to find my way."

"Same thing." She pointed to the door behind her. "Just so you know, if you're looking for direction, the Church of the Wand can help."

"Actually, I am looking for directions to the Hidden Castle. No one here seems to have any clue—"

"I didn't mean literal directions," she interrupted. She stirred in her seat while giving Jerlone a once-over. "You got some magic in you?"

He hesitated before answering, "Don't we all?"

"Yeah, but you're different, like a reactor leaking radiation."

"And how would you know that?"

"I'm tapped into the right things. I feel magic pulsating everywhere. I know when someone is directionless—disappointed, yearning, struggling—you know?" She raised an eyebrow.

Jerlone knew. He wasn't sure if he should divert from his main objective, but there was something calling to him. "I don't even know your name."

"Kleros. Now, you can either introduce yourself and we can go inside and have a nice warm talk, or you can keep going about your way 'cause I have no idea how to get to the Hidden Castle."

Jerlone looked around. He was supposed to be getting directions, but this felt important. This felt like the pathway to knowledge, and there was nothing he valued more than knowledge.

• • • •

Kleros led Jerlone through the church hallway. It seemed impossibly long. The walls were made of a blue salt rock. Little bursts of light traveled through the walls like veins, creating a haunting glow. The ceiling was in a half-crescent shape and hovered just a foot above their heads. The space was wide, yet there was a sense of containment.

Kleros continued her story. "I woke up one day not knowing what to do. Everything seemed pointless. Nothing mattered, and I needed help. This was when I was at university. I changed my studies from accounting to religious philosophy and magical theory. I became so captivated by what I was reading, I needed more time to digest everything. I took fewer classes so the ones I did attend could receive more attention. It took me an extra four years to finish the program. That was the result of doing the research my way. I was slow and meticulous and didn't have the pressures of some arbitrary deadline."

"I've found that's the only way to research." Jerlone nodded. Visions of his time in libraries flashed before him. The smell of parchment was one of his favorites. These thoughts made him eager to get to the Hidden Castle's library. "Unraveling the mysteries of the universe is not something that can be achieved while being timed. So, when all was said and done, what did you decide? You find any meaning in this life?"

She shrugged. "Who's to say what really happens? That's an impossible answer. There was one theory I liked, though. It proposes we live the same life over and over. What we do today will echo forever; we just won't be aware of it. I like this notion, because we get to reunite with our loved ones. Yes, we have to re-experience our pains, but they keep us humble. There are some very convincing papers written by psychics. They are able to study this subconscious past life much easier. They would seem to suggest something similar to this time-loop theory."

"That's what you believe?" Jerlone was shocked by her grim opinion. He was not entirely sold on the crazy theory.

"I've had some moments of déjà vu so powerful, I had to have lived through them before. So, yes, I am a believer."

"That's preposterous." Jerlone shook his head. "Events would have to unfold with variations. Those differences would set a life off track. Nothing would line up as intended, especially multiple times."

"I think you'd be surprised. Destiny is a powerful force, even if we don't understand it. Each life probably has little variations, but I still think the big moments come around and end the same. Our human nature leads us there."

"I don't know. When I think of my prior life, it feels different."

"We change as time goes on. Some days, I wake up and don't recognize the face staring at me in the mirror. Maybe those little changes were enough to make you feel you were someone else. Or, maybe one day, you'll have a better understanding of what you saw because you'll have become it."

"Well, if existence is just one life on repeat, that sounds terrifying. Unhappy, heartbroken, socially unaccepted people who have to live an eternity like that? That would be akin to Hell." He feared he would be one of them.

"Maybe with the variations in their next life, they don't end up in the same place. That life was a tragic one, but the next will be better. Perhaps our trauma follows us from one life to the next. It subconsciously guides us to where we need to be. It helps us evolve and better ourselves."

"I hope you're right." Jerlone walked over to the salt-rock wall and touched it. A blue light passed by his hand, and he marveled at the wonder of it all.

"You said you were drawn to this church, right?"

"Yes, it's a magnificent piece of architecture. Anyone who sees it must be drawn to it."

She laughed. "You think we get a lot of visitors?"

"I imagine so, yes."

"No. You're the first this week. Services these days are quaint. We seem to be fading." Her voice seemed to be fading too. She let the silence echo before continuing, "But that's beside the point. You felt inclined to come here. What if you had no control over that? Some may call it destiny, others fate—or did you choose it yourself?"

Jerlone found these questions fascinating. He was too analytical to believe in fate, but the idea intrigued him. He wanted to believe there was some sort of higher calling.

"These other Mystics you're traveling with," Kleros continued. "Why are you with them? It seems like everyone has a different agenda."

He wavered before answering. "I had a feeling it was what I needed to do."

"Excellent. More evidence for the destiny theory. Even though you're reconsidering things, you know you need to do this."

"I never said I'm reconsidering things."

"And I said I'm tapped into things. Maybe you just don't realize it yet, but you don't want to be with them. You're not going to find what you hope to find at the Hidden Castle. I know you want to help them, but you have to do right by yourself first."

He sighed, knowing she was right. "I'm worried how Sephra will react if I abandon them."

"She will have to learn to deal with it. Always do what's best for you."

They reached the end of the hallway. Kleros fumbled through her garb for a set of keys. She unlocked the door, and they entered the sanctuary.

Inside, there were thousands of candles, both big and small. They created a beautiful, orange glow within the room. The tiny flames generated enough heat to keep the room nice and toasty. Jerlone wondered how many hours it took to light all of them.

A few dozen rows of pews stretched from the entrance to the podium. An antique pipe organ sat on the stage underneath a massive stained-glass window. Mystics and magic were depicted on the window in a colorful array of spectacles.

Spirit permeated the room. That was the first time Jerlone became aware of it surrounding him. It was a calming energy that put him at peace.

"This church is so beautiful," he said, looking around. "I don't see why it's not busier."

"Well, we've had our issues." Kleros scratched the back of her head.

"Must be pretty big to keep people away from this."

"The Nan Clan wants to silence us." Her demeanor lost levity. "Magic can be a controversial subject. There are those who want to keep it hidden from the world. Some think it should only be for an elite few of their choosing. We've received threats. A few times, people have shown up, trying to intimidate us."

"This world seems to be built by magic, according to your myths. I would think everyone would already understand its existence."

"People only know of magic through legend. It's rare to see it with your own eyes. Even when they do, they think it's a trick. Somehow, time eroded people's sense of wonder. We are trying to show them the light, but the interest just isn't there."

Jerlone paced around, thinking of her situation. "Does the Nan Clan wield magic? Is that why no one has been able to help you?"

"Some of the more senior members are magic users, but the others are just followers of a cult. Our patrons dabble in magic, but they aren't warriors. Many of them are elderly or in poor health. We're a church, not a military academy."

"What about someone else? What are the authorities doing to help?"

Kleros shrugged. "No one helps. We've alerted the proper channels, but nothing has been done. I know just enough spells to keep them at bay."

Jerlone couldn't help but be a little paranoid. He began to wonder if she was using him. Assuming the worst in people was a common mistake he made. He tensed. "I know what you're doing."

Kleros looked at him. "Excuse me?"

"You've lured me in here to fix your problem."

"Why would I do that to you?"

"Because you think I can stop them!"

"I'm sure you could, if you wanted to, but that thought never even crossed my mind." She maintained her cool, even in the face of an elevating situation.

Jerlone stared at her, not sure what to believe.

"Not everyone's going to try to use you," Kleros assured him. She walked over to him and held his hand. Together, they went to a pew and sat down. "You're having a hard time trusting, huh?"

Jerlone was deep in thought, a tear in his eye. "I just feel so lost." He paused. "I'm trying to accept this new life, yet nothing's slowing down to give me a chance to acclimate. The situation with the Sauros was terrifying, and I don't want to end up there again." He looked her in the eye. "I'm sorry I took it out on you. I realize now that you didn't mean that." He felt bad for getting hot like he had.

"It's okay. It happens—and don't worry about us. Any time those punks have come here, I've sent them crawling home."

His voice raised. "Are you a Mystic?"

"No, but a Mystic trained me. He started this church just before he died." She closed her eyes and bowed her head in respect.

"I may not know him, but," Jerlone looked around, "I think he's still here."

"Oh, I know. He never left. He keeps us safe … somewhat." She went quiet. "I hope he's not disappointed in how I've run the church. I wish it were doing better, but it isn't."

Jerlone put his hand on her shoulder. "You're doing your best. It's not your fault outside forces are causing trouble."

"Thank you." She smiled and looked him in the eyes. Abruptly, she stood and walked off. "Follow me," she instructed. They went to a wall covered in white wands. "Is there any calling out to you?"

He studied them for a minute. Then, he reached out, feeling the energy around them. Before he realized it, one zipped into his hand. Moving it around, he became acquainted with its weight and feel.

"They say wands were constructed back during the Early Wars. The wood is taken from the Vand trees, which are now extinct." She pulled out her own wand and marveled at it. "They may not seem like much, but they are great instruments for summoning magic."

"I don't know what it is about this one, but it feels familiar." Jerlone couldn't take his eyes off it. He examined every centimeter of it, twirling it in his hands.

"Take it with you. It'll do you well in your upcoming journey."

"I couldn't take this; it belongs to someone else."

"Wands are meant to be used. Whoever owned that before you would be proud to see it in your hands. These are from the fallen, yes, but that does not mean their purpose should be retired. It flew into your hands because it knew you two share a path. Another example of destiny? Who's to say."

For the first time, Jerlone leaned into the idea of a destiny. This weapon felt significant, and he was glad they'd crossed paths. There was just one thing missing.

"I don't know how to use it," he said. "I can feel the energy in it, but I think I need some help."

"I can teach you the basics. A little practice on your own and you'll be proficient in no time. Then, if I'm lucky, you'll come back and save us from the Nan Clan." She smiled, winked, and playfully nudged him in the ribs.

CHAPTER 17

EMIT TRAIN STATION
DUSK

"**DAMN, WHERE ARE** they?" Sephra watched the giant clock over the entrance. She had been waiting for an hour outside the Emit Train Station and her frustration was at a boiling point. For some foolish reason, she'd thought everyone would be early.

She worried they could be hurt. There was also the possibility they'd abandoned her. Selfishly, that idea scared her a little more. Danger they could handle on their own, but could they deal with her?

The Emit Train Station was located on the western outskirts of Civis. The terrain resembled a desert, unlike the lushness of Streawberige Field. Tracks ran every which way across the sand, coming and going constantly.

Two hundred yards from the entrance sat a majestic fountain. Water spurted from the top to greet visitors as they passed by. While waiting for her companions, Sephra walked laps around it.

When Gala and Dagnarone finally arrived, Sephra was none too pleased to see them.

"I see Jerlone isn't here yet, huh?" Gala said with some charm.

"No, no, no!" Sephra yelled at him. "Don't try that! Do you know what time it is? I've been waiting for over an hour!"

Gala pulled out his pocket watch. "Okay, well we're only forty-five minutes late, so fifteen of those minutes are on you."

She waved off his comment. "I was worried something happened to both of you!"

"We were *fine*." Dagnarone slurred her words a bit. "We were at Happy Holiday Tabern, and … I don't think we're allowed back." A small trace of blood began dripping from her nose.

"Why is your nose bleeding?" Sephra screeched.

"Oh, *nertz*," Gala looked at her. "Dag, you've gotta tilt your head back and apply pressure." He demonstrated himself. "Another few minutes and you should be fine."

"Ugh," Dagnarone groaned as she followed instructions.

"What happened?" Sephra demanded.

"I showed a guy who was boss," Dagnarone droned.

"Gala!" Sephra glared at him, fuming.

"To clear up a few things," Gala started, "*She's* banned from the bar, not me. I'm still a valued customer."

"Gala!" Sephra was losing her patience.

"Sorry! But don't worry, she's fine, and the guy deserved it." He looked at Dagnarone and beamed with pride. "She may try to act like a pacifist, but she's got a little fight in her." He looked back toward Sephra, who was steaming. "Contrary to how this looks, I was there the whole time, ready to intervene. Which, by the way, she never even came close to needing my help—just to drive that point home."

"I did a good job," Dagnarone boasted, looking as proud as one can with a bloody nose.

"Yes, you did!" Gala encouraged her. "Her first bar fight! You never forget your first. Mine was on the Borr Islands, a small yet prosperous—"

Sephra cut him off. "Is this relevant?"

"No, but I find the story entertaining." He could see she was not amused. "Alright, fine, but you're missing a hilarious punchline. Anyway, don't worry about it. Sometimes, a little fight breaks out when the good times are rolling. If anything, we learned she's a passionate fighter with a little booze in her. Tolerance level is only thing she's gotta work on. But, like a twenty-one-year-old finally hitting the bars, she just needs a few bad nights to figure that out."

"I thought you were supposed to be getting us set up, not drinking."

"And I did! It's called multitasking." He motioned to the bags on his and Dagnarone's backs. "Apology accepted. I also set you up with bank accounts and a few other documents. We can go over all that when we're on the train."

"Well, I still think it's rude to keep me waiting. We could have missed our train!"

"I'm sorry, Sephra!" Dagnarone continued to slur, dragging out each r, even with her head tilted back.

"That was rude of us," Gala concurred. "I am sorry for making you wait. As for the trains, they leave every fifteen minutes, and keep in mind, I'm the one trying to get somewhere in a timely manner. So, if I'm not complaining …" he trailed off. "Speaking of which, you get the directions?"

"Yes," Sephra answered. "I wasn't ready for people to be so aggressive. I didn't think asking for help would be that big a deal, but apparently it was."

"I know." Gala smiled. "God bless, 'em."

Sephra pulled out her notebook. "Thankfully, I think I got good advice from one man. A couple spots he was a bit unsure of, but overall, he gave me detailed notes."

"Do you mind if I look them over?" Dagnarone grabbed them before getting a response. She grimaced. "I don't think this is right. We shouldn't follow the river; we should cross it."

Sephra wasn't a fan of being questioned, especially from a drunk. "I didn't think you got directions while you were at the bar," she snarked.

"I have a feeling, and we'd be wise to trust me," Dagnarone slurred.

"There were actually a few people who gave me the same advice."

Dagnarone was adamant. "But the forest changes, and I think they're wrong. I can feel it in my bones."

"There's a fork in the road at the blue barn. Do you know which way we're supposed to go?" Sephra challenged her.

"No idea, but I can try to feel it out when we get there."

Sephra turned to Gala. "You have any thoughts?"

"Been too long," he shrugged. "I don't even remember a river, but I was last there thirty-plus years ago."

"Come on," Dagnarone whined. "You can trust me. I've got a good sense of these things! Why won't you trust me?"

"You fell out of the sky yesterday with no knowledge of this world," Sephra bluntly stated. "Also, you're drunk right now."

"Hey! That applies to you too!"

"I'm not drunk!"

"Sure, not now, but someday you will be!"

Gala spoke up. "Careful, Seph. You don't wanna get on her bad side when she's like this."

Sephra took command. "Here's what we will do. When we arrive at that point we will stop and evaluate the situation—see if we have any other bits of divine inspiration between now and then. Sound good?"

Dagnarone smiled and stumbled backward. She caught her balance before falling down. "Glad to do business with ya," she affirmed.

The Mountains of Glimmen eclipsed the sun, creating the magic hour. The streetlights leading back to Civis were ablaze to combat the encroaching darkness. With the night came the cold.

Sephra was eager to get on the train, but they were still awaiting Jerlone. She sat on the rim of the fountain, hoping everyone who approached would be him. This had been going on for close to thirty minutes.

Eventually, Jerlone jogged toward his companions. "I'm so sorry," he apologized as he huffed for air. "I lost track of time."

Sephra did not look happy. She was furious at everyone for being so inconsiderate about her time. She wasn't asking for anything difficult, yet they couldn't even accomplish that. In this moment, she didn't want to talk to anyone but knew she had to. "Where were you?" Her voice was uncompromising.

"I found a church. The woman there taught me some lessons on—"

She cut him off, her face showing obvious disapproval. "Wait. You weren't even getting directions?"

It took him a second to respond. "No."

"We asked you to do one thing!" Sephra rolled her eyes while throwing her arms in the air.

"I'm sorry, I should have done that, but I found this place and—"

"Come on," Sephra cut him off again and tossed him his bag. "We've got a train to catch." She turned and went for the entrance. A part of her questioned if she was too harsh on Jerlone. If she was, she didn't care. She was tired and upset. If everyone else wasn't going to take her into consideration, then she saw no reason to do it for them.

She thought of the goodwill she and Jerlone had earned earlier and wondered if they both just threw it away.

Dagnarone watched as her friends walked toward the door.

She'd played with the fountain for the past half hour. She scooped magical bubbles of water into her palm and tried to clean the filth away. She was getting the hang of it but was not quite there yet.

This was her last attempt before catching up with them.

She closed her eyes and blocked out the world around her. She visualized successfully purifying the water. Within her hand formed a translucent half-ball of energy. She dipped it in the water and pulled out a gallon.

The half-ball closed up, trapping the murky water within. As she twirled her hand, the liquid began to get wavy. Clouds formed and little flashes of light popped. A sound emanated and changed pitch. The ball steamed during these climatic moments.

When everything calmed down, the ball opened back up. The water inside was clear as it had ever been. She wafted for odors but could not detect any. She was proud of herself. This felt like her first major accomplishment since falling.

She looked down and realized she would have to drop the clean water back into the festering fountain. As she pulled her hand back, the water splashed into its home.

Before leaving, Dagnarone took one last look at the fountain. It was one of the largest in the world, but it was dirty. It could be magnificent if they only gave it the chance.

At that moment, she realized how badly she wanted to clean the world. It made her feel good and gave her purpose. One day she would come back and clean all this water, revitalizing it to its former glory, but first, she would have to survive her adventure with Sephra.

CHAPTER 18

TRAIN CABIN
NIGHT

GALA JUST FINISHED sharing a big dinner with Dagnarone and needed to lay down. The drinks were hitting him, but he felt great. He was enjoying the company of his new friends and was excited about the days to come. His heart beat particularly fast when he thought of reuniting with Isra at the festival.

Stumbling through the train, he eventually found their cabin.

He opened the door to find Sephra sitting in the window seat, channeling the unknown. The room flashed a multitude of colors from her energy globes. Her legs were crossed, back straight, and eyes closed.

"Whoops, sorry." Gala started to leave.

"It's okay." Sephra opened her eyes. "I was just finishing up." The globes dissipated and the room returned to normal.

"You sure? I was going to come lay down for a bit, but I don't want to bother you."

"It's okay; please join me."

Gala stepped into the small cabin. There were bunks to the left and right. He walked to the window seat and sat beside Sephra.

"That one of your rituals I walked in on?" Gala asked her.

"I was just centering myself," she answered. "I can feel my power grow by the hour. This keeps me in check. I don't want to lash out and hurt someone. Meditation helps give me a greater balance." She shifted in her seat as her face became filled with concern. "A thought haunts me where I spend my life seeking power. It's easy to want more. By giving myself this quiet time, I can process these feelings and respond with reason. It's healing for my soul."

Gala stared at her, some wonderment in his eyes. "What's it like to summon magic?"

She shrugged, as if it were nothing. "It's simple. It just happens. Sorta like breathing—actually, more like sneezing. It takes a bit of a toll on you, but it's instinctual. It can be draining, but once you have a taste for it, you want more."

"That must be something. You act like it's so casual, yet it's a miracle."

"Is it really a miracle if anyone can do it?"

Gala didn't understand what she meant by that. "What do you mean anyone can do it? I've never seen anyone do what you do."

She shrugged. "They probably just haven't taken the time to try to learn how."

"You know, Dagnarone was saying something similar."

"You're hoping one of us will teach you how to conjure this power, aren't you?"

"Well," Gala shrugged, trying not to look too eager, "if someone wanted to show me, I sure wouldn't turn them down."

"It takes some discipline. Do you think you have any discipline?"

"Some here and there."

"You've pulled a couple fast ones on us. Not sure it would be wise to teach you this power."

"What? You think I'd go and use it for evil?"

"No, because it would be easy to stop you."

"Come on, you know me. You've known me your whole life! A guy like me has a power like that, well, I'll just be using it to stop another Sauros when one attacks me again."

"I suppose when all is said and done, you are harmless." She gave him a once-over, her eyes narrowing. "You'd have an easier time summoning because you've seen it in person. Once you see it, it opens up a door. Of course, if you don't have confidence in yourself, you'll never ignite even a tiny spark, but something tells me you won't have that issue."

"Thank you."

"That wasn't as much of a compliment as you thought it was."

"Oh." Gala put it together. "Gotcha."

She grabbed his hand and placed it palm up. She hovered hers inches from his. "Feel this. Don't think about what's going on. Just watch it and live in this moment."

Small traces of multicolored energy rose from Gala's palm. It was as if Sephra's hand was a magnet, attracting it. Slowly, the streams of energy combined into a small globe.

Sephra removed her hand, yet the magic stayed with Gala. When he moved his hand, it moved in conjunction. He felt control and had a basic understanding of how it operated. A moment later, the globe evaporated.

Gala sat there, unable to comprehend anything. His body tingled, as if he experienced a burst of dopamine throughout his whole being. The world felt different. Everything he saw around him had a new glow to it. Deep within his soul, he felt an eons-old power readily available. Yet interesting enough, he had no desire to call on it. There the power sat, a reminder to him he could take on anything.

Gala thought of Isra. He was excited to show her what he could do. All he really wanted was to impress her. Having this cosmic power would be quite the advantage the next time they went on an adventure. He thought of their fight against the demon Loff and how much easier that would have been, had he had this power.

After that moment of euphoria, Gala felt the burning sense of responsibility that came with this great gift. Gala was a man who looked out for himself but was still known to save a life. The spirit of his parents reached out to remind him of who they raised. He couldn't hear their message, but he felt their presence in his heart. As he had a hundred times before, he promised them he wouldn't let them down.

Sephra broke the silence. "That resides in every single one of us. Most people allow that beauty to drown out. Yet, if we give ourselves the opportunity, we become magnets to the fantastic. We can make anything happen if we set our minds to it. Whether we fall from the sky or rise from the ground, we can all be spectacular. You just have to believe."

Gala was still processing what had happened. He ran his fingers across his palm, trying to feel some sort of aftereffect.

"Now, do it without me," Sephra commanded.

Gala laughed and shook his head. "I doubt I can."

"Well, if you don't think you can, then I'm sure you're right. Any time someone says they can't do something, they are right."

Gala was easily provoked. He readjusted himself in the window seat and put his hand out. His face scrunched as he tried to do something, but to no avail.

"Remember the feeling," Sephra gently said. "Tap into what your body's telling you."

They continued to sit there while nothing happened.

"Is there something I should be thinking of?" Gala asked Sephra.

"No, in fact, thinking will only mess you up. It's okay if it doesn't happen right away. Let it be."

Gala flexed his arm, thinking his strength would produce magic. He was wrong.

"Don't do that," Sephra advised. "You're just trapping your energy within. You want it to be fluid, not rigid."

His arm relaxed, yet no magic appeared. He closed his eyes and breathed, but still, no success. He started to worry he wouldn't be able to impress Isra with this new trick.

"Try thinking of a magical moment in your life," Sephra suggested. "It should be something special, a moment that made life feel meaningful, a feeling that can only come from love."

He thought of Isra. His second year of knowing her, they'd explored a series of waterfalls. The sun reflected off the water in such a romantic way. She'd looked perfect and provided him comfort unlike anyone else. All he wanted was to be there for her and provide the peace she gave him.

His breathing slowed, and his body relaxed. All of this was reflexive; he was not cognizant of it. Small particles of energy began sprouting from his palm. They were not as strong as the previous attempt, but he was doing it by himself.

"Remember to borrow from your surroundings," Sephra guided. "It's not all supposed to come from you. Borrow the energy around you to build on the foundation, but remember: you're not taking the energy, it's just assisting you. It will have to return to where it came from when you're done."

Gala could feel that power around them. He attracted that energy to his palm. A globe formed and grew, but not large. He was getting the basic understanding. After a minute, he was exhausted and could not conjure anything else.

A few seconds later, the energy fizzled out.

Gala wiped sweat from his brow. He did not realize how taxing the situation was. When he tried to stand, he failed to do so and sank back down on his seat. He took a few heavy breaths to try to catch back up.

Sephra beamed. "Practice it when you can," she said. "It will be more of a struggle for you. Listen to your emotions and work on making small progress. You don't have to use much magic to be effective." She winked at him.

CHAPTER 19

TRAIN CABOOSE
NIGHT
• •

T WAS COLD at the back of the caboose.
Jerlone stood outside on the platform and watched the night sky pass him by. He wasn't sure what to do. Most of the night, he considered it a mistake getting on that train. There was a stop coming up, and he was considering getting off. He hadn't talked to anyone in his group, and as far as he could tell, no one seemed to care that he was upset. He assumed if he left, they would be annoyed, but inevitably, fine without him.

He heard the door open and turned to find Dagnarone. She looked scared to continue on outside.

The train was rickety, and they were passing through the Mountains of Glimmen, thousands of feet in the air. The mountain sparkled and reflected the stars in a dazzling display of light. That only helped illuminate how high off the ground they were.

"Doesn't seem that safe out here," Dagnarone said, swaying in what looked like a small tinge of vertigo.

"Not really safe anywhere when you think about it," Jerlone replied. "Safety is just an illusion. People think they aren't safe in one land because of a person ruling. They think they'd be safer elsewhere, but what's to stop tragedy from happening there? How do you know the evil person you fled from won't attack you? There's this misunderstanding some people have that animals are safer than humans. Yet, even in nature animals attack animals. You can live life as peaceful as a bird, but all it takes is one wrong step and something more vicious has snatched you up. We can try to avoid violence in this life, but it will find us. If it can find even the most innocent of creatures, what chance do we stand?" He was sure his uncertainty was plain on his face. "So, safety… who knows if it even exists."

"That was a lot more than I was expecting." Dagnarone scratched her arm. "Mind if I join ya?"

"As long as you don't hassle me."

"Nah, that's Sephra's job." She chuckled while cautiously taking a step onto the platform.

Jerlone reached for her. "Here, let me help you."

She grabbed onto him, and he pulled her over. Together, they clung to the back rail and watched the Mountains of Glimmen shimmer in the night sky. The rock reflected the moon and created a dazzling effect.

"Speaking of Sephra," Dagnarone continued, "You mad at her?"

"What tipped you off?" Jerlone looked away from her.

"Well, she cut you off, and since then you haven't really said anything, so call it intuition or … the obvious."

He nodded. "I found something that I was excited to share with everyone. I finally felt a sense of purpose. When she cut me off, it was like a boss disciplining an insubordinate employee. I didn't appreciate that. It put me in a mood."

"I've noticed her do that a few times," Dagnarone agreed.

"I get the sense that she's using us. She has some plan that she hasn't told us about, and we're her pawns."

"I don't think she's that devious." Dagnarone shook her head.

"She wants to save the world. Those types of people are always like that."

"Okay, I see what you mean, but I think she's different. Difficult but different."

"We both know we've lived lives with her before. We should know what we're getting into. Even if it's on a subconscious level, we know her game. Do we really want to make that same mistake again?"

"Well, uh, I guess it's too late now. We're stuck on this train." She shrugged.

"It's not too late. It's never too late." He leaned into her, as if about to tell her a secret. "All we do is get off the train and walk the opposite direction. We never have to see her again and maybe, just maybe, that will give us a chance at living a peaceful life."

"And walk off to what? We don't know anything about this world, and we don't even know where we wanna go or what we wanna do. At least, being with her, we have some sort of direction."

"We can go off and find a purpose together. She's not the only one handing out reasons to live."

Dagnarone seemed to consider it for a second but then shook her head. "I wouldn't feel right doing that. I told her I'd go to the Hidden Castle with her, and I just feel I have to see it through."

Silence lingered in the air. Jerlone was not happy with her answer, and the disappointment was palpable.

"Last night, you said you felt the same thing," Dagnarone continued. "That there was some sort of feeling urging you to join this adventure. What's changed?"

"Just had time to think about it," he answered. "I still have that feeling, but I wonder how much I need to listen to it. Am I just repeating a pattern that's become human nature, or am I actually in control of my life? What if leaving meant I finally got to live the life I always wanted? Why wouldn't I do that? I know I've been eternally unhappy with how life shapes up, and maybe walking away would be the best thing for me to do. Everyone would rightly judge me for it, but what if it is what I need? At what point do I start putting myself before others?"

Dagnarone looked sad. "What if … I forgave you for killing the Sauros?"

"Huh?" Jerlone was confused by her offer. It seemed irrelevant to the subject at hand.

"I'm still salty about that. I'm coming around to understanding there wasn't another choice. It was more on instinct than malice. I've yelled, and we've had our moment, and I'll forgive you. I won't hold it over your head anymore or judge you for it, but if I do that, will you please stay with us?"

Jerlone did not know how to respond. He appreciated the offer but didn't know if he wanted to accept it. "I, uh— you, uh," he stammered. "I-I don't understand why you're so desperate for me to stay."

"Gala leaves us tomorrow. If you leave, too, then it's just me and her, and I don't really want that. I'll definitely get swept up in her shenanigans if that happens. Also, more importantly, I do like you. You're fun to be around—even when I'm mad at you."

"That's kind of you." He smiled. "I enjoy your company too—except when you're yelling at me."

"Good." Dagnarone smiled back at him. "We both like each other but with stipulations."

He thought about what she had to say. He made his decision faster than he spoke, thinking it would be good to leave her hanging. "I'll stay," he paused for a second, "but only so you aren't stuck alone with Sephra. I mean, what would you two even talk about?"

"Justice." Dagnarone chuckled.

Jerlone laughed hard. "That sounds about right. You'd get a lot of lectures, and she would probably try to impart a lot of wisdom upon you too."

"That'll still happen, even with everyone here … assuming Gala isn't hogging the conversation with stories of his glory days."

"That's why I don't speak a lot when we're together. They'll fill the silences, and you won't get a word in edgewise."

"Glad we're on the same page."

They stood and enjoyed the night sky.

"What did you want to share with us?" Dagnarone eventually asked.

"I found a church that deals in our magic. The woman running it was able to teach me a lot about Mystics and how we use our energy. She even gave me a weapon." He pulled the wand out of his breast pocket. "Apparently, there aren't too many of these around anymore. I was in the middle of a lesson when I realized I was late."

"Gala and I were literally at a bar, but I guess since we arrived first, we were off the hook."

"Really?" Jerlone was a little off put hearing that. "I would have assumed if you were late, she would have scolded you as well."

"I mean, she tried, but we defused the situation—Gala more than me. I wasn't in the best state to defuse."

Jerlone shook his head. He didn't understand why Sephra treated him like she did Hearing Dagnarone say that was humiliating. If he hadn't promised her that he'd stay on the train, he would have surely left after hearing that.

"So," Dagnarone began, changing the subject, "is this church somewhere you want to be? If you weren't with us, would you have stayed there?"

"I'm not sure, but it felt right. If I did go there, I wouldn't become some devout follower. It would be for educational purposes." He paused. "She also mentioned they were having some trouble from a local clan. Wouldn't be the worst if I leant them a hand with that."

"Thought you wanted to avoid a violent life?"

"Well, a smaller fight here and there is one thing. We've all gotta fight to survive, and god knows, sometimes I feel I've got the fight in me, but I'd rather avoid being in a war, and that's what Sephra is leading us toward."

CHAPTER 20

ONE WEEK PRIOR
THE HIDDEN CASTLE: THE THRONE ROOM OF KING COART
NIGHT
. . . .

THE ROTUND KING Coart sat alone on his throne. Like every day, he spent it brooding.

The throne room was atop the castle tower. He had the most amazing view, yet it never made him smile. He was too busy berating his subordinates. As far as he was concerned, they were always doing something wrong. His favorite downtime activity was picking them apart. Everyone knew how critical he was, especially the three ex-queens. It was a source of constant ridicule, which he was unaware of, since he thought he was the most beloved in all the land.

Everything in the room was green. The carpets, drapes, flags, chairs, maps, and weapons were all some shade of the color. Coart even draped himself in green, making sure his lavish robes matched his emerald crown.

Diamonds and jewels lay about on tables just to show off. Some trinkets, Coart claimed, were infused with magic. This was a lie. He desperately attempted to create an illusion of wealth and intrigue, unaware it came off as pathetic.

The stairwell doors swung open, and General Afua entered with purpose. This was unusual. Typically, she would stop and bow, per the usual pomp and circumstance.

She wore an emerald-colored armor, decorated with dozens of honors. There was a sword by her side. There were scars on her black skin from years of battle. Grays were starting to show in her hair. Still, she walked at a brisk pace, right up to the king.

"Why are you bothering me this time of day?" Coart snarled. It was too late as far as he was concerned. Once the afternoon passed, he began winding down for the night. When he noticed the jolt in her step, he began to worry.

"Your Majesty, word has come of an impending attack against the province of Larkin," Afua informed him. "Fascio has amassed an army and will be arriving shortly. We need to deploy right away and provide them additional support."

"Not my beloved province!" Coart jumped to his feet. "My vacation home will be in great danger! If they attack, I'm sure they'll destroy it just to spite me!"

He walked off the throne and began pacing the spacious room.

In an emergency, the room could hold two thousand people. The irony was that there were never more than ten people in at a time. Coart kept his circle tight but wished Afua did not have to be a part of his coalition. She gave him headaches, but she had also done right by the kingdom many times over. Frustrating as she may be, he had to keep her.

"You did the right thing, coming to tell me this," he muttered. "Do we know how many troops they're sending?"

"Intel believes close to fifteen thousand. He may even arm them with weapons."

"Really? He hasn't given his soldiers weapons in a long time. At least not to that scale."

"I know," Afua followed his pacing. "It doesn't make sense, especially since the province is not well armed."

Confused, Coart shook his head. "What does he plan to do with the land? It doesn't have any resources he would want. He can't have his people drink ocean water! Although, they're such sickos they probably would." He stomped his feet. "It's just beachfront property!"

"We're still trying to understand the logic behind the attack, sir. Regardless of the reasoning, we need to immediately dispatch additional troops. The Larkin army is three thousand strong, and their population is ten thousand. Those numbers don't play in our favor."

"And we can't forget the property damage they'd cause!"

The circular room was covered in windows. The vertical openings were spaced out every few feet. Right then, all of them provided a breathtaking view of the Forest of Light. The trees illuminated the city, providing a natural streetlight.

Coart walked to one of the windows and looked out. His patriotism swelled when talks of war came about. He smiled a little and felt like a big man. His posture even corrected itself as the conversation progressed. Of course, he was not considering the cost of war; he only thought of his image. He pictured this being a defining moment in his legacy, if done right. There's no place he was more proud of than his vacation home, and he would do anything for it.

"We will fight them," he announced. "What's the word on my vacation house? I assume it will have an extra set of security, correct?"

Afua rolled her eyes. "I'm sure it will be well protected, sir. But, right now, we need to talk about deployment. The Generals Assembly recommends sending eleven thousand of our troops to help. Swords are literally being sharpened as we speak. I need your official decree to start our march for Larkin."

Coart turned from the window and faced Afua. His face solemn, he waited a moment before speaking. "Send all our troops."

"Excuse me?" She sounded befuddled, and there was a hint of a laugh within the two words.

"Losing fifteen thousand troops would be a huge blow to Fascio. If we send all our resources to help, it will be an easy victory. That will stop them from ever stepping foot on our beaches."

"And what about here? You're going to leave the castle completely defenseless?"

"Fascio wouldn't move more than fifteen thousand troops at once. If we know he's sending them to Larkin, then we don't need to worry about some sneak attack here."

"That is a childish way of thinking about this," she said, stern and distraught.

"Don't you question me!"

"You would be leaving these people open for a massacre if something happens here!"

"The forest will protect us!"

"That has not always been the case!" Afua took a few imposing steps toward Coart.

"We are sending everyone because it will get the job done faster!" Coart took a few unimposing steps toward her. "Strength in numbers. You know what that's like. In fact, I even want you to call in the reserves."

"That is absurd!" she nearly screeched. "We do not need to send that many people to battle! Why do you need able-bodied people in their fifties to fight?"

"Because we are going to win!"

"We can win with significantly less troops! You are putting needless lives in danger both here and abroad!"

Coart pointed at her, and this time the gesture was a bit more imposing. "Let me tell you something, lady. You're the only person on my side who is against me. Anyone else from the Generals Assembly or the Senate does my bidding! I've tolerated your insolence because you've produced results. Well, I'm tired of it! If my orders are not followed to a T, I will have no choice but to view you as an insurrectionist! Is that clear?"

She glared at him. "I understand that if I don't follow orders, you will just arrest me and replace me with someone who will. You've damned the troops, regardless of the choice I make."

"So, what'll it be, General?" Coart enjoyed playing with her conscience. "You gonna take responsibility for them, or am I going to have to get someone else?"

Her eyes sunk low. "I will follow your orders, *my king*." She spit out her final two words.

"As I knew you would." The smile that spread across Coart's face would enrage anyone. It was of a cruel man enjoying the moral misery of others.

"The next order of business is handling the evacuation," Afua said.

"If they wish to leave, they are welcome to." Coart turned and made his way to the throne. "Clearly, our time and resources will be better spent preparing for the battle. Have the province issue a warning and let the citizens deal with it themselves."

"We can't just let them deal with it themselves. We need a strategy. Traffic is a major issue, and if everyone leaves at once, it also puts them at other risks, like encountering an approaching army that wants to annihilate them. Then, once they leave, they need a safe place to shelter until the battle is over."

"I'm sure they have family out of town they can stay with." Coart plopped back down on his chair.

"We can't assume that. These are things we have to—"

"General!" Coart barked. "I have a battle to plan, as do you. Tell someone else to deal with their evacuation. It doesn't matter to me where they go. Frankly, if they want to stay, I don't think they will even have an issue. With the amount of troops we have in our corner, the enemy will never set but a foot past our borders."

"Yes, sir." Afua conceded. "We'll get to it then."

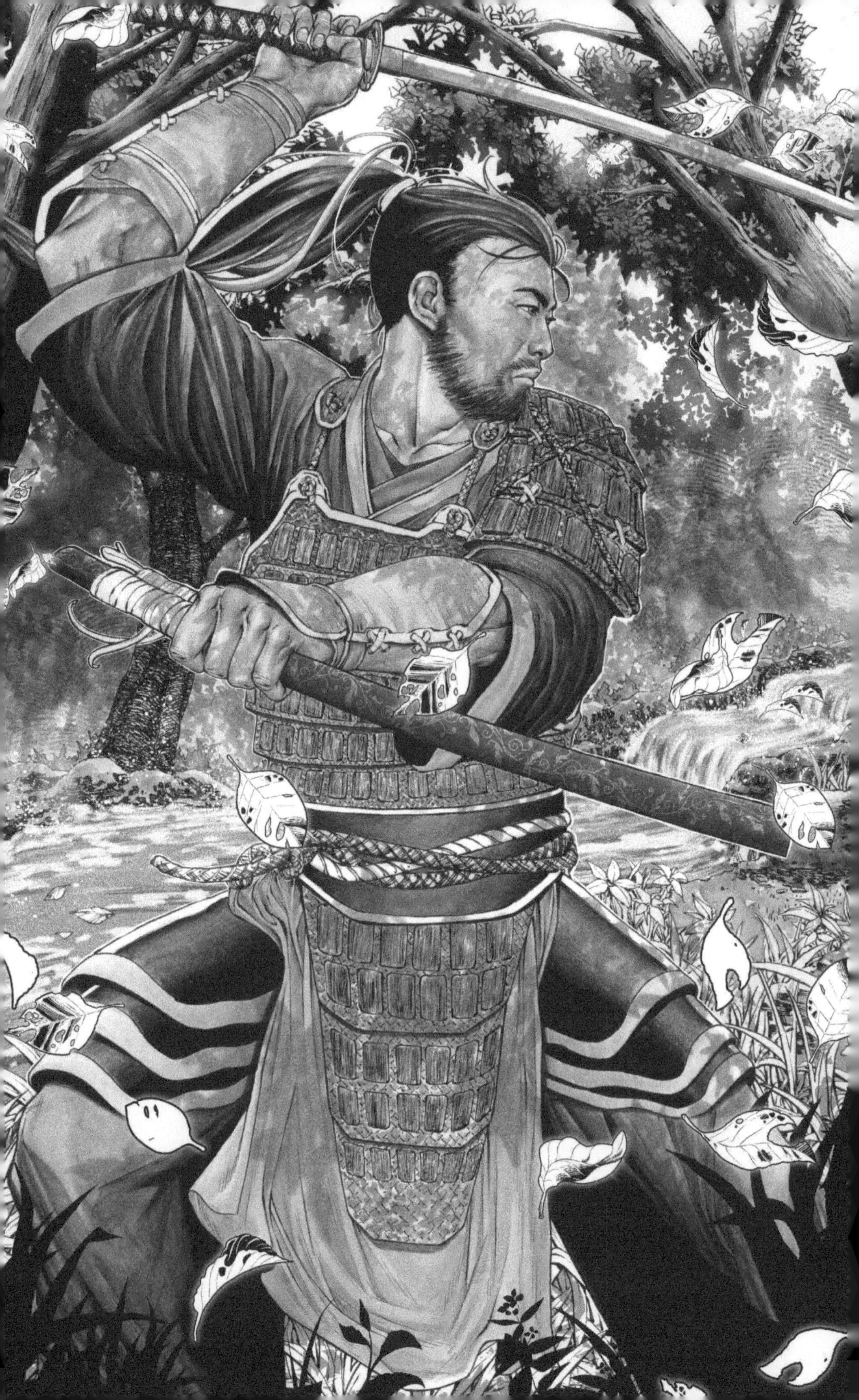

3
A MATTER OF MYSTICS

CHAPTER 21

THE HILL VALLEY OF IGNATUSKI
DAY

WITH AN OVERCAST sky, the wind blew the changing of seasons. The warm summer days were coming to a close as the chill of autumn returned to the air.

Gala and the Mystics made their way through a valley of green mounds. They spent a few hours walking through this monotonous, albeit serene, view. As soon as they made it over one mound, another began. Up and down, nonstop, for hours.

Over the past half hour, the forest had become visible upon the horizon.

"So, I says to him, I says, 'You may have beaten me the last four rounds, but the next five are a different story!'" Gala boasted. "I find, a lot of times, I get a second wind during the latter half of a fight." He smiled, as if this were something to be proud of.

Jerlone rolled his eyes. "And how badly did he beat you the next five rounds?"

"He didn't! Well, that is, not the next *four* rounds, but he did win that last match, which made him the victor. Point of the story is, *if* I had beaten him in that last match, I would have won, and it all would have been thanks to perseverance."

"But you lost," Dagnarone reminded him.

"Yes, in this case my perseverance was actually my downfall, but in another life, it would have been my inspiration."

"I don't think this story has the lesson you think it does …"

Sephra spoke up with a smirk across her face. "Come on, don't beat Gala up. He already has enough people doing that to him."

Dagnarone and Jerlone guffawed.

"Laugh it up," Gala grumbled.

"It's okay," Jerlone said between chuckles. "It sounds like you tried your best."

"You think my best results in me inevitably losing?"

"I mean, based on the evidence you've presented so far, and from what I've seen …"

The final mound was about a half-mile from the forest. This one was a little steeper than the rest. The group stopped for a second to catch their breath.

"Well, I guess this is where I leave you," Gala declared in a dramatic fashion. He walked before them, as though he were accepting an award and addressing an audience. His back faced the forest. "It's been a short time, but we've had good times. I feel like I've known you my whole life." He smiled absentmindedly. This attempt at saying good-bye did not feel heartfelt at all, just theatrical. "Next year, you should consider coming to the Third Island Festival. We can have a drink and catch up on our lives. It'll be a merry time. That is, of course, assuming you're all still alive without my help."

"More like if you're still alive without us," Jerlone mumbled.

"I do just fine, thank you." Gala smiled as he corrected him, then took a deep breath. "A wise man once said—"

Sephra cut him off. "Gala, are you sure there's nothing I can say to convince you to join us?"

He shook his head. "I'm sorry, but I've gotta get to that festival, and I'm already running late." Now he felt genuine, as he realized it was about time to leave them. "Y'all are gonna do fine without me. Don't worry about anything."

One by one, the Mystics noticed a commotion coming from the forest. Their heads tilted as they looked past Gala.

Twenty-five Fascio soldiers walked out of the woods. These troops wore armor, which was unusual. Gala recognized them as part of a scouting group. They weren't the average soldiers; they were elite. Some had swords, while others appeared weaponless.

Two Mountain Folk wandered from the trees and stood at the forest's edge. Their elongated arms dangled, and their heads slowly swayed. It was an unnerving and foreboding sight.

"Who're they?" Jerlone asked.

"The Fist of Fascio," Gala answered. "This is … not what we wanted."

Sephra defended the directions. "But, I was told this would be a safe passage. Babineau told me Fascio never travels this far. It's too out of the way."

"He's right; this is unusual. They could be a … rogue group that got lost?" Gala tried to think of what else could bring them there. "They could be letting others know the path is clear?"

"I could redirect us," Dagnarone offered. "I'm getting a sense of the land. The closer we get to the forest, the more I can feel it."

In unison, the Mountain Folks each raised an arm and pointed to Gala and the Mystics.

The soldiers began their charge.

Sephra turned to the group. "No. They've seen us, and they'll chase us. We have no choice but to fight back."

"Those are six-to-one odds," Gala reminded her.

"We beat a Sauros; we can beat them." She readied her bow.

"Uh, I don't like this," Dagnarone whispered.

"We need a plan. Something fast and effective."

"I got a plan." Jerlone took a few steps toward the incoming horde. "We kill 'em fast."

"No, I meant along the lines of teamwork and strategy!"

Jerlone kept walking, not bothering to look back or acknowledge Sephra.

"Not surprised he'd respond like that." Dagnarone's voice quaked.

"He can be the first line of attack," Sephra said. "The three of us will hold a united front."

"Or …" Gala trailed off as he completed his thought. "I could go join him, and you two could be a united front."

"What? Why? How is that better?"

"'Cause it's two teams of two." Sephra stared at him, not understanding his logic. "Well, we can't just leave him to fight by himself!"

"Why not?" Dagnarone questioned. "He put himself in that situation; he can deal with it."

"If the three of us work together, we can save him," Sephra said.

"Here's the thing …" Gala took a few steps toward Jerlone. "I've never been good at following plans. The two of you will do much better without me tripping over you."

"Gala! We need to be coordinated!"

He continued walking and waved a hand in the air. "You'll do fine, don't worry!"

• • •

Dagnarone wanted to throw up, but now was not the time. She saw the enemy approach and knew there was no escape. She would have never admitted it, but she was starting to regret not finding a weapon.

Sephra kicked her foot on the ground and grunted. "Imbecile!" She looked at Dagnarone. "I know you don't want to fight, but I really need your help right now."

"I don't want to kill anyone," Dagnarone bemoaned. She truly felt cursed, having to engage in a fight this early in her life. She couldn't save the Sauros, and it tore her up inside. Now she was ready to fight humans. Not even three days old, and she already felt like she was failing in life.

"I know you're against killing, but there are ways you can help. I'm sure you can feel the energy from the roots underneath us. You could summon them out from the ground and restrain our attackers. You could also cast shields around us and be an extra set of eyes."

Dagnarone thought Sephra had some good ideas. It was possible to get into a fight and not kill someone. Her biggest struggle would be managing her strength and not accidentally hurting someone. Her visions showed her she was a proficient fighter; now, it was time to be confident in her movements.

"What do you say, Dag?" Sephra asked. "You with me?"

Dagnarone nodded. "I've no choice. I doubt the lot of you will walk away without my help."

Sephra smiled. "There ya go! Nothing wrong with roughing them up a little, is there?"

Dagnarone frowned at Sephra, still not okay with violence.

• • •

Gala hustled over to Jerlone. He was looking forward to this fight. Nothing felt as good as punching fascists, and he had some aggression to work out.

"You think Sephra will convince Dagnarone to fight?" Jerlone asked.

"She may be giving peace a chance right now, but once a sword is swung at her face, she's likely to sing a different tune." Gala replied. The enemy was a quarter-mile away and still charging at them full speed. "Any ideas on how to handle them?"

"Beat the hell out of whoever gets closest to you."

Gala took one step away from Jerlone. "That works for me."

He watched as Jerlone pulled out the wand from his breast pocket. Gala hadn't seen this item before and wondered where Jerlone had come across it. He hoped his friend knew how to use it, because otherwise, it would be quite the hazard. At the very least, Jerlone looked confident, as far as Gala could tell.

Gala readied his whip on the left and his pistol on the right. He was a bundle of nerves, even though he walked with his typical swagger. The odds of this fight were not in their favor, but with a couple of Mystics on his side, they would hopefully win.

Gala broke the silence. "Everyone has a different opinion on how to deal with anger. A lot of smart people would recommend dealing in nonviolent ways. Personally, can't say I've ever subscribed to that. I think tapping into those emotions in certain *situations* can be therapeutic." He pointed at the incoming horde. "This is one of those situations. I know you're mad about being here, and what I did to you, and what Sephra did to you, but keep those in mind and see what it does for ya."

"What're you tapping into right now?"

"My parents' death." With those three words, Gala's demeanor changed. His jovial, fast-talking persona dropped, and the vulnerable child appeared. These were sullen eyes with a face of steel. This was a man ready to take it out on the world.

They were seconds away from clashing with the soldiers.

"One last thing to keep in mind." Gala tensed up, feeling the fight about to happen. "Unlike the Sauros, these jerks deserve it. Ain't nothing but a bunch of damned fascist followers, so put a little extra *oomph* into it!"

CHAPTER 22

THE EDGE OF THE FOREST
DAY

WITH THE CRACK of Gala's whip, the scuffle began. Jerlone's wand conjured globes of energy, downing multiple enemies. This took a toll on him. He was out of breath and wobbly, but thankfully, that attack stopped the soldiers in their tracks.

As Jerlone took a step forward, his leg gave out. He dropped to the ground and watched his foes rush him.

Gala jumped between them and cracked his whip, but the soldiers did not slow down. He cracked it again, this time even harder. Still, they did not slow down. When he took a step forward and snapped his whip, it hit the leader of the pack. He turned and struck two others running toward him. They all fell but survived.

With a burst of adrenaline, Jerlone sprung to his feet and fired a spell from his wand. The attack drained him, and he immediately fell back down. He was embarrassed that was all it took to exhaust him. If anyone else shot one spell and then needed to sit, he would have ridiculed them for some time.

The had enemies retreated a few yards when a barrage of arrows rained down. Sephra was responsible, firing one after another. Some targets were killed, while others were clipped. Some arrows missed entirely.

Dagnarone was just seconds behind. Her hands twisted and tangled in peculiar forms as she summoned energy shields for her companions.

Jerlone watched an attacker charge toward him. Seconds later, the enemy ran into a blue energy shield that Dagnarone had summoned around him. Jerlone could not touch the shield himself, but he knew it wouldn't last long. He looked to Dagnarone and smiled, thanking her for the assist.

The four companions united.

"Did a plan get formed?" Jerlone asked.

"Going with yours," Sephra informed him. "Kill 'em quick."

Together, the four stood, ready for battle.

• • • •

Sephra had four arrows left. One felled an enemy, but the other three missed.

When the first soldier reached her, she struck with her bow. It only took two hits for her to defeat them. She latched the bow to her back and grabbed the pair of sai from her hips. She twirled them, ready for combat.

The next enemy arrived, slashing with a sword. She dodged to the left and then the right. With each movement, she felt a sharp slice of wind as the steel passed her face. There was no fear in her, just the enthusiastic adrenaline of competition.

When their blades clashed, sparks screamed across the metal.

The soldier was a more proficient swordsman. When an opening presented itself, the enemy cut Sephra along her forearm. She gritted her teeth and used that surge of pain to her advantage. She leapt forward and struck her enemy down.

As she removed her sai, the next foe attacked, wielding two swords.

She conjured a tiny amount of red energy onto her blades. With one swipe, they cut through one sword. With a second swipe, the other one was also rendered useless.

Weaponless, her enemy trembled before her. She felt no mercy for them. With one jab to the throat and another to the stomach, her enemy fell. Sephra moved on to her next duel before the body hit the ground.

Two soldiers with clubs fought gallantly. Anywhere Sephra struck, they blocked. They exchanged blows until one of them whacked her back.

With a dazzling display of speed, she turned and got her revenge within seconds.

The other clubber realized they would not win and ran.

Sephra pointed her hand at the fleeing soldier. Seconds later, a globe of energy shot forth. It caught the target, nullifying the threat.

Even though she took some bruising, she felt good about herself and was ready for more.

• • • •

Gala needed to reload his pistol. Then again, it wasn't like it was doing him any good. Like always, the trigger was jamming up, and when it did fire, the bullet veered way to the side.

A fist swung at his face. He dodged and struck the attacker with his own punch.

Three new enemies were approaching fast.

Gala's pistol called out to him. He wondered if it were possible to shoot magical energy from it. He'd practiced once that morning and was able to conjure it, so he believed he could do it then. It would be exhausting, but this was a desperate time.

He pointed his weapon and remembered what it felt like to summon the energy. His hand began to tingle. It was right in the tip of his fingers, ready to release.

The enemy was just feet from him, brandishing a sword above their head.

Like a jolt from a sneeze, a small energy bullet flew from the pistol and into the soldier. It pierced the armor, no issue. The soldier's momentum carried their body forward a few more steps before they collapsed. Their soul was long gone before even hitting the ground.

There were still two others to deal with.

Gala pointed at his next opponent and pulled the trigger—another energy bullet and another victory.

Exhaustion crashed into Gala. He could barely stand.

The final soldier had no weapon in hand, so they tackled Gala to the ground.

Gala's pistol fell out of his hand, landing inches out of reach. The soldier pinned him to the ground and pummeled his face. Gala squirmed, eventually freeing his right arm. As another punch came hurtling down, Gala grabbed the fist. He tossed it to the side and delivered a painful headbutt.

Both combatants cried out in pain.

Gala pushed the soldier off him and scurried toward his pistol. To his surprise, another weaponless soldier had already grabbed it. Gala found himself staring down his own barrel.

The soldier pulled the trigger, but nothing happened.

Gala smirked, pulled out his whip and struck the enemy. He wished he had a witty quip, but he was too exhausted.

Casually, he walked over to retrieve his pistol. He twirled it and put it back in its holster.

• • • •

Jerlone could not continue using the wand. He did not have control, and it was draining too much energy. He had to be on his feet. Reluctantly, he put it back in his breast pocket.

He punched the air, as if to reload his arms. It didn't matter if his enemy had a weapon; he wasn't scared.

The first soldier to attack had a sword, which did them no good. Jerlone dodged the attack, and with one punch, knocked them out cold.

Another soldier approached. Five strikes to their torso and chest and they were done.

Jerlone felt good. This was an effective way to get his anger out. The wand was powerful, but it wasn't the same experience. As much as he didn't want to fight, he had to admit it was fun—and he was damn good at it too.

Four soldiers arrived, and his luck changed. Only one of them had a sword. The unarmed troops went after him first.

Jerlone was good at blocking attacks from three people while also delivering strikes. He could take a hit and keep moving, but soon it got to be too much. The three got the upper hand and clasped his arms behind his back.

Slowly, the soldier with the sword approached.

Jerlone squirmed, but they held him tight. He was desperate to escape and wracked his brain for a plan. With a great big stomp of his foot, a wave of energy knocked the enemies down.

A flurry of punches and kicks took out all four soldiers in the aftermath.

Jerlone thought he'd won until he saw two Mountain Folk heading straight for him. Their arms swung as they ran in such an unnerving way. They had to have been at least eight feet tall. Drool poured out the gaps between their ravaged teeth.

Each creature came down with an overhead strike, knocking him to the ground. They kicked his ribs, and for a moment, he took the beating. Anger washed over him with each hit.

Being on the ground, he realized, he had an advantage. He pulled out his wand. With the snap of his arm, globes of energy blasted his opponents. Exhaustion flooded him, and his vision went black.

A second later, his eyes jolted open. He was exhausted, yet ready for more.

• • •

Dagnarone allowed panic to cripple her.

The group splintered apart, and the chaos surrounding her was overwhelming. She did not have an instinct as to where to go or what to do.

Three soldiers charged at her.

With a wave of her arm, she conjured an energy shield. Her enemies ran into it and knocked themselves out.

An enemy approached from her side. She turned and cast a spell that turned grass to quicksand. The enemy was trapped and sank down to their knees.

She was starting to feel confident. She understood how to use her power, and if she wanted, she could use it in a much more lethal manner, but she had no intentions of that.

Out of nowhere, a sword nearly slashed her face. She stumbled backward while trying to gain her bearings.

The attacker rushed in for another strike.

Dagnarone dodged the attack but fell over. With a quick roll to her side, she had a second to think.

Her foe prepped for the next attack, honing in on her.

To her left was a root sticking out of the ground. She knew what to do.

With the flick of her wrist, roots shot out of the ground and wrapped around her opponent's leg. First trapping the soldier, they then pulled him down to the ground and pinned him there.

As Dagnarone stood, she realized her companions had migrated toward the forest and ran to catch up with them. After a few seconds of running, she felt winded. It took a moment to hit her, but after conjuring magic, she needed to rest. Thankfully, she was within walking distance of everyone.

• • • •

Hidden just within the trees, a man watched the fight unfold. He studied everyone's movements and appreciated the spectacle. It didn't take long for him to realize this was what he had been waiting for.

When the man with the whip and the Mystics reunited, everyone was bleeding from somewhere. Bruises were forming, and the group looked exhausted. Sweat covered their foreheads, and everyone's shoulders slouched. It seemed as if they could only muster to limp as they inched toward the forest.

When they were only twenty yards from the trees, ten more soldiers revealed themselves.

The man could see the Mystics hearts break. They were in no shape to finish the fight, but with little choice, they reached for their weapons.

"We can do this." The woman's voice wavered. Her hands shook, but she held her sai at the ready. "We're not going to let people like them stop us."

Slowly, the others got their weapons ready for a fight.

Unable to let them die like fools, the man started walking toward the battlefield. He pushed tree limbs out of his way as he strode forth. When he revealed himself from the forest, the world went quiet. All eyes looked to him, no one knowing who he'd pledged allegiance to.

His blue robes shimmered in the sun. A golden trim outlined various parts of his attire. Wooden armor covered his chest and left shoulder. Little, multicolored lights were burrowed into the wood. Red gauntlets matched the sash around his waist. A sword hung by his side. His black hair was pulled back into a tight ponytail. With just enough scruff on his face, he truly looked mysterious. For him, there was no question about who was on the side of the righteous.

He raised his hands, pointing them at the soldiers. With a flash of light and a loud crack, globes of energy hurtled toward the fascists. Colors flashed and danced throughout the field as he unleashed the energy.

Not every soldier was a victim of the spell cast. Three ran. The man grabbed the hilt of his sword and chased the survivors.

As he approached the first victim, he withdrew his sword and swung. The steel screamed death as it hissed through the air. With that cut, the soldier fell.

The second victim foolishly stopped to watch, making for an easy target to slay.

The final soldier ran, but to no avail. The swordsman caught up, and once again, one slice was all it took.

The man turned toward the Mystics, and he could read their indecision plain on their faces. They weren't sure what to do. While he had just helped, would he now turn his wrath toward them?

The man approached as nonthreateningly as possible. He rolled his right shoulder back, followed by the left. He sheathed his sword, and a smile spread across his face. *"Kon'nichiwa,"* he said.

The other man holstered his pistol and put away his whip. With a smile on his face, he approached and greeted the man. "Well, hello there. Just to make sure it's clear, we are not with them," he motioned to the soldiers on the ground, "but we are big fans of what you just did here."

The man laughed and grabbed the speaker's hand, delivering a mighty shake. "It was my pleasure. I always enjoy helping those who so desperately need assistance."

The Mystics exchanged befuddled glances.

The man locked eyes with the woman who'd fought with sai, and his world felt different. Seeing her was like seeing a long-lost love. He didn't know the details, but he was captivated by her.

"I'm Sephra." She stepped forward. She gestured to the others as she introduced them to him. "Thank you for helping us."

"I'm Yawonte," he replied. "These parts aren't typically dangerous. First time I've seen something like this since living here." He looked at everyone and felt the energy around them. "You're all like me, except ... new."

"We're what?" Jerlone questioned.

"You probably fell a few days ago?"

"How would you know that?"

"I noticed how quickly your power drains you. You're summoning spells, that in a month's time, will be no more challenging than blinking. It took me some time, too, but I eventually built up the muscle. What brought you here?"

"We're on our way to the Hidden Castle," Sephra answered.

A horn blew in the distance. They turned to see an army rounding the curve of the forest. Even though it would take them time to arrive, a sense of urgency now filled the air.

"That can't be good," Jerlone grumbled.

Yawonte walked toward a soldier wrapped in roots. "Are those your people?"

The soldier ignored him.

Yawonte drew his sword and pointed it at him. "Where are they going?"

Still, the soldier said nothing.

Yawonte twisted his hand in the air, and the roots squeezed together.

Now, the soldier screamed. It did not take long for him to beg for mercy. "The Hidden Castle!" The soldier screamed repeatedly.

"I thought it was impossible for an opposing force to invade?" Dagnarone questioned.

"Not impossible ... just ... improbable." They could hear the despair in the soldier's voice as the roots continued to crunch him.

"Then, there's no time to waste." Sephra turned to the group. "Gala, you've gotta get going."

Gala looked out at the valley and then toward the approaching army. "It's safer for me to go with you."

"But the festival!" Dagnarone objected.

"I can take a hot air balloon in the kingdom. I'll get there for the last day, which is fine by me as long as I get there."

"Thank you." Sephra's voice trembled.

"Don't thank me. Ain't got any other choice."

Sephra then turned to Yawonte. "Will you accompany us and teach more about our magic? I won't lie, it will be dangerous."

"Of course!" Yawonte was thrilled. "You don't understand, I see things. What I've seen is our group united and changing the world. I have the eye of prophecy, and we are all meant to be together!"

No one said anything for a moment after that comment. A few of them looked at one another, but none challenged the statement.

"Alright ... if you say so." Sephra pointed to the forest. "Now, into the woods we go."

CHAPTER 23

THE FOREST
DAY

YAWONTE LED THE group along the trail at a great speed. The first hour, there was little talk, just hustling. They had to jump over logs and duck from branches. Their feet slipped in mud, and their bodies ached.

Sensing everyone needed relief, Yawonte slowed down. "We should be far enough ahead."

The trail was very wide. The five walked side by side and they could have added another ten people and still had space. The scent of cinnamon lingered in the air. Tall, thin trees lumbered over them, their orange and red leaves raining down.

It would be a moment, if not for the army following them.

Yawonte turned and gave Gala a once-over. "You are different. You didn't fall?"

"You got that right," Gala answered. "I'm just a regular ol' human being."

"Yes, but you've also got some magic in you."

"Maybe a little. Sephra showed me how to tap into it."

"With practice, you'll be proficient in no time." He pat Gala on the back in an encouraging manner. Looking around, he knew he was with a good group of warriors. They may not have had it together yet, but they would be a force to be reckoned with once he taught them more.

Sephra spoke up. "Yawonte, what did you mean earlier about us being together?"

Yawonte was silent, unsure how to explain everything. "I fell from the sky nearly fifty years ago. Sapphire clouds dropped me in the Forest of Light. The trees were ablaze with energy as lightning pierced the night sky. It was a sight unlike any other. The chaos of the storm raged above me, yet on the ground, everything felt at peace, as though I was watching the terror through a window. I marveled until the storm passed, and then I began my journey."

"No one else fell with you?" Jerlone asked.

"It was just me." Yawonte was at peace with this. "I had no clue what to do or where to go. For years, I wandered the woods, discovering my magic. I was able to slowly learn how to master it. I had not encountered anyone else then, but I had been seen by others. The Mystic of the Woods is what they call me. Legend grew that I was responsible for shifting the forest around. Nonsense. I was but a child, searching for purpose. The shifting of the forest is thanks to our ancestors, the great Mystics of old."

Gala chuckled. "I remember hearing about the Mystic of the Woods when my family and I traveled through here. Scared the hell outta me!"

"Yes, when I learned the myth, I was not happy. I am not some monster who bewitches children and sacrifices the pure! They attribute the tragedies I've stopped to me. I'm the one who put end to the Gremlin of the Dale[6] and slew the Witches of West Wode[7]! Yet, they give me this awful reputation!"

"Maybe if you left the woods and introduced yourself to people, that would help," Dagnarone suggested.

"I've had plenty of pleasant encounters with people, but once a rumor like that gets going … there is no stopping it. People would rather believe the outlandish if it gives them a form of entertainment. Now, all I can do is claim I am not the Mystic of the Woods." He paused and thought about where he was. "After a few years of aimlessly wandering, I stopped to better myself. I began my meditation phase. For ten years, I would sit and tap into the vastness of the unknown. For hours on end, I would only focus on my trance. I still ate and slept but did nothing else. During that time, my visions of the future started coming into play. There were two things I repeatedly saw: war and the four of you. The eye of prophecy gave me guidance. Spirit told me to stay in the forest. I trained myself to become a warrior for when our time came. At points, I lost faith, but something kept me holding on."

---

[6] See Section V: Myths for more information.

[7] See Section V: Myths for more information.

"So, you believe these visions were of the future?" Jerlone scratched his chin. "Do you not think they could be from the past?"

"These visions are from all directions. I have seen events come to fruition. Other times, I have experienced moments that, in my heart of hearts, I know I have lived before. It is a sense of déjà vu that is so haunting it can't help but stay with you."

"I've felt these moments of déjà vu too," Sephra concurred. "I had it when we met you."

"As did I," Yawonte replied.

"I did too," Jerlone added.

"Same ..." Dagnarone agreed.

Everyone looked at Gala. He shrugged. "I think I felt a little something too?"

"That is why I believe we share a destiny." Yawonte smiled and held his hands behind his back. "We are meant to change the world together."

Dagnarone looked a bit uncomfortable. "So, you've seen us fight in war?"

"Many times."

"Everyone? Including me?"

"Oh, my, yes. If not for you, I think we would have lost over and over."

Dagnarone's face dropped and she sighed.

"What did you do after your time meditating?" Sephra asked.

"I continued my journey through the forest," Yawonte answered. "With it ever changing, there was always something new to see. Views change, but the spectacles never cease. I also got myself into trouble with the lawmen of Moralis and battled the Warlock Damnáre[8]."

"Sounds like you kept yourself busy," Gala remarked.

"See, they say I haunted this forest, but all I did was protect it from the evil that lurked within. Many fools hide here due to the ever-changing land. All I did was try to bring them to justice."

"How admirable," Sephra praised.

While everyone else rolled their eyes at Sephra, Yawonte smiled. Her words touched his heart, and he felt it begin to race. Seeing Sephra was like feeling love for the first time. He wanted to know everything about her. The twinkle in his eye had to have been obvious, but he didn't care. "Had to look respectable for when you got here," he said.

---

[8] See Section V: Myths for more information.

CHAPTER 24

THE FOREST RIVER
DAY

A FEW HOURS LATER, the group came to the controversial river and bridge.

Being there only made Dagnarone hold strong in her belief that they should cross the bridge. Her bones and intuition were burning with that advice, but in the end, it would not be her decision. She looked over to Sephra, who was nervously scanning the area.

"Well, this should be our first crossroads." Sephra pulled out her notes and looked at them.

The wind picked up, flying in from every which direction. Capes, cloaks, and jackets all fluttered dramatically.

Sephra looked at Dagnarone. "You still think we cross the bridge?"

Dagnarone knew her answer but wanted to make sure she was right. If she were to lead them astray, no one would trust her again. If she wasn't going to be some great warrior, she'd have to earn her keep somehow.

She closed her eyes and listened to her soul. It still pointed her across the bridge. When she walked along the river, each step felt like she was going to trip. Then, she took a few steps onto the bridge. Now she was walking with confidence, as everything felt correct. Each movement only emboldened her. She looked to them and smiled. "This is the way."

Sephra's facial expression gave no indication of which way she was leaning. She gave each option one last look. "Alright," she said. "As much as I trust Babineau, I trust you more, Dag. If you think we cross the bridge, then we cross it."

Dagnarone did not expect that response. For the first time, she felt like a valued member of the group. She curled her hand into a fist and victoriously jabbed it into the air. "Woohoo!" she cheered. She was so happy, she spoke faster than usual. "Thank you! I promise you won't regret this, and if it is the wrong way, then I'll get us back on track—but don't worry, this is the right way, so you've got nothing to worry about. If there's one thing I know, it's the right way to do things."

Sephra walked next to Dagnarone and put an arm around her shoulder. "Just remember: if you're wrong, everyone will yell at you." She slapped Dagnarone's back and meandered down the bridge.

CHAPTER 25

THE BLUE BARN
NIGHT

SEPHRA STARED AT the blue barn, which sat between a fork in the road. The barn had a lot of wear and tear, appearing to have been abandoned decades prior. It was a relief they'd made it there, but now they were stuck.

The sun set hours before, and it was getting cold. There was no visibility in the forest, and they were still too far from the castle for the trees to light up. All they had for light were a few makeshift energy globes the Mystics had conjured.

Everyone was watching Sephra, waiting for an answer. Most of their arms were crossed and their faces did not appear welcoming. Sephra was actually afraid to turn and get another glimpse of them. She knew they were fed up, but she was too invested in the mission to take their feelings into consideration.

Sephra walked down one path and then the other. She sniffed the air, but could not smell anything to indicate the direction, like Babineau had said. The others watched her as she paced back and forth, hoping to find some indicator.

"Uh, she does know we're going to rest for the night, right?" Gala questioned the group.

"I doubt it," Jerlone replied, deadpanned.

Sephra walked back to them, fidgeting with her hands. "Anyone have a sense of things? Dag, you're pretty cocky about this stuff. And you were right last time, so you must have some sort of idea."

Dagnarone shook her head. "I think we need to get some rest."

"And we will, but just to gauge your opinion, which way do you think we're supposed to go? Just take a look, and then we can get some sleep."

Dagnarone sighed and walked down the left path. Then she backtracked and walked down the other. "I guess this one?"

Jerlone frowned and walked toward Dagnarone. He stood on the left path for a minute, looking around. He then walked to the right one and did the same. "I don't think she's correct, it's the left path we want."

Dagnarone snapped to attention. "What do you mean it's that way?"

"I'm just getting the sense it's this way. What makes you think it's that way?"

"I just have a sense!"

"So, we have the same reasoning then!" Jerlone raised his voice to emphasize each word.

"Alright, everyone, calm down," Sephra instructed. Her attempt at playing the leader did not work, as the bickering continued. If anything, it got louder. "Hey, come on!" She tried again but still to no avail.

"There is an energy emanating from this path," Dagnarone explained. "That energy will bring us where we need to be. That path had no energy!"

"Exactly," Jerlone countered. "We don't want any encounters. We want the path of least resistance and it's down here!"

Dagnarone stared at him before delivering her rebuttal. "No."

"No?" Jerlone scoffed saying the word.

"Yeah. No. You're wrong!"

Jerlone stood there, mouth agape. "Excuse me? I may be wrong in the end, but you cannot make that declaration at this moment in time!"

"Can you please calm down?" Sephra pleaded.

"What do you know about anything?" Dagnarone hurled at Jerlone.

Jerlone was incensed. "What do I know? I know more than you! I can tell you THAT! I'm a scholar and you're a … a … a botanist!"

"Was that an insult?" Dagnarone tilted her head.

"In this regard, yes." Jerlone finally lowered his voice.

An awkward silence hung in the air.

Sephra turned to Yawonte. "Do you have any idea which path to go down?"

Yawonte looked down one path and then the other. He did not bother taking a single step toward either. "I think we should sleep on it. Let our subconscious figure it out."

"I think that's an excellent idea," Gala agreed.

Sephra sighed. "Fine, let's settle down."

CHAPTER 26

THE BLUE BARN LAKE
NIGHT

G**ALA NEEDED SOME** time to himself before going to sleep. Even though he was exhausted, he wanted to sit back and have a sip from his flask in peace.

There was a small lake near the blue barn. Gala trudged through the woods, tripping a couple of times along his way.

The lake was a serene place. The moon glistened off the water, illuminating the surroundings.

Gala slumped down by a tree and took everything in. He undid the cap of his flask and savored that first sip. Gala realized that, for the first time in a while, he was actually excited by an adventure he was on. The adventures he'd had with Isra were great, but he never wanted to go on them. He just wanted to spend the time with her. This was different. This was the first time he felt like he was doing what he was supposed to.

Gala shuffled through his satchel until he found the Diamond of Farrokh. He sat it in his lap and thought of Isra. Not being at the festival was frustrating. He was terrified he'd miss his chance to be with her and have to wait another year. A lot could happen in that time. *Hell, a lot could have happened in the past year,* he thought. What if he got there and found her with someone else already?

Overwhelmed, Gala took a long sip from his flask.

Behind him, a twig broke. He whipped his head around to find Sephra walking toward him. "I could sense ya coming," he told her. "Is that part of this magical power?"

"No, I think that was just listening with your ears," Sephra answered.

"Damn, thought I was getting better at it."

"Do you think we should try to break into the barn to sleep there?"

"With the way this week's going, I wouldn't. With our luck, it'll turn out haunted. Maybe infested with killer cannibals or a Book of the Damned. Those are popular out in the woods."

"So, what brings you out here?" Sephra slumped down next to him.

"Just trying to get some time to myself …"

"Oh, I can go."

"Nah, it's fine. One person I can handle. Four … that gets a little much."

Gala offered the flask to Sephra, but she declined.

"So," Sephra began, "I hear you're going to this festival because you're smitten with some singer?"

"First off, she plays the guitar. Yes, she also sings, but she's a guitarist at heart—and if I'm being objective, her voice isn't the greatest. It does what it needs to, but I doubt she would win a contest, but her guitaring is great! Secondly, I told that to Dag in confidence!"

"She didn't tell me about it, Jerlone did."

"What! How does he know?"

"I can only assume Dag told him."

"You know, for cosmic beings, y'all sure are a bunch of gossips!" Gala shook his head and took another swig from his flask. "By the way, I'm not smitten with anyone either, okay? That term makes me sound all cute and cuddly or something."

"That's not what I heard," Sephra mumbled.

Gala grunted. He didn't know how, but she knew exactly what to say to make him flustered. Even though it had only been a few days, Gala felt like they had spent a lifetime together. It was like he was sitting with an old friend, catching up.

Sephra looked at the diamond in Gala's lap. "I mean, you did get that diamond for her, right? That's cute and cuddly! And here you were, alone in the woods, looking at it. You were thinking of her, weren't you?"

"I hate this conversation so much." This topic was Gala's worst fear. He put the diamond back in his satchel.

"Is her band actually good, or are you too biased to answer that?" Sephra said with a smirk.

"I like her music. It's got a good energy and beat going. Her lyrics speak to me."

"Her lyrics speak to you because you're a sensitive soul."

"Damn it!" Gala got up in a huff. "Maybe I can't even handle one of ya!"

He walked over to the water and knelt down. From his pocket, he grabbed a clear vial and a pill. He scooped some water into the vial and sniffed it. There was no odor—a good sign. He then dropped the pill into the vial. A second later, the water turned blue.

"Good news ... it's safe to drink," he said. He poured the vial on the ground and began pacing. "You know, my second year at the festival, she inadvertently got into a bar fight."

"Inadvertently?"

"Yeah, she thought someone was talking to her who wasn't and—uh—to be honest, it was kinda hot."

"Not surprised you'd think that." Sephra shook her head.

"I mean, if she got her ass kicked then it wouldn't have been."

"Gala!"

"What? I'm just being honest! There's a confidence in winning a fight that— I'm just saying, it got me going."

"Gross." Sephra closed her eyes and made a face. "And did those people even deserve it?"

"Sure, they weren't talking to her, but their content was still in very poor taste."

"What's her name?"

"Isra Isolé," he smiled after saying it. "By the way, I stepped in to help with the fight. I kinda got in her way, and she had to save me, but that's beside the point."

"What was the point?"

"That I'm a gentleman and I helped her fight off the attackers she provoked."

"Glad chivalry isn't dead," Sephra replied sarcastically. "And that's the story of how you fell for her?"

"Nah, fell for her the first night we met. Funny story, the next day she dragged me along to steal the Crackle Daggers[9] in Cadogan Mountain. You see, there's this myth about these swords that's really fascinating. They—"

---

[9] See Section V: Myths for more information.

He could see Sephra did not care about them. "Never mind. Long story short, she's now the owner of some of the most powerful weapons ever forged. Which is ironic because she's not really a fighter."

"Didn't this story start with you telling me about her getting into a fight?"

"Well, yeah, she can fight but that doesn't mean she's a fighter. She's just smart enough to know how to defend herself. I don't see her running off into a war like you, even though using the Crackle Daggers could really be advantageous."

"So, your plan is to go to this festival and confess your love?"

Gala laughed. "No one said anything about confessing my *love* to her."

"But you stole that diamond for her, right?"

"Yeah, but giving a gift ain't confessing *love*. I mean, hell, I wouldn't say I love her. First off, I'd be coming on too strong, and second, I'm not even sure if I got any love left in me."

"You obviously do, since you're expressing feelings for her."

"Could be lust instead of love."

Sephra studied him. "No, I think it's love."

Gala didn't know how to respond to that, so he did what he always did. He took out his flask and had another drink.

"You keep sticking with us to avoid her, don't you?" Sephra asked.

"Excuse me?" Gala pointed a finger at her.

"After you got the diamond, you could have left."

"Yeah, but y'all saved my bacon, and I feel like I owe ya. It's called doing the right thing!"

"And that's something you're known for doing?"

Gala knew her words were true, and worst of all, he didn't have a snappy comeback.

"I think you're scared to admit how you feel for her. You're worried she won't reciprocate. Or, maybe worse, she will feel the same as you. You already can't help but picture how things will be a few years down the line once the fire has faded. Right now, she's this perfect, untouchable being that seems to be the pinnacle of life. You two start a relationship and you know that'll change. You like the illusion you've created. Gives you something to strive for but to never have to be responsible for. Am I wrong?"

Gala gritted his teeth and looked away from her. "Ya ain't wrong, damn it! Maybe I did stay with y'all out of fear. If I miss her at this year's festival, then I've gotta wait another year, and maybe I'm just hoping I'll feel more confident then? I don't know." Gala sighed. "I want to tell her, but I'm just terrified of the repercussions. Whether they're good or bad, our dynamic changes, and I like the fantasy I've built in my head too much."

"It's not easy for you to be emotionally open with people, is it?" Sephra looked deep into his eyes, connecting with his soul.

"Darlin', it ain't easy for anyone."

Once again, he offered her the flask. This time she accepted. She sniffed it and then took a shot. Her face scrunched up, clearly not enjoying it. To her credit, she never made a groan. Gala could respect that.

Gala broke the silence. "You know, it's a little unfair you get to psychoanalyze me when you've got no romantic history to speak of."

"I know, it's frustrating," Sephra replied.

"Dag can remember love. Why can't you?"

"I'm willing to bet she prioritized it more than me. I don't think I prioritized correctly. I always feel like something needs to get done when, in fact, it could probably wait. I sacrifice my own happiness for it, yet at the same time, It's the only thing that gives me joy." She stared off into a daze. "Sometimes I wonder if love could do the same."

Gala felt sorry for her. He wasn't sure if he should try to hug her to make things better. He decided against it and sat back down. "Have you tried thinking about love? I mean, Dagnarone had to focus on it; maybe you can do the same."

It appeared as though Sephra just sat there, but Gala suspected much more was going on than he could imagine. He gave her the time she needed to search her soul.

Sephra finally spoke. "I remember love. There was someone who was my equal." Her words were slow, and at times, her voice quivered. "And we were dumb. It was never easy for us to admit our feelings either, and worst of all, I feel it ended in tragedy."

"One way or the other, they all do."

Sephra turned to him, making eye contact. "Don't run from the feeling, Gala."

Her words reverberated through Gala's soul. As soon as they reached the Hidden Castle, he would go off and find Isra.

CHAPTER 27

THE BLUE BARN
DAWN

DAGNARONE WAS FAST asleep until she felt something sniffing her ear. She opened her eyes to find an adorable, little woodland creature crawling all over her.

Upon seeing the creature, she yelped and grabbed onto her branch. She fell asleep about ten feet up in a tree and was now holding on for dear life.

She looked around to find all her companions being terrorized by the little creatures. Not everyone was awake yet, but they would be soon.

The creatures themselves were small, furry, and had scrunched-up faces. They mostly walked on all fours, but some were prowling on their hind legs. When standing upright, they were about a foot and a half tall. They were ambidextrous, but most of all, sneaky. The creatures chuckled and nudged each other as they pulled off their heist.

Gala slept in a hammock, grasping onto his satchel. As soon as two creatures crawled on his legs, he opened his eyes. He went from sleeping to screaming in no time. "Wudulonds! Thieves!" Gala yelled. "We're being robbed! Everyone, grab your valuables!"

With that, the two Wudulonds lunged for his satchel and latched on with their teeth. Gala shook the bag and did everything he could, but the creatures would not let go.

"Come on, buddy," one of the Wudulonds growled at him, stretching out the last word.

"Scram, you blasted beasts!" Gala hollered back at them. He kicked his legs and flailed his arms, but they held tight.

"Gala," Dagnarone yelled over to him, "why are you freaking out so bad?"

"Look at what I'm currently dealing with!" At that moment, another two Wudulond ran onto the hammock and fought for Gala's bag.

"But outside of right now, what's your issue?"

Gala hesitated to answer. "I got robbed blind by these jerks years ago."

The Wudulonds laughed and pointed at Gala.

"How could you let them rob you?" Jerlone chuckled. He was over on a flat rock, playing with the Wudulond near him. "They're so tiny."

"I didn't *let* them rob me!" Gala yelled. "I was … tricked." The Wudulonds keeled over laughing. "It wasn't funny! I had some very valuable treasures in there! Cost me a fortune."

"Don't worry." Yawonte grinned. He was feeding the critters some nuts and berries from his pocket. "I can help keep an eye on your valuables. They won't be bothering you."

"Ha-ha, very funny. Let's see how you like it when you find yourself destitute and alone 'cause these critters target you!"

"I've come across them many times in my travels. They have never bothered me. If anything, they've always been quite helpful in giving me directions."

Dagnarone looked to Sephra and saw her lying in the grass, petting her Wudulond. If anything was going to happen, Dag needed to take command of the situation.

"What're you doing here?" Dagnarone asked her Wudulond.

"We live in the woods," the Wudulond replied in its native tongue, Wudhuy. Their language had a lot of 'lu' 'wu' and 'moo' sounds. It was a wobbly noise that alternated up and down.

"But why are you harassing us?"

The wudulond shrugged. "It's what we do? You looked like you probably had some shiny treasures on you. We like shiny treasures."

"My name's Dagnarone, what's yours?"

"I'm Eddie."

"It's nice to meet you, Eddie the Wudulond."

"You seem to understand Wudhuy pretty well. Usually gotta speak in one of your tongues to be understood."

"To be honest, I need a little more time to get all the intricacies of it down, but I think I can manage for the most part. Language comes naturally to me, not to brag, but it is cool."

"I had a feeling you were the smart one." Eddie winked at her and clicked his mouth. "You and your friends finding everything you need? Food and shelter going okay?"

"Yes, thank you, Eddie the Wudulond. We've only spent one night in here, but so far … actually, we do need help."

"We're good at helping." Eddie's tail began to wag.

"We need to get to the Hidden Castle and fast. Should we take a left or a right?" She pointed to the fork in the road.

Eddie leaned off the branch and sniffed the air in both directions. He pointed to the right. "If you go that way you can follow us home. Our village is just a few miles from a bridge. That'll connect you to a path that we take anytime we go there."

"Do you go there often?"

"Oh, yeah. We like to see the lights. There's some tribes over there we like to play games with too. It's a nice change of pace."

"How delightful!"

"We live our best lives." Eddie smiled a mischievous grin. "You know what else we do? Sometimes, we steal things from the castle! Pretty cool, huh?"

"Oh, that sounds … like what Gala accused you of doing."

The Wudulond shrugged.

Dagnarone climbed down the tree with Eddie on her back. She walked over to the fork in the road. "My new friend, Eddie, gave me directions." She announced to the group. "He says we should go down the right path."

"Hmm," Jerlone grunted. "How convenient he would tell that to just you."

"Don't be grumpy just because my path's the right one."

"We don't know that it's the right one yet."

"Come on, Jerlone. Just be a gracious loser here. I was right and you were wrong, and that's okay." She was frustrated that he wouldn't let it go. She got them there from the river and felt she deserved a little credit.

Jerlone put his hands up, acquiescing the point.

Eddie crawled atop Dagnarone's head. "Hello, everyone," he spoke in the Wudhuy language. "We would be happy to assist you in getting to the next marker in your journey. We will not even charge you much!" The little creature laughed at his joke, as did his companions. "I kid. I kid. In all seriousness, we would be happy to bring you to our village and feed you. From there, we can set you on the path we use. It's fast and will save you days. All of this, of course, free of charge."

"I don't know what he just said, Dag." Sephra stood up and joined her. "But if you think he's telling us the truth, and that's our fastest path to the Hidden Castle, then we have to take it."

Dagnarone looked to Eddie, and he nodded to her. She looked back to Sephra. "He's confident."

CHAPTER 28

THE FOREST
MORNING

JERLONE WAS MISERABLE. The Wudulond were fast and well ahead of everyone. The creatures had an annoying habit of whistling while they scurried, and the sound was maddening. The same eight-second loop was repeated without pause for over an hour. They were like a small team of workers heading to the job and happy to tackle the day.

His companions weren't making things easier. They were either too focused on running or telling inane stories one after another.

"The whip was my mother's grandmother's," Gala droned on. "She passed it down to me when I was about eight. I know most people would say that's too young an age, but I only suffered a few bad cuts. Frankly, anyone learning this is gonna take a few hits, no matter how old they are." Jerlone noticed Gala beamed with pride when he talked about his family. "I think they gave it to me because they always said I was sharp as a whip."

Jerlone glanced at the weapon. "Nothing about it looks sharp. Are you sure that was a compliment?"

Gala paused, thinking it through. "Yes?"

When the Wudulond started to slow down, everyone else followed suit.

Jerlone needed space and slowed his stroll to a crawl. He was frustrated with everyone except Yawonte. Gala still hadn't fully earned his trust. Dagnarone enjoyed arguing a little too much. Sephra didn't care about anything but her own objective. All things considered, it was easy for him to feel lost in the shuffle.

The Church of the Wand weighed heavily on Jerlone's mind. With more consideration, it really seemed like the place for him. Their knowledge of the mysterious enticed him the most. Outside the church, Civis had many libraries and universities, making it a treasure trove of education. With those resources, he would have a much better understanding of the world around him, satiating his quizzical nature.

He decided that when they reached the Hidden Castle he would take a few weeks to study. If he was making the trip, it may as well be beneficial. He thought nothing of the army also en route. It was his assumption someone else would handle that mess.

For the first time, his path forward started to seem clear.

Lost in thought, Jerlone didn't even notice when Yawonte found his way next to him.

"Do you mind if I join you?" Yawonte asked.

"As long as you don't hassle me," Jerlone bluntly replied.

"I will do my best," he said with a chuckle. "Are you enjoying this world so far?"

"Really got nothing to compare it to. Seems to have some nice views."

"Yes, the views are spectacular."

"How would you know?" Jerlone cocked an eyebrow. "Thought you just stayed in this forest your whole life?"

"I figure if this small forest has so many marvels, the rest of the world has to be filled with them too."

"For fifty years, you only stayed here. Seems to me like a bit of a waste."

"To you, yes." Yawonte shrugged. "At one point, I was imprisoned. I had no choice but to stay here. Besides, I knew my time outside the forest would eventually come. Until then, I needed to be here for all of you to find me."

Jerlone wasn't sure if he believed in this shared destiny, and his look said so. "You're really convinced we're all supposed to spend life together, huh?"

"I have the eye of prophecy, and I know for certain we are entwined in each other's lives. Yesterday was my second birth."

"I don't know. It's hard for me to imagine us staying together. I feel everyone has a different goal in mind, and none of them align."

"Oh, you'd be surprised. Fate is funny. Today we may be working toward opposite objectives, but in another month, we could be united. You just lack the vision to see our potential. We may still be learning how to work together, but once we do, we will be something spectacular."

"Alright, if you say so," Jerlone dismissed him.

Yawonte stared at Jerlone for some time before speaking again. "I have to know, and I do not mean this in a rude manner, but why are you here? You project this energy that says you would rather be anywhere else."

"Well, not quite, but yes." Jerlone thought for a moment, considering what else he was willing to reveal. Yawonte was a calming presence, and he felt surprisingly open around him. "I've had my doubts. When Sephra proposed this idea, it was like something compelled me to agree."

"That was Spirit influencing you to accept your fate."

"Sure, it was." Jerlone wasn't a believer. "Truth be told, I think I was scared of leaving behind the only people I know. Deep down, I'm an introvert and don't need anyone, but I don't think I'm ready for that just yet. I know I don't connect to them as well as they connect to each other. Still, I want to be with them, even if our desires are spreading us apart."

"Our desires may separate us from time to time, but that does not mean we don't share a connection. There will be times we fall apart only to reunite when we need it the most."

Jerlone thought about that statement. He pictured what his life could be like with this group. It didn't seem the worst way to spend a life, but he wasn't sure if it was his ideal way to spend it.

Yawonte continued to walk next to him in the silence. Feeling rude for going silent, Jerlone looked for a new topic to discuss. When he caught a glimpse of Yawonte's sword, he felt a power manifesting. "Where'd you get your sword from?" Jerlone asked him.

The smile on Yawonte's face faded as his eyes focused straight ahead. "My meditative years concluded with the challenge of the Cutlery Cult," he said. "I witnessed their cannibalistic ways from afar. I'm no longer ashamed to admit they terrified me for some time. They were demonic with the little magic they conjured. Their horrors haunted these woods for many a year. I spent too long avoiding them and running."

"As you tell it, there sure is a lot of evil in this forest," Jerlone replied, concerned, looking around to make sure no one was stalking them.

"Yes. Even in the light, there can be great darkness." Yawonte fiddled with his sword's hilt. "Within this forest, there is the Black Swamp, a place where life does not dwell. Trees sit dead and mud covers all ground. It was a favorite gathering spot for the Cutlery Cult. One night I observed them dragging twenty drugged bodies for their rituals." Yawonte shook his head. "I had to intervene. Now, at this point in time, I was nothing but a man in rags. With no weapon nor armor, stealth would be my best strategy. I hunted my first target and waited til he stepped away from the others. When my opportunity came, I struck. He never saw me. I did my best to make it quick. I may have condemned him to death, but he did not need to suffer for his sins." Yawonte withdrew his sword. "This belonged to him. I'm fortunate the Cutlery Cult are collectors and crafters of fine blades. Any one of them would have made a worthy weapon." He stared intently at the steel. "Keeping this reminds me of the path I have chosen to walk down and why I have done it." As if snapping out of a trance, he put away the sword. "Fate has a way of drawing us to our weapons, you know?"

Jerlone's wand emanated an energy upon hearing those words. This weapon was more than just wood; it was sentient in its own way. "Yes, I do know." Jerlone pulled out the wand. "Did you feel it go off just now?"

"No, for I do not have that connection. Your weapon speaks to you. That's important. It will make the two of you stronger." Yawonte studied the wand. "I observed you using it against your first wave of attackers."

"Still working out the details." Jerlone scratched the back of his head, embarrassed to think of that performance.

"You did fine. It's a hard weapon to use." Yawonte gestured toward it. "Would you mind if I …?"

"Be my guest."

Yawonte gently grasped it and slowly examined the intricacies. For Jerlone, it just looked like a stick at times, but Yawonte could see the history of the wood. He sniffed it and even held it to his ear. With every movement, he swooned like he were holding a child. "Yes," Yawonte said. "This is a powerful weapon. From a Vand tree, correct?"

"As I understand it."

"Probably made by one of the Wand Whittlers of old. This weapon will respond best to visualization. Imagine conjuring without becoming exhausted. Picture massive eruptions of energy. See yourself standing over your foes with the wand held triumphant! The wand will connect with you by doing this."

Jerlone's mouth was agape. "That sounds absurd."

"Magic is nothing if not absurd."

"I just don't see how visualization is going to help. That's wishing for an outcome. Wouldn't I become more proficient with some sort of practice?"

"Sure, do that too." Yawonte shrugged. "I doubt you know this, but the Vand tree was once known as the wishing tree. People would cut a piece off as they revealed their hearts' desires."

"I don't understand how that can work. It sounds like a superstition."

"It's magic, my friend; of course it's a superstition. You don't have to understand how all of it works, you just have to believe in the process and yourself. The day I stopped worrying about how it happens was when it clicked."

Jerlone mulled on that thought for a moment before changing the subject. "You didn't finish your story. After you got your sword, what happened?"

"I cut down my enemy." With crestfallen eyes and a face like stone, Yawonte said nothing more of the matter.

CHAPTER 29

WUDULOND WOODS
DAY

S**EPHRA WAS NOT** impressed. After all these hours, the Wudulond simply led them to a clearing in the woods. No civilization, just some scattered leaves in between trees.

The Wudulond stood around, talking in their language. They seemed uptight, yet offered the humans no explanations.

To collect her thoughts, Sephra walked away from the others. Focusing on one of the nearby trees, she realized it was abnormally large. She stepped back to see how tall it was and noticed something unexpected. Above them was a whole civilization scurrying about, multiple layers of treehouses and bridges with little Wudulonds moseying through their days.

As Sephra looked around, she noticed the elevator descending to pick them up. She couldn't help but smile knowing she'd get to see their home up close.

Sephra walked back over to the group. Two of the Wudulond seemed to be arguing with Eddie. They kept tapping their wrists, apparently complaining about how long it took. What should have been one hour took three. Eddie kept brushing them off with the swipe of a hand, but the others were relentless. Even angry, they were still adorable.

While the elevator brought them up to the city, the Wudulond continued their bickering in the Wudhuy language. Everyone else, respectfully, kept quiet.

When they reached their stop, the argumentative Wudulonds scuttled off. Eddie stayed behind and climbed onto Dagnarone's shoulders.

Dozens of Wudulond passed by as the humans stood there. They didn't seem the least bit interested in them. A couple stopped to sniff them but kept moving.

By Sephra's count, there appeared to be eight levels above them. Even from down there, it was evident all levels were crawling with the critters.

Tree leaves played a big part in this civilization's design. The orange-and-yellow growth decorated their homes and lined the massive, wooden walkways. They were almost like a set of flowers. It was a unique experience seeing the foliage intermingled within the society instead of ruling from above.

"Alright," Eddie addressed the group in his native tongue. "Why don't we go get something to eat and I can give you the directions you're looking for."

"He says we're gonna eat while he gives me the directions," Dagnarone translated for everyone.

Gala gasped and his face lit up. "Are we getting a Wudulond breakfast?"

Eddie nodded and gave a thumbs up.

"Wow! I hear these are out of this world. I never thought I'd get one, 'cause you know, we have history, but here I am!"

"It really seems like you're living your best life." Jerlone's tone was flat and unimpressed.

"Just you wait. This is gonna be the highlight of your short life."

"Really? It'll be even better than when you almost caused a Sauros to kill us?" Jerlone spit the words with contempt.

"It won't make for as interesting a story, but you'll have a better time. Also, you're acting like I asked the Sauros to try to kill you. It tried killing you 'cause that's what they do. That part's not my fault!"

"Isn't it a little late for breakfast?" Sephra interjected. She felt it would slow them down, even though she was hungry.

"They serve it all day here," Gala responded.

"You sure do know a lot about their eating habits," Dagnarone chided.

"When you live on the road like I do, you need to know these things. Free meals are an important part of being a vagabond."

Sephra knew she was not going to get her way and decided to concede. "Alright, well, we should get a move on." There was a hint of annoyance in her voice. "We don't want the army beating us to the castle."

As they followed Eddie, they saw little homes carved into trees. Wudulonds poked their heads out as the Mystics passed. Not a lot of detail was visible from the outside, but one appeared to be a cozy, little, one-bedroom home. These were very social creatures, not known to keep to themselves. The house was really just a place to get some rest. Their sleep schedules were not consistent, so someone was always home trying to catch a few minutes rest.

Ten minutes later, they arrived at the dining hall. It was the centerpiece of the city, with multiple bridges encircling it. No matter where they were in this city, it would be easy to get here.

On their right was a view to die for. Independent of one another, Sephra and Yawonte stopped to take it in. Wudulond Woods surrounded them, brown, orange, yellow, and red as far the eye could see.

Looking up, they saw how far and wide the city ran. It didn't seem possible for something that massive to float above in the trees so gently.

"My god, what a view," Sephra marveled.

"I can only imagine how many generations it took to construct," Yawonte said.

"Fascinating creatures. Wouldn't expect something so small to be capable of something so massive."

"Hopefully that teaches you not to make your estimations based on stature."

They took a moment to enjoy the view in silence.

Yawonte glanced over at Sephra, but she was oblivious to it. "Do you remember the Lightning Lakes?"

Sephra thought something sounded familiar. "The chain of lakes that are struck by lightning every couple of minutes?"

"Yes, it's a goldmine of stored energy."

"It's ringing a bell." She nodded. "We'd just fought off a small platoon and were taking in the surroundings. It was—" She stopped short of saying the word romantic.

"I don't recall the fight, but that would explain why we looked like a mess. Is there anything else you remember?"

Sephra hesitated. "Yeah, I remember being disappointed."

"Disappointed?"

"A little bit."

"Because of me?"

"I'm not sure." She stopped to think about it. "It was just the two of us there, right?"

"Don't forget the enemy we smote, wasting away by our feet."

"I can't remember all the details, but when I think of the moment, I just remember this feeling of wanting something more. By the time we walked away, it just ... wasn't what I was expecting."

"Interesting."

She made eye contact with him, and her nerves flared. "Why did you bring that moment up?"

"It's something I've had many dreams about."

"And I'm there?"

He broke eye contact. "Always." He blushed as the words came out.

"You know, some people would be creeped out by that answer."

"But you're not, are you?" He turned and looked at her with a confident smirk.

"No, because ... I know you. We just met, but I've never felt more comfortable around anyone in my life. When I see you, I feel like I'm home."

"Same."

For the first time since falling, Sephra was not thinking about the mission. Right now, all she wanted was to stay in this moment with Yawonte.

When she realized their shoulders were touching and their heads were leaning in, she snapped out of it. She didn't know what had come over her or how she'd become so enchanted. She backed away and turned, as if something got her attention. It was time to get back to the mission and be a leader.

"So, uh," Sephra stammered as she hoped to make things less awkward. "You said before that you have the eye of prophecy. How do you differentiate visions of the past with things to come?"

"When my past comes to me, it is always in black and white," Yawonte explained. "When I see the future, it's vivid. The colors are more exaggerated than reality. It's like an artist left big streaks of paint on the canvas. When I see the past, I feel calm ... even when it shows me something devastating. When I see images of the future, my heart fills with dread."

"Dread?"

"Yes." Yawonte appeared despondent, like he was looking through

Sephra and gazing into the cosmos themselves. "Gala has set into motion events larger than he could ever understand. What we are doing here is, well, it's going to change the world, and I find that when you change something, even if it's for the better, a little part of you must always dread the outcome."

"I don't understand." Sephra shook her head. "What's going to happen?"

"I don't know, but at least we will all be together." Yawonte flashed a fake smile.

Sephra looked at him, unsure what to say. She was already a bundle of nerves, and this was not helping. "Maybe we should go get something to eat."

CHAPTER 30

WUDULOND DINING HALL
DAY
• •

JERLONE WAS FEELING too salty to be impressed with the Wudulond dining hall. The facility was beyond huge, which made no sense to him since it housed the smallest of creatures. The wooden smell was overpowering, so much so he couldn't even smell the food.

"Wow, wow, wow," Gala repeatedly uttered. Unlike Jerlone, he was more than impressed. "I tell ya, these buggers know what they're doing. I don't mean to be rude, but I'm getting food and finding us a table. See you there!"

Jerlone and Dagnarone watched as Gala dashed off to the buffet. Eddie shuffled alongside Gala, so the two finally shared a moment to bond.

"For someone so suspicious of the Wudulond, he sure is making himself at home," Jerlone said.

"That's Gala," Dagnarone replied. "Suspicious for a second, then happy and dumb as a dog."

"I'm surprised to hear you say something so mean."

"How is that mean? I compared him to a dog. That's the nicest thing I could say."

"If you say so," Jerlone grumbled.

"Oh, no. Don't tell me you're more of a cat person!"

He shot her an annoyed look.

"Jeez, guess you're not an animal person." She rolled her eyes. "What's your deal? You seem grumpy."

As far as Jerlone could tell, he had never felt so antsy before. Even though he enjoyed his conversation with Yawonte, he had been annoyed since. His life was coming into focus, and this wasn't the right path. That frustrated him, yet dealing with the problem seemed impossible. He knew he was lashing out but was hopeless to stop it.

"I don't know if I should be here," he told her. "If I left, you'd no longer be stuck with just Sephra. Gala is still around and Yawonte has joined up. You'd be in good company."

"Wait, what are you saying? Are you about to abandon us?"

"Why do you gotta use that word?"

"Fine, is there a synonym you would prefer?" Dagnarone snapped each word.

"I thought you would be more understanding." Jerlone raised his voice. "All of you really just want to use me for whatever needs you have, huh?"

"How is wanting you around using you?"

Jerlone felt like fire was shooting from his eyes. "This is manipulative. You're not listening to my needs. No one is listening to me or trying to give me what I need!"

"Do you realize how selfish you sound?"

"How is it selfish to take care of myself? I'm not asking anything of you! I'm asking to be left to my own devices for some time! Am I not allowed to try to live my life how I want?"

Dagnarone's shoulders relaxed as her defenses dropped. "I'm sorry, you're right. You do deserve that. I guess I just feel stuck here, and I selfishly liked you being stuck with me."

They were both quiet. The high-energy fight was done.

Jerlone broke the silence. "I don't think either of us feel in control of our lives." He spoke slow but with a power. "You could come with me. We can get out of here and avoid all the trouble Sephra is about to get into."

"But, Sephra needs us now more than ever."

Jerlone thought she would say more, but she didn't. He couldn't believe she stopped there. "Are you serious? You literally have an army chasing after you right now, and you just think you're supposed to stay on this path?"

"I don't like it either, but I feel I have to be there for her."

"When that army arrives, you're going to have to fight." He maintained his composure. "You won't be able to just subdue your attacker next time, you'll have to kill. That's the life you wanted to avoid. If we leave, then you can still make that a reality."

Dagnarone scratched the back of her head. "I always envisioned a life of peace, but I know that's not going to be the case. Trouble finds me. I'm sorry, but I've gotta stay. There's too many people in danger."

"And those people … you'll die for them?"

"I'm not worried about dying. I'm worried about looking back and realizing I had the opportunity to do something—to have a chance to make this world better—and if I pass up that moment, what will it say about me? I have to do what I believe is right, and staying the course with Sephra is the right thing to do. Spirit's telling me this is where I need to be, even though I don't want to."

"But, Dag, what about you and your needs? You know this is just forcing you to relive that cycle of violence over again," Jerlone pleaded. All he wanted was for her to realize they didn't have to do this.

Dagnarone spoke up. "People are going to need me, and they're going to need you too. I know you don't want to do this, but it would be for a worthy cause."

Her words hit him hard. He did tell her he wasn't against a fight if it were for the right reasons. His logic told him that, with the Hidden Castle's army, there probably wouldn't be much of a struggle to win. This could all be over in a few days, and then he could go about his way. He wanted to leave, but he also didn't want to let down Dagnarone like this. "Fine," he said without sounding happy at all. "I'll stay."

Dagnarone smiled. "Thank you."

Jerlone did not acknowledge her.

They finally began walking toward the buffet. The first few steps were in silence and Jerlone felt that Dagnarone knew something was wrong.

"Do you ever feel there's trauma that's so ingrained in our souls we carry it from one life to the next?" Jerlone asked her.

She paused before replying, "Yes, I do feel that, but I also think happiness engrains itself on our souls too."

He took her words in. "I hope so."

"Are you feeling okay?"

"I'm just wondering if this longing I have is because of something that happened to me at another time, and I'd like to feel different."

CHAPTER 31

WUDULOND WOODS
DAY

SEPHRA STOOD ON the outskirts of the community, twiddling her red cape. She was waiting for the others so they could depart the Wudulond community. It felt like they had been there for hours. It was time that would have been better spent on the road. Once again, she found herself waiting for everyone else.

Dagnarone was the first to arrive. There was an awkward silence between the two at first.

Dagnarone finally broke the tension. "You have some breakfast?"

"A little bite," Sephra replied. "I dunno, I didn't think it was so great."

"Can't say I'm surprised."

Sephra shook her head, annoyed by the comment. She turned and began pacing.

Dagnarone approached her. "Hey, what's wrong?"

"I'm just upset, and comments like that don't make me feel better."

"Okay, jeez. I was just kidding around; sorry. What's got you in a mood?"

"We should be walking toward the castle instead of having a soiree with little, furry creatures!"

"I think it's too early for it to be a soiree."

"That's not the point!" Sephra yelled and threw her arms about. After a big sigh, her shoulders slumped. "Am I a fool to think I can save this world?"

Dagnarone looked like someone who was caught in the act, unsure of what to say. "Well, I mean ..." she mumbled and struggled to think of the right word. "Yeah. You are kind of dumb to think that, but I don't think that should stop you."

"Maybe it should stop me. Maybe I'm making a huge mistake trying to undertake this."

"Yeah, maybe, but maybe not? Where is this coming from? I thought you've seen previous lives where you did this exact thing. Heck, I've had visions of you doing it."

"I'm just worried I'm doing this wrong." Sephra could not look at Dagnarone as she revealed her vulnerabilities. She took a few steps, hoping the distance would help comfort her. "I've seen myself fight hundreds of battles and kill who knows how many. What if the violence I've used as a means to an end was actually just a symptom of what I was trying to fight against?"

"Sounds like you finally heard something I had to say." Dagnarone beamed with pride.

"Well, uh, yeah … also, when I got the directions from Babineau, he said something similar—said I can't save the world just using a sword."

Dagnarone's face dropped. "Are you kidding me?"

Sephra turned back to her friend. "Do you really think I'd get to this point without our conversations too? There was just something about the way he said it that resonated with me. I've been thinking of it ever since."

"So, do you have a new plan to save the world? I don't know if you remember, but there is an army chasing us."

"I'm not saying I'm putting down my weapons. There's no getting out of the fight ahead of us; I'm talking about after. I'm going to have to do more than I initially thought, and I'm scared I'm not good enough to be effective."

"You know, you don't have to save the world alone."

"Sometimes it feels like I'll have to." Sephra feared the day Dagnarone and Jerlone would leave her. It was inevitable, but something she would have to come to terms with. The dreams she had of them fighting side by side would most likely not come to fruition. She'd have to think of something else, a new way to spend her days, and that made her sad.

Dagnarone walked over to Sephra and playfully punched her in the arm. "Come on, you'll be fine. If you want to change the world without resorting to violence, I think you should get into politics. It's probably the most effective means of really trying to make a change."

Sephra laughed, thinking the notion entirely foolish. "I don't know how much I like that idea."

"Well, if you want to accomplish your goals, then you may have to do a few things you don't like."

CHAPTER 32

THE FOREST
AFTERNOON

THERE WERE NO longer many leaves on the trees; they now littered the ground, withered and crunchy. The brown tree limbs were thin and pointy. Some had small, bulbous lights scattered along the bark. This time of day they provided a faint light, an encouraging sign they were headed in the right direction. The closer they got to the castle, the brighter the lights would shine. It was another spell placed by ancient Mystics in their travels to beautify this world.

Yawonte trailed behind, thinking of their progress. Since joining, he had barely been able to impart any wisdom. He'd told them a few things, like *good posture helps conjure spells*, but for the most part they had not begun their education. He was ashamed by his lack of discipline, getting swept up in the conversation of gossip instead of focusing on his purpose. War was on the horizon, and now was the time for action.

"When we make camp tonight, we need to spend time training," he said. "You all have bad form. It's embarrassing watching you fend off your opponents. Simple adjustments would make a world of difference."

Everyone turned to look at him with a bit of surprise.

"Cut 'em some slack." Gala waved his hand. "They just fell out of the sky three days ago."

"You're as bad as them. What's your excuse?"

Gala stopped in his tracks. "You'd better watch it, pal." He pointed at Yawonte. "If you don't, I'll show you just how bad my form is."

Yawonte snickered. "I'm glad you've survived as long as you have, but it's shocking." He walked right past Gala. "Makes me wonder if you've even encountered half of what you claim. Or could it all be talk?"

"Hey, I don't make up nothin'!" Gala followed after him. "You know I'm real, because I tell plenty of stories where I get my hat handed to me! Like when Bert beat the snot out of me! You think I'd make that up?"

"Exactly. You lose a lot; therefore, you have bad form. I'm trying to help you get better. But you're going to let your ego stop that from happening."

"Wouldn't be the first thing I've let my ego stop, pal!"

Yawonte turned and looked at Gala. "You keep calling me pal. I know we are friends. You don't have to keep saying it."

"He means it in a threatening and ironic manner," Dagnarone informed.

"Oh." Yawonte chuckled. "Well, consider me threatened." His laughter increased.

"Hey, my threats are not funny!" Gala yelled in his own defense.

Dagnarone walked over to Gala and patted his back. "Come on. We don't need this right now. Everyone here knows you're an adequate fighter." She looked to the others for confirmation, yet they stayed silent. "Okay, well, you know when to run."

"Hey! I don't run!"

"Dagnarone," Yawonte grabbed her attention. "Do you carry a weapon with you?"

"No," she shook her head. "I don't need one. A weapon will just corrupt my soul."

"It will give you strength!"

"If I have a weapon, then I'll use it and—"

"I'm not here to talk about the philosophy of when we should fight. I'm talking about having something that can channel your power. An extension of yourself. Call it a weapon, call it a totem, call it what you want. You can cause damage or heal with it. Our magic is endless. How you choose to conjure is what matters."

Sephra addressed the group. "I think Yawonte is right. We could use the training and shouldn't pass this up. Everyone needs to be able to admit they have room for improvement."

"I don't mean to condescend to any of you." Yawonte apologized. "I only wish for us to grow as a team. I've been fortunate enough to have time to prepare for this moment. I have made such silly mistakes, and I wish to keep you from doing the same. It took me time to get where I am, and I don't even know if I am ready for my first battle. I can only imagine what the rest of you are going through, but I think, with my guidance, we can navigate our way through this. You're lucky our fates are entwined."

Jerlone scoffed. "Ha! We're lucky! You know, you sure can be arrogant. If anyone else here spoke like that, you wouldn't be taking too kindly to it."

Yawonte nodded. "That's true. If anyone here were to tell me they had the experience to better me, I would laugh in their face. Only I can walk this talk. Jerlone, being a man of knowledge, how can you laugh in the face of this opportunity?"

"It's not the opportunity I'm laughing at, it's the superciliousness of it. How you lord it over us."

"I am doing no such thing."

"I don't think you're aware of it, but you are."

"Jerlone," Sephra interjected, "he's not doing that. Stop."

Jerlone scowled at Sephra, and she glared right back.

Yawonte broke the silence. "Perhaps I can give a piece of advice now. When casting a spell, don't come at it from a place of hatred. Anger drains you. You may feel that extra rush of adrenaline, but it will only hinder in the end. Your emotions play into your spellcasting, and you need to be aware of them. It may feel counterintuitive, but the calmer you are, the more powerful you are."

CHAPTER 33

THE BRIDGE
EVENING

SEPHRA LED THE group and managed to keep the peace. For two hours, the group talked about their powers. They discussed borrowing energy from the world around them and how it could aid them in their struggles. The conversation stayed civil, and everyone was engaged—at some point or another.

The sound of rushing rapids was audible, indicating they were on the right track. Once they crossed the bridge, they would truly be in the Forest of Lights.

The trees thinned as they came to a clearing. They were on the edge of a cliff. Down below, a ferocious river flowed. Across from them was a similar precipice, continuing their path.

A rickety rope bridge ran across the chasm. It was dilapidated and looked like a hundred-yard death trap. It was not stable; the slightest breeze battered it in every direction. There were missing planks, and those that remained looked ready to fall with the slightest touch. Two pillars sat ten feet from the cliff's edge, the bridge's ropes bound to them. The rope holding it up was so thin and worn, it was a miracle it still stood.

Sephra realized this was the bridge Babineau had warned her about. She shook her head, furious that they'd listened to the Wudulond. She looked to the group's navigator, Dagnarone, expecting an explanation.

"So," Dagnarone scratched the back of her head, "I guess for something the size of a Wudulond this isn't a big deal …"

"Alright," Gala said, "let's do some walking and find an alternative route."

"Eddie said this is the only bridge nearby."

"It'll take us days to backtrack and find the other one," Sephra interjected. "That's something we don't have time for." She stepped forward and looked around. She was trying to figure out what they could do to cross. "We're going to have to find a way. If we aren't at the Hidden Castle by tonight, then we may be too late."

"I understand that," Gala raised his voice with each word, "but we ain't getting there by way of that bridge!"

"What if we climb down the cliff," Jerlone suggested. "We then swim across the river and climb back up the other side."

"The current looks too strong," Yawonte observed. "It would take us out with ease."

"Can't you cast some spell to slow it down?" Jerlone jibed.

"Guys, come on," Gala said, attempting to calm them. "We're not gonna do anything that involves swimming. I hate getting wet, and it would ruin these shoes."

Sephra walked to the edge of the cliff and studied her surroundings. She touched the ground, closed her eyes, and listened. Once tapped into that spiritual place, she no longer heard her companions. Even though the wind whipped wildly, she felt she could control it. Her soul told her not to fear any of the elements, for they were there to aid her. Even the rapids below lost their power over her. She opened her eyes, looked at the bridge again, and visualized her plan.

She walked back to the others.

"A *raft?*" Dagnarone asked Gala. "And how exactly are we going to build a raft?"

"We get some branches and twigs and tie 'em together," Gala explained. "Don't worry, I've done it once before. Well, I was with someone and they did most of the work, but I paid close attention."

Dagnarone mumbled something in her native language.

"What did you just call me?" Gala fired back at her.

"I have an idea." Sephra walked to the bridge as she spoke. "It won't sound like the most logical idea." She studied the rope. "But, if you're willing to trust me, I think we can still make all of this work." She looked at the bridge from a few different angles as she continued to envision her plan.

"You're starting to worry me by saying all of this as you look at that bridge," Gala murmured.

"Yawonte, is it safe to assume you have no problem coupling energy to an object?"

"With ease," Yawonte responded. "Just keep in mind, the more magic we exert, the greater the price we pay."

"I know, so everyone else is gonna have to be fast." She walked back to the group. A small smile spread across her face. She was excited and nervous at the same time. "Alright, team, here's the plan. I cross the bridge. Then, Yawonte and I cast a shield spell over it. Once that energy has covered the bridge, the three of you cross it. Fast but gentle; that's the key. After that, we just need Yawonte to cross, and we can continue along our merry way."

Gala stared at her with his mouth open. "Sephra, that is the worst plan I have ever heard, and I've suggested some doozies! So, the fact that I'm self-aware enough to know it's terrible should really emphasize how bad a plan this is! First off, you didn't even tell Yawonte how he can cross. You just left it up to him!"

"Do not worry about me," Yawonte said. "I will find my way. I do not fear the challenge."

"How? *How* are you going to cross it?"

"Carefully."

"You— that— I— *That is not an answer!*" Gala threw his hands about.

"Do not worry for me, Gala Goda. This is not my time or place to die. I may bruise myself in the process, but I do not fear this gauntlet."

Gala stood there, shaking his head, looking at the ground. "Fine. You want to get yourself killed, then see if I care! I only met ya yesterday; it's not like we have some strong bond. And just to reiterate, when I'm saying something is a bad idea, it usually is!"

Yawonte smiled with all the confidence in the world. "I guess we will see which of us is right."

"Come on, there's gotta be some other way. We just need to stop and explore our options that don't require crossing this bridge!"

"We don't have time." Sephra stepped forward. "We need to get to the castle, and nothing can stop us. This is just a challenge we'll have to overcome."

"This is never gonna work," Jerlone mumbled loud enough for everyone to hear.

"Yes, it will! Besides, what're you worried about? You're part of the easiest phase. All you have to do is walk across our magic."

"That's assuming nothing breaks your concentration and we fall to our deaths."

"That won't happen."

"Why? Because you said so?"

"In part, yes." Sephra believed every word of it. While she knew this would be dangerous, she believed in their ability to make it across the bridge. She could feel it in her soul that this was the right thing, and it was almost time. She saw them succeeding in her mind.

"I don't think we would die if we fell." Dagnarone looked at the drop, which was a few hundred feet. "We've fallen from a greater height than this."

"We could survive," Yawonte agreed, "but there would be a cost. It would not be pleasant. The first time we fell was a cosmic occurrence. Reality is different in that moment. It is a birth, and certain protections are in place, but now we are in the real world—one where we bleed if we are cut. Pain and death will be inevitable in our lives; don't forget that."

"Then, shouldn't you be showing more concern about getting across?"

"I have my worries, but I welcome this great challenge."

"What a weird way to look at something so terrifying."

"Perhaps, but at this moment, you are filled with fear while I'm brimming with excitement."

Sephra looked at the bridge. It was time. She had not been this nervous before. She took her first step toward the bridge. "Alright, then; anyone have final questions?"

"We're doing this right now?" Gala asked, clearly more worried than ever before.

"Can't lose any more time. We need to warn the castle."

"Sephra, stop! We need to think about this! No one has even agreed to your plan!"

"This does seem rushed," Dagnarone agreed.

"And I'm not sure if you have our best interests at hand," Jerlone added.

"Trust me," Sephra brushed them off. "This will all work out. You three have the easiest part." She placed her backpack on the ground, the less weight on her, the better.

"You really need to reconsider." Gala grabbed Sephra by the arm.

She shoved his hand off her. "I'm sorry, but there's no other choice. We have to do this. Believe in us and I'll see you on the other side."

With that, Sephra stepped onto the bridge, and there was no turning back.

The first ten yards felt safe. Being so close to the edge gave her a sense of comfort. The rope was taut, providing a sense of security.

One missing plank was easy to step over. Two took more confidence and a greater focus on maintaining balance.

Sephra went at a slow, albeit steady, pace.

She felt a connection to the bridge and had to move in accordance with it. Once tapped in, it was easy to feel out.

Forty yards out and the bridge swung with ferocity. This part lagged, creating a droop.

Each step took longer than the last.

When the wind picked up, she stopped and waited for it to calm. During these stressful minutes, she kept her legs loose and didn't resist the motion of the bridge.

She maintained her focus on the destination. It helped keep her calm, as it was always getting closer. She did her best not to think much of the dangers surrounding her.

In the dead center of the bridge, three planks were missing. Sephra slowly reached her foot out and gently pressed down on the next plank. She held on tight to the rope as she lifted her back foot.

The forward plank wobbled, and she knew it wouldn't stand long.

Quickly, she swept her back foot forward and landed one plank ahead. Without a moment's hesitation, she brought the other foot forward.

The plank she had just been standing on fell to a watery grave. There were now four missing planks in a row.

The bridge warned Sephra that she needed to hurry. For the first time, she picked up the pace.

Planks trembled and fell as she passed over them, but she remained vigilant.

Twenty yards to her destination, her confidence returned in full bloom.

With one wrong step, a plank fell out right from under her. She stumbled and her foot dropped into the gap.

Her grip on the ropes tightened, saving her from plunging down. Even under this circumstance, she did not panic. Her face scrunched as she focused on getting back up. The bridge bounced and bobbed as she worked to recover. Getting up was not an easy task; the pull of gravity never felt stronger.

The chaos made her feel queasy and disoriented. She closed her eyes in an attempt to quiet her senses. Her foot felt more isolated than ever, especially when the breeze passed.

With one final tug, she summoned all her strength and pulled herself back up. She regained her balance and strode forth.

The final yards were uneventful but stressful nonetheless.

Upon reaching solid ground, she was hyperventilating. All the suppressed stress hit her at once, in an explosion of emotions. She collapsed to the ground, needing to catch her breath.

When she was ready, she stood and waved to the others. This was to let them know she was about to get into position. She walked to a pillar holding the ropes in place. With her hand atop it, she was ready to conjure the spell.

Dagnarone was not thrilled with heights. Dropping into the river below would be a less than ideal way to spend her afternoon. Even worse, if they did not make it across, everyone was sure to give her a hard time for leading them there.

Yawonte touched one of the pillars, and within a matter of seconds, a blue energy poured from his hands and onto the post. It spread along the ropes and across the planks. The energy even filled in gaps, creating a smooth, continuous surface.

On the other side, Sephra was crafting the same spell.

When the two energies met, they created a magical bridge of light.

"Guess we've got no choice but to do this," Gala muttered as he took the first step onto the bridge.

Dagnarone looked to Jerlone, hoping he would go next. He looked terrified and motioned for her to go first. Knowing she'd have to go eventually, she decided not to put up a fight.

Her first step onto the bridge was terrifying. She thought it felt even less stable than she'd imagined. After a few steps, she started to gain confidence. Each step was still slow and methodical, but she was moving.

Dagnarone felt the bridge sway when Jerlone stepped onto it. Now that all three of them were crossing, they were moving as a unit. Each step they took affected the motion of the bridge. They all had to work in conjunction, or failure was inevitable.

Halfway across, Dagnarone found herself enjoying the view. Even though it was a terrifying spot to be in, she sure thought it was pretty. Without thinking, she looked down and froze upon seeing the rapids. There was something about them from that point of view that made them extra terrifying. She realized how high up they were and started to feel dizzy. Both her feet and mind stopped working. She was a shell of a person.

Jerlone bumped into Dagnarone. "What's the hold up, Dag?"

She didn't respond.

"Dag? What's going on?" Jerlone asked again.

She still didn't respond.

"Did you look down?" Jerlone asked.

"Yup," Dagnarone squeaked out.

"Well, that's not good."

"You two okay back there?" Gala yelled out to them. He was a ways ahead and wasn't stopping. "I really don't feel confident turning around, so if you're not okay, then I'm sorry I'm not a better help!"

"Just keep going, Gala!" Jerlone yelled back at him. "Okay Dag, we've gotta get going, alright?"

"Yes, let's get going," she managed to say.

"Good! A response is good. So, let's just take a step forward."

He moved forward, but she did not, resulting in their second collision.

"Hey!" Dagnarone yelled. "Watch it!"

"I thought you were going to move!"

"I wasn't ready yet! Didn't you see me standing here?"

He was quiet for a moment before replying, "My eyes are closed."

Dagnarone shook her head. "Some tough guy you are."

"Alright, let's get moving on three. How's that sound?"

"We say three then go? Or we go on three?"

"Whichever you prefer, but we have to get going!"

"Okay, we say three then go."

"Fine!" Jerlone snapped.

"Alright, start counting."

"One, two, three. Go!"

Dagnarone took a step forward, and they were off. They were moving even slower than before, but that was better than not moving at all.

Looking at Sephra, it was obvious she was straining to keep the spell conjured. This helped motivate Dagnarone to pick up the pace.

Gala stepped off the bridge to safety, but Dagnarone and Jerlone still had ten yards to go.

The bridge began to shake just as Dagnarone was closing in on solid ground. She leapt to make it there and ran another ten feet for safety. Her heart was pounding, but she kind of loved the experience. She was terrified, but in a good way.

She walked over to Jerlone, who still had his eyes closed. "You missed an amazing view," she told him.

Jerlone opened his eyes and looked at her. "Glad I had the view I had. If I had seen what you saw, I don't think I would have made it."

"And I don't think I would have made it without you." She smiled.

Sephra walked over, a stupid grin on her face. "See," she bragged. "I told you there was nothing to worry about. I had the hardest job, and you didn't believe me."

They rolled their eyes.

"I'd wait until Yawonte is safe before making any of those declarations," Dagnarone said.

After taking a minute to rest up, Yawonte stood. He grabbed Sephra's bag and tossed it across the chasm.

He tightened his belt and made sure his sword was secure.

At the bridge, he plucked on the ropes. They slacked and needed tightening. He rolled his wrists and a golden energy formed. The ropes began to move and curl around the pillars. As the bridge stretched some planks fell while others held on for dear life.

When the spell was done, the ropes were nice and taut through and through. Yawonte plucked them again, this time getting his desired results.

"If you can," he shouted to his companions. "Please focus on keeping the bridge stable! Connect with it and be its shield! Don't try to move the ropes or anything of the like! Just focus on keeping the bridge in place!"

"You got it!" Sephra hollered back.

Yawonte watched the three Mystics find their places. Dagnarone and Jerlone sat by the pillars holding the bridge. Sephra stationed herself a few feet in front of them. Gala, meanwhile, hung off to the side standing at the ready.

Like the flip of a switch, the wind stopped blowing. Yawonte knew it was likely Dagnarone creating that effect. He smiled, impressed by the display of power.

The plan was to tightrope walk across the bridge. To accomplish that, he needed something to help with balance.

Yawonte walked to the edge of the woods to look for the perfect stick. He weighed a few, but inevitably tossed them back. Eventually he found a long, slender stick that worked just right.

As he walked back to the bridge, he reminded himself he could do this. He was nervous, but he refused to be scared. Over and over, he told himself this would be done in a matter of minutes, and he would be all the stronger for it.

Gently, he hoisted himself up onto the rope. Breathing in, he appreciated his surroundings.

With his first step, he felt a small bounce. Looking down, he saw the rope beneath his feet beginning to rip apart. It was a thick piece and would take some time, but the process had begun.

Time was now of the essence.

After a few steps, Yawonte was on a roll. He balanced his stick in conjunction with the turn of the world.

The rope continued to unravel.

There was an energy flowing through the rope. He knew it was from Sephra and Jerlone. All Yawonte had to do was connect and trust in them.

As he passed the halfway point, he foolishly thought he might be able to make it. With that arrogance came his downfall.

The rope severed.

A split second before it happened, Yawonte felt it coming. He prepared mentally for the drop. Reaching his hand out, he grabbed the rope as he fell. In one fluid motion, he swung into the cliff wall.

His ribs slammed into the rocky cliffside, almost shattering them. Yawonte screamed out in pain and grasped the rope tighter. As he swayed there, loose planks began raining down on him. They smacked into his head and shoulders, further breaking his concentration. His attempt at lifting an arm to cover himself only resulted in him sliding down the rope a few feet.

As soon as the planks ceased, he withdrew his sword. With five quick slashes he cut away most of the bridge. The remains crashed into the water.

Yawonte sheathed his sword and began his ascent. His shoulders were sore, but he had no choice. If he didn't climb, then he would die.

• • • •

Gala looked over the edge of the cliff and was relieved to find Yawonte climbing. "You okay down there?" Gala hollered.

"I've been better, thanks!" Yawonte yelled back up.

"Hey, at least you're not dead!" Gala turned to look at something behind him, and his face dropped. "Ah, *nertz*." He turned back to Yawonte. "Hey, I've gotta go look at something, okay? You just keep climbing—and the faster the better! Not to put any pressure on you or make you worry, but the faster the better!"

Gala raced back to the pillar. The rope was unraveling, and it wouldn't take long for it to all come undone. He wasn't sure what to do, but Yawonte didn't have much time. He looked to his companions for an answer.

The Mystics were out of their trance but disoriented and too weak to stand. They needed time to get back on their feet.

Gala's panic overwhelmed him. *Gotta do* everything *myself*, he thought.

He ran back to check on Yawonte again. It was disheartening to see how far away he still was. Loose pillars continued falling down on him, whacking him over and over.

"Not to put any pressure on you, but," Gala started clapping his hands with each word, "Faster! Faster! You must go faster!"

The Mystics were still not on their feet. They were close, but not there yet. Gala prayed they'd be ready to help soon.

The rope unraveled from the post. Gala ran back just in time to grab hold of it. Of course, the weight was much too great for Gala to do anything. Even worse, Gala saw other tears in the rope forming.

Yawonte dropped a few feet but held tight.

Gala pulled and tugged the rope, but it dragged him toward the cliff. He dug his feet into the ground, but the force was too great. Even when he was inches from the edge, he had no intention of letting go.

Suddenly, everything stopped.

Gala looked down and saw his toes dangling just over the cliff. He didn't know what was happening.

"Pull!" Sephra yelled.

Gala turned his head and saw her standing behind him. She grasped the rope with ease, steady as a statue. Behind her was Dagnarone and Jerlone, pulling the rope with all their might.

Yawonte continued to climb, and the rope continued to fray. He was ten feet from the top, but Gala wasn't sure if he was going to make it.

As the tear in the rope reached its crescendo, Gala dropped to the ground and Yawonte leapt toward him. They managed to lock wrists but were left dangling in the wind.

The strain on Gala's arm was intense. Even worse, he didn't have a plan to get back up. He wasn't able to lift his arm or do anything to help his situation.

As Gala hung there, he realized how big a drop that was. A shiver ran through his whole body, as all he could see were the rushing rapids hundreds of feet below. The blood raced to his head, disorienting him even further. The world spun, and he was sure he would slide off the cliff any second.

Without realizing it, Gala began moving backwards. He turned his head and saw Jerlone and Dagnarone dragging his feet from the edge. Sephra was then by his side, helping get Yawonte to solid ground.

Gala was out of breath and almost in tears. He may have found that scarier than their encounter with the Sauros. His chest felt so many different pains, he wondered if he was about to throw up.

Looking around, he saw everyone was collapsed on the ground, trying to catch their breath. Yawonte chuckled to himself, but no one else seemed to be in the mood to laugh.

Gala sat up and looked at the ruins of the bridge. "Well, Dag, I don't think Eddie's going to be too happy we destroyed their bridge."

CHAPTER 34

THE SCARLET TREE
LATE NIGHT
....

ALL THE TREES were lit up. Tiny lights, mostly white, were engrained along the bark and buzzing with life. An eerie glow enveloped the Mystics as they settled down for the night.

Yawonte stood before the scarlet tree; its essence captivated him. He was seeing red and feeling a bit disoriented. The menace of the tree was radiating and all-consuming. The tree's glow haunted him. His mind spiraled and his angst turned toward his companions. He knew they were getting ready for sleep, even though they'd talked about training.

Turning away from the tree, Yawonte realized how powerful its glow was. A quarter-mile radius was covered in a red light. It seeped into every crack. Animals didn't even congregate around the tree, as the light would be too bothersome.

While everyone else was doing their own thing, Yawonte studied them. Sephra was the only one doing something constructive, as she was training with her bow and arrows. Yawonte could see she was becoming faster and more proficient. Gala was helping Dagnarone set up a hammock while Jerlone was curled up against a tree.

"This is unacceptable," Yawonte announced, standing in the middle of everyone. "You have an opportunity to expand your magic, yet you waste it prepping for slumber?" He did not make any attempt to mask his displeasure.

"Look," Jerlone grunted. "We've been on our feet all day and almost fell to our deaths. I think we earned a moment's rest." He closed his eyes and leaned back.

Dagnarone crawled into her hammock. "And let's not forget, it is the middle of the night. If we don't sleep now, then when will we?"

"Being tired is nothing compared to being unprepared," Yawonte scolded. "We are but a day away from war, yet you refuse to become better warriors? I hope you're aware that plucky attitudes won't save you; only honing your skills will."

"I don't disagree with you." Sephra stopped firing arrows and faced him. "But I don't disagree with them either." She put down her weapon and walked toward Yawonte. "The conversations we had earlier taught us much, and we are grateful, but if we don't sleep then we will be useless. We all know the dangers that await us, so tonight we need to rest. Tomorrow, when refreshed, we can begin the physical training."

"And if the army arrives before we have that opportunity?" Yawonte began pacing. "We have a moment right now to better ourselves, yet we are squandering it!"

Gala walked toward Yawonte, motioning for him to calm down. "You should really relax. Y'all ain't gonna be the only ones fighting that battle. You'll be alongside the whole Mervelliere army. Also, just so you know, Fascio doesn't typically supply his troops with weapons. So, all you're really fighting is a horde of people, not some warriors of legend. All things considered, should be able to handle them with ease."

Yawonte studied Gala before speaking. "You act as if you aren't fighting alongside us?"

"Well, as I have also said repeatedly, I have somewhere to be. So, once we get to the Hidden Castle, I'm finding my ride out of there, but I'll be wishing you all the luck in the world."

Yawonte was disgusted by Gala's insolence, but not surprised. "Come here, my friend. I'd like to see how your magic is evolving."

"My magic's fine. Better than it was a week ago, but not as good as it'll be after a good night's rest." He smiled and winked.

Yawonte pointed straight down at the ground before him. "Get. Over. Here."

Gala made a face. "Don't appreciate that tone—unless it's coming from a pretty woman, of course." Gala walked toward Yawonte. "But, hey, if you wanna see my magic so bad, then you've got it."

"Thank you. I'm sure you'll show me *amazing* things."

Standing beside Yawonte, Gala lifted his arm. His posture was not proud, he slouched, and his limbs were not firm. His body was barely able to stand, let alone conjure the unknown.

Yawonte grimaced. He would have to find a tool to correct Gala's mistakes. Nearby was a fallen branch covered in violet and blue lights. He grabbed it and whacked Gala's back and elbow.

"What the hell was that for?" Gala screamed while rubbing the pain.

"You call that a warrior's stance?" Yawonte demeaned.

"No one said I had to be a warrior!"

"Conjuring magic isn't for some sort of cheap trick! It should only be summoned by the most noble and brave individuals! From what I have seen, that is not you."

Gala's jaw dropped. "I didn't even do anything!"

"Exactly." Yawonte stared him down. "Your stance matters! You cannot produce exquisite results with such a disrespectful body! One must stand tall and proud when summoning magic! Magic doesn't respond to a wrinkly, broken body of shame and exhaustion. If you choose poor form, you are destined to fail." He moved behind Gala and straightened his arm and back, molding his stance. "Now, try it again. Remember: your body is the conduit." He went from condescending to encouraging.

Gala took a second to breathe and center himself. A second later, red energy formed in his palm, but before he could do anything with it, Yawonte's branch came crashing into his arm.

"What the hell?" Gala screamed. "What was that for?"

"Your arm began to slouch," Yawonte shot back at him.

"It's what my body told me to do!"

"And who told you to listen to your body? It is your mind you must listen to when the body is weak! Channeling magic is draining, but you *must* fight that urge! You can't always give up when it gets hard. It's time to leave that life behind and step forward into what you were meant for."

"Like I need you telling me what to do with my life."

"Oh, Gala, that is your problem. You can't take constructive criticism. Your ego prevents you from becoming a better version of yourself. Imagine the great Gala Goda not being so great. I want you to succeed. This isn't me being mean for the sake of being nasty, but I can only take you so far, and you'll only take yourself so far without that ego in check! You'd be surprised how much power comes from acknowledging our weaknesses. You will only transform if you take responsibility as both the teacher and the student! I can't teach you anything; only you can do that. I can squawk silly words of motivation, but in the end, if you don't want to learn something, you won't. You have to put your heart, mind, and soul into it!" Yawonte walked right up to Gala and quietly delivered his final message. "All of this—everything that happens to you—will come down to you."

Gala looked at Yawonte with his mouth slightly open and his eyes wide. It looked as though the message was getting through to him.

"Now, do it again," Yawonte instructed. "This time with power."

Gala raised his arm and took a minute to find the right stance. First, he looked too rigid, then too relaxed.

"Magic has to travel from your soul to your hands," Yawonte reminded, using his gentlest voice. "That only happens if the right paths are available."

Gala's globe of energy increased in size. Energy pulled from their surroundings, crafting little traces of light. Magic littered the air, and everything felt alive.

When the spell was the size of two fists, a slight push of Gala's hand shot it forth. Fifty yards away, a tree was the recipient of the attack. It smoldered and left a mark. Gala smiled and looked to his teacher for validation.

"That was it?" Yawonte was genuinely disappointed.

"What was wrong with that?" Gala's legs gave out and he fell to the ground. He gasped for air.

Yawonte lifted his arm to the side. Without looking, he summoned a globe much larger and shot it. The energy shattered a tree, sending bits of wood everywhere.

This did not bring a smile to Yawonte's face. If anything, he looked more upset.

"He showed you," Jerlone chimed in from across the campground.

"Shut up," Gala grumbled.

"Perhaps if you shut up, you could do the same," Yawonte chided.

"Alright, I'll show you." Gala attempted to stand but failed. "Uh … just give me a second here …"

Yawonte lifted his arm and repeated the spell. Another tree fell. He locked eyes with Gala. "Do my legs even shake?"

"Stop hurting the trees!" Dagnarone yelled from her hammock.

"Relax," Jerlone said. "They haven't hit either of your trees. No need to complain."

"No need to complain? They're killing living beings! Just because it takes a different form than us doesn't mean it's an object!"

"So righteous." Jerlone rolled his eyes.

"I'd rather be righteous than apathetic. You'll sit there and laugh, yet once your tree is hit, then it'll be a big deal. Once it affects you, you'll sing a different tune."

Jerlone ignored her and continued staring at Gala and Yawonte.

"Look what I've accomplished," Yawonte lectured. "Even my first few spells weren't as weak as yours. Surely, a worldly man like yourself can do better."

"First off, you're a natural and I'm just … normal." Gala finally made it back on his feet. He was wobbly, but he managed to stay up. "Only learned how to do this a day or so ago. I'm sure I'd be doing great if I was like you and made of magic."

"You know what you're made of? Excuses." Yawonte let the insult linger in the air. "If you changed your attitude, then you could accomplish the same as me. That really shouldn't be too difficult for you, since you're such an arrogant man. Refocus that energy and you'll be a success. I've learned three important lessons that I cannot stress enough. A Mystic is only as strong as they are confident, stand tall and proud when channeling your power, and above all, you must breathe with intention!"

"I don't even know what that means …"

"It means don't waste your breath," Sephra approached them. "Know your purpose and work toward it. A guy like you is easily distracted if he doesn't stay on task. You can either use this power for nonsense or to save the world. Which will it be?"

Gala paused. "Is there somewhere in the middle I can fall?"

"This is not a joke!" Yawonte's fist was ablaze with red energy. With all his speed, he threw a punch at Gala, missing by less than an inch.

Gala jumped back and cracked his whip three times.

"Is that supposed to intimidate me?" Yawonte asked as he withdrew his sword. He paced around Gala.

"Come on, calm down," Sephra cautioned.

Yawonte charged, brandishing his sword overhead.

Gala cracked his whip, but Yawonte swiped it away with the sword.

"Your whip is useless!" Yawonte screamed, slashing at Gala. "Only your magic can defeat me!" He slashed again. "Now, defend yourself!"

Gala stuck his hand out, and without realizing it, conjured a globe of energy at Yawonte.

A blue-light shield flashed around Yawonte. When Gala's globe made impact, it evaporated.

Yawonte smiled, proud of how quick his student progressed. Still, there was no time for respite. He charged at Gala, swinging his sword like a madman.

Yawonte swung his blade before Gala's face. It was obvious the explorer was already exhausted, but he managed to dodge each attack. Gala fought back by cracking his whip, but Yawonte was too skilled to be bested.

It was soon a dance between steel and leather as the two combats went back and forth.

Eventually Gala wrapped his whip around Yawonte's sword, but the Mystic was ready for that. He tightened his grip, almost making the sword and his arm one. Gala attempted to yank the sword from his hand repeatedly but failed each time. Yawonte had a magical grip on his weapon that would only break with death.

Yawonte felt it was time to mix it up, so he snapped his fingers twice. Thousands of minuscule globes of light bombarded Gala from all over. The little pebbles of light slammed into Gala repeatedly and relentlessly. None of this energy came from Yawonte, just from the surroundings.

"When your opponent is magical, you must fight differently!" Yawonte yelled as his attack continued. "If you use all your energy on one big attack, then you will have nothing to defend yourself with."

A dulled arrow flew toward Yawonte's back. Once again, a blue flash of energy popped up, protecting him.

Yawonte stopped his attack on Gala and turned to face his new attacker.

Sephra stood with a sharp arrow now strung in her bow.

"Now it's a jamboree." Yawonte smiled. He was excited for this challenge.

"Let's see who will be the first to take me down. I suspect it will be neither of you." He readied his sword for the challenge.

Sephra coupled energy to her arrow, covering it in a neon crimson. With the spell fully cast, she fired.

Yawonte conjured a shield, but the arrow broke through. He turned and the projectile missed him by a hair.

He raised his hand and magic flowed forth. Globes of energy of all shapes and sizes chased Sephra. Most shimmered red, while others were blue and some even green.

Sephra dodged the barrage of luminous globes. She fired arrows, popping the energy globes. The green globes were the only ones that she could not penetrate. She cast shielding spells with a couple swats of her hand, protecting her from the attacks.

Yawonte was impressed with her skills. There was not much he expected to teach her. If anything, he thought she might give him some helpful hints. To really test her, he increased his attacks.

Sephra strapped her bow to her back and grabbed the pair of sai on her waist. She twirled them once and ran toward Yawonte. Magic hurtled toward her, but she moved to her left and right, dodging and ducking each attack.

Yawonte stopped summoning magic and gripped his sword. When she reached him, their duel began. The sai was just as powerful as the sword. Yawonte was on the defense as Sephra went after him with a barrage of attacks. To his surprise, it was a challenge keeping up with her.

With two quick swipes of the sai, Yawonte lost his sword. It landed twenty feet away but that did not slow Sephra down. If anything, now that he was defenseless, he had to move faster. He fought back using his mitts but could not land a punch. No matter how fast he moved, Sephra was a little faster.

"There's nothing I can teach you," Yawonte said, hoping this compliment would distract her.

● ● ● ●

Jerlone enjoyed watching the fight from afar. At times, the players moved toward him, but they inevitably bounced away.

He saw Gala get knocked down and then get back up again. A blast of energy tossed the man into a tree. Jerlone chuckled, feeling Gala was getting his comeuppance. He didn't wish to see the man hurt, but a little battered would be fine.

The next time Gala ran back to fight, Yawonte sent him flying toward Jerlone.

By the time Jerlone realized Gala would be crashing into him, it was too late. An attempt to stand was derailed, and the two men found themselves entangled.

"What're you doing?" Jerlone grunted as he pushed Gala off him.

"Relax!" Gala snapped while brushing the dirt off his jacket. "You think I wanted to end up here?"

Jerlone turned to see Yawonte and Sephra going at it. With the quick sweep of a foot, Yawonte knocked Sephra onto her back. Without a second's hesitation, he pivoted and jumped toward Jerlone and Gala.

The men hustled to their feet and moved just before Yawonte crashed down. A powerful force rippled out upon his impact, causing them to trip.

Even though Yawonte was unarmed, he was still a threat. He coupled magic to his knuckles and lunged at his opponents. They were fast enough to dodge but not fast enough to counterattack. They were playing a game of survival.

With a wave of his hand, Yawonte tapped into nature. Tree branches came alive and thrashed about. The ground cracked open while flames shot up. Mud changed to cement, trapping Gala in the process. It was chaos all around.

Jerlone withdrew his wand and fired at Yawonte. To counter, Yawonte cast his own attack. Opposing globes clashed, creating massive sparks. It was like a strobe light, flashes so intense they were disorienting.

"Our powers are more than just explosions!" Yawonte yelled. "If you're creative, you can do amazing things. Your magic's limitations are always expanding."

• • • •

Dagnarone quietly stood by while Yawonte went about his grandstanding.

She was light on her feet as she approached him from behind. As soon as she was close enough, she tackled him.

When they hit the ground, Yawonte's spells broke. The globes of energy fizzled out, smoking for a second and gone the next.

With Yawonte on the ground next to her, Dagnarone crawled atop him. She wasn't sure her exact plan, but she knew she didn't want to hurt Yawonte much. She punched his chest a few times, hitting his wooden armor.

"That's not going to do much, dear," Yawonte taunted her.

His right hand caught her next punch. As he squeezed down, Dagnarone yelped in pain. Her hand was trapped there, and she couldn't think of a way to get it free.

When she saw Yawonte smirk, she wished she had punched him in the face. His eyes went wide, and his expression turned aggressive. With a sudden thrust, Dagnarone was sent flying through the forest.

She smacked into a tree and crumpled to the ground. She grunted to acknowledge the pain but otherwise refused to focus on it.

Something caught her eye just a few feet away. There was a branch, about four feet long, encrusted with multicolored lights. It was as if this branch were calling out to her. She could not take her focus off it. Each step toward it felt like she was walking toward her destiny.

When she touched it, everything felt familiar. As she moved it through the air, the motions felt comfortable. Yet, there was something that was off. This branch was more than a branch. It was crooked and bumpy, something that would make for a clumsy weapon in its current state.

With a twirl of her hand, she spun the branch and did not stop. A purple energy formed around the wood as it rotated, becoming stronger each second. Dagnarone felt the power surrounding it and had a control over it. The branch began whittling down as soon as the energy touched it. Wood clippings flew everywhere as Dagnarone's magic smoothed everything out. She moved her hands around, smoothing out the bends in the branch.

Within no time, the branch became a staff.

Dagnarone took a second to marvel at her handiwork. The wood was nice and smooth with a nice glossy sheen over it. She even created a golden trim to showcase the blue and green lights at the edges.

Now, everything felt perfect. The staff cut through the air with ease. It was so light, it felt like nothing at all.

Dagnarone saw Yawonte approach her. She didn't see where anyone else was and she didn't care. She was ready for a second round.

The combatants charged at one another and wasted no time with pleasantries.

Her staff was strong enough to block his sword and not even get a scratch. It was also durable enough to clash into the sword and knock it back. This weapon was powerful, and each move helped her learn more.

As the two went back and forth, Dagnarone realized she enjoyed fighting. She was ashamed to admit it, but it felt like a dance. The physicality made her feel alive. It didn't hurt that she was good at fighting. Seeing her success only encouraged her to try to take things further.

She jabbed her staff into Yawonte's ribs and watched him keel over. She knew he bruised them on the bridge and felt partially bad for taking advantage of that.

Yawonte looked up, his face painted with anger. He threw an arm up, and a light started strobing. Wind howled past Dagnarone, and her hair whipped about in all directions. She planted her staff into the ground and held up one hand. She braced for the impact as she channeled her own spell to keep her safe.

When the attack ended, Dagnarone stood ready to finish the fight.

The crack of a whip grabbed her attention. She turned to see Gala next to her.

"So, you'll get a weapon to fight him," Gala pointed to Yawonte, "but when I ask you to get one ..."

"Well," Dagnarone grumbled, "maybe you weren't entirely wrong."

Sephra and Jerlone joined them.

"We need to surround him," Sephra said. "Then, we strike together. Once we best him, the training ends and we can go to bed."

"What spell are we casting?" Jerlone asked.

"We're not casting a spell. We're taking him by hand. A spell could be too dangerous."

"So? You don't think he's hurt us?"

"He can't physically take us all on at once. Besides ... it'll be good practice."

Yawonte stood underneath the scarlet tree in a warrior's stance. The crimson light pulsated, encompassing everyone in a red glow of doom. Yawonte suspected the tree was driving them all mad. A snow flurry began, making it seem as though blood were dripping from the sky.

It was dead silent.

Sephra led the troupe as they encircled him. Behind her, Jerlone cracked his knuckles and clenched his fists, Dagnarone stretched with her staff as she got into place, and finally, Gala snapped his whip and cocked his pistol.

Yawonte waited for the first person to make a move.

Sephra looked Yawonte in the eye. He knew what was coming. She pointed her sai at him and yelled, "Now!"

Her sai and his sword were the first to clash. Many times, her weapon came close to blinding him, but he did not take offense; he laughed it off.

As they charged at Yawonte, he cast a confusion spell. Within seconds, everyone attacked one another. Sephra and Dagnarone engaged in a battle of staff versus sai. Gala and Jerlone had a shoot-out between pistol and wand.

Yawonte returned with a powerful blast of energy, knocking his challengers to the ground.

Singling out Jerlone, Yawonte jumped toward him, his sword at the ready. He sliced down as he landed, cutting Jerlone's arm.

Jerlone yelled out in pain and grabbed his arm. A steady stream of blood poured from the wound.

When he looked up, he saw Sephra firing an arrow at him. It was meant for Yawonte, but he dodged it just in time. Jerlone was helpless as the arrow sliced past his ribs. As the blood spilled from him, he dropped to the ground.

Sephra put her bow away and ran toward him. "I'm sorry." Her face was adorned in panic as she apologized. "That wasn't meant for you. What can I do to help?"

Jerlone struggled to get back on his feet. His breathing was loud, and each huff sounded like it could be his last. "You did that on purpose!" He yelled at Sephra, using the remainder of his strength.

"What? Why would I do that on purpose?"

"'Cause you don't care about me!"

"So, you think I'd attack you like that? I was clearly aiming for Yawonte! If anything, you should have been paying attention and dodged it."

"So, now it's my fault?"

"I didn't say that!" Sephra screamed in his face.

"May as well have!" Jerlone turned his back and walked away.

Sephra followed him. "I don't understand why you're getting so upset. You know we were training. These types of accidents happen."

"Are you even sorry it happened?"

"Yes! That was the first thing I said!"

"I've had enough." Jerlone grabbed his bag. He packed his knapsack as he talked. "I've been lied to. I've been conned into joining multiple misadventures. I've been condescended to throughout. Now, I've been hurt, and I've had enough! There are other things I want to do in this life than go off and fight in some damned war that I don't even care about! I've had enough of this and enough of all of you!"

Everyone was quiet, watching from the sides.

"But— but— you can't leave us now. We're almost there." Sephra stayed next to him.

"Still just worried about your own goals, huh?" Jerlone shot her a look. He took out some gauze from his bag and wrapped it around his injuries. "I've told you this wasn't for me, but you never actually paid attention to anything I said. You were too damn worried about getting your own way!"

"That's not true! I care about your needs, but I don't know if you happened to notice this mission is time sensitive! So, I'm sorry if I couldn't cater to you!" Sephra said passionately, pointing with each word. "If we don't warn the castle of this invasion, then people will die! We have a responsibility here!"

"No. I don't have any responsibility to those people. That isn't my problem, and I'm not going to make it mine." Jerlone winced as he finished patching himself back up. "Have fun if that's what you want in life, but it ain't for me." He turned and started to walk away from everyone.

"Just because it isn't your problem today doesn't mean it won't be tomorrow." Sephra chased after him.

"Then I'll deal with it when I'm forced to. Until then, I'm out of here."

"Please," she grabbed his hand. "You're a great warrior, and we're going to need you when the battle breaks out."

"That's all I am to you? A soldier?" He snatched his hand back. "I'm just someone who can take out a lot of your enemies, right? Suppose you're hoping for me to be quiet now? Time to be a good little soldier?"

"I'm sorry. Of course, I don't view you like that."

"Then how do you view me?"

They both stopped walking and looked each other in the eye.

"I view you as my brother." Tears formed in her eyes.

Jerlone had felt alone and was worried that feeling would never go away.

"Don't go," Sephra pleaded. "We can do better. Please!"

Jerlone stared at her. "I'm sorry. I wish you all luck. Maybe I'll see you again … or maybe I won't." He waved to the others, then turned and walked into the forest, alone.

Everyone stayed silent for a minute after he left.

Gala spoke up. "I hate to say it, but he's right." His body ached, and when he thought of the tropical islands where he was supposed to be, he hurt even more. His patience wore thin, and he was never good at masking that. "You're putting your neck on the line for people you don't even know, and if you got to know them, who's to say you'd even like them? You're looking at things through children's eyes. You think you can save this world? You're going to get killed doing it! Worst of all, you won't even get any credit for trying. You want my advice? Burn this whole mission down to save your life."

Sephra shook her head. She turned to Gala with a sneer. "Yawonte is right. You are made of excuses."

"Hey!" Gala pointed at her. "I'm a realist, okay? I've seen the world! I know what I'm talking about, unlike someone who fell out of the sky two days ago!"

"I'm not abandoning the mission!"

"What if you get yourself killed?"

"Then I'll die doing something worthy!"

"And what if you get someone else killed?" Gala looked at their two remaining compatriots.

Sephra crossed her arms and frowned.

"Sephra," Gala said with compassion, "not all worlds are worth saving."

She turned back to him. "*All* worlds deserve saving."

Just like that, Gala was annoyed again. "Lady, you ain't got a clue!" He turned to Dagnarone and Yawonte. "What about you two? You gonna stay with her and fight?" He looked directly at Dagnarone. "Because keep in mind, if you're with her, you will *have* to fight."

"I'm with her for as long as she'll have me," Yawonte said with a smile.

Gala rolled his eyes, not surprised that answer was so over the top.

"I told Sephra I would help her." Dagnarone looked unsure. "And I intend to keep my word."

"You've gotta be kidding me," Gala huffed. "You want this the least! What could possibly make you feel compelled to stay with this train wreck?"

"It's like she said … we're family." Dagnarone looked to Sephra. "I feel too much of a responsibility. As much as I've denied it, Spirit is telling me I'm supposed to be here. At this point, all I can do is accept it for what it is."

Gala shook his head. "Everyone, get your bags. We're getting to the castle tonight."

"You said the drawbridge will be up till dawn," Yawonte reminded him.

"It will, but I want us to be there as soon as it drops. I've got places to be and I'm tired of being held back."

CHAPTER 35

**THE HIDDEN CASTLE: SOUTHERN GATE
DEAD OF NIGHT**

GALA WAS EXHAUSTED. It took another two hours to get to the Hidden Castle. Worst of all, no one said anything the entire time.

Once they were deep in the Forest of Light, the castle was not hard to find. The trees glowed brighter the closer they got. It was well-lit enough to create a calming atmosphere. Forest wildlife grazed in the distance, but none of it seemed threatening. Even the larger Wulpa were as docile and obedient as house dogs.

When they arrived at the Hidden Castle, it was not an impressive sight. All they could see was the miles-long eastern wall—no grand city or castle, just the defensive wall. They walked southward and made their way to the drawbridge. There, they set camp for the night.

Gala was eager to abandon everyone. Being the middle of the night didn't help his attitude, but he was over the adventure. All he wanted was time to himself and to make it to the Third Island Festival.

He watched as Dagnarone struggled to nail her hammock to a tree. It was even more frustrating since he had shown her how to do that multiple times. He needed to let his frustration vent, and she would be the unlucky victim.

"Are you okay with dying?" Gala snapped as he approached her.

She turned to look at him with a cocked eyebrow. "What?"

"You're getting yourself into a fight, and what if you get hurt? Is this something you're willing to die for?"

"Earlier, you said not to worry …"

"You're still walking into a battle! Even with the best defense in the world, something can go wrong." He paused, not sure how to say the next thing. He looked around, thinking the words would come to him. When they didn't, he just blurted it out. "You could come with me, ya know."

Dagnarone looked surprised, and a little put-off. "Didn't think I was invited."

"Yeah, well, I hadn't thought of it till now."

"Once again, I made a promise to Sephra."

"So?" Gala shrugged. "People break promises all the time. I broke, like, three today, and everything has turned out fine.

"What about the people who need me?"

"Come on. You are not responsible for keeping the world safe! That's not who you are, and that's okay. Besides, I think once you get to see this world, you may realize it's not worth putting your neck on the line for."

"Worlds least deserving of saving need it the most."

"What is that, like, your team's catchphrase?" Gala rolled his eyes.

"I just feel I need to be here."

Gala couldn't believe her. He knew just as well as she did that she didn't want to be there. The fact that she wouldn't say it out loud was offensive. He shook his head. "You do remember Sephra tricked you into joining this foolish crusade, right?" His tone was no longer calm. "You thought it was going to be a hike and now it's a march to war. I don't see how you can come to terms with the weight of this and still carry forward."

"As I've said, Spirit is telling me I'm needed here."

"That's not some sagely spiritual advice about destiny, that's your ego! Trust me, I know a thing or two about that."

"If you have such an ego, then why don't you want to stay and save the world with us?"

"'Cause I'm the guy who's gonna pick the girl over doing the right thing."

"How romantic." Dagnarone made a face.

"You think so?" Gala smirked. "That something I should tell her when I see her?"

"You think professing your love by telling her how you abandoned your friends in their hour of need will make her swoon? You'd have a better chance by going there and telling her you saved the world alongside us."

"Alright, we need to clear something up. You are entering a battle, not saving the world. Unless this kingdom was burnt to the ground and all the leadership was killed, the world will live to see another day!"

"Why did you come over here just to bicker?" She threw her arms up in the air. "Gala, you ever been on a life-changing adventure?" Her voice was exhausted. "What is your purpose? What are you here for? I see enough specks of gray smattered in that hair, and I can't believe someone would make it this far into their life and not have a clue! You go day-to-day looking for food and finding a way through. You take in all these amazing things, but what do you give back? Is it always just going to be about you and what you want?"

Gala didn't know what to say. His mouth was ajar as he searched for the words to fight back with. "First off, I've had plenty of quests like that," he sneered. "And guess what? They don't change ya like you hope they will! So, you're right, I am just trying to make my way through this world. Once you start living, you'll do the same." He turned away from her. "Finally found myself someone I could settle down with, and everything's trying to keep me from her," he mumbled.

"If she were as important as you make her out to be, then why aren't you at the festival right now?"

Gala looked around in disbelief. "Because I'm here helping you!"

"Are you? Or were we just a convenient excuse? Tell me, at this point in your life, do you really want to settle down and give this up? 'Cause I don't think you'd be able to do that."

Gala knew it was true but wouldn't let her know she was right. "You know … that's … I … you've got some nerve!" He pointed at her. "Just because we've known each other for a few days doesn't mean you know me!"

"Tell yourself whatever gets you through the night but know I'm right. I am a cosmic being of insight, and you'd be wise to listen to me. You really think the three of us needed your help to get here? You're here 'cause you want to be."

Gala had nothing more to say. He walked away, regretting his decision to help them.

● ● ●

Yawonte felt guilty for dividing the group. He knew it was too late to apologize to some, but not to the one who mattered the most.

He walked over to Sephra. She was in her sleeping bag, staring up at the beautifully illuminated trees.

Yawonte sat on the ground next to her. He fiddled with a twig before speaking. "I'm sorry for being so aggressive earlier." His voice was gentle. "I hope I did not overstep and ruin everything. It was not my intention."

"Things got out of control, but they were probably destined to." Sephra spoke slow and sounded weary. "Hopefully, we all learned something we can use in battle."

"At least Dagnarone has a weapon now."

"Assuming she doesn't ditch it."

"True." Yawonte stopped playing with the twig and made eye contact. "Seeing Jerlone walk away felt familiar. In the grand cosmic scheme of existence, I do not think that was the first time we've witnessed that."

"His reaction was ... upsetting," Sephra looked guilty. "I didn't realize how much I had done to drive him away. If I had been a better leader, I would have seen that and changed my approach. I wasn't trying to unite us; I was trying to get my way. Now he's gone, and ... I'm afraid to think about how much I may have seriously hurt him." She sighed. "I didn't think life was going to be this complicated."

"What a foolish thought," Yawonte said with a chuckle.

"I thought these powers would give me a leg up, but ... I don't know if I'm confident enough to do all this. I mean, look at us ... we're falling apart. What kind of leader allows that to happen?"

"Stop being so hard on yourself. People fight, and you can't stop them from having those moments. You're only four days into your mission. You must be patient."

"But I've lived hundreds of lives before! Why hasn't that knowledge traveled with me?"

"Because we constantly have to start anew. That's been one of Jerlone's main points of contention with this life. Did he not express that to you?"

"Oh. Huh ... must not have heard him."

"Just know, with some patience and focus, you'll get back to where you want to be."

"Do you think I'm taking on too much in this life?"

He was nervous to answer. The last thing he wanted to do was hurt Sephra. He knew she didn't like her authority questioned, and his response was close enough. "Let's see … your goal is to save the world and make justice universal, right?"

She looked a bit miffed. "I don't know if I'd phrase it like that, but along those lines."

"It's a bit *ambitious*. Now, I don't know if this helps, but I would fight in your revolution."

"Some revolution. Right now, it's just you and me."

"We can find some simple-minded people to join us. It's easy to appeal to the masses when you offer them bogus solutions." He laughed, but she did not. It was clear she was too wrapped up in her own head. Yawonte hoped to put her mind at ease. "When all this nonsense is said and done, what do you want to see in this world?"

"I don't know. I hadn't thought of it." Sephra sighed heavily. "I've thought about what I want my purpose to be, but I never thought about how I want to enjoy myself."

"No point in having a purpose if there's nothing to enjoy. Too many people get swept up in their responsibilities and forget what they're really here for."

"So, what are you here for? You spent fifty years just in these woods … that can't be your full purpose. What do you want to see?"

"An ocean." Yawonte zoned out. With each breath, he tried imagining the smell of the beach. He so desperately wanted the sun to shine down on him, reminding him that everything would be alright.

"An ocean? Just an ocean?"

"I've met birds who rave about them. They say standing on the shore makes you realize the enormity of the world around you. All that water in one place sounds … majestic."

"And that's it?"

"Some things are that simple. I want to feel my toes in the sand, watch the sun rise and fall, take in the scenery, and allow myself to … be."

"How long do you plan to go for?"

"Until I feel content."

"And will you swim?"

"If the mood strikes." Yawonte shrugged.

"Do you know how to swim?"

"Somewhat."

"Somewhat? That's not very reassuring."

"I won't venture far. Don't worry, I'll keep myself safe."

"It sounds nice but, I don't know, a little boring."

"Life doesn't always have to be about thrilling adventures. Sometimes, you just need a day at the beach."

"I know, I'm just … not that person. I don't remember much about my past lives, but I know I was always working. It's hard for me to take time for myself. It makes me feel … irrelevant? It reminds me that my time is ticking and it's so easy to be swept away into the recesses of it. I've robbed myself of life and neglected those I care about. I don't want to do that again in this life, but it seems I've already started. You speak of destiny, and I wonder if hurting those closest to me is part of mine. I've done it before, and I know I'll do it again, because I'm selfish. It's probably why I want to be in charge." A look of remorse crossed her face. "People meet me and get to know me, then, one day, I'm out of their lives. I become an old, forgotten acquaintance. It makes me worried I don't have any true connections."

Yawonte gave her a warm smile. "If you're cognizant enough to recognize that, then you can change."

CHAPTER 36

THE HIDDEN CASTLE: SOUTHERN GATE
DAWN
· ·

GALA OPENED HIS eyes just as the sun began to rise. Everyone else was still asleep.

Atop the wall, two gatekeepers arrived to lower the bridge.

Gala wasn't good at saying goodbye. Sneaking off was more his style. It was a better way to avoid dealing with his feelings. Even though he'd only known these people for a short period of time, he felt a great amount for them.

Regardless, he had to do what was right for him. Getting swept up in a battle wasn't on his agenda. He didn't risk his life for the Diamond of Farrokh just to not give it to Isra.

Quietly, Gala stirred and packed his belongings. A part of his soul screamed for him to stay. It felt right being with them, but then there was that part reminding him he was a loner. It was time to do what he always did: look out for himself. It was a trait that stopped him from growing, time and time again.

Gala walked halfway to the gate when he stopped to look at his friends one last time. To his surprise, Dagnarone was up, watching him leave. With two fingers, he waved goodbye. She returned the gesture.

With a deep breath, Gala turned back to the gate and left.

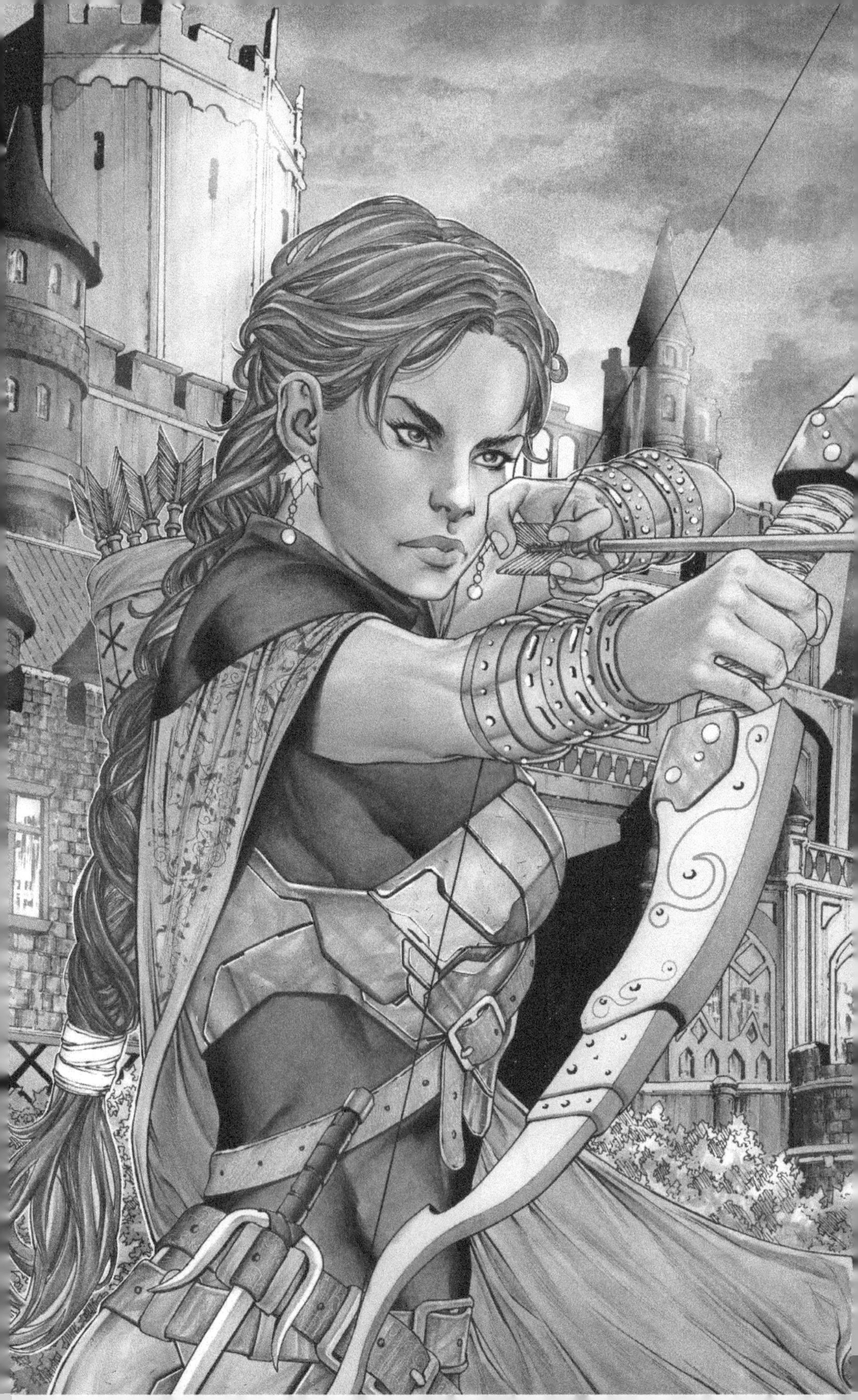

4
BATTLE FOR THE HIDDEN CASTLE

CHAPTER 37

THE HIDDEN CASTLE
MORNING

YAWONTE HOPED, AFTER a night's rest, Gala would change his mind. Instead, he couldn't even give them the courtesy of a proper goodbye. Yawonte wasn't offended by this action, but he was sad to see Gala leave. He may have given Gala a hard time, but he did enjoy some of his stories.

As they walked through the streets, Yawonte gazed in astonishment at his surroundings. He'd visited small communities within the Forest of Light, but this was unlike anything else. Even though this neighborhood was a little dilapidated, there was still a whimsy to it. The neighborhood consisted of small, two-bedroom homes with a kitchen, living room, and not much else. Brown and red houses were scrunched next to each other with dying lawns. Rickety picket fences lined everyone's property. In the distance they could see the luxurious homes of the elite, and the discrepancy felt insurmountable.

The kingdom's walls formed a pentagon. The southern wall was near the lower class. Dead center was the king's throne, surrounded by the business district. The remaining space up north was filled with the extravagant homes of the senators and the rich.

Sephra and Dagnarone walked ahead, gabbing about animals and if they could ever see themselves owning a pet. To no one's surprise, Dagnarone was in favor of having a pet, while Sephra seemed horrified by the idea.

Yawonte meandered behind them, occasionally walking over to something and examining it. There was a calm as they walked down these streets. He imagined a life for himself there, one where he worked a menial job and came home to a place like this. Being a man without his responsibilities seemed nice. It wasn't a surprise for him to feel this way; he had thought about it before. It was something he desired but didn't expect to receive.

As more people left their homes, Yawonte noticed a common recurrence: everyone was either child or elderly. It made no sense to him. He wondered if it could be a coincidence, but to see it on that level seemed suspicious. "Has anyone noticed everyone here is either young or old?"

"I have," Sephra answered. "It seems suspect to me."

"Everyone else could be at work," Dagnarone suggested.

"We could be in a retirement community? People watching their grandkids?"

Yawonte was unable to take his eyes off an elderly man rummaging in his yard. There was a curiosity there that needed to be scratched.

The man circled a large, filthy, tree stump. The ground around it was dug up. Yawonte could see thick and gnarled roots tangled in the dirt. It was obvious decades were spent trying to remove this eyesore, but to no avail.

Yawonte walked over to the man's fence with a smile. "How are you this morning, sir?"

The man looked up and grimaced. "Every day, I spend thirty minutes trying to get this stump out of my yard," he said. "You wanna take a guess how long I've been at it?"

Yawonte shrugged. "A couple years?"

"Close … about sixty-five years."

"You started early."

The man laughed. "I don't know what I'm gonna do. At this point, I've accepted that stump is going to outlive me."

Yawonte stared at the stump and knew the roots ran deep. There was a time when the tree was grand and powerful, but now it clung to this world with its final breaths. "My name is Yawonte, and perhaps my friends and I could help you."

The man walked over and shook his hand. "I'm Orville, and I appreciate the offer, but there's no way you're getting that stump out. My grandfather tried, my father tried, I've tried, my boys and girls have tried, and now, so have their kids. That sucker may as well be part of our family at this point. We seemed to be cursed with it. You'd have to be magic to get it out."

"Why don't you let us give it a try." Yawonte smiled. "Besides, you've probably loosened it over time."

Sephra leaned toward Yawonte. "You remember we have to see the king immediately, right?"

"If you're gonna see Coart, you'll be waiting a few hours," Orville told her. "He gets up well after the sun rises."

"Sounds like we can spare a few minutes then." Yawonte walked toward the gate.

"But there must be someone we can talk to instead," Sephra protested.

"What's going on?" Orville asked. "Why do you need to see Coart so urgently?"

Yawonte looked at Sephra. He didn't think it would be wise to alert the people before conferring with the king.

Sephra hesitated before answering. "It's nothing," she finally replied. "I'm just an impatient and selfish person, and I have matters to discuss."

"Wow." Dagnarone stood there in shock. "That took a lot of courage to admit that out loud. I didn't know you had that insight—"

Sephra turned and glared at Dagnarone.

"Oh!" Dagnarone's eyes went wide with her realization. "I was just kidding about that."

Sephra shook her head and walked into the yard.

Yawonte knelt by the stump and ran his hands over it. He did not tug at it; he wanted to familiarize himself with its texture. Holding onto it gave him insight. He knew how this stump dug itself into the planet. He leaned his head in and sniffed. For something that looked so rotten, it still smelled like the great tree it once was.

Releasing his grip, he buried his hands in the surrounding soil. He rubbed the dirt into his hands, intending to connect with nature in a stronger manner.

"It's an ornery stump, that's for sure." Orville spoke as a defeated man. "We never make the progress we hope for. One day it almost seems gone, and the next it's reinforced itself. It regroups faster and better than we ever do. Really makes a man feel hopeless."

"Have you ever considered moving?" Dagnarone asked.

"And abandon our home? We can't just leave because of an inconvenience."

"Yeah, but it's such an eyesore …"

"No home's perfect. Anywhere you go, you'll find issues. This one ... I can live with it for the most part. Look, just to let you folks know, I can't offer you much for helping. Best I can do is the best breakfast you've ever had."

"I dunno, we had a pretty good one yesterday," Dagnarone mumbled.

"Orville," Yawonte said, "would you be kind enough to get us a gardening edger?"

"I'd be happy to." Orville left for his toolshed in the back of the house. Yawonte motioned the women over. "If we're to remove this, then we're going to have to be creative. Dag, I need you to connect to the stump and cradle it. You're going to have to reach all of it and I suspect the roots run deep. You'll feel how it's anchored down."

Dagnarone nodded. She knelt down and closed her eyes. Touching the stump, she started her process.

"Sephra, you're going to be doing the heavy lifting. You'll need something that can give you leverage." Yawonte leaned in toward her and spoke softly. "Maybe put a little energy on it for some help."

"And what're you doing?" Sephra surveyed the stump.

"I'm grabbing it and guiding it out. I can cast some spells that I think will help loosen everything. We may have to adjust and turn once we're in position. Be ready to move *with* the stump, not against it. Visualize it coming out, or else we are doomed to failure."

Orville returned with the gardening edger and handed it to Sephra.

The three Mystics circled their wooden opponent, looking for the right spot. Slowly, their pacing eased, and they sank into positions.

Dagnarone sat to the side, her hand gently touching it. An outsider wouldn't think she was helping at all.

Sephra dug the edger into the ground, cutting into a chunk of the wood.

Yawonte stood across from her, his hands grasping onto the top.

"What do you want me to do?" Orville's voice trembled.

"Stand back," Yawonte responded.

Orville stepped back and crossed his arms. He didn't look confident in their plan.

"On three," Sephra commanded. "One, two, three!"

Red energy jumped from her hands onto her tool. She sliced into the root, latching on for leverage. It was evident that she was experiencing lot of resistance. She flexed her muscle and the wood moved slightly. She cranked her arms again, and it budged.

Dagnarone swirled and twirled her hands, untangling the roots below. You could hear the faint sound of branches snapping. Her hands helped wiggle the edges of the stump and loosen things.

Yawonte pulled the stump but to no avail. Spirit told him to reposition himself. He moved next to Sephra and pushed. This worked much better.

"Everything on three!" Sephra commanded again. "One, two, *three!*"

The stump began to rise but suddenly dropped back into the ground. It was as if the tree was resisting and trying to burrow back down.

Orville took a few steps back. His face now looked a little less pessimistic.

Sephra shifted to her right, and everyone followed. She dug the edger in again. "More!"

The stump thrashed and thumped as they increased their magic.

"I need a hand," Yawonte requested.

"Give me a second." Dagnarone stood and scurried to him. Together, they pushed and lifted the stump. "Sephra, move to your right and dig in. I think it's weak there."

Sephra removed the edger and took a step over.

"One more step," Dagnarone requested.

With another step, Sephra planted the tool. She struck a root that she couldn't break through. "I could use some help with this one!"

Dagnarone stopped pushing and clapped her hands.

Sephra struck once more, this time breaking through.

They gave it one final push and the stump ripped from the ground. There were roots sticking from the soil, creating a whole new mess to deal with. But at least the massive eyesore was gone.

Orville couldn't believe his luck. He walked over in shock. "How in the world …?"

"We've got a special touch," Dagnarone gasped for air.

"I can see that …"

"You need us to dispose of the remains?" Sephra offered.

"No, that's fine, thank you. We can cut it up and use as firewood." Orville looked around at the aftermath. His yard was a mess. "You know … a small part of me questions if it actually looked better with that stump there."

CHAPTER 38

ORVILLE AND YUMA'S KITCHEN
MORNING
. . . .

D**AGNARONE LOVED THE** quaint, little kitchen. Heirlooms and knickknacks decorated every spare inch of the room. It was all handmade and old, with paint chipping away and new screws needed.

Smoke filled the air, bringing the aroma of bacon and eggs to the visitors' noses.

The three Mystics sat cramped at the table, while Orville and Yuma finished preparing the meal. Even though they were elderly, they could move about their kitchen as though they were in their prime.

"I know it can still be bad out there," Yuma flipped the bacon, "but you should have seen it sixty years ago. Back then, you were only safe in the big cities. Small towns were regularly overrun by Mountain Folk. They'd annihilate whole communities overnight. That's what led my family here. It was one of the few safe havens, assuming you could find it. Once we got here, I never left."

"Are you serious?" Dagnarone asked incredulously. "You've just stayed here since you were a child?"

"That's right."

"So, you haven't seen the world?"

"Just through books and the stories people have told me."

"How is that living a life? I can't imagine all the wonders you've missed out on." Dagnarone had no clue she was coming across as rude.

Yuma tucked her gray hair behind her ear and smiled politely. "Yes,

I understand that, but everyone prioritizes differently. Some people want adventure, but that's not me. I wanted a safe place to love a family, and thankfully, I got it."

"Must be some family," Dagnarone mumbled to herself. She looked at one of the countertops and saw a photo. It showcased a few generations of the family. Yuma and Orville had four children and close to ten grandkids. Dagnarone was humbled but still felt strong in her opinion.

"Why didn't anyone help the smaller towns?" Sephra asked.

Yuma walked over with the bacon and served it. "These attacks were so sudden and vicious. There was nothing anyone could do to respond fast enough."

"But why didn't they form militias to protect themselves?"

Orville sat down with the eggs. "They formed 'em, but they were often overrun by their attackers. It may be hard to believe, but it really was a different world back then. The old Fascio regularly dispatched his Mountain Folk. Now, they're only used in case of emergency. He finds them too valuable. Hate to give this newer Fascio credit, but he keeps them within their border."

"We're only safe when they're told to stay there," Yuma interjected.

"Which is most of the time."

"Do you even remember having to defend our land, or are you too old and forgetting things?"

"There were barely any Mountain Folk at the siege! We fought off humans, not those creatures."

Sephra shook her head. "I just don't understand why no one has put an end to Fascio's rule. These leaders really are too cowardly to do anything, aren't they?"

Orville took a sip of his coffee. "It's complicated. You take him down, and a chain of events starts. No matter what, his people would suffer. It's most likely that a new regime would take over. It would be one of his generals, and they would continue the reign of terror. I think our leaders would rather deal with the enemy we know—someone who's behavior we can predict—but for us to even consider taking him out is a logistical nightmare. Navigating through the Gray Mountains that surround his castle would be damn near impossible. His people know how to get in and out through their secret paths, but we don't have that luxury. He's barricaded himself in tight."

"The last Coart attempted an invasion." Yuma scraped food onto her fork.

"But only because of ulterior motives," Orville argued.

She threw her silverware down. "Stop it! He was a good man! You just never liked anyone from that family!"

"Can you blame me? Why should I like him? He's the worst kind of politician—one you can't vote out!"

"He kept you safe during his reign!"

"And then he handed the crown over to the biggest screw-up to ever wear it!"

"It's his son, what would you expect?"

"When it comes to leadership, you put that aside!" Orville slammed his palm on the table.

"We'll discuss this later." Yuma motioned to their guests.

"By all means, don't let us stop you," Dagnarone said with glee. She was fascinated by their fight. She didn't know how they could both be so passionate, yet believe such different things. Still, they were charming.

"Sorry," Orville muttered. "We both get a little loud. Never saw exactly eye to eye on some subjects."

"Lots of subjects," Yuma chimed in.

Yawonte pleasantly squealed and moaned as he chewed with his mouth open. He was a factory of sounds. When he finished, he slammed his hand on the table, grabbing everyone's attention. "A wonderful meal! Thank you for this kind invitation. It warms our hearts, truly."

"Always happy to help a person in need."

"Lots of people come here in need?" Yawonte daintily wiped his mouth.

"Everyone's in need of help. A lot just won't bother to say it out loud."

"I have to be honest with you, there is a lot about this world that I do not know about. I've gathered my *assumptions* and am trying to wean my way through which are accurate, but one thing that has occurred to me is that Fascio and Coart are opposite sides of the same coin."

"Let's see," Orville stroked his chin. "They both inherited their thrones and continue a war their ancestors started. Pride and ego influence most of their decisions. Innocent civilians who want nothing to do with the squabble are regularly silenced. Both have brainwashed their people into thinking they are the altruistic society. Those same citizens believe the other side needs to be annihilated in order to keep themselves safe. Their tactics and coat of paint may differ, but yes, they are the same."

"I've often thought about how a society reflects its leaders. When insecure bullies run the show, those traits trickle down. That turns people from victims of circumstance to perpetrators of opportunity. If I may be so bold to ask, you see the corrupt and nasty side of this society, so why stay?"

"If the decent people leave, then who will fight for the better tomorrow? Like I said about the stump, every place has a problem. The thing that keeps us here is our safety. We've always been able to eat tomorrow," Orville shrugged, "and we love the people. Our leaders are awful, and while there are those who support them, it isn't everyone. These are kind people around us. Even those we disagree with, we know their hearts are in the right place."

Dagnarone felt connected to Yuma and Orville. When she looked around the house, she could tell those were good people. They were just trying to find a sliver of happiness in that scary world.

"You were here during the last invasion?" Sephra took the last bite of her meal.

"Yes," Orville became grim. "About forty years ago, they attacked. I helped fight that night on the western wall. Most of us were stationed there 'cause it's the easiest to climb. Lots of vines and overhanging branches from the forest. My buddies and I held that line. I lost some good friends, but we did what it took to protect our people. That was my only taste of war. I still have nightmares about it." He went quiet and became lost in a gaze.

Yuma put her arms around Orville. It was evident he needed her touch in that moment. She kissed his ear. "You did everything you could," she told him softly. She looked at the Mystics. "I would have been by his side, but I was pregnant with our second child." She turned back to Orville. "We bicker about everything, but I'll always be proud of you for protecting us."

Dagnarone watched this display of love, and it tore her apart. She worried about keeping them safe from the incoming invasion.

Yuma must have seen the look in her eye. "What's wrong?"

"Hmm?" Dagnarone tried to act nonchalant.

"There's something you're not telling us. Is everything alright?"

Dagnarone could feel the intense glare of her companions burning into her. In the most convincing manner possible, she nodded to the elderly woman. "There's nothing to worry about," Dagnarone reassured. "I'm just someone who always looks distressed and thinks everything's about to fall apart, but it's fine, I promise."

"I hope so," Orville replied. "Grandkids and I've got a fishing trip planned in a few days. Would hate for anything to happen to it."

CHAPTER 39

THE HIDDEN CASTLE: BUSINESS DISTRICT
LATE MORNING

SEPHRA WAS STRESSED and eager to talk to King Coart. She couldn't believe it took him this long to start his day. The army could arrive at any second, and they still needed time to prepare. Thinking about it increased her anxiety. She rubbed her hands together in the hope of calming herself down.

It was turning into a cloudy day, and a rumble of thunder could be heard on occasion. A particularly loud and long rumble grabbed everyone's attention.

"I keep thinking that's the army arriving," Sephra said.

"When they arrive, we will know it," Yawonte told her. "We will feel a change all around us. The sky may be dark now, but when it is time for war, then we will know true darkness."

In the center of the kingdom was the throne tower. It reached ten stories tall and could be seen from any spot within the walls. The winding stairwell rotated up to the throne room at the very top. Everything about the tower seemed large and exaggerated, just the way Coart liked it.

Orville led the three Mystics through the business district. It did not live up to its name. Instead, it was more akin to a ghost town. Impressive architecture sat unoccupied, and the sidewalks were mostly empty. This time of day, horse drawn carriages typically littered the streets. By the Mystics' count, they had seen three.

It seemed as though everyone was already evacuated.

A small group of a dozen elderly individuals passed them. They were dressed in black and gray attire, nothing very fashionable. Chatting among themselves, they appeared happy to be out. It was as if they didn't have a care in the world.

Sephra watched the people pass them by. "Are you two noticing this?" She asked her companions.

"Yeah, the fashion sense is really lacking around here." Dagnarone sighed. "Nice people, but they could really use a splash of color and flair."

"You know," Yawonte looked around, "she's not wrong. I hadn't noticed it before, but it's all I see now."

"She's obviously right, but that's not what I'm talking about!" Sephra yelled in frustration. "We're *still* only seeing the elderly. Since we entered this land, I have yet to see someone who we could fight alongside. I'm really concerned about what this means."

Yawonte scratched his chin. "Hmm. Perhaps any able-bodied individual is already getting ready for battle?"

"I don't think it's that. Something feels off."

"I agree." Dagnarone looked around, suspicion in her eyes. "Spirit is telling me something is amiss."

Sephra stood there, wondering, in horror, what they would do if there was no one to fight alongside them.

● ∘ ∘ ●

A moat surrounded the throne tower. Bridges connected the streets to a small landing before the throne door. Sephra was surprised to see the tower's door was not constructed of the finest materials. Instead of metal, it was a wood that dilapidated over the decades.

"Well, here we are," Orville said, stopping before crossing the moat. "I wish you the best of luck with your mysterious mission."

"Thank you for everything." Sephra hugged him. "I can't thank you enough for the hospitality you've shown us. I promise we will pay you back."

"You don't owe us anything. The pleasure was ours."

"Please, thank Yuma for the delicious bread." Dagnarone patted him on the back. "If we survive this thing, I'm coming back for that recipe."

Orville stared at her, his face drawn with concern. "What do you mean, 'if we survive this thing'?"

Sephra glared at Dagnarone, biting her lower lip in annoyance.

Dagnarone looked around, searching for an answer. "Oh, you know, survive this … crazy thing called life?"

The color drained from Orville's face. He leaned in and spoke quietly. "I need you to be honest with me. Do I need to get my family out of here?"

Sephra stepped in close to him. "I think it's safest for you to stay here at this moment. If you leave, I think you'll run into even more danger—but don't worry, we're going to make sure everyone's protected. Listen to any official decrees and follow their orders. We'll take care of the rest, just like we did with the stump."

It took a moment for Orville to say anything. "You did take care of the stump so … I'll trust you." They shook hands and went their separate ways.

Dagnarone tried to slink away from Sephra, but she was not fast enough.

"Dag!" Sephra yelled at her. "Why would you say that to him?" She worried if the citizens learned of the danger too soon, then a plan could not be effectively executed. Part of this was her ego and need to control everything. It was nerve-racking enough having to talk to the king; now she had to hope a panic didn't start in the streets.

"It was an accident!" Dagnarone said defensively. "And, if I'm being honest, I think I had a pretty strong recovery."

"Is that what you think?" Yawonte questioned her.

"I know it could have been a lot worse!"

"Okay, well do me a favor." Sephra looked her in the eye. "Stop talking."

CHAPTER 40

THE HIDDEN CASTLE: THRONE ROOM
LATE MORNING
· ·

SEPHRA STUDIED THE stairwell. It was wide enough for five people to comfortably walk side by side. A red, velvet carpet lined the stairs while cold, gray slabs of stone decorated the walls with disenchantment. It was a long and repetitive trek to the top.

As they climbed, Sephra went over the plan. First off, no one would use magic. She feared it would frighten Coart and turn him off. Sephra would lead the conversation, and Dagnarone would say nothing, no matter what. Yawonte was allowed to speak his mind. The gist of the battle plan was for Sephra and Yawonte to each lead half the troops. One would fight from the wall and the other on the ground. Dagnarone would set up a shelter for the injured and cast healing spells. If need be, she was willing to run onto the field and pull someone aside.

Atop the stairwell sat the throne room door. Unlike the one below, this was made of an exquisite steel. Patterns of flowers were ingrained into it, creating a beautiful collage of wealth and arrogance. Sephra ran her hand over the doors. Just by touching them, she could tell they were heavy. Using her power, she swung them open into the room.

The throne, like always, was primarily a showcase for the king's treasures. Yet the glimmering diamonds and piles of gold didn't impress Sephra. She strode in with a confidence unmatched.

Closest to the door sat the senators. They were hunched over a round table, counting their gold. They seemed most disturbed upon seeing the intruders. Quickly, they huddled close to their money and stared down the strangers.

The Mystics walked past the senators without any acknowledgment.

Four soldiers made Coart's security detail. They rushed halfway across the room and stood with their weapons at the ready. A woman who looked like a general stood in between the guards and the king. She grabbed the hilt of her sword, ready for an attack.

The Mystics stopped out of respect.

The plump King Coart sat on his throne. His arms quickly covered his torso, as if to prevent himself from being exposed. Everyone heard his little squeal when the doors opened, a truth he would adamantly deny.

"King Coart," Sephra curtseyed.

"How dare you?" Coart shouted. "There were no appointments today! You have no right to be here!" He stood and stomped his feet.

"I apologize, but we come with urgent news. Are you aware of the approaching army?"

"Yes, to the province of Larkin." Coart suddenly seemed bored of the conversation.

"The province of Larkin?" Sephra raised an eyebrow.

"Yes!"

"Is … is that another name for here?"

"Woman, are you daft? Do you really not know the difference between The Hidden Castle and the province of Larkin?" He plopped back down in his chair. "Rest assured, we've dispatched the troops, and tonight will bring us another victory in the war against Fascio."

Sephra looked at Yawonte and Dagnarone. They appeared just as confused as her. She turned back to Coart. "I don't think you understand me. There's an army marching its way through the Forest of Light right now. They could be here within hours."

The color flushed from Coart's face. He looked around the room for help. The silence was deafening. "You m-m-m-must be m-m-m-m-mistaken," he stammered. "The arm-m-m-m-m-my-y-y-y is on its way to—"

"Here," Sephra interrupted. "Even if somewhere else is being attacked, there is an army marching here right now!"

"How do you kn-n-n-now this?"

"We were attacked by a small platoon. We interrogated a survivor, and he told us of the plan to invade. As we left, we saw the larger army approaching. There had to have been thousands of them."

Coart stood and walked toward his general. He looked as if he could smash something to smithereens. *"Afua, why is there an army heading here?"* His screeching echoed throughout the chamber. "You told me the province of Larkin was being attacked, *not here!"*

"That's what our intelligence told us, sir." The general, Afua, maintained her composure.

"Well, the intelligence was clearly wrong! You idiots can't get anything right, can you? Ought to just do everything myself!"

Afua turned to address Sephra. "How many troops are en route?"

"Thousands," Sephra answered. "We need to gather your remaining soldiers and start planning our defense." No one replied. Everyone looked at one another, as though they had something to say. "You do have an army … right?"

"Not at this moment," Afua informed her.

Sephra's eyes went wide. "What?"

"They were deployed to the province of Larkin."

"But, surely, not all of them."

Afua did not reply. She glared at Coart, who was oblivious to the conversation.

"All of them!" Sephra looked for confirmation, desperate to be told she was mistaken. "No reserves! Nothing?"

"King's orders," Afua answered finally.

"Why would you send everybody?" Sephra looked at Coart. Rage boiled in her soul, and she had to contain it. She wanted to lash out at this oaf and cause him harm, but she knew that would only complicate matters. "Didn't you take into consideration the people here?"

"I did what I did to protect the most beautiful vacation house in the world!" Coart stomped his feet. "If you could see the real estate down there you would understand what I'm talking about, but I doubt a Philistine like yourself has ever experienced such a … spectacle of the eye!"

Sephra couldn't believe what she was hearing. "How are you the leader of these people?"

"Through hard work, sacrifice, and a little help from my dad."

Sephra shook her head, terrified of what was to come. She looked to

Afua, the only person she felt she could trust in this administration. "Then, we need to make some sort of evacuation plan."

Coart clapped his hands in agreement. "Excellent idea! Guards, get my emergency bags and warm the chariot. I need to grab a few things from the royal bedroom, but I should be ready to depart within the hour."

"You're just going to leave?" Sephra turned her attention back to Coart. "You're not even going to wait and make a plan for everyone else to evacuate first?"

Coart stared at her with this mouth agape. "My lord, woman. Are you obtuse? If I die, then who will lead them? No, my safety is of the utmost importance. Perhaps the senators will stay to help?"

The senators shook their heads and incoherently mumbled. They stood and slinked past everyone, not to be seen again during that dire hour.

"So, you'll just let everyone else fend for themselves?" Sephra asked, looking for confirmation one final time.

"They're welcome to leave," Coart said as he went for the royal elevator. He was walking away from Sephra, not bothering to look at her while talking. "Some will survive, and some won't, but as long as I live, so will the country. I am the spirit of our dream and as long as I survive, so will our people. I shall avenge them! Fascio will not get away with this! This transgression will unite the world, and we shall strike back!" He took a deep breath. "Thankfully the only people we're losing in this debacle are the elderly and … unkempt … for lack of a better term."

"What about the children who will die?" Sephra screamed, her voice echoing in the chamber.

"Oh, yes. Them." He reached the elevator and turned to look her in the eye. "They will always be in our thoughts and prayers. Now, if you'll excuse me, I have a few things to gather. General Afua, meet me downstairs."

The elevator doors shut, and Coart was gone.

"Is there no one who can aid in the fight?" Sephra asked.

"I doubt it." Afua shook her head. "He dispatched everyone but the elderly and the children. Everyone who remains wouldn't last an hour in battle."

"What can we do?"

Afua shrugged. "I don't think there's anything we can do."

"There has to be something we can do." Sephra remained adamant.

"Some of these people are stubborn. They'll only take an order from their king … no matter how foolish an order it is."

"If we don't do anything, then people will die."

"And if we do something, people will die as well." Afua stood and walked toward the stairwell door. "It's a hopeless situation, and you'd be smart to run."

CHAPTER 41

THE HIDDEN CASTLE: THRONE TOWER
DAY

THE THREE MYSTICS walked down the stairwell in silence. When they stepped outside, Dagnarone noticed the clouds were even darker than before. There was a chill and a dread in the air.

Dagnarone broke the quiet. "Well, he lived up to his terrible reputation."

"I can't believe him," Sephra spat her words. "What kind of leader picks up and abandons their people?"

"A common one," Yawonte replied. Everyone stopped walking. "Now is the time to decide our role in the upcoming battle. If we stay to fight, we will likely die. If we leave, then we are cowards, but will live to fight another day."

Everyone stared at one another while the world carried on around them.

"The way I see it," Sephra said solemnly, "we don't have a choice. These people will die without us. We were not sent here to stand idly by while the innocent are massacred. Should it lead to my death, at least it will be a worthy one."

"We aren't going to be enough." Dagnarone shook her head. Her heart raced when she thought of death. With all her being, she wished she wasn't there.

"I know, but we can't just leave them." Sephra put her hand on Dagnarone. For once, Sephra's eyes looked compassionate as she went on, "I'm just as scared as you, but we have to force ourselves to be brave. I'm not asking you to do this for me, but for the people." She removed her hand and looked at Yawonte. "I will do everything I can to protect them, but I will need your help. I cannot do this alone. Only together do we stand a chance." Her voice rang true, like a trumpet of justice. "What say you?"

"As long as I stand, I shall fight by your side." Yawonte grabbed the hilt of his sword and stood proud. "We were brought here for a reason, and I'm glad to have finally found that purpose."

They looked to Dagnarone, awaiting her answer.

People had warned her about this moment, and she'd said she would accept her fate when the time came. Now was that time, but she did not feel ready. The world spun around her as thunder cracked in the distance. Anxiety overwhelmed her body and kept her quiet.

Deep down, she knew what she had to do. She looked at her staff and felt the power radiating from her palm. A calm began to wash over her. A voice spoke to her, reassuring her everything would be okay. This was her purpose, and even though it scared her, it was time to accept it. The people needed her to save them.

She took a deep breath and nodded. "As much as I don't want to," she said, "I will stay and fight by your side, and if that means dying by your side … then so be it."

CHAPTER 42

THE HIDDEN CASTLE: HOT AIR BALLOON DISTRICT
DAY

LOCATED SOUTH OF the throne tower was the hot air balloon district. Depending on the weather, there were typically eight-to-ten vendors set up. The balloons were colorful and came in a variety of shapes and sizes. All together, they created quite the spectacle.

Gala Goda was deep in negotiations with one of the elderly vendors, Lyle. He thought they would have opened for business hours before, but that turned out to not be the case. This society's relaxed work ethic was stressing him out. He felt the clock ticking and wanted to be with Isra, but so far, no one was willing to help.

"And you're sure we'll be there by tomorrow?" Gala groused.

"Should be there by six," Lyle replied.

Gala shook his head. "I've gotta get there earlier than that. Any way you can speed it up a bit?"

"A little extra might speed it up a little extra."

Gala rolled his eyes. He knew he was being conned, but there was nothing he could do about it. "You know, you people really do find a way to make a living off suckers like me, huh? You see how desperate I am, and ya keep adding the fees! Real noble line of work you've found yourself in!"

As Gala reached into his satchel to pull out more coins, he felt something change in the air. He looked up to see Sephra, Dagnarone, and Yawonte standing before him.

No one said anything.

"I got a real bad feeling, seein' you folks," Gala mumbled.

"We just saw Coart," Sephra told him.

"Let me guess … it didn't go the way you wanted?"

"There's no army here to protect them."

"Yeah, well, like I was telling ya—" Gala froze, realizing what she said. "Wait. What do you mean there's no army here?"

"Coart sent everyone to protect his beach house in the province of Larkin."

"Okay, that … sounds about right." Gala turned to Lyle. "Is this true? Everyone's in Larkin?"

"Yep," Lyle confirmed. "He's got a beautiful piece of property down there. Would be a real shame if it were burnt to the ground."

Gala looked away from everyone. He knew what they would be asking of him, but he couldn't face that reality just yet. His heart pounded harder than ever before. Even though it was a cool day, he suddenly felt hot. He shook his head in the hope of waking himself from the nightmare, but to no avail. He wiped the sweat from his brow with his yellow jacket.

"Coart's packing as we speak." The desperation in Sephra's voice was obvious as the panic seeped into her face. "The three of us have decided to stay and fight. We know the odds aren't in our favor, but we have to do something."

"What's going on?" Lyle stepped forward.

Gala finally turned to face Sephra. Staying here would surely bring about his death. He wasn't ready to meet his maker, but then again, who ever was? "You're really going to stay and fight?"

"We have no choice," Sephra answered with confidence.

"You'll be killed."

"Perhaps," Yawonte interjected, "but perhaps we win."

"I wouldn't put money on it."

"We are capable of summoning the impossible. Fighting an army of men will be child's play for beings such as us."

"Love that confidence, but this is insane! Standing to fight isn't going to save these people. You've gotta get them out of here somehow. Fighting this army to save the world just ain't gonna work! You'll get killed!"

Sephra spoke up. "We don't get to choose our time. We're here to answer a call. We know the odds are stacked against us and that death is likely, but we are the only ones standing in their way. If we die, then at least it's from helping good people."

Gala sure did want to run, but he continued to waver.

"Come on, Gala," Dagnarone encouraged him. "You've survived impossible battles before."

"Yeah … by running," Gala reminded her.

"Oh, never mind then."

Sephra walked over to Gala and grabbed his hand. "Please … we need you. Right now, this kingdom's population consists of its most vulnerable. Just because they're people on the edge of life doesn't mean they aren't worth saving. Allow your love of the everyman to speak to your soul." She gazed deeply into his eyes, vying for a connection. "Please. Help us."

Gala thought of Isra. He pictured them walking along a beach, her long brown hair blowing in the wind. There was nothing he wanted more than to be with her. After years of missed opportunities, this was supposed to be his time to tell her he had feelings for her. He thought of that moment a thousand times over throughout the past year. Every word was planned out, even if he'd never admit it. Until that moment, there was nothing that would have stopped him from getting there.

He thought of what it would be like to tell Isra he'd abandoned these people in their hour of need. Even if he explained it meant staying for his inevitable death, she would have felt he should have done the right thing. She'd roped him into adventures because she wanted to save people, and if she were there, she'd be doing it again. Stealing a diamond for her wasn't going to do anything to win her over if he wasn't a righteous man.

The wind picked up, and Gala's jacket flapped in the breeze. The young and old walked around him, oblivious to their encroaching doom. He knew what he had to do but didn't want to say it. Once he said it, then it would be real.

Anxieties about death and dying alone swelled within Gala's soul. He told himself that he would at least be reunited with his parents if he were to die. Still, that did not make anything better. That only showed him how much he wanted to live and how much he wanted to be with Isra.

It was then that an odd thing happened. Gala's anxiety disappeared, and a calm rushed over him, as if a higher force told him he was meant to be there and that all would be well.

Gala accepted his destiny. "I will help you." His face was no longer that of an adventure-seeking youth. Now, it was grim, like a man who had seen too many winters. He looked back at the hot air balloons. "Can't say I was willing to miss this year's festival for anything, but … I guess you've gotta sacrifice something in your life before it's over." A lump formed in his throat.

"Don't go into the fight expecting defeat," Sephra said.

"Yeah, well, the odds of four people beating an army are pretty slim."

"Just because the odds aren't good doesn't mean it's impossible."

The breeze passed, and a change occurred. It was no longer time to fear the inevitable; it was time to save the world.

"Alright then. What's the plan?" Gala asked.

Sephra looked at the hot air balloons towering over them. "First, we get as many children out as possible. If we can use these balloons, then we have the perfect method for escape. Everyone else, we corral into the throne tower. That way, they're centralized and we will know they're safe."

Gala turned to Lyle. "Ya hear that? We're gonna need your help evacuating the city."

"Is that what you think?" Lyle remarked with an attitude. "Last thing I'm doing is waiting around for an army to show up. I'm gathering my wife and grandkids and we're getting out of here. Good luck!"

"But these people need you." Dagnarone stepped toward the frail, old man.

"Not my problem. If it comes to my family or theirs, I'm always gonna choose mine." He turned to walk away.

"What will it cost?"

Lyle stopped in his tracks. "You serious?"

"Yes." Her honesty showed on her face. "Help us load as many people as possible. Then, at the end, you and yours can leave in the final balloon. You'll save a lot of people. Not only will you be considered a hero, but you'll also get paid."

Lyle nodded his head as he thought about it. "I'll do it for ten thousand."

"You know, Lyle," Gala grunted. "This is something of an emergency. Maybe you could find it in your heart to help your fellow man?"

Lyle stared at him for half a minute before responding. "Fine. I'll do it for twelve thousand."

"Gala!" Dagnarone scolded her companion.

"Hey, don't get mad at me!" Gala said defensively. "Yell at him! He's the one being greedy."

"How about this," Sephra stepped in between everyone. "Gala and Dagnarone, stop negotiating for the group. As for the money … we will pay it, but we need you to start right now."

"Show me the money and I'll start."

Sephra, Dagnarone, and Gala all dug through their bags and grabbed the corresponding coins and jewels. Lyle counted everything twice before smiling and accepting it.

"Bueno?" Dagnarone asked for confirmation.

"Everything checks out," Lyle said with a smile on his face. "Just gotta go tell the missus and we can start the evacuation!"

"No, no, no, no, no," Sephra corrected him. "You start evacuating now. We will send for your wife and grandkids. Gala, think you can handle that?"

"Not a problem," Gala replied.

"Yawonte, you talk to the vendors and find some way to get them to help. Coordinate a safe drop-off, far from the army and their path. Dagnarone, you start gathering people. Form lines and work to keep the order as we load the children. They will need a chaperon. Do what you can to get that going." Sephra looked back toward the throne tower. "While you're doing that, I'm going to talk to Coart one last time."

CHAPTER 43

THE HIDDEN CASTLE: THRONE ROOM
AFTERNOON
. . . .

SEPHRA STOOD BEFORE the throne door. The last time, she was nervous to walk in there, but this time she was more determined. With the flick of her wrist, the doors burst open.

Coart sat lounging on his throne, buffing his fingernails. Upon seeing Sephra, he rolled his eyes. "Ugh," he snarled. "Why have you returned, woman?"

Sephra knew she had to approach this carefully. If she wasn't delicate, then everything would fall apart. "I'm so glad I caught you," she claimed. "I'm sure earlier was unpleasant for you, which is something I completely understand." She received no response. "So, after I left I got to thinking, and I realized something. You inspired an idea that I think could save everyone. Would it be alright if I shared it with you?"

Coart shook his head and blinked a few times. "Well, I wasn't expecting to be anyone's muse when I awoke this morning." A smile creeped across his face. "Yes, by all means, please, tell me more."

"Thank you." Sephra smiled. "Let me ask you something. Where is the safest spot in this kingdom?"

"Why, that would be my throne, of course."

"Exactly. So, I was thinking, if you were to allow the citizens to take shelter here, I could then protect them from the invaders."

Coart looked more confused than ever before. "You'll protect them?"

"Yes."

"All by yourself?"

"With a little help from my friends."

"And how exactly did I inspire this idea?"

"Oh, it was from ... seeing you— your ... savvy?" Sephra's performance here was less than stellar, something she thought was obvious.

"Yes, my savvy is legendary." Coart nodded. "Still, this is foolish. I worry about what the lot of them would do to the throne. They'd mess it up for sure, get their sticky fingers all over the velvet, and with all the treasures I can't carry with me. I don't know if I can allow it. I mean, what if something were to break?"

Sephra inched toward him. "But, my king, this is the perfect opportunity for you to simultaneously take action while also absolving yourself of the repercussions. This is what they will write about you in the history books—how you protected your people while still getting yourself to safety. It will show such resolve and ... admirable qualities."

"I do like when I exhibit those traits." Coart seemed to be coming around to the idea.

"We all do, and think, if things go terrible here, then the history books will write about how I failed, not you."

Coart nodded with a smile. "You're right, I would look good. No matter what, I win."

"Well, like I said, I would have never thought of this on my own. Only through seeing your ... brilliance ... was I able to even muster such an idea."

"Yes, I have heard tales like that many a time throughout my life." Coart looked proud of himself. He put a hand on Sephra's shoulder. "It's brave of you to make this sacrifice. The people will remember you, uh—what was your name again?"

"Sephra."

"Yes, Sophia, you will be a legend to the survivors, and we shall sing your name with merriment." He removed his hand from her shoulder and began walking away.

"Thank ... you." She rolled her eyes. "Sir, if I may, could you ask the people to do the following? Anyone with children needs to convene in the hot air balloon district to evacuate. They will get the little ones out of harm's way. Everyone else must gather here in the throne tower. I know it is asking a lot, but they will only listen to you." She hated saying these things to him, but she needed to stroke his ego just right. Even though it seemed like she was laying it on too thick, his reaction indicated anything but.

Coart spread his arms in a dramatic fashion. "My dear woman, it would be a pleasure to address my people."

Attached to one of the windowsills was a horn. The massive, flared bell was positioned outside, while a mouthpiece and crank were inside. Coart walked over to the contraption and rotated the crank. The city alarm blared. After five loud bellows, Coart leaned into the mouthpiece.

"My loyal subjects," Coart announced in an almost regal manner. "It has come to my attention that we will be expecting some unwanted guests soon. For your safety, I am asking you to do the following. Anyone with children, please report to the hot air balloon district. Vendors there will lead you to safety. Everyone else is to gather inside the throne tower. Please keep your hands to yourself when here, as there are many priceless artifacts out in the open. Please be respectful of this rich history that comes before us. If everyone can please follow my instructions and execute them in an *orderly* fashion, then you will survive."

Sephra looked to Afua. The woman was already shaking her head in disbelief. It was a relief to see the General was aware of how insipid Coart was.

Coart turned to the women, still beaming from his speech. "Well? How'd I do?"

Neither woman responded to his question.

"Sir." Afua stepped toward him. "I won't be joining you. Your chariot awaits and your security detail will accompany you, but I must stay."

"If you insist." Coart did not look concerned. "You'll likely be killed, but that's no skin off my back. You and I always had our *issues*, but you've made your decision, and frankly, it's one I support." He looked around the room. "I think I have everything of value I want. I wish you ladies the best of luck." Without waiting for a response, Coart walked over to his elevator and left.

"Truth be told, we're better off without him." Afua stepped toward Sephra.

"Yeah, I was getting that sense," Sephra replied.

"So, you and two other people are gonna defend us from an invading army?"

"We've recruited another."

"Still don't like those odds."

"Me neither, but they're the only odds we've got."

"So, what exactly is your plan?" Afua cocked an eyebrow.

"The plan is to be a force of nature," Sephra said with a wink.

CHAPTER 44

THE HIDDEN CASTLE: HOT AIR BALLOON DISTRICT
EVENING
....

HOT AIR BALLOONS came and went all afternoon. As soon as one arrived, another departed. It was nonstop for Dagnarone and the vendors. Between weighing and loading people, there was always something to attend to.

The balloons delivered the children to a village west of the forest. It was part of their kingdom, and the people were more than happy to help. It was a short enough ride; still, there would not be enough time to evacuate everyone.

The sun would set soon, and darkness would follow. The clouds maintained their foreboding shade, but it never rained. The air was just chilly enough to add an extra layer of dread to everything.

Dagnarone had not stopped moving since Sephra asked this of her. For hours, she ran around, not even stopping for a sip of water. The vendors eventually convinced her to take a break, but not without a mighty argument. When they reminded her she needed her strength for the battle, she conceded.

She walked down a few side streets, looking for a comfortable curb. Upon finding the perfect spot, she sat and realized how sore her feet were. Closing her eyes, she attempted to center herself and take away the pain, but nerves plagued her spirits, preventing the healing process.

When Dagnarone opened her eyes, she saw Gala standing before her. The hot air balloons ascended behind him.

"They tell you to come get me?" Dagnarone asked him.

"Something like that." Gala also seemed exhausted. "We need to do a little preparation before the invasion happens." He sat down next to her on the curb.

"Thought you said we had to go?"

"We've got a few minutes to spare." He surveyed the scene. "You know, you did real good here today. Lot of people are safe because of you."

"I could have saved so many more." Dagnarone was still worried about the people who wouldn't escape.

"You still will. Just in a different way."

"Not if we die."

"Yeah, well, you don't know that we'll die."

"Gala, you told us repeatedly we would die! That has been one of your major talking points!"

"Yeah, but you've gotta keep in mind, I was only saying that to try to convince you to leave them. I was angry, and I know you don't want to do this. I tried to hype it up and make it seem awful … which, in all fairness, it is. Look, if we're gonna be stuck in this position, we've gotta head into it with a better attitude, gotta believe in ourselves, and that starts with self-talk." Gala smiled and seemed oddly optimistic. "No point in doing any of this if we're just gonna focus on our deaths."

Dagnarone looked toward the ground, tears welling in her eyes. "You're right, but I can't stop thinking about all the things I could miss out on. There's still so much I want to do."

"And you'll do them. I promise."

Dagnarone shook her head, a little annoyed at his optimism. "Why are you being like this?"

"'Cause it's what we need right now."

She knew he was right and needed to hear it. "What's your biggest regret? You know, assuming we don't make it out of this alive."

"A couple of investments I shouldn't have made and a couple I passed on."

Dagnarone was not amused by his response.

He seemed to notice, because he added, "Outside of that … not making it to the festival this year." Now, there was an actual sincerity in his tone.

"You don't regret not telling her all this sooner?"

"Yeah, probably would have gotten me out of this jam." Gala took out the flask from his breast pocket.

"Or she'd be here with us."

"That'd increase our odds pretty significantly." Gala took a swig from the flask. "Alright, one big regret I have with her. Last year, I had the perfect chance to kiss her and … didn't."

"Yeah?" Dagnarone leaned in. "Tell me more."

"Well, if I'm being honest, there were a couple of times. The night before we stole the Golden Pernula, we were on a private beach watching the fireworks, and it could have happened then."

"What stopped you?"

"Probably just worried I wasn't enough. Fear of turning a good thing into a real thing." He took another swig of his flask. "And you know, sometimes … sometimes people just miss a moment. It just doesn't happen, and you didn't even realize it until it was over, and I don't know, maybe it wasn't supposed to happen, and that's why … that's why I'm here now." Gala looked up to the sky. "And if I had just told her I liked her instead of getting this stupid diamond, it probably would have saved my life."

"That doesn't sound healthy."

"Wow, I'm not handling my emotions in a healthy manner?" His voice dripped with sarcasm. "I surely never thought of that until now."

"Maybe that's something you can get fixed if we survive this."

"Fix my emotions?"

"Yeah, I think it would help you. Don't worry, you'll get your chance to tell her next year."

Gala reached into his other breast pocket and pulled out another flask. He handed it to Dagnarone. "Got ya a little something for tonight. Just make sure you space it out and don't have it all at once."

"Gala!" Dagnarone stared at the flask in her hand. "We're going into battle, we shouldn't be drinking!"

"I get that, but hear me out. Remember laying out Khurl? That wasn't like you, but thankfully, you're an angry drunk. I think you need to tap into that side of yourself tonight. Every thirty minutes, you take a swig; that'll get you through the night alright. It's what I plan on doing."

"This is such an irresponsible idea."

"Dag, what have I been saying? You've gotta get into the right headspace! This is war we're talking about here! This can help fuel you. You may think it will dampen your senses, but you claim to be a cosmic being of might. I think you'll manage. Besides, all the great generals in history were notorious drunks."

She opened the flask and sniffed. "Ugh, it smells terrible."

"Tastes terrible too."

She took a swig and proceeded to gag. "Yuck! Why would you drink that?"

"Ain't drinking it to quench my thirst. Makes me feel good, like I'm a big man … except when I'm not. By the way, you're gonna want to keep some water with ya tonight. Hydration is important." A water cantina hung around Gala's shoulder. He took it off and handed it to her.

They stood up together, but Gala had to help Dagnarone keep her balance.

"This really isn't a good idea," she told him.

"Yeah, well, none of this is a good idea," he stated bluntly. "Besides, first shot hits the hardest. Everything after this will keep you in a nice warm place, and you'll be all the more violent for it. We can deal with the way we handle stress tomorrow. Right now, we've just gotta do what we can to survive."

CHAPTER 45

THE HIDDEN CASTLE: THRONE TOWER STAIRWELL
LATE EVENING
....

YAWONTE AND SEPHRA spent the majority of their time assisting the elderly up the stairwell. It was a slow ordeal, but walking together helped pass the time.

Their conversations revealed a few details about their past lives. When they talked of food, Sephra was very critical. Yawonte was not surprised to learn she was a picky eater. As the conversation continued, Yawonte had visions of fixing shoes but not particularly enjoying the activity.

These were small details but important to their sense of identity.

The more they thought about their past lives, the more war they saw. These visions were frightening, dissuading them from diving further into the recesses of their minds.

Having just escorted a couple to the throne, they walked back down the stairwell. Others were slowly trudging their way past them, everyone looking mortified.

"They are almost here." Yawonte could feel evil energy moving toward them.

"Good. It is time to show them we are not to be trifled with." Sephra's voice did not waver.

"I must confess, I am a bit nervous," he said apprehensively.

"You're nervous?" She guffawed.

"Just a bit. A tad. Nothing extreme." He looked away from her.

"But you've got more experience than any of us."

"True, but I've never gone against an army. A platoon, yes. A troop, sure. But an army? No. Nothing that size."

"Just remember: you're not doing it alone." Her voice was confident. She sounded so matter-of-fact, it seemed as though she was not scared at all. This bravery inspired Yawonte. "You know, only a fool wouldn't be nervous. We're all having our doubts. Ignore that voice. You know what we need to do, focus on that."

"Yes, you're right." Yawonte nodded.

"Remember the premonitions you've had. We must do alright if you're seeing us on future adventures."

"Perhaps I'm only seeing that because we flee before the bells of doom toll."

She shook her head. "That's not who we are—maybe Gala, but not the rest of us." They laughed, and then she added, "So, you're sure you don't regret joining us?"

"No, this is my destiny. It's what I've waited my whole life for. Without you and this mission, I would be incomplete. There will be hard and painful days ahead of us, but I will not shy away from them. The universe united us to save this planet; now, our time has finally come."

"And if things don't go our way?" Sephra cocked her head. "Are you afraid of dying?"

"No. We are Mystics, and to face death is our responsibility." His baritone voice delivered each word as if it were fact. "These powers burn away at our soul, a fire we can never extinguish. If we do not use our magic it will itch away at us, forever plaguing our minds. I have never thought of my life as something pleasurable. I could never abandon this mission, no matter how lonely it makes me." He let out a long exhale. "I do not know what happens to us when we die, but I feel it will be okay. I am nervous for the battle, but if it does not go our way, I do not fear what comes next. I've just found enough joy to hold onto in this life to make it worthwhile, but if death is what it takes to keep these people safe, then a worthy death it shall be."

Yawonte grabbed Sephra's arm and they stopped walking. With smoldering eyes, he met her gaze. Here was a soul he'd spent lifetimes with, not just two days. Her face was everything he needed in that moment to stay calm. Even though they were about to fight a war, she made him forget all of that. His heart did not race with anxiety, and his mind thought not of his worries. He did not know how to express any of that to her, so all he could do was smile and enjoy the moment.

"Well, whatever happens to us," Sephra said, "it has to be better than shoe cobbling."

"You know," Yawonte chuckled, "I have reason to believe I was the best cobbler there ever was."

"I believe that." Sephra smiled.

Yawonte reminded himself that this was what he would be fighting for.

CHAPTER 46

THE HIDDEN CASTLE: THRONE ROOM
NIGHT
....

"WE WILL DO whatever we can to get them through the night," Sephra said to General Afua. The two women were in the throne tower along with the remaining citizens. "No matter what, you must stay here to protect them. I pray it doesn't come to that, but if it does, you will be the last line of defense."

"I have spent my life protecting these people, and I will not stop now," Afua replied.

Sephra shook Afua's hand. She trusted the general to do right by these people. This was the type of leader they needed, someone willing to stay and fight for them.

The room sat in a dreadful silence. Many said their prayers as religious figures offered solace. People were huddled together, holding hands and trying to comfort one another. Others lined the walls, looking out the window, hoping to catch a glimpse of something.

As Sephra went for the door, she saw a familiar couple. Orville and Yuma walked toward her, their faces looking beyond worried.

"I really wish you would have accepted our offer to evacuate you," Sephra told them.

"Wouldn't be fair for us to cut to the front of the line," Yuma said.

"Could have gone with the grandkids and their other grandparents."

"And that probably would have resulted in some kid being left behind. We stand by our decision."

"Besides," Orville chimed in, "we've got you to protect us. Nothing to worry about."

Sephra grimaced. "I hope so. Speaking of, I have to join up with the others, but I want you to know … I'll be thinking of you two."

The couple looked overwhelmed with emotion but did not say anything. At the same time, they both hugged Sephra.

Sephra put her arms around them and held as tight as she could. Even though they had lived good lives, she did not feel they deserved an end like this. No one deserved an end like this.

With that goodbye, she left and began her descent down the winding stairwell. Halfway down, she started hearing the drums. That meant the army was in the process of setting up.

She picked up her pace and was soon running down the stairs.

The drums beat louder and louder. Soon, there was chanting as well. Cries from depraved humans echoed in the night sky and reverberated through the stairwell chamber.

When she reached the bottom of the tower, she stopped to secure the door. There wasn't much she could do to protect it. The wood was old, and if enough people went for it, this would be an easy obstacle to overcome. Praying it didn't come to that, she ran off toward the eastern wall.

CHAPTER 47

THE HIDDEN CASTLE: EASTERN WALL
NIGHT

SEPHRA REACHED THE top of the wall and saw a breathtaking view of the Forest of Light. All the trees were illuminated, creating a glow bright enough to make it feel like late afternoon. The view was so spectacular, she could understand why people chose to live in such an isolated place.

As she stared, she noticed the trees rustling. It had to be the enemy spreading out and encircling the castle. There would be no escape.

Minutes later, Sephra found her companions. They were also watching the trees.

The drums of war beat louder.

"It will take them some time to finish surrounding us, but it won't be long." Yawonte perched like a gargoyle with one leg between the wall's small merlons.

By their feet were boxes and satchels of weapons, some even scattered along the ground. Blades and arrows and other weaponry that would do wonders in a battle lay at the ready.

Sephra noticed the cache and pointed to it. "What've you got there?"

"Found some stuff that'll help," Gala answered. He picked up a grenade from one of the boxes. "We've got about fifty of these suckers." Everyone stared at him with blank expressions, not seeing the threat. "Right ... probably not familiar with what this is." Gala motioned to the grenade. "So, you've gotta pull this pin, then you throw it, and an explosion will happen, and that will kill a lot of people."

"Oh," the three Mystics acknowledged in unison.

"If we add some magic to it, that can cause even more damage." Sephra began removing her earrings. "But we have to use these wisely. Make sure you throw it into large crowds. We may have to wait a bit for them to fill in before we unleash these, but as soon as you think you can be effective, light them up." She put her earrings in her pocket. "We don't want to use these within the kingdom's walls. Maybe, if we're lucky, the attack will scare some of them off. Realistically, we only win this battle if we can drive them out. We have to make them realize they cannot beat a force of nature."

Gala passed around the grenades while everyone else gathered last-minute items. There was so much going on, no one heard the approaching footsteps.

"You lot look like you could use a hand," a soft-spoken Jerlone said.

Sephra's heart burst with joy upon seeing his face. Throughout the day, she'd wished he was by their side, and this felt like a dream come true. "Thank you." Sephra sped over to him and squeezed him tight. She had never been so happy to see him, nor possibly anyone else.

"I knew you'd be back." Yawonte nodded. "I'm glad to see I was right, but I must know, how did you enter the kingdom?"

"The vines on the western wall," Jerlone answered. "They're pretty easy to climb. We may need to do something about that."

"Just like Orville told us."

"You just helped us significantly," Dagnarone said to Jerlone. "I mean, you are putting yourself at much greater risk, but our odds are significantly better."

Jerlone tilted his head in confusion. He looked around and seemed even more befuddled.

"I'm happy you're back too." Gala checked the chamber of his pistol. "And, just so you know, I also stormed off."

"Glad to hear I wasn't the only one." Jerlone continued looking around.

"If I may ask," Sephra said, "what brought you back?"

"First off, as soon as I turned my back, I felt guilty. I knew no one meant anything by it, yet I allowed other feelings to cloud that. I should have handled myself better and expressed everything in a different manner. I'm not apologizing for how I felt, but I am sorry for how I conveyed it."

"And I'm sorry for making you feel that way." Sephra was sincere.

Hurting her brother was not her intention, and she wanted to set it right. "I've been blinded by this mission, and I owe all of you an apology." She turned to look at Dagnarone specifically. "Sometimes it's hard for me to take others' feelings into consideration. While I'm glad you're all here, it was wrong of me to drag you into this. I hope I can make amends one day."

Jerlone accepted her apology. "Thank you, but don't even think of that now, for there are much larger matters to attend to. As I tried to flee the forest, I came across the army. They appeared even more massive than when we first saw them, and I knew you would need my help. But I have to ask … since I've entered the kingdom, I've seen no signs of our soldiers. Where are they?"

Sephra looked to Yawonte, Dagnarone and Gala in turn. All of them stood silently, waiting for someone else to speak.

"We are the army," Sephra finally explained. "Long story short, Coart called in the reserves and stationed them elsewhere, along with all his other soldiers. Now, we are all they have."

Jerlone's jaw dropped, and desperation clouded his eyes. "Please, tell me you're kidding." He fell to the ground, breathing harder with each breath. "The five of us won't be enough. Their army is in the thousands!"

"We know," Sephra knelt next to him and held his hand.

"And you're just going to stay here and fight?"

"There's people to protect." She looked him in the eye. "None of us like this, but we can't leave them to die. We have the power to do something, and we must. Should we die, then this is a good death—an honorable death."

With a blink and a nod, he faced her. "Alright, then … what's the plan?"

Sephra looked at each of them. All day, she strategized in her head. This was the moment she had been waiting for—the chance to step up and be their leader. "We each take a wall." She was determined and confident, and she held it in her voice. "Yawonte, I think you'd deal with the vines on the western wall best. Gala, you should take the northwest wall. I'll guard the northeast wall. Dagnarone, you protect the eastern wall. And Jerlone, would you be willing to defend the southern wall? The gate is there, which is going to be their main target."

"I'll handle it," Jerlone said without hesitation.

"The most realistic goal we can strive for is to drive them away. We need to hit them hard. We shall rain magic down upon them! A cosmic storm of light and death shall be their gauntlet!" She walked back and forth. "Nature is your ally; use it wisely. Remember to pace yourself, especially while we have the high ground. Using this much energy will be exhausting, so be aware of that. Should they break through the gate … that is when we will need to work together the most. We will assemble at the throne tower. They can burn the city down if they must, but we will not let them go near the citizens!"

The drums beat louder. The hooting and hollering of the army rose above the trees. They sounded more deranged than wild animals. Like monsters of the night, only blood would satiate them.

With everyone ready, it was time to go their separate ways.

"It's time." Sephra looked them over. "Remember: we can do this. We were sent here to protect, and that's exactly what we're going to do. We won't let these supporters of violence and fascism overtake this land! We will save them, because there's no other choice! This is what we are meant to do! We have a chance to do something with our lives and make this world a more beautiful place! This is our moment to be spectacular!" She raised her bow in the air. Everyone else followed, thrusting their weapons up. "Believe in the power of tomorrow and we will make it through this night."

CHAPTER 48

THE HIDDEN CASTLE: NORTHWEST WALL
NIGHT
• •

THE TREES SWAYED with more force than before. From what Gala could see, the castle was almost surrounded, and battle was ready to commence.

His nerves were causing him to overheat. Temperatures like this would usually make him cold, but not tonight. He was too focused on the mission to worry about his comfort.

From what he could tell, the wall would not be easy to climb. It was relatively smooth, which would make grasping it tricky, and the terrain below looked muddy and uneven. He hoped that would be enough of a challenge to deter them. If they were able to climb up there, then Gala would be responsible for defending two miles of wall. He shook his head, knowing it was too large a space for him to cover by himself.

As far as Gala was concerned, all he needed was his trusty pistol and whip. He took out the firearm and stopped walking. He stared at the weapon, remembering where it had come from. He thought of his parents, suddenly missing them a lot. As a powerful gust of wind blew past him, he knew they were by his side. They would always be there to protect their son, and not even death would stop that.

Gala wondered what his life would have been like had his parents survived. Would he be facing down the inevitable right then? Would he and Isra have met? Could they have settled down? A vision of multiverses passed through his mind, and he saw all the ways life could have played out.

All those lives seemed better than the one he was currently living.

When this was over, he needed to make a change. He couldn't keep going on meaningless adventures for treasure. He needed someone to be there for him. Flying solo was getting old, even for him. All this just showed him how alone he really was.

The enemy was getting louder as the first few soldiers stuck their heads out of the forest.

Gala reached into his breast pocket and took out his flask. He opened it and brought it to his lips. "This one's for you, Isra. Enjoy the party." He threw his head back and took a shot. He wiped his mouth and put it away. Grabbing his whip, he uncurled it and gave it five loud cracks.

Gala was ready for the fight of his life.

CHAPTER 49

THE HIDDEN CASTLE: NORTHEAST WALL
NIGHT

SEPHRA STOOD LIKE a statue in the middle of her wall. She knew she looked both elegant and intimidating. In reality, her sweaty palms clenched tightly around her bow. Grasping her weapon helped keep her calm and reminded her of the power she possessed. She wished they could just get on with it, as she found this intimidation act silly.

A horse cried out from the trees, the shrill screams haunting the night. The beast stomped about with such intensity even that was audible. When it burst from the forest, a rider sat astride with something in his hands.

Sephra grabbed an arrow and took aim. She noticed the rider was clad in armor. A sword even hung by his side, another unusual trait for this army, according to Gala. It must have meant he was of importance, possibly a general.

The general rode right up to the wall and held up Coart's bloody head. "We have taken your king," he snarled. "Surrender, and we will be merciful." He spit on Coart's head and tossed it to the ground.

This sight did not scare Sephra. As far as she was concerned, the world would be better without Coart's leadership. "We will not stand down!" Her voice echoed throughout the land, like the voice of a god.

The general grinned like a devil. He raised a hand, and troops began walking out of the forest. They were in no rush, as there was no need to be.

Sephra added magic to her arrow and fired. It pierced her opponent's armor without any resistance. With one last gasp of air, the general fell from his horse.

CHAPTER 50

THE HIDDEN CASTLE: SOUTHERN WALL
NIGHT

JERLONE SAT PERCHED atop the gate. The invaders were assembling battering rams and other weapons that could pry it open. It would take them time, and Jerlone was happy to watch them while they worked.

He looked behind his left shoulder. In the distance, he saw Sephra's trail of neon red energy. Moments prior, he'd heard her battle cry. He admired her dedication and bravery. Without those traits, it was unlikely she would have inspired him to join in this foolish adventure.

He closed his eyes and contemplated things. Mostly, he wondered if he'd be able to protect the gate. He didn't want to let the others down. It would be too embarrassing if he were the weak link who ruined everything. This was a big responsibility, but he was up for the task.

Exhaustion didn't concern him; he could push through that. Mentally, his head was in the game, and he wouldn't let anything slow him down psychologically. Only being overpowered would stop him.

Before returning to reality, he visualized their victory. He imagined the sun rising as they stood victorious with the enemy on the run. They were bruised and battered, but they were walking out of it alive. He imagined what that would feel like as he prayed for it. Most importantly, he saw the wand in his hand, knowing it was the true hero.

Jerlone opened his eyes to find more enemies on the battlefield. There were only a hundred yards between the trees and gate, and that area was starting to fill in.

To his side was a plethora of weapons. Plenty of projectiles and sharp blades would be ready at a moment's notice, including an ax that called to him. It was heavy, but it could serve him well.

He took out his wand. It knew a fight was brewing and buzzed with anticipation. There was a weight and legacy within, making it feel all the more powerful.

"You fools." Jerlone stood up. "You have no clue the magical explosion you've walked into."

Lightning and thunder clashed overhead.

With the battle ready to commence, he took a final moment to get into the right headspace. He thought of his memory loss. Beneath his surface was a burning pain of loneliness. He didn't understand where this fear came from, but he knew it was time to channel it into bravery.

Jerlone did not know the people of this kingdom, but he was going to protect them.

CHAPTER 51

THE HIDDEN CASTLE: EASTERN WALL
NIGHT

AT FIRST, DAGNARONE could hear birds chirping and critters scurrying throughout the woods. Since the enemy moved into place, her furry friends had been silenced. Now she heard an angry mob charging through nature with reckless abandon. They had no weapons, but they could tear the world apart with their hands.

Dagnarone was not feeling well. The butterflies in her stomach were so intense she thought she could faint. She needed a distraction to help her concentrate. Pulling out the flask, she took a swig. Her face clenched as she grunted, but seconds later, she felt better. Her confidence went up as she accepted her reality.

With this new state of mind, she looked around excitedly. The glowing trees captivated her. Even in this moment of terror, she was able to stop and appreciate the surrounding beauty. Nature was something worth fighting for.

Time to show everyone how much of a bruja you can be.

She sat with her legs crossed. Her spells required concentration, so she closed her eyes. She mumbled an incantation as she gestured with her hands. She was connecting with nature and spreading her energy through the roots.

The trees began to thrash about. The branches stretched and bashed the nearby soldiers. The little lights on the trees burned bright and shot out energy. A deadly white light soon flew every which way inside the woods.

Roots sprung from the ground and dragged the enemies to Hell. This section of the forest came alive in a terrible symphony of carnage.

Those who escaped the trees met a minefield of quicksand and ice. They sank into the ground and slipped into fire.

For someone claiming to be a pacifist, Dagnarone knew how to fight.

With the snap of her finger, the spells were in place. She could now focus her attention elsewhere.

Standing up, she grabbed her staff and gave it a twirl. The only other weapons she brought were the grenades, but it was too soon to use them.

She felt disgusted as the enemy fell into her traps. Within just a few days, a pacifist life was no longer possible. Here she was, a sorcerer of chaos, the antithesis of what she wanted to be. She knew there were people down there who did not deserve such a grisly fate.

Needing a reminder as to why this was worth it, she looked to the Throne Tower. Orville and Yuma were up there with likeminded people who deserved to have someone stand up for them. Those people didn't ask for war, but the invaders did. With that in mind, Dagnarone could live with her actions.

Even though she kept it together, she knew her soul would never be the same after this night.

After some time, breathing became difficult. There were too many spells cast and Dagnarone felt the strain. She had to pull back. With a wave of her hand, the trees stopped shooting energy. On the field, quicksand turned to mud. There may have been less danger, but there was still plenty of opportunity for the soldiers to meet their demise.

CHAPTER 52

THE HIDDEN CASTLE: WESTERN WALL
NIGHT

YAWONTE HELD HIS sword at the ready. Even though he would not use it for some time, the steel made him feel powerful. He no longer looked concerned, but instead looked like a man who'd fought a thousand battles and won them all.

The enemy continued to leak out of the forest. They were rowdier by the minute. Some who saw Yawonte attempted to throw rocks at him, but none hit their target. This angry horde was just as ready for this fight as the Mystics.

Throughout the day, Yawonte had found time to meditate. It was only ever for a few minutes, but that had been enough to center him. He wished he could squeeze one more in, but now was not the time. He could feel the explosion that was about to happen. If ever there was a time for spiritual guidance, it would have been then.

He paced and studied his enemies' movements, looking for some level of insight. What he saw was an untrained group of fools. They had numbers but no discernible skills.

Something whispered to Yawonte's soul, telling him it was time for battle.

"Today, we face our gauntlet, our crucible and maybe our destiny. It will be a challenge, but we will overcome." He pointed his sword at the invaders. "And today, you face your defeat. We be but a small group of Mystics, but we are mighty!"

He lowered his sword and took out a grenade. A red energy engulfed it, charging up the explosive. When tossed, a scarlet trail followed in its path. Upon impact, the grenade exploded. Orange and red flames erupted all around, but with his magic came an extra flair. Blue, green, and purple energy zipped around the destruction. Flames of multiple neon colors burned, taking out swaths of troops.

With this, the assault of grenades began.

CHAPTER 53

THE HIDDEN CASTLE: THRONE TOWER
NIGHT
. . . .

GENERAL AFUA JUMPED when the first explosion went off. She'd initially thought it was the enemy's attack. As she watched the scene unfold, she realized there was something different about the flames. They were more colorful than usual, and the fire lingered, burning in a different manner.

The citizens gathered around the windows to watch. The nervousness showed clearer and clearer on their faces the longer the explosions erupted. They continued to hold each other tight.

This went on for fifteen minutes, with each blast a more vivid shade than the last. It felt as though the fires of Hell were bursting all around them.

"Everyone, stay calm," General Afua instructed. She walked to the door, making sure all the locks were latched. "Even if, somehow, they get through the gate, there's no way they make it up here."

"That's a load of junk," one of the citizens yelled out. "What makes you so sure about that?"

Afua knew she couldn't make them believe, but she had to present an optimistic front. "I just have faith."

Everyone went back to the windows. Even after the explosions calmed down, they were still glued to their spots.

Their night of terror was just beginning.

CHAPTER 54

THE HIDDEN CASTLE: NORTHEAST WALL
NIGHT

SEPHRA WATCHED SOLDIERS march over the bodies of their fallen comrades. The storm of grenades did not turn them away. If anything, they screamed louder, as their thirst for blood swelled.

Before the battle, Sephra had lain quivers filled with arrows along the wall. She started in the south and slowly walked north, firing every few steps. As soon as one quiver ran out, a new one would be waiting by her feet. Hundreds of arrows had already slain foes, and there were still a thousand arrows left.

Her muscles ached, but she told herself it was easier than fighting them all by hand. Adding magic to the tip of every arrow was taxing. That energy would burst on impact and ricochet into others. It was a good way for one arrow to kill three or four soldiers, but if she kept that up, she would quickly run out of juice. She returned to firing without magic.

She gasped for air in between each shot. Every breath felt like it could be her last, but now was not her time to die.

Her willpower pushed her forward. She ignored the exhaustion and focused on winning.

Another mounted general rode toward the wall. The man aimed his bow at Sephra and fired. The arrow whizzed past her head, grabbing her full attention.

Sephra fired back but missed her target by centimeters.

The two exchanged blows with a ferocity rarely seen. For Sephra, this was like a ballet as she dodged and attacked. She would lean to the side a split second before an arrow whizzed past her. Seamlessly, she would grab an arrow and fire while diving away from another attack. Her legs lifted into the air as she twirled and fired an arrow at the same time.

Sephra was becoming frustrated with her target. The skilled warrior evaded each of her attacks and was always ready with a counter. Even when Sephra attached magic to an arrow, it still missed. The magic energy may have blown apart the ground, but the general was always just out of reach.

Reaching for an arrow, Sephra realized her quiver was empty. She looked to see her enemy fire at her. With a swipe of her hand, she grabbed the arrow midair. In one motion, she strung it in her bow and fired it back. With that, she performed a cartwheel maneuver that brought her over to the next quiver.

She strapped the new quiver to her back and began firing. Each shot missed. "Blast it!" Sephra screamed at her enemy. She was losing all patience in this fight, which only made her sloppy.

One lucky shot tagged Sephra in the shoulder. She grunted but did not scream. That was a satisfaction she would not allow her opponent. Dropping her weapon, she grabbed the arrow. She clenched down on her teeth until her mouth hurt. One big yank and her shoulder was free of that savagery.

As she evaded another attack, she grabbed her fallen weapon. In one fluid motion, she aimed the bloody arrow and fired.

Her enemy had no time to respond. He saw something coming toward him and then was on another plane of existence. His lifeless body fell to the ground, and the horse scurried into the woods.

From her pocket, Sephra pulled a small vial of cleansing alcohol to sterilize her wound. She cried out as she applied it. The burn was fierce, but she knew it would only be for a moment. She covered the spot with her other hand. A golden glow began to shine from her palm. Magic could not fully heal her, but it could help. These holistic spells were just a bandage, and tomorrow she would have to deal with the ramifications of this war.

She attempted to fire another arrow, but her injury threw her off. She missed the target, and her arm felt like it was about to rip off.

"You're gonna have to push through," Sephra mumbled to herself.

Blood ran down her arm while she grabbed another arrow. Her head felt light, and the world spun, but none of that mattered; she was determined to fire her weapon. Drawing the bowstring was the hardest feat she'd ever attempted. She held it there before letting go. All the pain rushed from her arm and into her head. It felt like she was on the verge of collapsing.

She watched as her arrow found its victim. It was reassuring that, even though she may be slower, she could still be just as accurate.

As long as she kept herself motivated, she could do her part. Turning around, she peered to the castle, wondering how Afua was holding up.

CHAPTER 55

THE HIDDEN CASTLE: WESTERN WALL
NIGHT
. . . .

YAWONTE WATCHED THE enemy climb toward him. Vines covered the western wall, but he was in complete control of them. They twirled around soldiers, squeezing them into submission while flinging others to the ground.

With great difficulty, the first invaders reached the top of the wall and rushed Yawonte.

Faster than a blink, Yawonte withdrew his sword and cut a man down. Before he could turn to his next attacker, he was struck on the back of the head. He stumbled forward and turned to his assailant.

Four soldiers stood ready for a fight. One held a billy club, but the others were unarmed. There was a bounce to their stance as they waited for the fight to commence.

Yawonte leapt forward, and with two wide slices of his sword, cut the four down. The dead did not suffer before dying, for the Mystic knew exactly where to strike. With a pile of enemy smote at his feet, the man felt humbled. Their ghastly faces reminded him of the human cost of war. They may have been his enemies, but their lives were still precious.

More soldiers scurried atop the wall. Seeing their fallen comrades proved Yawonte was a foe they could not best. No one else attacked him; instead, they fled down into the city streets.

Yawonte felt it was time and sheathed his sword and use his magic.

He leaned over the wall and saw hundreds of soldiers climbing it.

Grabbing hold of a vine, he mumbled a spell, and his hand began to glow orange.

When he removed his hand, a flame burned forth. This was not a typical fire—it blazed shades of purple and blue inside the red inferno. The more it spread, the more it changed color. It was hypnotic and threatening all at once.

Soldiers attempted to jump from the vines, but many found themselves crippled from the fall. Still, that was a better fate than those cooked alive.

Even atop the wall, the heat was overpowering. Yawonte stepped back and covered his eyes. He was blinded by the light, and the smoke clouded his vision.

The vines burned to a crisp within minutes. While incinerating, the flame latched onto the wall itself. Yawonte noticed this and ran to extinguish it. As soon as he was done there, another spot caught fire. This blaze would not stay contained, endangering the whole wall.

"Oh dear. This is no good at all."

He ran to the next renegade fire and doused it with magic. He knew he needed a better strategy and racked his brain for a solution.

A spell came to him that would stop the fire from advancing. The wall would burn, and he hoped the structure could handle the heat. After the battle, he could finish extinguishing everything and help the citizens repair their damaged property.

He twirled his hands and chanted ancient words of magic. The flame burned brighter. He shook his head, realizing that was not helpful.

"Wrong way," he corrected himself.

The right enchantment wasn't coming to him. He tried a few variations of what he thought was correct, but to no avail. He was sure the frustration was clear on his face.

Finally, it occurred to him. He screamed the ancient words, and a blue wave of energy shot from his hands. It rippled across the wall, containing the fire. Everything still burned brightly, but it would not spread into the kingdom.

CHAPTER 56

THE HIDDEN CASTLE: EASTERN WALL
NIGHT
• •

DAGNARONE DID THE most while doing the least. She sat with her legs crossed and eyes closed. A constant flow of energy emanated from her, which was exhausting. Concentration was key in maintaining her enchantments. Staying off her feet helped keep that focus.

It was as if she were a master of the elements. The trees fought as though they were soldiers. Roots strangled the life out of their opponents and broke their bones. Wind howled with a ferocity few could push against. The ground even opened up, swallowing a platoon or two.

Dagnarone was the architect of this pandemonium, and she did not plan to let up.

A projectile flew toward her. Inches before contact, she shifted her torso to the left. The arrow flew past her face, and she did not flinch. It was as if her body was on autopilot. She knew what to do and would not be stopped.

Four soldiers made their way past her spells. With claws on their hands, they scaled the wall. Dagnarone was unaware of this. She had so many plates spinning, they were able to sneak past her senses.

When the four reached the top of the wall, they saw Dagnarone in her meditative state and went for the attack.

The first assailant tackled her, disrupting the spells. With the battlefield quiet for the first time, the troops rallied.

Dagnarone was pinned to the ground, her enemy pummeling her. She took two punches to the jaw that she wasn't expecting. She gritted her teeth and scrunched her face, bracing for the next impact. Now, each strike was just fueling her.

She reached for her staff, but it was just out of reach. The tips of her fingers could touch it, but she was unable to make it roll toward her. She felt the kick of another enemy, all while her main opponent continued to hit her. Calling upon a smidge of angry magic, the weapon rolled into her hand. With a wide swipe, she bashed her opponents away from her.

She stood and twirled her staff, feeling a familiar tingle in her hands. This weapon was ready to work with her.

Twelve soldiers were now on the scene. They stared her down, and she glared right back.

The aftertaste of booze still lingered in her mouth. The sluggish effects of the poison were in full swing, but she was ready for a fight.

The enemy attacked Dagnarone with their metal claws. Slicing and dicing, every movement more acrobatic than the last.

Dagnarone fought back but still took a scratching. The claws ripped at her arms and shoulders, making her a bloody mess. The searing pain made it hard for her to keep a rhythm. Even though she had plenty of targets, she couldn't hit anything. After minutes of failure, she stumbled back to reset herself.

The twelve approached her, smirking like devils.

Dagnarone spit up blood and wiped her mouth. She was not bothered by that, because she was too focused on her incoming attackers. Her body hurt because of them, and she planned to make them hurt just as much.

She twirled her staff again, this time with more ferocity. A red energy covered the weapon as she stood at the ready.

With a skip forward, Dagnarone unleashed a flurry of strikes. The staff moved on instinct. The next attack started before she was even aware of it. She smacked and jabbed the twelve repeatedly. With the aid of her magic, she ended their lives without even intending to.

She stood victorious among the dead. Her breathing picked up, and she was soon close to hyperventilating. Guilt washed over her and burrowed into her soul. This was the first time she had killed someone up close. Death was different once she could see the details in their face. The consequences of her actions felt real—horrific—and she could only wonder what it was like for those on the battlefield.

Needing a reminder of what she was fighting for, she turned to look at the throne tower. Thinking of good people like Orville and Yuma helped calm her nerves. If she were not there to stop these invaders, then innocent people would die.

Looking back toward the battlefield, she saw her traps stopped. With the swirl of her hand the destruction flared up once more. Hoping to avoid more close encounters, she turned up the heat. Towering over her enemies, she unleashed her inner witch.

CHAPTER 57

THE HIDDEN CASTLE: NORTHWEST WALL
NIGHT

GALA STRUGGLED TO keep up.

The battle raged for hours, yet the enemy was not letting up. They had no qualms trampling the fallen to make gains on the battlefield. They screamed obscenities into the night as they raged forth.

Gala had enjoyed watching the grenades go off. He'd found some joy in annihilating his foes with explosions. Also, that tactic was easy.

Now, he was conjuring energy and shooting it from his pistol. He leaned over the wall and aimed, taking out soldiers one at a time. This was a lot more exhausting than the explosions. Every shot drained him. Needing a minute and a half to recover wasn't uncommon, but he knew this pace was too slow.

Gala turned around to see how the others were doing. There was a lot of neon energy flying through the sky. Those powerful attacks made him feel inadequate. He reminded himself he was still learning and it was okay if it took him time.

A grappling hook caught the edge of the wall, followed by a few more. Soldiers were successfully climbing.

Gala rolled his eyes and grumbled. He shot the rope off a grapple and watched the soldier plummet.

One soldier reached the top of the wall and charged Gala. The two tussled until Gala got the upper hand and tossed him over the edge.

As another soldier approached the top, Gala punched him in the face, and he dropped.

Gala ran along the wall, shooting ropes off grapples. Those who made it to the top had him to contend with, and he was in no mood for them. Gala took out his whip and struck an incoming group. One soldier dodged the attack and walloped Gala right in the face. Retribution came with the shot of his pistol. The soldier dropped never to rise again.

Of all the damned places to be tonight. Gala rubbed his chin.

More and more soldiers breached the wall. Once atop, they jumped into the city to run amok.

Looking toward his feet, Gala found a miracle: an unused grenade. With great speed, he grabbed it and removed the pin. He scanned the battlefield for the best target. A small crowd moved toward the wall, and Gala set his sights on them. He pulled his arm back and adjusted his aim.

As Gala was about to toss the grenade, a soldier slammed into him. The explosive dropped and fell off the wall. When it landed on the soil, it erupted upon impact.

The ground beneath Gala burst, tossing him to his right. Brick and mortar littered the air. The scene was pure chaos, as nobody could comprehend what had really happened.

To Gala's surprise, he stayed atop the wall. He was covered in concrete and dust, but he was still in one piece. His head was in a daze, and everything spun. A ringing blared through his ears unlike any before. He was in no shape to fight a war.

The wall now had a massive hole in it. The debris created a slope, which soldiers used to their advantage. It was not the smoothest path, but it was easier than climbing with a grappling hook. The invaders were bloodthirsty and would go any lengths to quench their wicked desires.

Gala attempted to stand but stumbled. A few soldiers saw this opportunity and ran toward him. Gala knew he did not have enough time and panic set in. With a burst of energy, he made it to his feet. He blindly pointed his pistol and pulled the trigger. His magic bullet skimmed one of his attackers. Gala pulled the trigger a few more times, each shot making contact.

Six enemies surrounded Gala. No one wanted to make the first move.

To Gala's left was the city. From the corner of his eye, he could see a flagpole hanging off a building. Just past that was a rooftop.

An idea came to him, but it wouldn't be easy to execute.

Slowly, he reached for his whip. "You just had to come here to be savages, didn't ya?" Gala brandished his pistol about, trying to grab their attention. "Y'all wanna get nuts?" Gala screamed, selling his desperation. "Then, let's do this!"

Gala fired his pistol, striking one of the soldiers. With lightning quick reflexes, he dashed to his left and snapped his whip. It wrapped around the flagpole, and he seamlessly swung to a nearby rooftop.

As soon as his feet touched solid ground, Gala turned and fired his pistol.

There were soldiers who attempted to jump after him only to find themselves crashing into the streets below.

With a moment's reprieve, Gala took some time to breathe. He was exhausted, and it didn't look like things were about to get easier.

He noticed the western wall ablaze and cocked his head, not sure how he missed that earlier. He wasn't sure how the enemy lit bricks on fire, but he feared what that meant.

With the wall in shambles, it was time to assemble at the throne tower.

CHAPTER 58

THE HIDDEN CASTLE: SOUTHERN WALL
NIGHT

JERLONE WAVED HIS wand like a conductor. Energy gushed from the weapon and onto the battlefield, decimating dozens. With his strength annihilated, it was hard to even keep hold of the tiny wand. Heavy pants escaped his lungs while his muscles desperately yearned to collapse.

Below, the enemy chipped away at the gate. Most of the night had passed, and they'd made a significant dent. Hooks pried into the wood had torn chunks apart. Battering rams slammed into the doors, weakening the structure. It wouldn't be long before their weapons broke through.

A general sauntered around the battlefield, taunting Jerlone. The man lumbered over seven feet and weighed hundreds and hundreds of pounds. He was the constant target of attacks, yet he somehow managed to survive. His swiftness continued to come as a surprise. He leapt through the air and dodged explosions like a child playing tag. Derogatory language spewed from his mouth to motivate the troops. On his back was an ax, and he looked desperate to use it.

Jerlone took in all the destruction. That small piece of land used to be beautiful; now it was dirt and divots. He may not have had the appreciation for the environment that Dagnarone did, but it still enraged him to see it like that. To him, it was a visual representation of those monsters. He hated that there were people willing to invade someone's home and destroy everything beautiful just to spite them. He had seen it too much in past lives, and it was a pattern that never ceased.

The gate was ready to fall, and Jerlone needed a new tactic. He had to give the magic a rest and allow it to recharge. Looking at his cache of weapons, he once again saw the ax. The steel spoke to him, crying out to be used. Jerlone grasped it tight. Even though his muscles were sore, he could see himself using that weapon. A smile crept across his face.

By his feet sat a bundle of rope. One end was tied to a pillar and the other left untethered. Jerlone took the rope and threw it over the edge. With one hand, he slid down and landed on the battlefield with a great thud.

One heave of his ax and many a foe fell. His rampage cleared the surrounding enemies and shattered battering rams. When all was done, Jerlone stood back against the wall.

With a thousand enemies before him, Jerlone was not scared. He waved his weapon, confident no one would be able to best him.

The general stepped forward. He repeatedly smashed his fists together as an intimidation tactic. Grunts and other ungodly noises bellowed from his gut. With one final gesture, he grabbed his own ax, ready to cleave Jerlone in two. "I am General Vi, and I have never lost a fight," Vi snarled. "I don't intend to lose one now." Drool dripped out the side of his leathery mouth. "I was the great victor of the Whirring War and the Battle of Cannons. I have eaten baby dragons alive! You think one magical *fool* can stop me?"

As the two challengers stepped into the arena, the battlefield went quiet.

Jerlone was about to duel one of that world's most skilled warriors and thought nothing of it. It didn't matter how tall, broad, or fast the General was, Jerlone had all the confidence in the world going into the fight. He didn't expect to slay his foe immediately, but in the end, he knew he would walk out the victor. He was so cocky he didn't even plan to use his wand. His ego wouldn't allow it. He wanted to show this man he was just as much a physical threat as he was a magical threat.

The combatants rushed each other and wasted no time before exchanging blows. It was not a fast fight. Each swing of their ax was concise and with power. Metal clanged as the weapons clashed.

Vi clipped Jerlone, but that didn't slow him down. It was just a little blood running down his side; it was manageable. As long as his limbs were attached, he wouldn't back down.

General Vi jabbed his ax's handle into Jerlone's face, knocking the Mystic backwards. Another chop caused Jerlone to slip and fall in the mud. Not wasting a second, Vi jumped atop Jerlone and pinned him down.

It was hard for onlookers to tell exactly what was happening while the men were on the ground. It was clear Vi had the upper hand, though. The general wrestled Jerlone's arm and locked it behind his back. Then, he shoved Jerlone's face in the dirt for further insult.

Jerlone could barely breathe. Mud entered his mouth as he struggled to free himself of the brute.

The wand called to Jerlone. It would be an easy way to win that fight, but he wanted to beat his opponent with fisticuffs. As his face was pushed deeper into the soil, he realized his wishes were no longer a realty.

With great effort, Jerlone shimmied his other hand and grabbed hold of the wand. Then, with all his might, he pushed back against his enemy and freed himself.

Mud covered his eyes, but Jerlone did not let that slow him down. He stood and fired his wand at Vi.

There was a loud, wooden crack, followed by a crash.

Jerlone wiped the mud from his face to see his attack had missed Vi. Instead, he'd delivered the finishing blow to the city's gate. Splinters covered the ground, and anyone could easily walk into the city now.

Jerlone's spirit dropped upon realizing what he did. The enemy swarmed past him. No one bothered to attack him—and why would they, since he finished off the gate for them?

General Vi, on the other hand, had unfinished business. Going against the crowd, he approached Jerlone as though he were a hundred feet tall and indestructible. He lifted his ax, ready to deliver the killing blow.

Jerlone had bigger issues than Vi. On instinct, he grabbed his wand and blasted the opponent into the next life. Seconds later, his feet trampled the fascist's carcass.

With a slight tug of the rope, Jerlone propelled back to the top of the wall. He was too devastated to run right into battle. Panicked, he sat on the ground and watched the kingdom fall apart.

The western wall was ablaze, the northeastern wall had a massive gap in it, and now the southern gate was wide open for anyone to enter. Jerlone did not think things were looking good for them as a whole.

Like a wave, invaders flooded the city streets. They seemed to have no plan outside of causing chaos. They smashed windows and toppled monuments. Their screams echoed throughout the streets. There was no stopping them now.

Jerlone was overwhelmed. Any optimism fled his being. He stood there, taking in all the carnage, too indecisive to take action.

Death felt inevitable. Only upon acknowledging this did his attitude change. He knew, even if he died, his spirit would carry on. A smile spread across his face. There was nothing he couldn't do.

Jerlone jumped off the wall and landed in the city. He fired off quick, consecutive shots from his wand. The invaders attempted to avoid the attacks, but with little success. Pushed to the limit, he drained himself. His whole body ached, and even standing became a challenge.

One particularly brave soldier caught this moment of weakness and rushed the magic man. Jerlone saw the attack coming and was able to brace himself. The soldier crashed into him, but the Mystic did not budge. Jerlone glared at the soldier and then ended it. He did not need the assistance of magic then; his hands were enough.

Before Jerlone could celebrate his victory, he was attacked again. This time, he did not see the assailant coming. Suddenly, he was on the ground receiving an outbreak of kicks.

A staff whacked the soldier in the head, dropping them.

"Dag?" Jerlone questioned. Everything was spinning, and his vision was blurry.

"Looked like you could use some help," Dagnarone reached down and hoisted him up.

"This is all my fault. My magic went awry and blew up the gate. Now the castle is going to fall." He looked around, dismayed. "I did this."

"Stop being so dramatic. It's not *all* your fault. Did you see Yawonte's wall is on fire?"

"I saw."

"Even I screwed up. I conjured a spell wrong, and the trees betrayed me. They extended their branches and got the enemy atop my wall. I had to flee. That's why I'm here."

Jerlone leaned in and sniffed her breath. "You been drinking?"

"Well, uh … a little sip here and there to help me. Although, I think that may have contributed to the trees betraying me."

Jerlone chuckled. "Alright, let's give this a try then. And please, don't make nature betray us."

Dagnarone and Jerlone fought side by side, a dance of war and destruction. Magic flew like a wave washing over the attackers. Bright orbs of blue, green, and red poured from the Mystics and did not let up. The spells were exhausting, but effective.

Dagnarone gestured her arm up, and soldiers flew into the air. The ground split, and they crashed down into the abyss.

"You're really gonna destroy their roads by doing that," Jerlone remarked.

"Give it a try," she replied.

Jerlone moved his arms, and a gust of wind blew from his palm. It crashed into a building, toppling it onto a troop of soldiers. The building lay in ruin, and a main road was now blocked.

"We're both probably causing just as much damage as they are," Dagnarone gestured to the soldiers running past them.

"Agreed," Jerlone looked at her. "I think it's time we head to the throne tower."

CHAPTER 59

THE HIDDEN CASTLE: THRONE TOWER
DAWN
• •

YAWONTE STOOD GUARD at the base of the throne tower. More soldiers arrived by the minute, but they posed no challenge for the Mystic of the Woods.

His blade cut the air, striking enemy after enemy. He had not conjured any magic for some time, as he was strong enough to fight without the aid of bewitchments.

As one battalion fell, another arrived. They charged through the decorative moat that surrounded the tower, refusing to let it slow them down.

Yawonte met them head-on, not allowing anyone a chance to gain their bearings. Like everyone else, he was exhausted. His form was sloppy, but he refused to acknowledge it, for then, it would become his reality. He pushed through any pain and kept fighting.

Things looked bleak when three soldiers overpowered him. They brought him down with their unrelenting attacks. He'd given them their opening, and they were taking full advantage.

Three shots rang out in the desolation of night.

The attackers fell.

Gala Goda walked over and offered Yawonte a hand.

Too embarrassed to make eye contact, Yawonte stood without aid. Of all the people to save him, why did it have to be Gala? In fact, he didn't even think Gala would still be alive at this point.

"Why is your wall on fire?" Gala asked.

"A spell got out of hand," Yawonte said with a modicum of shame.

"Shouldn't you extinguish it? Looks like it's gonna burn the whole place down." Even at the throne tower, they stood in the fire's orange glow and felt the heat.

"Don't worry," Yawonte assured Gala, "the fire is contained."

"Huh? What do you mean? You can't contain fire!"

"I said it's contained!" Yawonte walked past Gala, watching the next wave of attackers approach. "Get ready. You take the three on the left and I'll take the four on the right."

As soon as the soldiers arrived, Yawonte and Gala both went to their right. They bumped into each other and fumbled around. Both looked annoyed as their enemies delivered a few painful punches.

"Gala!" Yawonte scolded.

"I thought you meant *their* left, not ours!" Gala retorted.

"Why would you think that?"

"I don't know, I guess I just got mixed up after staying up all night and fighting a war by myself!"

"Behind you!" Yawonte warned.

Gala turned right as a fist hit him in the face. He stumbled backwards and tripped over other dead soldiers. He tried rolling to recover but only got more tangled in the deceased. "Gross … gross … gross," he could be heard mumbling to himself. As soon as he regained his balance, he cracked his whip, clearly ready for some retribution.

As more enemies arrived, Yawonte and Gala fought side by side. They were often too close for comfort, knocking into one another and bickering. If success was their objective, they worked against that common goal.

Gala snapped his whip and accidentally tangled it around Yawonte's sword. "Stop getting in my way!" Gala hollered with a shove.

"You're the one in my way!" Yawonte barked back. "Your form is so sloppy, it's affecting others! This is why I stressed practicing!"

"Hey, I got plenty of practice! My whole life's been practice for this moment!" Gala pointed at Yawonte.

"Then why aren't you doing better?"

"You lit a wall on fire!"

"And you blew up a portion of yours!"

Six soldiers approached, all with sharp weapons. With the heroes arguing, the villains moved about unseen. Setting themselves up for the kill strike, they were about to achieve their first victory.

Arrows struck three of the soldiers. The survivors looked around for the attacker. Charging at them was Sephra, her sai ready to attack.

Yawonte and Gala stopped arguing and looked at the scene unfolding.

"Oh, uh … thanks, Seph." Gala scratched the back of his head, embarrassed to have missed them.

"You can't be like that." Sephra approached them. "You two are not in competition with each other!" She stood between them. "If we don't work together, then we aren't going to win."

"You're right." Yawonte turned toward Gala and put out his hand. Sephra would always get through to him. If she saw something one way, he didn't find it worth putting up a fight. "I am sorry. You're a skilled warrior, and I shouldn't doubt your abilities."

Gala did a double-take, then cautiously shook. "Don't worry about it. Besides, I do get my hat handed to me enough. You know, when this is all over, I'd love for you to teach me a thing or two."

With a smile, Yawonte put it behind him. But the smile did not last long. "Get down," Yawonte warned.

Without question, Gala dropped to the ground.

Yawonte lifted his hand and shot a red globe at an incoming wave of attackers. They fell among the rest.

• • • •

The enemy arrived with greater frequency and numbers, but Sephra led Gala and Yawonte in the fight and managed to hold the fort.

Sephra looked past the bridge and saw Jerlone and Dagnarone running toward them. As soon as Dagnarone and Jerlone crossed the bridge, they turned and threw their arms up. A blue energy rose from the moat, creating a shield around the throne tower. There was an eerie, gentle glow from the spell. Even the acoustics altered, and the outside world sounded muffled.

Inside the blue hue, the Mystics stood alone before the throne door.

"What's going on?" Sephra asked.

"The army is on its way," Dagnarone replied.

"We've already been fighting them." Yawonte sheathed his sword.

"Not this many," Jerlone cautioned.

"How long can you hold the shield?" Gala asked.

"Just long enough for us to catch our breath and form a plan."

Everyone turned to Sephra, looking for guidance. Whether or not she was ready to lead them, now was the time. Looking up to the tower, she thought of the innocents up there and the terror they must be experiencing in that moment. Death was coming for them, and all they could do was sit back and watch, but Sephra wouldn't allow that to happen. She looked back down at her companions and spoke with conviction. "The plan's simple," she said. "We protect these people *at all cost*! If this door breaks, then we fight all the way up the stairs! Should our enemy make it into the throne, then we fight them there too! We *only* stop if we die!"

The army arrived and scratched at the shield. The rapacious crowd was formed of a variety of people, some young and others old. They chanted for blood and desecrated all they touched. They harbored the deadliest weapon of all, hatred.

Sephra turned to find the enemy all around them. Even though she knew there were less soldiers after the night's battle, it didn't feel that way. Being on the ground with them made the army seem even more imposing. It didn't matter if they had already lost thousands; there were still thousands more.

This was Sephra's moment to show the world what she was made of. Everything led to this. Her heart raced as a surge of courage rejuvenated her.

"This is it." She stepped before her companions. "Yes, we are outnumbered, but DO NOT DESPAIR!" She stressed each word. "We're exhausted, hurting; we've been hit and can barely stand, but we're going to keep fighting because that's what we do! We push through the pain and don't stop! If we lose this day, then these people die, and I am NOT going to let that happen! We are Mystics! We have the power to dazzle this world into greatness, and we will NOT be defeated by a hateful mob!" She looked each of them in the eye. "When the shield drops, we climb our way out of this hell by showing them WHO WE ARE! The throne WILL NOT fall while we stand!" She armed an arrow into her bow. *"NOW, LET US FIGHT!"*

The shield dropped, and the enemy charged.

By no choice of their own, the Mystics scattered and left the door unguarded. This gave the enemy an opportunity to chip away at it. With their ferocity it would only take minutes for them to succeed.

Sephra used her sai with precision and speed. All it took was one hit to fell a foe. She coupled red magic onto her blades as they twirled through the air, stabbing anyone who got too close.

With one wrong move, Sephra stumbled, allowing a soldier the advantage. She took the hits in stride but struggled to regain her balance. The enemy swarmed. She was pushed to the ground as more flocked her.

Jerlone saw Sephra's predicament and went to help. With a flick of his wrist, magic shot from his wand, demolishing the attackers. He ran to her side and helped her up.

"Appreciate it," Sephra thanked him.

"Anytime," Jerlone responded with a smile.

• • • •

The enemy jumped into the moat to cross faster. It was seven feet deep with only three feet of water. Soldiers piled atop one another, trying to gain the leverage needed to pass through.

Dagnarone saw an opportunity. She swirled her hand, and a red mist materialized around her palm. With a slight push of her arm, she turned the water to lava.

Flames and screams shot from the moat. The trench was like Hell had cracked open and the damned were vying to escape. The heat was unbearable. Even though the enemy was being cooked alive, this did not stop them from charging forth.

Dagnarone watched the inferno go awry. The fire spread beyond the moat, setting ablaze the ground they stood on. A panicked yelp leapt from her mouth. She tried casting a spell to extinguish it, but to no avail.

Feet from her, Yawonte fought off four soldiers. From the corner of his eye, he noticed the ground burning. It demanded his attention, so with two swipes of his sword, he ended his duel. "I see you started a fire," Yawonte yelled to Dagnarone.

"Yes, and nothing I'm doing is putting it out!" Dagnarone was in full-blown panic. Sweat mopped her forehead. She'd never looked so rough before.

"Well, you are in luck. I have some experience with fires." Yawonte sheathed his sword and put his hands up.

Five loud bangs shot out behind them. Dagnarone turned to see Gala holding off incoming attackers.

Yawonte cast his spell, dousing the flames in magic. The lava cooled and dried, forever ruining the moat.

Dagnarone was relieved until she saw the worst thing possible. The enemy had ripped off the door to the throne tower and were about to ascend the stairs.

CHAPTER 60

THE HIDDEN CASTLE: THRONE ROOM
DAWN

SEPHRA SUMMONED A spell that knocked all enemies from her path. With that, she was able to run onto the stairwell and get in front of the invading army. Her companions were by her side, trying to keep up with her.

There was enough space in the stairwell for the five of them to fight side by side. Sephra took a few steps before them, each hand holding a sai that was drenched in blood.

The enemy filed into the wide chamber, trapping the Mystics. They did not strike; they stopped and waited for the battle to commence.

Sephra looked behind her left shoulder and saw Gala crack his whip. Dagnarone was next to him, twirling her staff. They both seemed ready for the fight. On her other side, Yawonte stood with his sword at the ready while red energy crackled around Jerlone's wand.

When Sephra turned her attention back to the enemy, she was without fear. She scraped her blades against each other. The screeching of metal was like a bell signifying the start of the fight.

The soldiers charged, and the battle began anew.

The Mystics' neon energy clouded the air in a haze. Bodies crashed into walls, taking out bricks. Limbs were severed, and people were trampled. No matter how much damage they took, the army kept pushing forward. They refused to stop.

Sephra worried most about Gala. It seemed like he could barely stand, and all his appendages looked akin to wet noodles. Every time she turned his way, he was getting punched, but she noticed that only motivated him. Anyone who hit him always got shot with a magic bullet. The more she saw this, the more she rooted for him to get hurt.

As the enemy continued to push forward, the Mystics began to slowly back up the stairs. They held their ground as long as they could but eventually had to relent.

Sephra felt like her heels were on fire and ready to snap. She wanted to collapse but refused to let that pain get to her. She screamed in the face of her enemy and pushed them back down the stairs.

"Keep fighting!" Sephra yelled to motivate her troops. Her shoulder was still bleeding from the arrow that had pierced it earlier. When she used that arm, it felt as though it were about to fall off. She reveled in the pain, using it to fuel each attack.

A soldier got the upper hand and pushed Sephra back a few steps. She tripped and landed on her back. Before she could respond, Dagnarone grabbed her arm and hoisted her back to her feet. As she readjusted herself, Dagnarone held off a few attackers using her staff and magic. As one soldier was about to attack an unsuspecting Dagnarone, Sephra leapt back into action. She took care of the assailant and fought by her friend's side.

Blood splattered the carpets and walls, while piles of bodies littered the floor.

The climb backward was never-ending and the most exhausting part of the night. Sephra couldn't tell how long they had been at it. She thought there was still some ways to go, but when she turned and saw the throne room door, she gasped. They were much closer than she'd expected, and there was still a sea of enemies before them.

Yawonte slashed his sword and ended up next to Sephra. She flicked red energy onto his blade as it swung through the air, cutting down almost a dozen soldiers. Fighting beside him felt right. She knew when to move one way so he could strike the other way. During a quick reprieve, Sephra saw Yawonte rub his ribs and wince in pain.

After a few more minutes of fighting, Sephra found her back against the throne room door. Her friends were by her side, but the enemy was still charging toward them. With a whip of her hand, a familiar blue energy materialized between them and the invaders.

The metallic door chilled her back. The steel felt heavy, yet delicate at the same time.

All she could see coming upon the stairs were soldiers. Every step was filled with six people crammed together. It seemed unreal that anyone could move in that abyss of people.

Keeping the shield up was difficult. Sephra didn't know how long it would last. The enemy slammed into it repeatedly, making it more of a challenge to stabilize. She flexed all her magic muscles to keep that blue energy alive, yet the strain was extensive. It was like holding something up while feeling its crushing pressure. Then, without warning, the tension let up.

Sephra turned and saw Jerlone next to her. She realized he was helping her channel the spell. Together, it was a much easier task, even with the repeated pounding of the enemy. Sweat mopped his forehead but he kept his attention forward. This dedication inspired Sephra, and she put a little more into her flex.

The enemy was not letting up. If anything, they were more coordinated than before. Together, they heaved and threw all their weight at once.

The Mystics held tight as their shield pushed them back. They squished against the throne doors. When the enemy crashed into them again, the throne doors cracked open for a second.

Sephra was desperate to think of a plan to get them out of this, but nothing was coming to mind. The only thing they could do was fight their way out. She started to fear they might lose the day. Then, she told herself to replace that fear with courage.

Again, the enemy crashed into the shield, and the throne door popped open. The screams of the citizens escaped into the hallway.

One more coordinated strike and the Mystics were pushed into the throne room. Their shield shattered and the doors swung wide open.

Sephra stumbled into the room and heard a thousand screams. She turned to see the innocent people in the back of the room huddled together. Orville and Yuma stood by the front, looking just as worried and desperate as everyone else.

The enemy sauntered into the room.

Sephra regained her footing and looked to her companions. Seeing them by her side inspired her. "Don't stop now!" She screamed her battle cry and ran toward the enemy. "DON'T STOP NOW!"

They charged behind her, knowing this was their moment.

Magic erupted into the hallway as the Mystics slashed and bashed their way down the stairwell. Sephra led the team, now playing offense instead of defense.

The enemy did not try to flee. They attempted to meet their match head-on, but found very little luck. The Mystics were an unstoppable force. Walls were decimated from the chaotic flurry of spells. The energy of the room changed, and it lent the Mystics more power than before.

When Sephra got halfway down the stairs, she thought they might actually win. There were less soldiers attacking her; more were trying to flee.

Gala pushed past Sephra, cracking his whip while magic bullets shot from his pistol. She didn't know where this burst of energy came from, but she was glad to see it. It was easy for her to underestimate Gala, but in this moment, he was putting up the fight of his life.

Dagnarone joined Gala, and the two took out hordes of soldiers. Dagnarone moved her staff like someone with a lifetime of experience. Neon magic shot from the tip and blasted enemies back. Her attacks were so powerful they made the ground shake.

Yawonte stepped next to Sephra with a smile on his face. His blade hit every target and did not stop moving. No matter where his blade swung, an enemy fell.

Sephra floated between enemies, never ceasing in her quest for justice. Her red cape flapped in the air, like a triumphant flag claiming victory. "KEEP FIGHTING!" Sephra screamed over and over. This was just as much to inspire herself as it was the others.

Jerlone conjured massive globes of energy from his wand. No enemy stood a chance against him. The man no longer even appeared tired, and he summoned the spells with ease. While everyone was running around him, he casually strolled down each step.

The sun was beginning to peek over the horizon. The light leaked through the windows and into the stairwell chamber.

Sephra and her companions were almost at the bottom of the tower. Their barrage was unrelenting and there was no end in sight.

The soldiers were no longer fighting back, most were trying to flee the mad Mystics. Even those not near the action were turning and running.

Sephra led her companions from the throne tower. Neon magic flew all around them in its various forms. The enemy continued to run and did not stop to look back.

Victory was theirs.

As the final monsters fled, Sephra put away her weapon. The rising sun felt warm on her face, and the morning air never smelled better. Looking around, she could certainly see destruction, but it was nothing that couldn't be rebuilt.

CHAPTER 61

THE HIDDEN CASTLE: DOWNTOWN
DAY

THE DEAD POLLUTED the streets.

Dagnarone couldn't take her eyes off the fallen, even though it made her stomach churn. Every face told a different story. These were people with goals and love and now none of that mattered. Their lives were wasted because they chose to follow hate. She questioned if she was any different from them.

There was a lot going on with her emotions, often changing by the second. Mostly, she felt the crushing weight of guilt. Her dignity was shattered after doing the one thing she swore not to in this life, and while there was some pride in saving the day, the cost was too great. This trauma would never leave her. These actions would forever plague her soul.

From the corner of her eye, Dagnarone saw Sephra walking toward her. There was a big smile on her face. It appeared as though Sephra felt no guilt for the casualties she committed.

"How are you, my friend?" Sephra put a hand on Dagnarone's shoulder.

Dagnarone kept her head down, staring at the corpses. She wanted to make it clear she was in no mood to celebrate. "I'm not my best."

"Do you want to talk about it?"

"Thank you, but I'm not ready yet. There's still a lot I need to process." Dagnarone finally looked Sephra in the eye. "And I'm not sure I'd choose you to talk with."

Sephra's smile faded, and her eyes narrowed as she bent her head. "I'm sorry I asked you to be a part of this." Her voice sounded sincere. "I— I never should have made you do anything you were against. Just know that, without you, we probably wouldn't have won."

Dagnarone hesitated before asking the next question, afraid of what the answer might be. "Let me ask you something. If you went back in time, would you ask me to do this again?"

There was a long pause before Sephra finally spoke. "Like I said, without you, I don't know if we would have won." They stared at each other, neither reacting. "Because of you, a lot of people survived."

They stood there, silent.

"That's what I thought," Dagnarone finally said. She was disappointed but not surprised.

At that moment, Yawonte walked over, covered in ash. Like Sephra, he, too, was smiling and reveling in their victory. "Ladies," he said, "General Afua will be arriving soon, and we need to discuss what comes next. The kingdom is still vulnerable, and their troops are a few days out. They will need protection and guidance even after they arrive. With no leader or clear heir to the throne, things could get out of line."

Sephra turned to Yawonte. "They're going to need a neutral body to help guide them into their next form of government. With this kingdom representing what it does, there will be many challengers, and with that will come much duplicity."

Dagnarone gave Yawonte a once-over. Gusts of wind were blowing the ash off of him and onto her. "I take it you extinguished the fire you started?" Dagnarone asked him.

"Yes," Yawonte said, blushing. "That was not my finest moment."

"I think you caused more property damage than the invaders."

"I know." Yawonte scratched the back of his head. "It won't be easy to explain when everyone returns."

"Maybe saving the castle will get you a pass." Dagnarone shrugged.

"That's what I'm hoping for."

"Although, it kind of feels like we inadvertently overthrew a government … doesn't it?"

"Coart was a victim of his own doing." Sephra shook her head. "If he'd stayed here, he would still be alive. Now, we can help them rebuild into something better—something stronger and more equal for everyone."

Gala and Jerlone had spent the morning piling bodies but were now en route to their friends. It was a warm day for that time of year. An autumnal smell was in the air, and the world felt perfect. Even with all the death surrounding them, everything looked bright and cheery.

Throughout his life, Gala had killed. It was never something he had done on the quick and easy. As far as he was concerned, everyone he'd offed had it coming. Sometimes, in life, you just have to lay a bastard out. He knew some of these victims didn't deserve it, but they'd made their choice. However, Gala wouldn't lose any sleep over what he'd done there.

To Gala's surprise, Jerlone had been quite chatty, but of course, he was pontificating about the morality of what they had done. It wasn't a fun conversation for Gala, nor was he an active participant.

"What disturbs me is the sense of familiarity," Jerlone droned on, "This was the first war I'm cognizant of, yet I don't feel bothered or traumatized. I'm not standing here shaking and worried about my soul being damned. What does that say about me? How can a person fall into reality and four days later almost win a battle singlehandedly? Is my existence purely to fight, and if it is, why am I cursed to that? I'm smart enough to know the terrors of war. I see how violence is like a snake eating its tail. War forever damns us to our selfish needs, and I see all of that … yet here I am."

"Yeah, that's something," Gala replied, having not paid attention to what was actually said. He couldn't stop thinking of Isra and didn't care about Jerlone's issues at that moment. All he wanted was to be on the beach with her.

Jerlone stared at Gala. "Thinking about that girl?"

"You know it. No way I can get there in time, and I've got no clue where she'll be after the festival. It sucks, and I'm feeling really sorry for myself, and I hope everyone else is too."

"You did save a lot of lives, though."

"Yeah, but I'd rather have—you know—she's so pretty and all …"

Jerlone gave him a blank expression. "I don't know what you're talking about."

Gala closed his eyes and shook his head. "Let's just say, as happy as I am to have saved the day, I'd rather be with her right now."

There was a pause.

"You think you saved the day?" Jerlone raised an eyebrow.

"Yeah," an overly confident Gala replied. "Well, okay, I know it was *all* of us, but the story sounds a lot better when I act like the main hero."

"That's insulting! You're not the main hero of this story!"

"If I'm not then who is?"

"I don't know," Jerlone shrugged, "but I'm glad to see your ego wasn't hurt in battle."

"*Anyway*, you should phrase it the same way when I'm not around. Take as much credit as you'd like in your retelling. We can both act like we never tried jumping ship."

"Actually, that's not too bad an idea." Jerlone chuckled and pointed at him.

"Hey." Gala stopped walking and Jerlone followed suit. The next words were hard to say, so they took some time coming out his mouth. "I'm sorry about getting off on the wrong foot." Gala finally looked him in the eye. "I was wrong to handle everything the way I did. I shouldn't have lied and, well, really dragged you into all this."

"It's okay, Gala, but I appreciate it." Jerlone put a hand on Gala's shoulder and smiled. "Honestly, it's probably a good thing you did drag me into this. Otherwise, I wouldn't have been here to save the day."

Gala laughed and felt closer to Jerlone than he'd ever expected. He threw his arm around Jerlone, and together, they continued walking down the street.

• • • •

Gala stood among the Mystics.

They were before the throne tower, the sun beaming a beautiful day down upon them. Even though the castle was in ruins, everyone looked happy to be alive.

Gala reached into his breast pocket and pulled out his flask. He took a swig, then offered it to Sephra.

"Gala!" Sephra scolded him. "The sun has been up for three hours!"

"Yeah, but we haven't slept all night." He smirked, took another shot, and offered it to her again.

Sephra stared at the flask, her expression hard to read. Finally, she grabbed it and took a long sip. "That's not bad."

"Got it from the Bewlay Brewery. Best booze in the world … or so their marketing says."

Sephra hiccupped and swayed. Gala suspected the effects were starting to hit her. Nevertheless, she addressed the group. "I'd like to talk about what comes next. First off, thank you all for accompanying me here. I know this wasn't what we expected, but if we weren't here, the world would be in ruins today." She looked at Dagnarone and Jerlone. "Still, it was wrong of me to strong-arm you into coming here. I know I put everyone through a lot, and I'm sorry." She took a breath. "I plan to stay here and help rebuild. When that's done, it's on to the next adventure. I'm not asking anyone to join me, but if you do wish to, you are more than welcome."

Sephra passed the flask to Jerlone. As soon as the liquor touched his lips, he recoiled. He spit out what he could in an overly dramatic fashion.

"Come on." Gala groaned. "It's not that bad."

"How do you do that?" Jerlone questioned.

"Give life another year and you'll be begging for it."

Jerlone shook his head and turned to Sephra. "I'm glad I was here in the moment of need, but I'm now needed elsewhere."

"I understand," Sephra nodded. "If you don't mind me asking, where do you plan to go?"

"I'll stay here for a bit and help in the cleanup. Once I get through the libraries here, it's back to Civis for me. The Church of the Wand is calling to me. I think there's a lot I can learn there about this world—and maybe even myself."

Sephra hugged Jerlone. "I hope it's everything you want it to be." She looked him in the eye. "Maybe one day we can reunite."

"I would like that." Jerlone and Sephra let go of one another. He passed the flask to Yawonte.

Yawonte sniffed the liquor before indulging. A smile spread across his face as the liquid poured into his mouth. "Ahh. Truly is a fine brew," he proclaimed.

"I know where to get good booze from," Gala gloated.

Yawonte turned his attention to Sephra. "It should come as no great surprise that I will stay by your side. My whole life has led to this adventure, and I could not be more excited."

"Me too," Sephra said with a twinkle in her eye. "Everything feels right when you're around."

"Agreed." Yawonte had never looked happier. The grizzled warrior was acting like some sensitive poet. Yawonte handed the flask to Dagnarone.

Dagnarone took the flask but shook her head. "Had way too much last night," she said.

"But it helped, didn't it?" Gala chimed in.

"Yeah, it got me in a fighting mood, but I'm not sure that's a good thing."

"You're standing here alive, ain't ya?"

"At least I got that going for me," Dagnarone mumbled. She turned to Sephra. "It's not my place to join you in your next adventure. You'll end up in some battle and that's not what I want. It's time for me to travel the world and bask in its beauty." She thought about it. "Maybe I'll meet someone special along the way and together we can help others in our own way."

"I understand," Sephra said. "Again, I'm sorry for the ways I've wronged you."

"Thank you." Dagnarone nodded. "I forgive you."

With that, all eyes were back on Gala. He took back his flask and finished it off.

"Well, Mr. Goda?" Sephra asked. "What's your next big adventure?"

Gala smirked. "I'd love to stay with ya, but I've gotta go see about a girl."

"I was hoping you'd say that." Yawonte beamed.

Befuddled, Gala said, "Okay, I know you and I didn't talk about her." He gave the others an evil glance.

"We didn't, but Sephra and I did. And Jerlone. Actually, Dagnarone and I discussed it too. Every new detail is exciting! You know, I'm a romantic at heart, and I'm really rooting for the two of you."

"Weird but also … if I'm being honest … a little flattering." Gala loved seeing people invested in his life. "Well, I hate to break your heart, but you may have to wait a bit to get a conclusion to the story. No way can I make it there in time, so I've actually gotta find her. Otherwise, I'll be waiting till next year."

"You don't know where she lives?" Dagnarone asked.

"She's a musician, so she's always on the road. Kinda like me," Gala said proudly.

"I don't think you're anywhere near as cool as a musician."

"No, I meant being on the road."

"Oh, you mean homeless? You like how she's also homeless."

"Neither of us are homeless!" Gala cried.

"Then what's your address?" Dagnarone quipped. Gala stared at her, unsure how to counter that argument. She added triumphantly, "My point exactly."

"It's crazy to think all this happened because I was trying to impress a girl," Gala said. "It really should stand as a cautionary tale to all men—"

"And lesbians," Dagnarone added. "Oh! When you see her, tell her she saved the world! That would be so romantic!"

"I could, but ..."

Dagnarone's face dropped. "You were going to tell her *you* saved the world, weren't you?"

Gala smirked. "Well, yeah. Otherwise, what would have been the point of doing all this?"

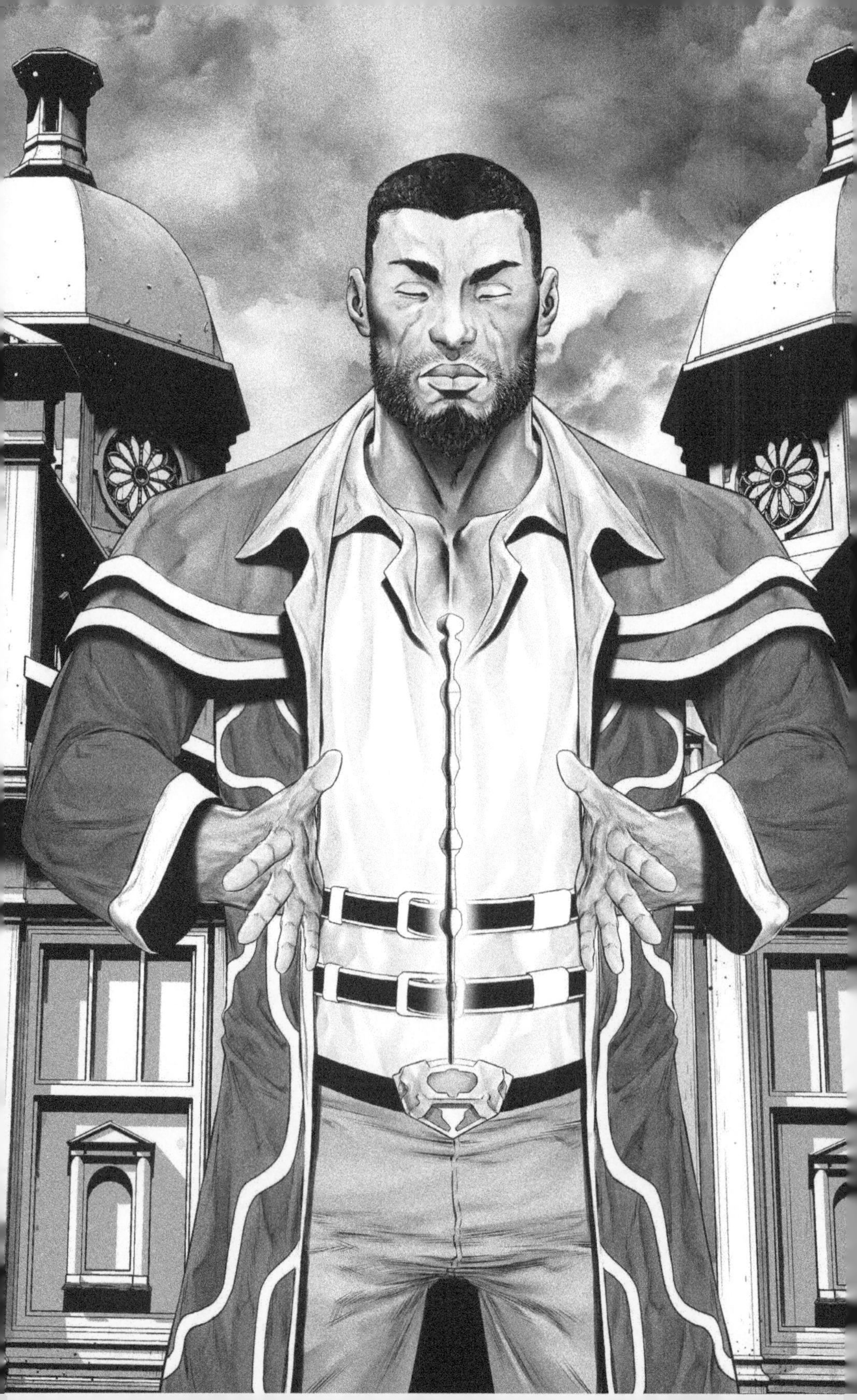

5
MYTHS

THE JADE FLOWER OF MAZ

EONS AGO, THE first flower blossomed in a secluded field. Its petals were blue, and there were small streaks of gold running throughout. It captivated anyone who walked past it, human and animal alike.

There was a power to this flower, and it caused people happiness.

For thousands of years, the flower flourished.

One day the Mystic, Maz, wandered into the field. She could immediately sense the flower and sought it out. Upon finding it, a great rush of dopamine coursed throughout her body. It was evident this was the flower's doing. As she looked around, the world was more beautiful than ever before.

Maz felt a calling and decided this was where she was needed. She did not want to disturb the flower, so she built a hut minutes away. Every day, she would come and visit it. There, she would meditate and search her soul for guidance. This meant something to her, even if she couldn't quite explain it.

Self-discovery was not her only objective when visiting the flower. She wanted to make sure it was protected as well. She knew that it would only be a matter of time before someone discovered the flower and tried to do something malicious. After years of nothing, she questioned if this was the right way for her to spend her time. Something still spoke to her and told her she was needed.

She would stay there for hundreds of years.

Eventually, the times changed and man invaded. This isolated field was the perfect place to dump their toxins. The pollution quickly seeped into the ground for the plants to absorb. Thick, green patches of grass became mushy tar. Everything warped as the ecosystem failed.

Maz asked the invaders to stop but they would not listen to her. Because of them, she spent all her time in the field, casting protection charms and curing ruined soil. Many nights, she was too exhausted to make her way home, and sleeping next to the flower became routine.

Maz fought this battle via nonviolent means for years.

Eventually, the flower began to wilt. This infuriated Maz. She tried everything she could to save it, but the healing spells did not take. She could feel the flower's fear and tried to console it, but even that was to no avail.

While out on a walk, an idea came to her. She raced back to the flower and conjured a spell. A blinding white light burned. When the light faded, it revealed the Jade Flower. Now crystallized, the flower was an image of its former, perfect self. Best of all, there was still an energy of love and excitement emanating from it.

Maz kept the flower for the remainder of her days.

At the end of her life, she built a temple. There, she put a curse on the flower. Only someone with a kind heart would be allowed to remove it. Their intentions had to be known, and the flower would judge if they were worthy.

It sat undisturbed for millennia.

• • • •

Time passed, and there were many who wanted the flower, including the Solum cult. They were greedy people who all proved unworthy. Like any obsessive, failure would not stop them. They became bitter as their indignation grew. Time and time again, they would repeat their trek to the flower in the hope that something would change, yet nothing ever did.

Growing up, Gala Goda's parents loved telling him myths surrounding Maz and the Jade Flower. They were nice foibles that didn't talk of derring-do. His parents always wanted to try to raid her ancient ruin and see if they were worthy of obtaining the flower. Sadly, they would not live long enough to go on that adventure.

Ten years after Gala's parents died, he decided to go for the flower. To successfully do this, he had to infiltrate the Solum cult. He was only a member for a few weeks, as he lied through every interaction he had.

In the dead of night, Gala went to the ancient ruin and made his way to the flower. When he grabbed the flower, he heard a voice. It asked him what he planned to do with it, and he answered. To his excitement, he was allowed to take it.

As Gala left the ruins, he encountered the cult. It was a fight he barely survived. He was battered and bloodied, but he ended up escaping with his prize.

Gala brought the flower to his parents' grave. Their headstone was at the world's biggest and nicest cemetery. Gala buried the flower between his parents. There, it would radiate joy and comfort to those grieving. Now, whenever they thought of their beloved ones, they would remember the good times and that everything was worthwhile.

BATTLE OF THE OMEGA SOLDIER

"**THE POWER OF** the Omega Soldier will save our kingdom!" Lord Fascio hailed throughout his land.

For decades, Fascio forced his scientist to study radiation. The hope was to weaponize it, all while evolving man at the same time. This project started fifty years back but did not find any success until ten years ago.

With a newfound formula, Fascio unleashed the Omega Bomb on his most loyal soldiers. This gas mutated them, increasing their height and strength. With this power, their stamina could now last them for hours. Those who survived the process were celebrated as heroes.

Fascio commissioned an elite death squad of Omega Soldiers for his most immoral missions. He dispatched them throughout the world to terrorize and assassinate. Their reputation grew at an alarming rate.

Two years later, things started to change. The soldier's skin was decomposing as their organs failed. Their bones were so brittle they snapped with a touch. When their minds started to go, they became more loyal. Soon, the soldiers could no longer feel pain. They would often push forward with limbs half attached without realizing.

They were walking nightmares.

Fascio demanded his scientists perfect the formula or they would die. Their efforts were in vain, and they were tortured for their failure. Still, wave after wave of faulty Omega Soldiers terrorized the world.

After months of terror, the world leaders reached out to Fascio. King

Coart, of the Mervelliere Kingdom, led the conversation petitioning for a peaceful solution. Fascio refused to deescalate. Eventually, it was decided that only battle would resolve the conflict. A time and date was set in the Desert of the Damned, as it was an unoccupied land.

Both kingdoms began a recruitment drive. Fascio enslaved subjects and forced them under the Omega Bomb. In Mervelliere, every family had a member who volunteered. Soon, all were enthralled in war.

• • • •

The Desert of the Damned was mostly populated by ghost towns. Out that way was also the entrance to the Sand Son Temple, and Gala Goda was on a mission to steal some treasure from there. Unbeknownst to him, war was about to break out around him.

When Gala walked out of the Sand Son Temple, he was in the middle of a battle. Monsters swarmed him as he dashed for an escape. He was fortunate to find a motorbike with gas in it. With that, he rode to safety.

The battle itself only lasted a few hours, but the Mervelliere army was decimated in one of their history's bloodiest attacks. Anyone who did survive became deathly ill from the offset radiation. Having made his escape as quick as he did, Gala avoided this terrible fate.

THE DIAMOND OF FARROKH

F**ARROKH WAS ONE** of the first Mystics. He was a musician who could play any instrument or sing any part. There was always a song in his heart.

Even though he fell before the Early Wars, he was not a soldier during them. He was one of the few Mystics who dedicated himself to his art rather than war. He was not someone to go on adventures to try to be heroic. All he wanted was to express himself.

He created the world's most famous melodies. Legend tells of him being the first music composer. His talent was not contained. He could write an opera or a pop song. Even outside of music, he was a renowned sculptor, and his poetry had a cult following.

Farrokh did not call a single place home. He was always on the road performing his music. During his travels, he fell in love with a man, Diamant. Their attraction was instantaneous, and their passion burned bright.

Diamant was a sculptor whose work was adored throughout hundreds of museums. There was no limit to his creativity. He shaped statues that were hundreds of feet tall and also painted elegant portraits. Like a sponge, he absorbed anything he could about the arts. The only person in the world who matched his talent was Farrokh.

Their life together was like a fairytale. They were loved by the masses. Their taste was elegant and lavish. For Farrokh, it felt like the honeymoon stage would never end.

One day, Farrokh was given a gift. Diamant presented him with a beautiful, green diamond. It was completely smooth, and all the sides were equal. Farrokh marveled at the delicate handcrafting it took to sculpt such a gem. To him, it was Diamant's most beautiful and honest work. The diamond was so magnificent, it was hard for Farrokh to accept it. He did not feel worthy of something so beautiful. Diamant assured him he was more than worthy.

Farrokh desperately tried to teach Diamant how to wield magic. No matter what argument he presented to Diamant, Farrokh was always shot down. Diamant did not want a steroid to boost his love of life. Farrokh begged him, wanting only for them to live long lives together. Still, Diamant refused, finding it unnatural.

Farrokh watched as Diamant got sick in his eighties. He wanted to heal his partner, but Diamant asked him not to. Farrokh wanted them to live long, beautiful lives together, but that was not in the cards. After months of struggle, Diamant passed comfortably in his sleep.

This was not easy for Farrokh to cope with. Being a Mystic, his life was doomed to be unnaturally long. Waiting hundreds or thousands of years to reunite with his lost love crippled him with depression. His sense of time was so warped that he was still in the honeymoon phase of the relationship. He was at a true loss. He wandered the world, unsure what to do. At times, he put himself in danger, since he no longer cared to live in this world. The only thing that gave him some purpose was singing.

Farrokh felt it his responsibility to tell the world Diamant's story. He composed music and brought the tale to life. Pubs and clubs wouldn't be big enough. He needed the masses to gather and pay their respect. Arenas were constructed to capture the majesty of what he was trying to convey. The show managed to deliver, and the people loved him.

Every performance started with him walking to the center of the stage and placing the diamond on a stool. He sang to it directly, as if it were his lost love. The diamond would glow and project images, creating a show in and of itself.

For a thousand years, he performed all over the world. His shows were sold out, even if it was the hundredth time he'd played in a city. The audience showered him with love and adoration, but he always felt alone. He met others, but they could never fill the void in his heart left by Diamant.

Over time, he found it hard to relate to others. He was isolated, and his depression grew. His human friends did not understand the power within him. They could not comprehend the world the same as him. Yet, when he talked to his fellow Mystics, they were too self-important to relate to him in matters of the heart. Everywhere he turned, he felt isolated.

One night while performing, something told Farrokh that his time was done. He sang his final song and announced his retirement. Later in life, he realized Diamant was channeling him to tell him to move on. Farrokh believed in the power of listening to Spirit and knew the choice was right.

During his retirement, he found himself at the Pimar Temple during the Reign of the Four Great Queens. He had known them since they were little princesses. All of them loved his music, and he adored them. They were the only politicians he ever trusted.

He spent years living among the students of the Temple. At times, the queens sought his wisdom, which was always vague and noncommittal. He did not like being asked about policy and war, as he feared causing more of it.

His time at the temple was healing. After many decades, he realized it was time to move on. As a parting gift, he left the Diamond of Farrokh there. He enchanted it with the love of music.

No one knows what happened to Farrokh after he left the temple. Legend tells of him occasionally performing in a bar. It was always unexpected and unannounced. It was the type of performance that happens once a decade, and it changes the people who witnessed it.

THE CHEST OF KING KHIRBY

WHEN THE WORLD began to rain Mystics, Khirby was one of the first to fall. He was incredibly powerful, but humble. His time was spent wandering the world, creating trinkets, and learning all he could about magic.

When the Early Wars began, he had no choice but to fight. He saw how fascism enveloped the world and knew it needed stopping. Aligning with the Mervelliere Kingdom, they fought for peace and equality throughout the land.

Khirby was a brawler. He didn't mind getting his hands dirty or jumping head-on into a fight. The man knew how to take a hit and keep pushing forward. Even though he was skilled at fighting, he did not enjoy doing it. As awful as he found the war, he knew it was necessary.

To aid the fight, Khirby assembled the Knights of Khirby. This group typically consisted of four soldiers who were the best of the best. They were the bravest and most selfless. These soldiers were loyal to Khirby and admired everything the man stood for. Together, they were able to take down dozens of enemy operations and free hundreds of prisoners of war.

Khirby had always been a crafter. During the war, he turned his talent toward weapons. He cursed them with the powers of the universe, creating the deadliest tools of all time. He forged a sword that could cut the land apart and a bow that could shoot an arrow halfway around the world. Nothing could stop their destruction.

Eventually, he realized how powerful his creations were and swore to lock them away. When asked why he would create something so powerful, he simply said he'd felt compelled to. He built a chest and gathered the weapons, planning to lock them away forever. This caused much controversy, but there were none who could stop him. His word was final.

The Early Wars raged for centuries. It would come to an end when Khirby led his knights against Beelzebub and her army of the damned. They fought along the Rocks of Rune in the Fire Seas of Plaisir. For three days they fought, neither giving an inch. Eventually, Khirby would gain the upper hand. With Beelzebub's surrender, the forces were vanquished and the wars came to an end.

Khirby continued his relationship with the Mervelliere Kingdom during the Great Settling. He helped expand the kingdom's borders by negotiating with other tribes and welcoming them into their community. King Stelen was not one to give others credit, and this was no exception. Even though Kirby did the majority of the work, history has claimed King Stelen was the hero who expanded their empire.

With the rise of the Fascio regime, King Stelen went to Khirby for help. He asked him to take his knights and wage war against the evil dictator. Khirby no longer wished a life of violence and politely refused. Stelen was not happy with this response and tried to convince the Mystic otherwise, but to no avail. When some time passed, Stelen summoned Khirby again, this time asking to use Khirby's cache of weapons. Again, Khirby refused, this time citing how incredibly powerful the weapons were. As the fight escalated, Khirby became more adamant that no one, not even himself, should use those weapons.

After some time, Khirby was visited by his knights. Even though he no longer fought alongside the king, he was still something of a mentor to them. They explained in great detail a meadow they found that was illuminated with colorful globes of energy. Their description immediately captured his imagination and intrigue. With just a little more coaxing, he agreed to join them and explore the area.

On the second day of their journey, Khirby sensed something was amiss. Instead of finding a lush meadow, they ended up in a desert wasteland. When they came across a factory, the ulterior motives were revealed. The complex housed prisoners of war who needed rescuing. Khirby felt betrayed. The knights explained how tight security was and how they needed an extra hand. Reluctantly, Khirby agreed to help them.

Khirby led his knights on a rampage. They plowed through the complex, annihilating any who chose to oppose them. It was not until they reached the prisoners when they encountered a Warlock. Like a Mystic, this was a magic wielder—except their intentions were evil. Khirby fought the Warlock while the knights freed the prisoners. It was a bloody, drawn-out slugfest. Their fight waged well after the prisoners and knights escaped. In the end, Khirby found an opening and managed to finish off his opponent.

Stumbling, Khirby left the factory and spent six days wandering home. At no point did he encounter any of his knights. There was no one waiting for him, ready to help mend his injuries. Their betrayal felt even greater as the sun burned his flesh during the hot, midday hikes.

He arrived to a ransacked home. There were small knickknacks taken, but the most egregious theft was that of his chest. It was obvious to him who would do such a thing. He stormed the castle to confront King Stelen. Khirby demanded his chest back, but Stelen refused. As Khirby escalated the situation, Stelen called upon the knights to protect him. Staring down his former pupils made him feel like a failure, but he would not back down. He knew how dangerous his weapons were and needed to make sure they did not fall into that lunatic's hand. The ensuing fight cost three knights their lives. Beaten and battered, Khirby was unable to finish the job. He fled, hoping to fight again another day.

Khirby did not return home; instead, he spent the next few years wandering the land. He wanted to get back in touch with his spiritual side, but that was hard, as his heart was bitter. He wanted revenge on King Stelen but knew that was not the right thing to do. Still, he worried about the power the Mervelliere Kingdom was accumulating. He knew it would not take much for a place like that to fall into full-on fascism. He turned to other world leaders, in the hope of forming an alliance to curb the rule of Mervelliere. To his surprise, most countries were willing to join him. Together, they found ways to issue sanctions and push back against Mervelliere's bullying tactics.

It was during this time that Khirby met Queen Roquette of Fifta Wrald. They formed an immediate bond. They approached problems from the same perspective. Talking to each other often inspired new ideas. Together, they accomplished many objectives in their cold war against Mervelliere. It was this that helped them fall in love.

Khirby and Roquette would marry and live a long time together. They did not have children. Her attempts at learning magic failed, and she never became akin to a Mystic. Khirby was able to extend her life a little, but in the end, she perished.

She wished for Khirby to take over the mantle, yet he was reluctant. He felt he was not meant to rule a people. During her final days, he realized how many vultures were after the throne. His visions foretold of terror should any of them replace her. In the hope of helping the people, he accepted the crown.

King Khirby was a good leader. He was not quick to risk soldiers or rule in favor of the greedy rich. The people loved him, yet he kept a humble spirit. Many said he was his harshest critic and that's what made him such a good leader.

Centuries into his rule, on a particularly dark day, King Khirby learned that Fascio had attained the Nebula Infinity Bomb. This was a weapon that Khirby had made during the Early Wars. It was powerful enough to unleash an atomic blast. The explosion was meant to grow miles wide and high. From there, it would have the power to continuously erupt as it traveled across the land.

The bomb was planted in the middle of Fifta Wrald. It was set, and there would be no deactivating it. While the people fled, King Khirby marched toward the bomb. He was the only one powerful enough to stop it from going off. He would have to absorb the explosion as it erupted. It would kill him, but he could not think of a more noble end.

When he touched the bomb, his life flashed before his eyes. Courage swelled in his heart, and he summoned the most powerful spell he'd ever conjured. The bomb erupted, but the explosion stayed contained within his hands. The fire rumbled and attempted to escape his magic grip but failed. A blinding, white light flashed every few seconds, and the bomb continued to strain and struggle. His whole being shook as he fought to suppress the attack.

For over an hour, the bomb erupted. The entire time, King Khirby dug his feet into the ground and took on the pain of the explosion. His screams traveled miles down the road. With one final flash of light, Khirby and the explosion were no more. The ground was littered with ash and nothing else. With his sacrifice, only a five-foot radius of their kingdom was harmed.

After his death, the Knights of Khirby reformed. Sadly, they no longer stood for anything he did. They were a corrupt bunch of power-hungry individuals. They hunted his artifacts, stealing from the people who deserved them, even managing to attain his chest. On the border of Fascio's kingdom, they set up their headquarters in a mountain. From there, they plan and plot their evil machinations as they continue to ruin the Khirby name.

• ◦ ◦ •

Millennia later, the Khirby Organization formed to fight back against the knights. Gala's parents, Hangen Goda and Luba Lunaire, were members. They believed that selfish men should not own Khirby's creations for their nefarious purposes. They became prominent members. Through this, Gala became well-versed in Khirby's history and deeds.

When word came down that the knights would be leaving their headquarters unguarded, the organization knew they had to strike. The Goda family took the charge. They found the codes needed and were willing to infiltrate. Gala was thirteen at the time and worked closely with his parents.

Gala and his parents broke into the knights' lair. Their main objective was to steal the Chest of Khirby. With that out of the knights' hands, the world would be safer. To the Goda's surprise, stealing the chest was simple. There was no one to stop them, but the treasure itself was heavy.

Hangen and Luba carried the chest while Gala scouted ahead. What they did not know was the knights had enchanted the chest. It would never willingly leave that cave. As the exit came into view, a mighty rumble grew. As Gala neared the exit, he turned to see the ground split apart, separating him from his parents.

Rocks fell from the ceiling as the cave shook. More of the ground collapsed into the widening abyss before them. The gap was too wide for Hangen and Luba to jump. Gala watched as hope left their eyes, knowing they wouldn't make it.

Gala ran to the edge of the abyss and told them to jump toward him. He thought he would catch them and they'd escape. His parents pleaded with him, telling him they stood no chance of survival. Gala had to get out and save himself, but he didn't want to listen. He told them how much he loved them as he refused to leave their side. Then, he watched as the ground below them crumbled and his parents fell.

Gala left the cave alone. He often jokes that he never really left.

THE TREASURE OF THE SVIMMA SISTERS

THE SVIMMA SISTERS were Mystics who fell into the ocean. They were part of the Mermayde species, a group of people who lived underwater and could swim faster than any creature. Their bodies were humanoid, but with webbed hands and a fin.

Like most Mystics, the sisters attempted to soak in their culture. They learned how the Mermaydes integrated with coastal cities. They traveled through city canals and lounged in exquisite water fountains. The underwater Mermayde cities were another place for them to explore. Those cities were constructed of sand. Most of their architecture resembled oval shapes. It was beautiful and deep in the ocean, where man could not bother them.

After years of exploring their communities, the Svimma Sisters heard the call to adventure. They were the first to explore the deepest parts of the ocean. There, they found countless treasures many thought were lost to time.

Deep in the abyss, they fought mythical monsters. The Geaunt Oktōpous and the Halja Schorck were their most legendary foes. Both creatures were enormous, making it difficult to see them in their entirety. Their rage was so mighty, it would not have taken much for them to destroy the world. The Svimma Sisters were there to stop them and any who dared disturb the peace.

The sisters became obsessed with hunting artifacts from before the Early Wars. These were some of the most beautiful trinkets they had ever come across. Mermaydes were not typically materialistic, but this soon became the sisters' character defect.

Off the coast of the Third Islands, the sisters created a home for themselves. They enchanted a water cave. It was a massive cave with many unexplored tunnels. The entrance was filled with treasure. It was a beautiful place that was so spacious it was inconceivable.

They spent their final years saving people from boating accidents. They would continue to collect treasure, but that thrill faded over time. Helping people never got old. To prepare for death, they turned their home into an ancient ruin. They put into place curses and spells on their treasure. There seemed to be no rhyme or reason as to why they cursed some objects and not others, but if you asked them, they'd say they knew exactly what they were doing.

After their deaths, a legend grew of their treasures. Many have gone to their cave to seek out riches, but few have had anything to show for it.

• • • •

Gala Goda and Isra Isolé talked about the Svimma Sisters legend for years. Isra's father loved the myth, causing her to grow up around the imagery. Gala learned of them during his days on the *Belafont*. He admired the sisters for finding some of the most beautiful treasure in the world.

Isra had a particular affinity for the Golden Pernula, so Gala claimed he did as well. This pearl was from the deepest and darkest depths of the ocean. It was perfect, and most would agree. The problem—it was hidden deep in the cave and not easy to get to.

For years, Gala and Isra talked of how they could steal the pearl. Gala went out of his way to try to get new information. Anytime he brought her a new piece of the puzzle, she dismissed it. There was always something else missing. He didn't know why he wanted to go on this adventure with her so bad, but he refused to let it go.

A year before Gala began his search for the Diamond of Farrokh, Gala convinced Isra to go on this adventure. They still didn't have everything they needed, but both of them felt a pull dragging them there. It was a particularly warm day, with the humidity out in full force. It was a record heat that made everyone sweat. Gala would always remember how hot it was that day.

They took a canoe to the water caves, where it was just as hot. The rocks above them glowed, and the water below them shimmered. Upon reaching their destination, they stripped down and jumped in the water. Gala searched for a key while Isra solved a puzzle. After accomplishing their tasks, they said the magic words and the ancient ruins opened up for them.

Mermayde's were at war with the Lauguana creatures. Gala thought this ancient ruin would be safe from that conflict, but he was wrong. There was a battle taking place within. Not only did they have to contend with traps but also war itself. After much struggle, Gala and Isra made it to the Golden Pernula. They claimed it and made their escape.

Back in the canoe, Gala and Isra were drying off. Their casual chitchat died down, and the moment struck. Gala felt that familiar flutter in his stomach. He had the perfect chance to tell her everything he felt. He'd thought about this over a thousand times and knew this was his chance. Somehow, he was more nervous to tell her this than he was at any point during their adventure. He rambled, leading to nowhere. It was clear to him his point was not getting across. Before he could explain in simple terms, she told him they should get back. He immediately misinterpreted what she meant and lost all confidence. The two awkwardly went back and forth as she tried to explain that she meant they should go back to her place. In the end, neither one of them communicated their feelings well.

The moment was gone.

Gala was crushed.

They said goodbye on Kornhellia Street. As a lonesome Gala walked away, he began thinking of another way he could tell her how he felt. That's when he thought of the Diamond of Farrokh and started formulating his new plan.

GREMLIN OF THE DALE

GREMLINS WERE NOT known to be kind creatures, but there was one that was particularly malevolent. Sick in the head, it loved to sing songs of terror and disgust. Its pale, white skin was gangly and deformed. Many who looked upon it screamed and fled, furthering the creature's insanity.

The Gremlin had a secret; it could channel magic. There was no Mystic or Warlock teacher, just a natural talent for it. However, having never nurtured that skill, it was not strong in the art.

After being cast into exile, the Gremlin relocated to a dale south of the Forest of Lights. This was a very popular place for local children to play every afternoon. When the Gremlin moved in, this serene place of beauty became a cursed land of terror.

The Gremlin disturbed the kids. Its conversations and songs chilled the children to their bones. Even the way it moved its arms and walked was aggressive and unpleasant. The children cried and begged the Gremlin to leave them alone, but it only laughed at their terror.

Weeks passed, and the children were continually harassed. A group of teenagers decided to confront the Gremlin, in the hope of putting a stop to the madness. When the Gremlin refused, one of the teens shoved it. That set it off. The Gremlin put a curse on the teenagers, paralyzing them in place. With the victims frozen, the Gremlin slaughtered them and feasted on their remains.

When news of their deaths broke, the town went into a frenzy. Within hours, the adults formed a posse and went to seek revenge.

The Gremlin was still chewing on the flesh of its victims when the posse arrived. Even seeing all those weapons, the Gremlin did not flinch. It was ready for a fight. Casting magic, the Gremlin made the scene even bloodier. When the Gremlin was hit, it would just laugh it off.

The Gremlin managed to survive the attack and flee into the woods. It felt good about killing a few dozen of its attackers. Now was a time for recovery. For decades, no one visited the dale. The legend and terror of the Gremlin grew, and everyone was too afraid to go anywhere near there.

As for the Gremlin, it hid on the edge of the woods, occasionally snatching up a new victim.

● ● ● ●

Fifteen years before he met Gala, Yawonte walked to the dale on his evening stroll. When a small boy ran up to him crying, Yawonte realized something foul was in the air. The child cried of a Gremlin who'd tried to eat him, showing the teeth marks left in his arm. With a gentle smile, Yawonte assured the child no harm would come to him.

While Yawonte walked the child back home, he learned more of the myth of the Gremlin of the Dale. His blood boiled hearing of the countless deaths caused by this creature.

Yawonte brought the child back home safely. He spent time talking to the parents, discussing why no one had stopped the Gremlin. He learned of the power it possessed and that there was no one strong enough to handle the problem.

Under a blood-red moon, Yawonte vowed to end this terror.

At the dale, Yawonte brandished his sword and called out for the Gremlin. He did not mince his words, he stated that he was there to kill the creature and send it back to the damned. "If you do not reveal yourself, then I will hunt you down and make your death a thousand times more painful!" Yawonte's voice boomed throughout the forest.

Finally, the Gremlin revealed itself. Its face was the victim of time. Skin sagged as if it were melting off. Snot oozed out its nostrils while drool sloshed from its mouth. Everything about the creature was repulsive.

Yawonte stared down his vile opponent. He ignored the chants and incantations the Gremlin attempted to complete. Yawonte was stronger than those cheap parlor tricks. They would have no effect on him. With each passing second, his hatred for the Gremlin grew as he thought of all its victims. He called out to their spirits, welcoming them to see their vengeance take place.

Yawonte raised his sword over his head. The moonlight glint off the steel.

The Gremlin cast a spell against Yawonte, but it did nothing. The energy evaporated before ever reaching the target.

With that, Yawonte charged forward, screaming for deadly retribution. He barreled through any magic shot at him. The energy may have burned his skin, but he did not care. He was too determined to feel pain. Death was all that would stop him.

Yawonte reached the Gremlin and sliced its chest. The monster fell back and was then carved up for the next two hours. Yawonte thought of all the dead children when he needed the extra motivation to keep going.

In the end, Yawonte was covered in blood, yet did not receive a single scratch. There was nothing left of the Gremlin's body, and the creature had felt every terrible cut.

With that, Yawonte brought an end to generations of terror.

THE WITCHES OF WEST WODE

THE WINNIFRED SISTERS, Balk, Bell, and Tru, were cursed. They grew up in the antiquated village of West Wode. Their peers considered them freaks and outcasts, isolating them. This loneliness formed an inseparable bond between the sisters.

In their teenage years, the girls became obsessed with witchcraft. All their time was spent reading the folklore and learning different theories. While their initial intentions were innocent, the inevitable results were anything but. Their dedication to the craft further alienated them from the entire town.

As the sisters entered early adulthood, government officials came and arrested their parents. They were doctors who performed controversial life-saving procedures. These were often frowned upon by the community. There was no trial, just imprisonment.

The Winnifred sisters would not let that stand. Using their magic, they tore through the town, sparing no one. Giant sparks of energy lit buildings ablaze and burned down entire neighborhoods. No one could stop them.

With their parents free, it was then time to escape the town. Except, by then, everyone had heard of their carnage and was ready to work together to stop them. The townsfolk made it ten times harder getting out. In the chaos of everything, their parents were killed. Their deaths pushed the women over the edge, and they burned the entire town to ash.

The sisters fled to a family cabin in the woods. Located in the Forest of

Light, this was secluded and would keep them safe. It did not take much for them to accept their new lives as the Witches of West Wode.

In the cabin they found a Book of the Damned. With this, they learned the dark arts. There was no spell too dark or dangerous for them. What started as a fun hobby then became an obsession that was devouring their souls. Like all who read from a Book of the Damned, it forever corrupted their beings. They morphed into something more hateful and destructive than they thought possible. In time, they stopped sleeping, which only drove them further into insanity. They were channeling demons and watching ghosts experience their eternal damnation. These sights only drove them further from reality.

Over time, the only thing that satiated them was the taste of human flesh. But not just any flesh would do; it had to be from someone who'd never loved before. Without this sustenance, the sisters were weak and queasy. They demanded the pure and hunted them down. When they ate the impure, they were sick for days.

For hundreds of years, the sisters haunted the woods. Anyone who dared approach them ended up regretting it. It seemed as though they would stalk the land forever …

• • • •

Forty years before meeting Gala, Yawonte learned of the Witches of West Wode. Learning of the town's demise disgusted him. He could not fathom the witches burning the entire town. He thought of the innocent people who must have suffered.

In Yawonte's youthful ignorance, he thought he could talk them out of their wicked ways. Upon finding their cabin, the wind howled and the trees warned him not to venture forth. Still, he knew what he must do. He felt fear but summoned courage and stepped toward the cabin.

There was no conversation to be had. Upon seeing his long, sharp sword, they knew he would cause trouble.

Yawonte attempted an attack but could not move. He was quickly aware they'd cast a spell on him, and he was rendered useless. His attitude shifted, and he happily became a docile and obedient subject. When they asked him to do something, he did it. He was aware of what was going on and did not like how things were looking for him.

Without any resistance, Yawonte handed his sword over to the witches. Internally, he knew this was not a wise move, but there was a higher power compelling him to do so. To taunt him, the women locked his sword in a chest and then displayed it on the fireplace mantel. It was a reminder of what they took from him and how close he was to having it back.

Every day, Yawonte would stare at the sword. It was his focus when the world got hard. Once a week, they would make him clean it. Feeling the steel in his hands drove him crazy, exaggerating his feelings of impotence. No matter how hard he struggled to use it, something stopped him. Whatever spell they cast on him would not break; he would not harm the women.

For the next five years, he was their faithful servant who was responsible for terrible acts. It was his greatest crucible.

One night, Yawonte had a revelation. The words to break his curse came to him in a dream. As soon as he awoke he muttered the chant, and lo and behold, he was a free man. His instinct was to flee and never return, but he wanted his revenge. With some consideration, he decided his best course of action would be to pretend he was still under their command.

For days, he continued the charade. He was so confident he didn't worry about one of them catching onto his scheme. Now, he was in charge, and it was time to have some fun.

It finally came time to clean his sword, and he smiled. The women gathered around to watch him. In a dramatic fashion, he removed it from the chest. He showed it to the women, and they examined it, calling out any dirty spots. Then, with greater care than ever before, he polished it. He was adamant to make it cleaner than it had ever been.

After the final spot was clean, he looked up to the women with a devilish grin, and they realized his deception. Before they could cast a spell, he was on his feet, slashing his sword.

Two minutes later, the Witches of West Wode were no more.

THE WARLOCK DAMNÁRE

DAMNÁRE FELL FROM a dark red cloud. He landed on the Rocks of Rune, in the Fire Sea of Plaisir. The flames burned, teaching him the terrors of this world all too soon.

Off the shore of the Fire Sea was the Ghost Light Woods. The trees called to Damnáre. There, he met a woman, Beelzebub. She was cloaked in darkness and hard to see. From what he could tell, she appeared as a middle-aged black woman with curly hair. Her necklace and rings would occasionally catch the light, but they were never truly visible. There was an aura of mystery about her. She offered him guidance, knowledge, and inevitable power. He accepted without consideration.

For years, Damnáre trained under her tutelage. She taught him to be vicious and unrelenting, traits that came naturally. There were no lessons of morality or pearls of wisdom. She attempted to motivate him with negative reinforcement, and he believed it made him a stronger person.

• • •

One day, Beelzebub's ramblings revealed her significance. She told Damnáre how she was one of the first Mystics to fall from the sky. The Early Wars had not occurred yet, and the world was still taking form. She met with other Mystics but soon found herself ostracized from them. They only borrowed energy from the world, while she stole it. "Use it dry and leave it to die," she would say. It was a selfish, albeit successful, manner of conjuring magic. It took less of a toll on the user and more on the environment.

With that rejection, she became something else—a Warlock. Unlike the Mystics, she was not there to use magic for the greater good. She would go about shaping the world to her liking, yearning for her selfish needs. She gathered pupils and taught them her wicked ways. When she had enough loyalists to form a small army, she began the Early Wars.

Her time fighting in the Early Wars has been chalked up to legend. The atrocities she committed seemed too great for one Warlock. Many question if she ever existed or was just a myth. When the war ended, she found herself on the losing side and went into exile.

Those who know she exists believe she is planning something, but she would deny that with a smile.

By the end of their training, Damnáre was her loyal servant. To prove his worth, she gave him one final test: to burn the Forest of Light to the ground.

● ● ● ●

Damnáre went to the Forest of Light, thinking this would be a simple task. He took his time wandering through the trees, looking for the perfect place to set his fire. As he cast his spell, he noticed a man standing nearby, holding a sword. It was Yawonte, and he was there to put a stop to those foul machinations.

The two fought in the blaze of fire. Yawonte doused the inferno, but Damnáre kindled the embers elsewhere. It was a cat and mouse game, all while engaged in combat.

After hours of battle, Damnáre found himself dueling on the edge of a cliff. Yawonte had trapped him, and there was seemingly no way out. A rapid river loomed hundreds of feet below him. Lost in thought, the Warlock did not know what to do, nor was he paying adequate attention. Yawonte stabbed him in the ribs, and he fell backwards, into the river. As he floated away, he saw Yawonte watch him. Rage filled his soul and gave his life new meaning.

Damnáre spent years recovering. He could not face Beelzebub in the

Ghost Light Forest. He was ashamed of his failure and knew she would be too. Instead, he kept his head low and practiced. With his muscles sore and bones near broken, he focused on his hatred for Yawonte. Whenever he was ready to quit, he felt his shattered ego cry out. Revenge would be the only thing to quench this thirst.

There were more attempts to burn down the Forest of Light, but all resulted in failure. Yawonte was always there to stop him. Even when Damnáre got the upper hand, somehow his enemy would put a stop to him. Yawonte would beg him to change his ways, even offering him his hand in help. This act enraged Damnáre more and drove him further into madness.

In the end, humanity always beats hatred.

It has been two years since Damnáre last saw Yawonte. He's just waiting and plotting for the right time to finally burn down the Forest of Light.

THE CRACKLE DAGGERS

IT WAS DURING the Mystic Reign when Meg-Gar fell. The Early Wars had come to an end, and the cosmic beings were in charge, shaping the world. Meg-Gar immediately knew power was not her purpose.

She wandered the world, feeding the poor and healing the sick. While perfectly capable of defending herself, she sought a nonviolent existence. To her chagrin, violence was so often at the root of those she encountered; it was inevitable.

As her legend grew, kings and queens extended a hand, hoping for her allegiance. She refused, knowing all too well that they'd planned to manipulate her for nefarious reasons. If she were to agree, they would send her to war, and that was not what she wished for.

In time, she met a man, Larks. He was not a Mystic but daydreamed of becoming one. She took him under her wing and taught him everything she knew. During this, they fell in love.

They traveled the world, trying to make it a better place. Their power was unmatched and their determination unbreakable. Together, they took on small-time gangsters as well as Warlock rulers. All who came to know their names feared them.

On Jones Island, they fought the monstrous Dwerg. It took five days and nights of nonstop combat, but in the end, they stood victorious. With that, they rid the world of a centuries-old evil. The following day, the cat priest, Hiroki, married them. It was a small gathering with close friends.

In celebration of their union, they traveled to the Fire Pits of Herza. There, Fabri the Blacksmith took them up to the lava baths. Together, they crafted their ultimate weapon. With the energy of their love, anguish, and hopes, the steel was blessed. A baptism in the lava took place, and the Crackle Daggers were born. The blades shimmered in the air and erupted with sparks of pure energy upon impact.

After their honeymoon, Meg-Gar began questioning the Mystic Reign. She saw cosmic rulers who could not be reeled in. Whatever these kings and queens wished became reality, regardless of what their people desired. Meg-Gar believed this attitude was driving their world toward the brink of annihilation. She knew these leaders were the type who would never step down. They were too powerful, and none were able to stand against them. None ... except Meg-Gar and Larks.

The two went on to perform the most memorable assassination spree in recorded history. They declared ten of the kings and queens no longer Mystics, but dreaded Warlocks. With this, they vowed vengeance for the injustices committed to the every man.

Meg-Gar and Larks traveled the land, handing out their retribution. Any who stood in their way met a similar fate. They were called terrorists by some and revolutionaries by others. Either way, they saw both as terms of endearment.

The Crackle Daggers always got their target. Their legendary sparkle put the fear into any soldiers. They'd killed more world leaders than any other weapon tenfold.

The end of the Mystic Reign came as they crossed the last name off their list. The world's fate was back in human hands.

With their mission accomplished, Meg-Gar and Larks decided it was time to hang up the daggers. They resettled to Cadogan Mountain and carved out a home deep inside the highest peak. Happy and content, they decided it was time to start a family.

For years, they lived in peace. They kept to themselves and avoided attention as best as possible. Meg-Gar knew they would never escape the heirs of those they killed.

As their children grew older, they made sure to train them in the ways of magic. There would always be a target on their heads, but they would be ready to face it.

Eventually, the ruse was up. All the heirs to the fallen Warlock kings and queens united and attacked Cadogan Mountain. Meg-Gar and Larks used the Crackle Daggers one last time to defend their home. They instructed the children to evacuate as they made their last stand. Even in their elderly age, they were capable of holding their own in a fight. It was a bloody fight, and in the end, there were no survivors.

Meg-Gar and Larks held hands as they lay bleeding out. Accepting their death was easy, as they were able to protect their children in the process. Together, they went into the next realm of consciousness.

The children eventually returned to their home. It took days for them to clean it and turn it into an ancient ruin. With that, they were able to pay tribute to their parents and the Crackle Daggers.

● ● ● ●

Five years before he discovered the Diamond of Farrokh, Gala Goda met Isra Isolé at the Third Island Festival. They spent the night talking of their past and flirting. She eventually brought up the Crackle Daggers and told him she wished to steal them. When asked why, her reasoning was vague. Enchanted as he was, Gala could not resist. The next morning, they set out and encountered more obstacles than they'd bargained for.

This adventure continues soon. Look for it in a comic shop near you!

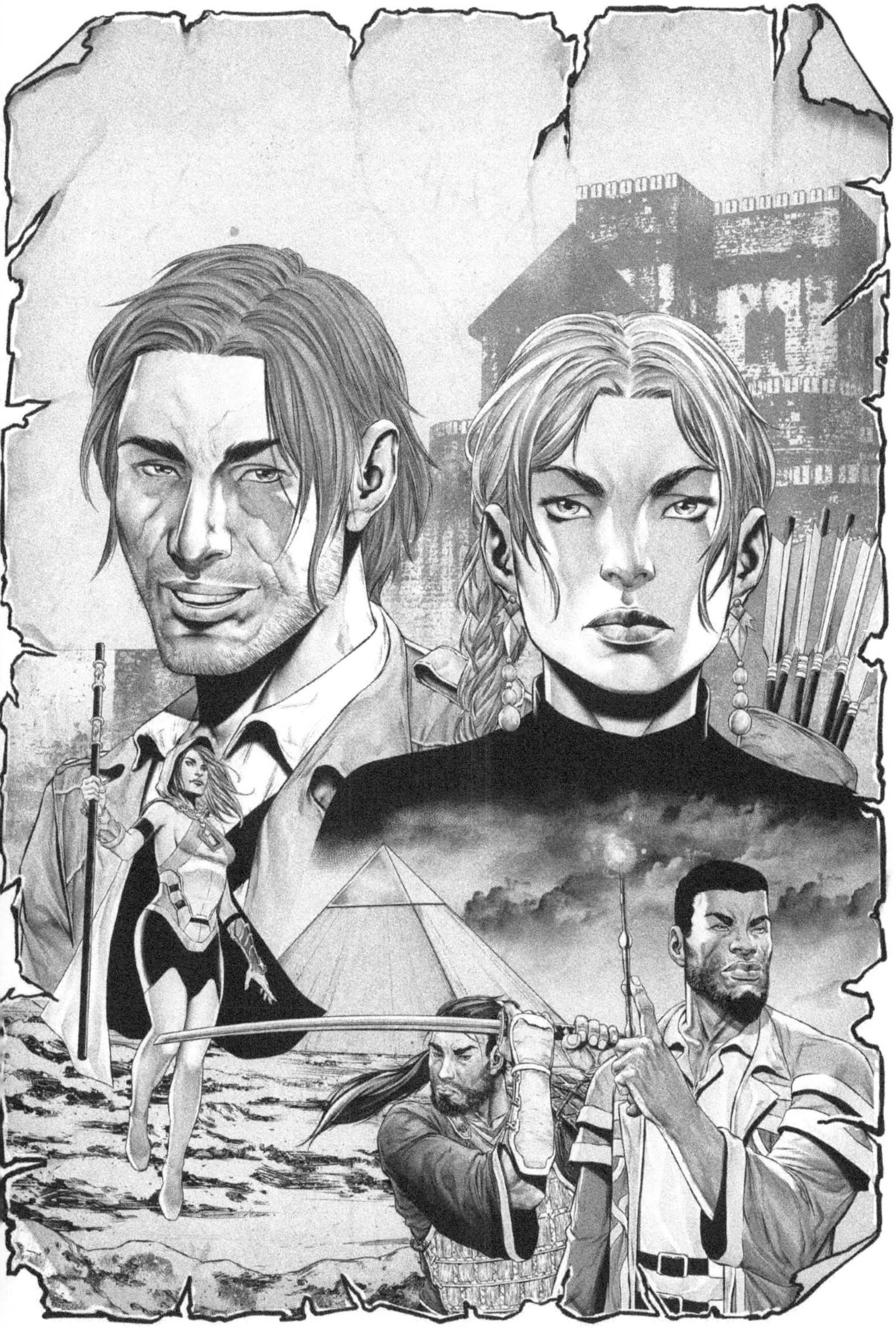

Milton Keynes UK
Ingram Content Group UK Ltd.
UKHW042039080724
445206UK00009B/56/J